# Ignited

BOOKS BY CORRINE JACKSON

*If I Lie*

The Sense Thieves series

*Touched*

*Pushed*

*Ignited*

# CORRINE JACKSON

KENSINGTON PUBLISHING CORP.
www.kensingtonbooks.com

KTEEN BOOKS are published by

Kensington Publishing Corp.
119 West 40th Street
New York, NY 10018

All Kensington titles, imprints, and distributed lines are available at special quantity discounts for bulk purchases for sales promotions, premiums, fund-raising, educational, or institutional use.

Special book excerpts or customized printings can also be created to fit specific needs. For details, write or phone the office of the Kensington special sales manager: Kensington Publishing Corp., 119 West 40th Street, New York, NY 10018, attn: Special Sales Department; phone 1-800-221-2647.

KENSINGTON and the KTeen logo are Reg. U.S. Pat. & TM Off.

ISBN-13: 978-0-7582-7335-2
ISBN-10: 0-7582-7335-5

First Trade Paperback Printing: June 2014

10 9 8 7 6 5 4 3 2 1

Printed in the United States of America


First electronic edition: June 2014

ISBN-13: 978-1-61773-295-9
ISBN-10: 1-61773-295-8

*To Stephen—*

*You've always inspired me and celebrated what I could bring to the page. Thanks for being part of my life's story.*

*Love,*
*MacDaniels*

# CHAPTER ONE

*I* hid in the alley, painted in shadows and praying that I hadn't stepped in whatever caused the putrid scent burning my nose. Across the street, a lone pay phone—the first one I'd seen in the last hundred miles—stood under the glaring spotlight of a street lamp. *Two more minutes,* I promised myself. *Two more minutes of cowering, and then run for the phone.*

Warm fingers pressed into my back, seeking comfort and offering it at the same time. My half sister, Lucy, waited behind me, and I could feel how she shook. These last four months we'd lived like hunted animals, and I knew what horrible thoughts might be running through her mind. At seventeen, she might only be a year younger than me, but our lives had been very different. I'd grown up used to violence, but this was all new to her.

My fingers trembled around the knife I gripped, and I used a cloth to wipe my warm blood from the blade. I lifted my thin T-shirt to tuck the weapon into the back of my jeans waistband and pressed a hand to my stomach when the torn muscles protested. The part of the plan where I had to be injured sucked.

"Well? See anything?" Lucy whispered into my ear, peering around me with wide brown eyes. Her heart-shaped face glowed white against her curly black hair, and she looked small and scared.

I shook my head and tucked a loose blond strand back under my ski cap. My body had frozen some time ago in the frigid January air, and I shoved my fingers into my bulky coat's pockets to thaw them. Then I dug for courage like it was buried treasure. One way or the other, this call would decide what path we would take next. We just had to make it out of this alive first. "It's time. Wait here. If anything happens or Asher signals, you run. You hear me?"

My husky voice sounded harsher than normal as I tried to swallow my emotions.

"Got it, Buffy."

She stumbled over the joke, her voice flat, but it didn't matter. That my sister could attempt to joke about me being as strong as Buffy nearly killed me. I could be brave for her. I lifted my chin, imagining my spine made of iron rebar, and looked down at her one last time. Then I stepped out of the shadows and onto the sidewalk where anyone could see me. Nothing happened. No Healers or Protectors jumped out at me.

Maybe we really had given them the slip two days ago. Florida had been too close. A Protector had gotten his hands on Lucy. If Asher hadn't managed to take the guy down, I might have lost my sister. We'd been lucky that he was alone. We couldn't seem to lose our enemies for long, but we couldn't fight back, either, when they overpowered and outnumbered us. They held all the cards as long as they had my father. If he was still alive.

I looked both ways down the deserted street. Maple, Alabama, could be called many things, but never a party town. Home to a whopping 863 people, the town had one stoplight, a gas station, a diner, and a few small businesses lining the main street where we stood. Everything had shut down around six, as people went home to their families. As far as I could tell, Lucy and I were the only ones out on the street. Well, the two of us, and Asher, who hid somewhere nearby.

Earlier today, our trio had crashed for a few hours at a tiny motel sixty miles down the highway. Then we had packed our few belongings into the car, knowing that we might have to run in a hurry after I made this call. There was a very good possibility that our enemies were hidden, waiting for me to come out into the open. I shivered again, and then rolled my shoulders back.

*Now or never, Remy.*

I marched into the street, walking straight though it sent spikes of pain to my stomach. My steps echoed, and the sound encouraged me. That meant I would hear others approaching if they tried to sneak up on me. I cast another glance around when I reached the phone. Something crashed nearby, and I jerked in reaction, wincing at the pain. A cat screeched, and I shook off the bout of nerves. Then I picked up the receiver, dropped some coins in the slot, and dialed the number I knew by heart.

I counted three rings before a male voice answered. "Hello."

Memories crashed and tumbled into each other at the sound of my grandfather's deep voice. I once thought we could be family, but François Marche was incapable of loving anyone.

"Hello?" he repeated.

I swallowed, suddenly mute.

"Remy." He almost purred my name, the confident bastard. "I wondered how long it would take you to call. You lasted longer than I thought you would."

Four months. It had been four months since I'd seen him, heard his voice, watched him threaten my family. My nails formed half-moon indentations in my palms when my hands tightened into fists. *Please let my father be alive.*

"Franc," I choked out.

"How are you, sweetheart?"

The fake concern reminded me of how naïve I'd been, taken in by this huge hulk of a man towering over six and a half feet tall with crazy white hair and a booming laugh. My grandfather called me "sweetheart" in his old voice, the charming voice, as if he hadn't destroyed my life.

I buried my rage, keeping my tone light. "I'm a little tired from ditching your guys so often, but I can't complain. How about you? Sacrificed any Healers to your friends recently?"

If the Healer community he led knew how he'd betrayed them to the Protectors, they might rise up against him. Franc rationalized that sacrificing a few of his Healers to the Protectors would save the larger community.

Franc sighed. "I do what I have to. It doesn't have to be like this, Remy. You could stop it all."

Take their place, he meant. Unlike full-blooded Healers, I wouldn't die from the things the Protectors would do to me. I could be their rechargeable battery. Bile swam up the back of my throat as I pictured Asher the night we rescued him from my grandfather. Tortured, broken, hopeless. That would be my life if I caved to my grandfather's demands.

"Never," I whispered with revulsion.

"Think about it. Nobody else has to die."

Disgust and fury sharpened my words. "I have thought about it. I've had nightmares about it since the day you suggested it. You remember that day, right? Because I do. By the way, how's your stomach?"

Franc had tried to force me to kill my father, but I'd escaped using the greatest weapon I had—transferring my injuries to those who hurt me. The last time I'd seen my grandfather and his Protector allies, they'd been bleeding out from a stomach wound I'd inflicted on myself.

"Healed," he bit out when I wondered if I'd gone too far bringing up the past. "You're more powerful than I gave you credit for. You caused me a lot of pain."

Smug satisfaction curved my mouth.

"You're lucky I'm not a man who believes in petty revenge. I don't think your father would survive what I'd do to him."

I gripped the cold metal ledge beneath the phone to stay upright. I had to try twice before I pushed the words past the golf ball wedged in my throat. "He's . . . He's alive?"

Four months ago he'd kidnapped Ben, my father. My Protector blood came from Ben and, despite using them against me, Franc hated Protectors. I'd almost lost hope that my father could be alive after all this time. Hope swelled inside me in one giant, yawning ache. *Don't hope yet, Remy. He lies.*

"Franc?" My desperation grew. "Please," I begged.

"He's alive," he said softly.

*Thank God.* The relief threatened to burst out of me, and I covered my mouth to contain it. Moisture seeped through my T-shirt, and I bent at the waist to ease my burning stomach. Soon I would grow faint from blood loss. *Just a little longer.*

Franc's deep voice coaxed and cajoled. "You could be with him tomorrow. Come home, Remy. Come home, and I'll let him go."

If I believed him, we could end the misery of these last months. My father could return home to Blackwell Falls. My sister could go back to her life and school and her boyfriend, Tim. They could start over in our small town. I wanted to give that to them.

As if he sensed my wavering, my grandfather rushed on. "Your mother wouldn't want this life for you. She would want you to help us."

Big mistake on Franc's part, thinking a mention of my mother would influence me. Anna had let my stepfather beat the shit out of me for years.

"Why did you take my father?" I asked.

"You already know why."

He wanted to control me and the powers I'd inherited with my mixed Healer-Protector blood. And he wanted to experiment on me. Healer powers descended through the women of our bloodline, but Franc wanted to change that—he wanted to create male Healers. Something in the air shifted, and I glanced around, the hair prickling on my arms. "I have to go."

I started to hang up and he shouted, "Remy, wait!" I paused, and he added, "He's alive because I believe you'll come to your senses. But I won't wait forever. Think about that."

How had I missed the kind of man he was in those months I'd lived with him? I would never forgive myself for exposing my family and friends to him. I hung up on his threats and hunched my shoulders while I leaned against the phone booth. My breath puffed clouds into the air, and I shuddered. Anyone watching me would think me over-come with grief, but another kind of pain plagued me.

It didn't take long for them to show themselves. Asher's quiet whistle—three low chirps—signaled their arrival. One chirp for each man. Their footsteps echoed like mine had, thudding heavily. Healers then, like we'd hoped. Pro-tectors could have attacked without warning, and these men sounded bigger and heavier than me. Lucky for us, the men of the Healer bloodline had no powers, despite Franc's efforts. My heart pounded in anticipation, but I re-mained hunched over.

Warm breath lifted the hair at the nape of my neck in a moist gust, and I shivered.

"Remy," a man said.

I looked over my shoulder. Three twentysomething men of varying sizes circled me, blocking escape. A stocky brunette with arms wider than my neck and a tattoo of a snake circling his neck. A whipcord-lean blond held a lethal-looking knife, but his hand shook as if he feared using it. He had to be shorter than my five-foot-ten height by at least six inches. The last man looked familiar, and I guessed I'd seen him in Pacifica when I stayed with Franc. Bald and sporting the ugliest goatee this side of the Mississippi, he lacked muscles and a belt to keep his jeans up. But then, he didn't need to be muscle-bound with a gun in his hand.

Goatee-Man eyed my tall, skinny frame with disdain. "That was a stupid move calling your grandfather. He's had a trace on that line for months."

I twisted around. "I know."

I dropped my hands to my side, allowing my coat to fall open. Their eyes fell to my waist. Blood stained my navy cotton T-shirt a deep violet. The blond's eyebrows shot up. Snake-Tattoo took a huge step back, and Goatee-Man froze. Too late. My energy snapped through the air in a burst of red lightning that struck all three men. Wounds opened at their waists, the injuries duplicates of the stab wound I'd inflicted on myself in the alley twenty minutes ago. The injury would stun the men, but not stop them indefinitely.

I aimed to kick away the gun, but my body rebelled against the use of my powers with quaking knees and a thready pulse. Lucy appeared beside me, hooking her shoulder under my arm. I had six inches on her more petite frame, but she held up under my weight.

"Got you," she said.

"Lucy, the gun!" I warned.

Goatee-Man raised the weapon. I swiveled to put my body between my sister and him. A grunt sounded behind me, and I turned. Asher had stripped all three men of their weapons and knocked them to the ground so they lay spread-eagled on their stomachs. My boyfriend hadn't regained all the weight he'd lost in the months Franc held him hostage, but he possessed enough Protector strength and speed to take down a few powerless male Healers with ease.

Asher shoved a foot in Goatee-Man's back. "Okay?" he asked me, the British lilt in his voice more pronounced than usual.

His question was our shorthand for *Are you okay?* and *Can you heal yourself?* I nodded. *I'm good.* Asher heard my thought, and the muscles in his face eased slightly at my reassurance.

"I can't believe you fell for that," Lucy muttered to the men.

In addition to the Protectors, my grandfather's men had stalked us for weeks, tracking us from town to town. We'd hidden in a series of vacant homes, getting by on cold canned food and rare naps. Then Florida happened two days ago, and it had become clear that our strategy of running and hiding wasn't working anymore.

The plan to use my grandfather to lure the men in had been Lucy's idea, and Asher had gone along with it, much to my surprise. Usually, he vetoed any strategy that would put us in danger, but he hadn't hesitated this time. Desperation and fear had infected our trio these last months, causing us to take chances we normally wouldn't have. We'd needed to know whether Ben was alive so we could plan our next move. It didn't hurt that we could use this to put some space between our hunters and us.

I wavered on my feet, a little light-headed from blood loss. *I can't believe I have another stab wound because of Franc.*

Asher frowned at my bitter thought and ground his heel until the man he held down cried out. I slammed my mental walls up to block Asher from my mind. He didn't need my thoughts inflaming his hatred of the men.

"Now what?" Lucy asked.

"I saw them get out of that truck." Asher gestured down the road at a vehicle I couldn't see. His Protector vision beat out my twenty-twenty eyesight, and he could even see in the dark, so I believed him. He handed me the gun. "We can use it to move them. Wait here. I'll go get it."

"Ash—" I started, but he had already shifted into a run, the blur of his body barely visible. I sighed. "He forgot the keys."

"You're a traitor to your kind, turning your back on us for a Protector," Snake-Tattoo practically spat at me.

I knelt down so he could see my face. My quiet voice sliced through the air. "He is my kind. Or didn't Franc share that bit of news?"

His lips pressed together like he didn't believe me.

These men had probably never heard of someone like me with both Protector and Healer blood. Nobody had, which was why both groups hunted me—either to kill me or to use me.

"My grandfather isn't who you think he is. Ask him what really happened to Yvette."

The blond's eyes widened at the mention of the dead Healer's name. Healer energy acted like a stimulant for Protectors, temporarily allowing them to feel the sensations of touch, smell, and taste that they'd lost decades ago. Franc had given Yvette to the Protectors as payment for their services, and they had tortured her to death to feel human for a few moments.

Snake-Tattoo looked away, and I gave up on convincing him. My grandfather had fooled them all into thinking he was their patron saint. I rose, wobbling a little as blood rushed to my head.

"Asher would make a killing as a thief," Lucy observed

with a wry smile. She pressed her scarf to my waist to stanch the blood flow.

I followed her gaze and watched a truck speed toward us. *Okay. My boyfriend knows how to hot-wire a car.* He pulled to a stop a few feet from us, and Asher and Lucy worked together to move the men into the truck bed with a combination of force and threats. Until I had time to heal my injury, I wouldn't be lifting anything heavy. Asher clambered into the back of the truck to watch the men, while Lucy climbed behind the wheel and I took the passenger seat, holding the scarf at my waist.

Lucy drove toward our designated spot, an abandoned barn about five miles out of town. The scenery consisted of farmland and more farmland. We took a dirt road part of the way, and I bounced in my seat, almost crying out when my stomach screamed in agony. A trio of moans sounded from the back of the truck, and I guessed the men were wishing they'd driven a vehicle with better shocks.

"What are you waiting for? Heal yourself already," Lucy said.

I shook my head. "Not yet. Not until we're away from them."

Healing myself or anyone else weakened me further. We couldn't afford for me to be out of commission. First, we had to take care of the enemy.

The headlights shone on the barn a few minutes later. The structure leaned to the right, and weather and hard use had aged the wooden walls to a pale gray. If it had been painted once upon a time, the color had chipped off long ago. The place looked like it would fall down any minute, but it would serve our purposes. Crops stretched into the distance with no other buildings in sight. That meant nobody would stumble across the men while we made our getaway.

I jumped out to swing the huge door open, and Lucy pulled the truck into the empty space inside. As soon as she hit the brakes, Asher launched out of the truck and dragged the men from the bed by their feet. They hit the ground on their backs, one by one, their heads bouncing off the dirt. They moaned in pain, but it had no effect on Asher's stony expression.

I shuddered at the violence in his movements. He'd changed since my grandfather's men had held him hostage this past summer. Lately, he alternated between rage and sadness, growing more and more distant. He'd been tortured for weeks before his brother, Gabe, and I had rescued him. Maybe it was too much to expect Asher to treat these men with compassion when they'd happily hurt him all over again if their positions had been reversed. Still, the easy violence in Asher's movements frightened me.

Lucy gathered the handcuffs we'd stashed earlier that day and helped Asher bind the men to posts a few feet away from each other. We'd also stored water for the men, and I placed a few bottles within reach of each of our prisoners.

"You can't leave us here," Goatee-Man said. "You can't leave us to die."

"Because you intended to show us so much mercy?" Asher asked.

A chill spiraled its way down my spine at the way he curled his hands into fists and stared at the man. Asher's energy buzzed in the air, his lack of control raising the hair on my arms.

"Let's go, Asher." *Please,* I thought. *My stomach hurts.*

Almost immediately, he snapped to attention. "Okay, *mo cridhe.* We'll go. Lucy, do you mind driving?"

"I'm on it," she said.

The three of us headed for the barn door, ignoring the men as they yelled. After we'd put a few hours' worth of distance between us and them, we'd call in an anonymous tip to send ambulances their way. We passed through the entry, and Asher swung the door closed behind us, slapping on a padlock that we'd picked up at the hardware store. Then we circled around to the back of the barn where we'd stashed our latest transportation—another truck, except this one was older and more beat up than the one we'd left in the barn. The last owner hadn't even bothered to apply a coat of paint to the gray primer, and dents lined every side of the body. It had been easy to steal because nobody would want it.

Asher tossed the keys to Lucy, and I climbed in the middle to make room for Lucy on one side and Asher on the other. A few minutes later, we rumbled along the dirt road back to town. At least the engine worked.

We hit a particularly bad dip as we turned onto the gravel road, and I moaned. An arm cradled my shoulders, and I looked up into Asher's eyes as we passed under a street lamp. Normally, their color—a clear, forest green— distracted me, but we hit another bump and my eyes crossed at the fresh onslaught of pain. Asher's forehead wrinkled in concern. He traced a finger across my brow and brushed my hair behind my ear, letting his hand come to rest under the thick waves against my neck. His breath warmed the skin there when he leaned close and whispered, "Let me help."

It had been too long since he'd looked at me like that or touched me with tenderness. The love that had once blazed in his eyes had been banked or burned out for months. He'd been through hell at my grandfather's hands, so I'd given him space, hoping and praying that he would return to me. I waited and savored every accidental touch and rare embrace.

My fingers curled around his wrist, as I closed my eyes

in concentration. Then I lowered my guard to let him in. With a little time, I could heal myself from most injuries or illnesses, but borrowing a Protector's energy hurried the process along. A second passed, and I felt it. Asher's energy floated over me and into me, and pins and needles prickled under my skin. I used his power, manipulating it to seek out my injury. I pictured the wound and imagined the torn edges of the skin tugging together. Flames licked my skin, burning me from the inside out. Left on my own, the healing process caused me hypothermia, but when I borrowed a Protector's energy, heat scorched through me. His power receded, and my eyes flickered open.

Asher's dark brown hair fell over his forehead. It had grown back into a tangle of waves, hiding the scar his tor-turers had left on his scalp. The night Gabe and I had found him, his hair had looked as if a knife had been taken to it. Asher's smile faded as I reached up to touch it, and he removed his arm, blocking me. He shifted toward the door, putting an inch of space between us. His physical and mental retreat cut deep when he raised his mental walls. I should have been used to the rejection after all these months, but every time he pulled away the pain rip-pled through me. I dealt with it as I always did—by pre-tending the pain didn't exist—and Asher pretended along with me. I was afraid of what would happen if we ac-knowledged the cracks widening between us.

Now able to think past my injury, I shifted to meet Lucy's worried eyes in the rearview mirror. Without pre-amble, I said, "Dad's alive. Franc said he's okay, and I think he was telling the truth."

Lucy's breath caught, and she gripped the steering wheel. She looked afraid to let hope in. I didn't blame her, but I hated seeing my happy sister so changed and sad.

"We're going to get him back, Luce."

Her knuckles spread on the steering wheel so my fingers could slide between them, twining our hands together. "Promise?" she asked.

"Promise."

*No matter what,* I thought. I owed her that.

# CHAPTER TWO

*W*e drove several hours before we stopped to send Franc's men help. Asher wanted to wait longer, but I insisted. I wasn't exactly of a mind to champion the men, but I didn't want them to die because we'd left them bleeding. That would make us like them, and I didn't want that.

After we called the Alabama police from another antiquated pay phone (and I'd changed out of my bloody T-shirt), Asher took the wheel. Lucy and I slept, leaning into each other and swaying with the movement of the truck. I woke when the engine shut off, the comforting roar fading into a deafening silence. I rubbed the grit from my eyes and looked around. We'd pulled off the highway at a truck stop. Harsh gray dawn light did nothing to improve the looks of the rundown café in front of us. The squat building sported dirty windows, and trash rolled through the parking lot like paper tumbleweeds.

It sucked sleeping upright, but I'd almost mastered the art. Lucy's head snapped off my shoulder as she woke, too. I stretched, cracking the bones in my spine an inch at a time. I sneaked a glance at Asher under my lashes. Who would he be today? The distant stranger or the loving boyfriend?

"Where are we?" I asked.

We'd been on the road all night and a good part of the morning, putting as much distance between us and my grandfather's men as we could.

"Somewhere in Arkansas," Asher answered.

Exhaustion drained the color from his tanned face, leaving his handsome features dull. I couldn't stop myself. I traced the growth of whiskers shadowing his jaw, and he dredged up a tired smile. He shifted and my hand fell away. It might have been an accident, except that it happened all the time. Avoidance hunkered down between us, a wedge that I couldn't budge.

I knotted my fingers together and stared at them until they blurred. "We should call Lottie to check on Laura and then find a place to rest," I said.

My grandfather's men had run my stepmother down with their car when they'd been making their getaway with my father, and she'd been in a coma for months. Never good with head wounds, I hadn't been able to heal her injuries. We'd been forced to hide her away in a Chicago hospital under a fake name, and Lottie, Asher's powerful Protector sister, had volunteered to watch over her.

"That's a good idea. I didn't get to call yesterday," Lucy said.

She tried for calm, but she couldn't hide the ache in her voice. She'd led a sheltered life before my father had brought me to live in Blackwell Falls. Since then, she'd lost both parents and been forced to leave her entire life behind. Sometimes I thought she would implode, but she surprised me every day with her strength.

Asher nodded and tipped his head toward the diner. "Let's eat lunch first."

Lucy glanced at the restaurant and grimaced. "Yum. I think my stomach actually cramped just now in protest. I can smell the grease and bacteria from here."

"Don't be a wimp," I teased her, sliding across the bench seat and exiting the truck after her.

"Yeah, you say that now, but wait until you have to heal my severe case of food poisoning."

She continued grumbling as we crossed the parking lot. The diner wasn't much better inside than out. In the middle of the room, a group of men sat along a long counter, sipping coffee and eying the ancient TV that hung over the window where waitresses dropped off orders and the short-order cook threw down dishes piled with steaming food. Booths formed a U around the bar, and most were occupied by truckers in flannel coats or the odd bedraggled traveler seeking a shot of caffeine before they hit the road again.

Our group waited to use the unisex restroom. I winced when it was my turn, knowing Lucy would freak out when she saw how dirty the small bathroom was. Sadly, it was better than some of the places we'd been to lately. Eating on the run meant grabbing food when and where we could, and home-cooked meals were a thing of the past.

*How far we've come down from our life in Blackwell Falls,* I thought. I missed our house with the sea glass in the windows and the view of the Maine shore.

I hardly dared to glance in the mirror, afraid of what I'd see. I'd given up on makeup ages ago because my appearance didn't seem important in the scheme of things. My daily uniform consisted of jeans, boots, and T-shirts. Apparently, plain features, freckles, and crazy cotton Q-tip hair worked for some guys, because Asher had seen me at my worst and liked me as I was. At least I had my father's height and navy eyes, something to remind me of him.

I exited the bathroom, stepping aside to allow Lucy to enter. I hesitated two seconds, long enough to hear her disgusted moan as she took in the filth, then I smiled before making my way to Asher. He'd chosen a corner booth overlooking the parking lot, a strategic spot that would ensure no one could sneak up on us. I sat across from him.

"I figured we'd call Lottie after we find a place to rest for the night," he said.

He didn't avoid my gaze. Rather, Asher's eyes appeared empty when he spoke, as if he'd retreated deep inside himself and pulled the door shut behind him. Times like this I considered flashing him to see if I could replace that look with something else. Desperation was an ugly thing.

"Okay," I said quietly. With my eyes, I begged him for more. *Give me something, Asher. Something to tell me you're still in there and that you care.*

He lifted his menu, but he might as well have tossed the Grand Canyon between us. He'd been avoiding me for weeks, maneuvering things so he never had to be alone with me. I couldn't go on like this much longer. We had to figure things out, because we couldn't fix what had broken if he wouldn't talk to me.

Out loud, I asked, "Do you think maybe tonight we could—"

"There's Lucy," he interrupted me. "Do you know what you want to order?"

Relief flickered across his face when Lucy pressed into the booth beside me, and I guessed he'd heard my thoughts. My bottom lip trembled, and I bit down on it. I busied myself with my coffee, emptying three sugars and four creamers into the ceramic mug. Once upon a time, I'd had to shut off my emotions to survive. That had ended when I'd left the nightmare of my stepfather's abuse and my mother's neglect behind. My new family and Asher had changed me, melting the glacier inside me. *Wouldn't it be easier to shut down again?* a traitor voice whispered. *Isn't that what Asher is doing?* The urge to close ranks and protect myself tempted me, but I'd worked so hard to change.

A waitress stopped at our table, and we ordered lunch. Our food arrived minutes later, and we ate with little enthusiasm, too worn out to bother with conversation. I'd gone for a salad, hoping for the best, but the thick coating of ranch dressing smeared across the limp lettuce in a way that canceled out my appetite. It had been weeks since we'd stopped long enough to eat a good meal. I missed macaroni and cheese, the good kind that oozed strings of cheese from each bite. And mochas with clouds of whipped cream sprinkled with cinnamon. And pizza smothered in toppings. My imagination ran until I sipped my doctored coffee and almost spat it out. I loved coffee, and even I couldn't keep this swill down.

Asher made a noise. One corner of his full lips tilted in the hint of a smile. I melted into a little puddle under the table. I'd missed his smiles. Lucy glanced over curiously, guessing that he had read my mind.

"Food fantasies," he told my sister with a shake of his head. "Shameless ones."

I flushed to the tips of my burning ears. "Shut up. Like you don't fantasize about food, too. I just have better taste than to imagine crumpets and tea."

He threw a fry at me. "Hey! I would never have shared my favorites if I'd thought you'd use them against me."

I ate his fry. "Your favorites are such sissy snacks. When I asked you what foods you missed, I thought they would be macho things like steak and potatoes."

I scowled at him, but truthfully, it felt good to be teased, even if it was about food.

Despite looking my age, Asher hadn't been eighteen for many years. In the late 1800s, the Protectors had tired of the Healers using them like slaves, and they'd fought back. When the war erupted, Asher had stepped into the battle, along with the other members of his family. He'd killed a Healer to defend his sister and accidentally stumbled onto what he thought of as a curse: Protectors could become immortal if they killed a female Healer and stole her energy. Immortality cost him his senses of taste, touch, and smell, a fate that all immortal Protectors shared and most hated.

He'd lived what he called an empty life, sleepwalking through the years until he met me. Our bond had changed him. His senses had begun to return, along with his mortality. For the first time in decades, he could taste foods again, could smell the sea air, and he'd felt my touch. Of course, the return of his senses meant that he'd also felt every bit of pain that Franc's men had inflicted on him.

The memory deflated the small bubble of happiness inside me. Asher avoided my touch. It made sense that he blamed me for how my powers had changed him. Where did that leave us?

I cleared my throat, pulling myself out of my miserable thoughts and back to the night before. Franc had said I could be with my father if I would go "home." As much as I hated to return to Pacifica, that was where we'd find my father.

I sipped my coffee. "About Franc . . . You all know that if we go to Pacifica we're walking into a trap, right? He didn't tell me about Dad out of the kindness of his heart."

Lucy's brown eyes narrowed. "He's using Dad as bait."

I exhaled. "Yeah. Not a doubt in my mind. Asher?"

He rubbed a hand over his square jaw. "Definitely."

From the beginning, we'd guessed that Franc had taken my father to lure me back to him, but these last months, we'd been too busy running to go on the offense. Sometimes the Healers found us, and sometimes it was the Protectors who got too close for comfort. Our only choice had been to keep moving. Keep hiding. Last night we had taken a stand and manipulated our hunters to get the answers we wanted—namely that Ben was alive in San Francisco. I was scared to admit how good it had felt to use my powers again to take down those men.

I shoved a sad-looking cherry tomato around my plate. "He'll have people watching the airports, bus stations, whatever."

He'd admitted as much the first time I'd met him. He'd established the security measures to make his community feel safe from their enemy. They made a point of tracking Protectors and knowing when one entered their city.

Asher ran a hand through his hair. "I was thinking the same thing. We should drive in. They'll be watching the motels, too. I'll ask Lottie to set us up with a house."

Thank goodness the Blackwells had more money than Jay-Z. I could have gotten by on very little, but the logistics required for three people changed things. Money made hiding easier, even if it couldn't solve our dine-and-dash problem.

"How are we going to find Dad when we get there?" Lucy asked, dumping ketchup on her fries. "Without getting caught, I mean."

I tapped a finger on the table. An idea had occurred to me last night, but it didn't sit right. Unfortunately, it was the only idea I had.

"What?" Asher asked me, noticing my hesitation.

"I was thinking that they know we're traveling together. They're looking for three people."

He picked up the thread. "You're suggesting we split up."

Lucy's mouth dropped open. For months, I'd preached that we stay together no matter what. To suddenly suggest that we break up our trio must have had her head spinning. I couldn't see a way around it, though.

I rushed on. "Just to follow them. We need to figure out where they're keeping Dad. I think Alcais and Franc are our best bets. If we separate, we can cover more ground and hold on to the element of surprise. They won't see us coming when we go in for the rescue."

Asher and Lucy didn't say anything. Alcais was a sadistic boy who had tortured Asher, and I hated to bring up his name. Lucy absently turned a butter knife over in her hand, the light glinting on the metal as she flipped it again and again. Asher studied the ceiling with his arms crossed. That went on for several long minutes until Lucy heaved a huge sigh.

"I'm sitting here trying to come up with a plan that keeps us together." She held up both hands, palms up. "I've got nothing."

"Me, either." Asher ran a hand through his hair, mussing it until it stood on end.

"So we're going to do this?" I asked.

Lucy balled up her napkin and tossed it on her plate. "I'm in. I'm tired of being the hunted. It would make a nice change to do the hunting for once."

Her fierce expression unnerved me, though I'd had the same thought moments ago. So far she'd listened when Asher or I had given her orders. We'd kept her safe, but this would be different. More dangerous. I wanted to hide her away somewhere, but there wasn't a place far enough away where she would be out of reach from the people after us. She wouldn't let me coddle her anyhow. Not when our father was held captive and we could save him.

Asher nodded. "I'm in, too."

"Okay," I said. "It's a plan."

It should have made me feel better to have a strategy. Instead, a creeping sense of dread tangled with my nerves. Our time in California had brought nothing but pain and terror. What would our return bring? And why couldn't I stop wishing that Gabe was here to help?

★   ★   ★

Two towns over, we found an empty house with a FOR RENT sign on the lawn. A little online research had helped us secure lodging more than once. Homes listed with descriptions of "available for immediate move-in" were right up our alley. That often meant that the house sat empty. If I felt guilty about breaking into somebody's place, I got over it pretty quickly when I thought about what my enemies would do to Lucy if they caught her.

At first, we'd stayed in motels, but we'd been too easy to track. People noticed three teenagers checking in without parents. Last October, we'd nearly been caught at a motel in North Carolina, and we'd had to adjust our strategy. If that meant my morals had adjusted, too, I could live with it.

The vacant single-story Tudor-style brick house sat at the end of a long lane of similar homes. We were far enough away from the neighbors that we felt safe using our camping lantern to guide us through the dark, empty rooms. It wasn't much: just two bedrooms, a bathroom, living room, and kitchen. Our quiet voices echoed, and shadows slid across the walls, as we unpacked the gear we traveled with.

I picked a bedroom and unrolled my sleeping bag on the bare carpet. Usually, I waited for Asher to choose first and settled beside him, but that habit was quickly becoming pathetic considering how he avoided me. The white paint and lack of furniture in the room gave no clue to the type of people who had once lived here. In the living room, I could hear Asher greeting his sister on the phone before he handed it over to Lucy.

"How is she?" my sister asked Lottie.

A few seconds later, she asked, "Can you tell her that I miss her and I love her?"

Every time we spoke to Asher's sister, Lucy had the same questions. And always, the hope in her voice soured to overwhelming disappointment because Laura hadn't magically woken up from her coma. I sank down on my sleeping bag and turned my hands over to stare at the useless limbs. I hadn't been able to help my stepmom any more than I'd been able to save my mother. It was the head injuries. My mother had died of hers. What if Laura never woke?

I stretched out, sliding into the sleeping bag to stare at the ceiling rafters, easing up on the reins I kept on my emotions. I wanted two minutes to hide and grieve. Two minutes when I didn't have to pretend everything was okay for Lucy. Two minutes when I wasn't trying to figure out how to be there for Asher when he hated being in the same room with me.

I sensed him before he spoke, and I steeled myself for another un-confrontation.

"You didn't want to talk to Lottie?" he asked.

Asher braced himself against the doorway, with a hand on each side of the frame. He wore an awkward expression on his face as if he couldn't decide whether or not to enter the room. I couldn't handle another rejection, so I didn't extend an invite.

I shrugged. "I overheard Lucy. Nothing's changed?"

He took one step into the room. "No. Laura is stable, but no change."

Four months of status quo. Lucy would cry herself to sleep tonight, and I couldn't fix things or make her feel better. We fought against a tide that kept coming no matter what I did. Tonight, I could be towed under the surface and drown if Asher said the wrong thing.

"Did Lucy get settled?" I asked, changing the subject.

"Yeah. She's at the end of the hall. She said she was going to turn in."

He took another tentative step forward. For a second, a blissful, hopeful second, I thought maybe Asher finally wanted to talk. I lowered my mental wall, and Asher took two hurried steps backward. *Let him go, Remy.* Defeated, I rolled to face the wall, flipping the switch on the lantern by my head.

"Alright. Good night, then," Asher said.

I sensed him lingering in the doorway. I used to be so in tune with him that I could guess what he was thinking, even though I couldn't read his mind. Now I had no clue where his head was at, except that he wanted distance from me. Well, he could have it because chasing after him was killing me.

"Remy. I'm sorry," he said, his voice a guttural whisper. "I'm not trying to hurt you."

I'd forgotten to raise my walls back up. He could hear my every thought. I sat up and faced him. Asher could see my expression with his Protector eyesight, but I could only make out his shape in the dark room.

"Talk to me. I don't understand what changed. We were okay until that day in Townsend Park. You've changed," I said.

The park with its labyrinth had been our place, until the day Franc followed us into our retreat. He'd used the woods against us, capturing Asher and luring me in after him. We'd escaped, but my family had paid the price.

"You haven't," Asher responded. Before I could question that bittersweet statement, he continued, "I have changed. The things they did to me . . . What happened . . ."

Everything in me yearned to reach out to him, but he wouldn't welcome it. "Will you tell me what happened?"

I knew only the barest details of the time Asher had been held hostage. During the weeks he'd been tortured, I'd thought he was dead. When Gabe and I had rescued him, we'd been stunned at the damage to his body. The wound from the bullet that had grazed his head. The weight he'd lost. A half-dozen broken bones, and more bruises and cuts than I'd been able to count. The way he'd carried himself had changed, too. Before he'd moved with a kind of arrogant confidence, but now he held himself back, tense and watching.

"Asher?" I asked when the silence stretched on. "Please, come here."

He wasn't able to talk about what happened. I could accept that. If he understood that I wouldn't push him, then maybe he wouldn't be afraid to be near me.

*It's okay,* I thought. *I just want to hold you.*

"I can't . . ." he whispered.

I squeezed my eyes closed and rolled away from him. "That's okay. I'll see you in the morning, okay?"

I was proud of how my voice didn't break when I wanted to crawl into a hole and lick my wounds. I should be used to this kind of rejection. My mother had avoided my touch, too. How could I fault Asher for feeling the same after everything that had happened to him? *I'd withstand ten times the pain to touch you,* he'd once told me. That was before my powers made him able to feel everything that Franc's men did to him. I fiercely wished we could go back to the days when the return of Asher's senses meant hours celebrating with kisses and heated touches.

I started when a warm hand sifted through my hair, lifting the strands off my nape. I hadn't heard Asher cross the room, but I sensed him kneeling behind me. I stilled as he trailed a hand over my shoulder and then down, down to trace the indentation of my waist and the curve of my hip. Even with the sleeping bag and my clothing providing a barrier between us, my skin lit up, awakening and leaning toward him like he was the sun. It had been so long since he'd touched me like this.

"I miss you, too, *mo cridhe*. It's not about you."

He'd been listening to my thoughts again.

"Isn't it?"

I didn't say Gabe's name, but then I didn't have to.

Somehow I'd bonded to both brothers, and they thought I had done it on purpose. They could both read my mind, and our powers had increased before my healing ability had begun to make Asher more mortal. I'd thought he no longer blamed me for bonding to Gabe, but maybe he couldn't let it go.

"It's not Gabe," Asher ground out. He reached for my shoulder again, pressing until I rolled to my back. "Can we not talk tonight? Let me hold you. Can that be enough?"

More hope unfurled inside me. I didn't know why he'd changed his mind, but I didn't care. I nodded. He unzipped my sleeping bag and slid in beside me, curving my body into his. Until that moment, I hadn't realized how cold I'd been, freezing from the inside out every time he shrank away from me. Asher pulled the top of the sleeping bag over both of us, his arm wrapped around my waist, a heavy, comforting weight. His lips touched my neck again, and I shivered, thawing as heat settled in me, around me, over me.

*I love you, Asher.*

"Sleep, Remy."

And I did, feeling more peaceful than I had in a long time.

# CHAPTER THREE

*I can't breathe.*

My lungs threatened to explode, and the haze of sleep snapped away as I woke to instant, complete terror. Hands crushed my neck, choking me. I fought them off even before I opened my eyes to a darkened room, but something constricted my movements.

I clutched at the fingers to loosen their hold, and my nails raked skin hard enough to draw blood. The grip loosened for a second, and I sucked in a deep breath. I threw out an elbow, and my other hand fisted in the cloth that bound me. The nylon slipped through my fingers. The sleeping bag. I remembered Asher sleeping beside me.

My eyes adjusted to the faint early dawn light coming through the curtain-less windows. The light threw shadows across Asher's face as he leaned over me, ignoring the arm I used to fend him off. Unseeing eyes stared into mine.

"Asher!"

The expression on his face didn't change. I pushed against his chest, trying to scramble away from him. The sleeping bag cut off my escape, and his fingers clamped around my wrist with brute strength.

"Asher," I croaked. "Stop!"

My scream turned into a meek whimper when his body

landed on mine, his weight heavy and suffocating. His hand covered my mouth and nose, cutting off what little air I had.

Pure animal instinct kicked in. I couldn't lash out with my legs, bound as they were by the sleeping bag, so I bucked my hips. Then I cuffed him in the temple with my free hand, hitting him over and over again with my fist. Nothing worked. Spots popped against my closed eyelids.

On the verge of losing consciousness, my powers took over. Hot red light sizzled through the room, and Asher's face blanched as my pain struck him. He focused and saw me beneath him, his hands wrapped around my neck. His eyes rounded, and he threw himself back, tearing at the sleeping bag's zipper to release us. Finally free, he shoved away until his back hit the opposite wall.

I gasped and coughed, my lungs greedy for air. My harsh breathing morphed into frantic sobbing as I stared at him.

*You tried to kill me.*

"No! Oh God, Remy. Not you. I'm sorry, I'm sorry, I'm sorry . . ."

His tortured apology went on and on. He held out a hand toward me. My heart launched into my throat, and I was on my feet before the thought of escape had fully formed. I raced out of the room, searching for the bathroom. I slammed the bathroom door behind me and twisted the lock.

*Asher tried to kill me.*

I braced myself against the counter, my knees too weak to prop me up without help. In the mirror, my eyes looked wild with my pupils swallowing the blue irises. My lungs burned, and my heart galloped around a track in my chest.

It had been my stepfather all over again. Dean used to hurt me, and I hadn't been able to stop him. If I hadn't used my powers on Asher, he would have . . . The violence and fear and adrenaline unleashed sobs that hurt my chest as they escaped out of me, and I shook uncontrollably as I sank to the floor. I pressed my chilled cheek to the wall, letting the tears fall as I relived the sensation of my boyfriend's hands around my neck, suffocating me.

This was a new kind of nightmare. Asher was coming apart right in front of me. He'd been the one person I could count on, the one person who had my back, but I couldn't trust him anymore. My feet had been swept out from under me, and I didn't know what to do.

I couldn't hide in the bathroom forever, though. A long time later, I fought back the tears and scrubbed my wet cheeks with a cheap, scratchy towel, pulling myself together before I opened the bathroom door. I peeked in the other bedroom first to check on Lucy. My sister had slept through everything, and why not? I hadn't been able to scream with Asher cutting off my air. I shuddered, glad that she hadn't seen what he'd done.

The walk to my bedroom took all of my courage. Asher hadn't moved from his spot on the floor. His elbows were propped on his raised knees, and his chest heaved as he gripped the hair at his temples in both hands. He'd been crying, too. Part of me, the part that loved him and knew he hadn't meant to hurt me, wanted to comfort him. Another part of me wanted to lash out at him for turning me into that thing I hated—a small, cornered animal. I threw up my mental walls to gain a measure of privacy, feeling too exposed.

He looked up and his gaze dropped to my neck. His face twisted in anguish. "Tell me you're okay," he pleaded.

"I'm okay," I said, but my husky voice belied my words.

I eased to the floor across the room from him, unable to bring myself to sit any closer. He was fighting his monsters right in front of me, but I couldn't help him when he'd brought all of my demons back to life, screaming for blood. My toes curled into the carpet, and I let my hair swing down to hide my face. I eyed him warily when he crawled toward me. One of his hands tentatively brushed my hair aside, and I jumped as if he'd hit me. He lowered his head, and his cheeks burned a fiery red.

"Will you let me help you?" he asked, his voice colored by shame.

I didn't need his help to heal my injuries. It was too soon for him to ask me to lower my guard when my anger and hurt were barely banked.

"Please let me do this."

He raised his gaze to mine, inviting me to see his naked expression. He was torturing himself for attacking me in his sleep, and he teetered on the edge of control as he waited for me to blast him. I could destroy him, and I think maybe he wanted me to punish him. *This is Asher,* I reminded myself.

I tipped my chin in a nod and lowered my defenses. His fingertips touched my toes, as if he didn't trust himself to get closer. With his help, it took only a minute to heal the wounds on my body. The marks disappeared from my skin, and the pain faded to a memory. I wished I could forget the rest as easily.

"What happened, Asher?" I asked.

He shook his head, his green eyes bleak. "A nightmare," he whispered. "I didn't know it was you, Remy. I swear it. I would never hurt you . . ."

His sentence broke off because he knew exactly how much he'd hurt me. Red marks marred the skin on his wrist and neck where I'd transferred my injuries, and bruises formed on his forehead where I'd hit him. I didn't know what to say, so I let the silence stretch on and on.

Asher moved to sit beside me, his shoulders hunched as he rubbed his neck. "I was dreaming. I was back in that prison with Alcais and your grandfather's men. The things they were doing to me . . ." He gulped. "Somehow I felt you next to me and you were one of them. I struck out. I swear I didn't know it was you."

The anger didn't fade so much as the sorrow out-weighed it. I leaned toward him, brushing his shoulder with mine. "I believe you," I said.

Dean had been an abusive bastard who'd enjoyed caus-ing pain. If I'd thought Asher was anything like my stepfa-ther, I would have taken Lucy and run as far and as fast as I could.

My words didn't make him feel any better. He jerked his head back, hitting his head against the wall once, and I started. "I'm so sorry, *mo cridhe*. What the hell is wrong with me?" he asked, his voice raw.

The past wasn't letting him go. I should have recognized what was happening to Asher. The edginess and over-vigilance. The distance he'd put between us. The constant sadness in his eyes. Hadn't I been like him when I'd lived with the constant threat of my stepfather attacking me?

I touched his jaw, turning him to face me. "They hurt you, Asher. We've been so busy running, hiding, surviv-ing that you haven't had a chance to stop and deal with what happened." I paused, knowing that his pain might never go away. Tonight was proof that my old wounds still lingered under the surface. "Maybe . . . Maybe it would be better for you to go to Lottie."

My chest ached as I forced the words out. I didn't want him to leave, but what if he needed the distance to find some measure of peace? It hurt him to be near me. He'd made that clear. I reminded him of everything that had happened to him, and everything that could happen if our bond made him more human. If he went to Lottie, he could at least be rid of that worry. Truthfully, he'd left me already.

Asher's jaw tensed as he read my thoughts. "Do you really think I'd leave you to find your father on your own? Give me some credit," he snapped.

His anger sparked my own. Nothing I said or did made him happy. I was trying to do the right thing, but where he was concerned I couldn't seem to manage it. "I'm sorry, but I'm not a damned mind reader like you. And you refuse to talk to me, so how would I know what you're thinking?"

"Then let me say it loud and clear. I'm not going anywhere."

We glared at each other, facing off. "Fine," I snarled. I moved to roll up my sleeping bag. There would be no more sleep this morning, so what was the point of trying? Asher moved to help me, and my anger drained when our fingers brushed. Last night had begun so differently.

I sighed. "This can't happen again."

I loved Asher, but I wouldn't be like my mother, making excuses for someone who hurt me. Not for Asher. Not for anyone. That kind of life chiseled the soul out of you, one small chip at a time.

"It won't. I swear to you it won't." His fierce promise soothed my raw nerves, and I pretended not to notice when he shifted out of reach. The expression on his face smoothed out as he stood as if he'd discovered a new focus. "Remy, I think we should give each other some space," he announced calmly.

The punches kept coming. I rocked back on my heels, crouching at his feet. The air fled my lungs, and my mouth dropped open. "You want to break up?" I sounded devastated, even to my ears.

"No! God, I'm making a mess of this." He rolled his shoulders back to ease the tension.

I froze. "I think you had better explain what *this* is because I'm thinking you just said that you're breaking up with me."

He grabbed my sleeping bag off the floor, tucking it under his arm. "No, I said we should step back to give each other space. I know you've felt the tension lately."

He shifted uncomfortably from foot to foot, and that hurt. I guessed that he'd been thinking about this for a while because when he said space, he meant space from me, and I thought I heard a whisper of anticipation in his voice.

"Semantics," I said.

"That's not fair, Remy!"

I squeezed my eyes shut and threw up my mental walls to block him out. I'd been fighting for him for months. Patiently waiting for him to turn around and see me there. The long campaign had worn me down to nothing. Like him, I didn't want to feel anything anymore. I didn't want to be hurt when he rejected me again because this ongoing agony was worse than any wound I'd taken on.

"Fine," I said in a flat voice. "I'll give you space."

He watched me with a frustrated expression as I pulled a change of clothes from my bag and blocked me when I tried to pass him.

"Please, don't sound like that," he pleaded. "I still love you, Remy."

I stared at his chest through burning eyes, as I clutched my clothes. I needed to cry, and I didn't want him to see me doing it. That would be the final nail in the coffin of my humiliation. "But not the same way, right? Because you changed and I didn't." I shrugged and swallowed past the lump in my throat. "It's okay, Asher. We couldn't keep on the way we have been. Something has to give, right?"

I hadn't expected that thing to be our relationship.

A sob rose up, and I shoved past Asher and ran to the

bathroom. An icy cold shower did nothing to make me feel better, but it covered the noise. I didn't come out until I'd shoved all the pain down inside me, and I wished I'd never learned to cry again.

Asher had ripped my heart from my chest and tossed it to the elements. The months of shutting up and putting up had taken their toll. Asher's bad temper, Lucy's growing depression, and dealing with the battering of guilt and disappointment had worn me out. Loving people sucked.

As we packed up to leave the empty house, Lucy noticed the bruises on Asher's throat and the scratches on his wrist from my fingernails. I hadn't healed him, and he hadn't asked. He wore the marks like a punishment. I told Lucy that we were taking a break. She hugged me and didn't push me to say more.

In the truck, I stared out the passenger window, blind to the passing scenery and hyperaware of every move Asher made as he drove. Conversations we'd had replayed through my head. His promises to love me forever no matter what. After Dean, I'd had walls six feet thick, but Asher had broken through them.

*Everyone you care about hurts you in the end.*

I'd thought I'd left that life lesson behind when I fell in love with Asher, but some things never changed.

Hours and minutes blended together as we drove to San Francisco. Asher ignored me except when he needed to ask me a direct question. I ignored him, except when I had to answer. And Lucy ignored both of us after her attempts to get us to talk crashed and burned.

By the time we arrived on the outskirts of San Francisco, the inside of the truck felt like a morgue where we all kept watch over the slow death of my relationship with Asher. His tension had ratcheted up until he spoke in grunts when Lucy gave him directions. I guessed it was because we'd returned to the place where he'd been kidnapped by my grandfather's allies. How would Asher react when we arrived in Pacifica, where he'd been tortured?

Lottie had found us a furnished three-bedroom house not too far from San Francisco State University, and the key had been hidden behind a planter. Living near the college would allow us to blend in with the students in our area. The garage took up the first floor with the living quarters on the second floor, and the second-story windows faced the street. The huge bay windows offered a view of the sparkling ocean and wind-whipped mounds of sand. A stray person here and there dared to walk the beach, leaning into the biting winter wind. This type of view had soothed me in Maine, but here in California, it did nothing.

I turned from the windows, more lost than I'd ever been.

"Don't you want to explore?" Lucy asked. She wore a look of concern, but I couldn't make this better for her.

Asher stood in the doorway to the kitchen, watching me with eyes that begged me for something. I couldn't begin to guess what he wanted from me, and I was so bone-weary. Normal girls got to nurse their bruised hearts in private, but I'd been forced to sit by Asher for hours on end, gluing myself together until this moment when I could finally escape. There wasn't a lot of space to be had on a road trip.

I avoided his gaze. "I'm tired. I'll explore later. When do you guys want to begin scouting?"

"Tonight after we all get some rest," Asher said. "I think you and Lucy should follow Alcais to Pacifica, and I'll track Franc at his house in the Presidio."

He thought I would argue. I could hear his expectation in the belligerence he'd injected into his tone. I merely nodded. "Fine."

I turned away to escape him. At the first empty bedroom, I entered and closed the door behind me. I flipped
the blinds down to block out the sun, stripped down to
my underwear, and crawled into the bed. And then I
shoved my face into the pillow so the others wouldn't hear
me as I cried myself to sleep.

Sometime later, I woke in the unfamiliar room. My head
felt as if someone had stuffed it with cotton. The house
seemed silent as if Lucy and Asher slept, too, and I wondered what time it was. I dressed and wandered into the
kitchen, where I devoured an apple to fill the yawning pit
in my stomach. The hallway off the living room led to
what I presumed were bedrooms. The doors were closed,
though, and I didn't want to wake anyone when I wasn't
ready for company yet. The clock on the microwave said
it was just after six, which meant I'd slept for five hours.

The water in the bathroom was hot, and I gratefully inhaled the steam of my first heated shower in weeks. After
cleaning up, I dressed in dark jeans and a black T-shirt. My
bare feet made no noise on the wood floors as I padded
into the kitchen, while drying my waist-length hair with
a towel. I froze in the doorway when I noticed Asher eating a bowl of cereal at the kitchen table. Much as I wanted
to turn around and walk back into my room, I couldn't.
We'd come here to find my father, and Asher was part of
that effort, despite the pain it would cause me.

Faking calm I didn't feel, I folded into the chair farthest
from him. He studied me with sad eyes, seeing the evidence of my tears in the swollen, bloodshot eyes and pale
cheeks that I'd noticed in the mirror.

"Are you ready for tonight?" I asked to distract him.

His brows rose in suspicion. "Worried I'm going to go
postal when I see Franc?"

I lifted one shoulder. "He brings out the worst in people."

Asher pushed his bowl away. "I'll be fine. What about you? Ready to take on Alcais?" His lip curled with hatred when he said Alcais's name.

"I can handle him," I said, and I wasn't bragging. I'd had my run-ins with him and walked away.

Asher took his bowl to the sink and rinsed it out. On his return to the table, he veered toward me, drawn as if he couldn't resist the pull of what we used to be together. The towel fell from my hand when he tugged on it, and I sat very still as he rubbed strands of my hair with the material to dry them. The scent of him filled my nose as I inhaled, and I savored the familiar smells of the forest and him. For a moment, I tilted my head, absorbing the heat of his hands through the towel. He'd done this once before when I'd been sick with the flu and unable to heal myself due to temporarily short-circuited powers. He'd taken such sweet care of me, and I'd fallen deeper in love with him. The memory hurt, and I snapped upright and yanked the towel from him.

"Please don't," I whispered. "It's confusing."

The muscles in his face tensed, but he nodded. His actions had been more habit than anything else, and I wanted him to touch me. But if I let him close, and he pulled away again, the pain would be a thousand times worse. I couldn't do this if I wasn't sure he really wanted me for good.

Lucy saved us from saying anything else when she entered, yawning and stretching in a series of pops. "I could eat a bear."

I got up to fix two bowls of Count Chocula, and I picked up the thread of the conversation about Alcais like the last few minutes with Asher hadn't happened. "Alcais thinks he's untouchable. He takes chances, and he'll make a mistake if we're patient."

The cruel boy had used Healers like Band-Aids, acting

recklessly because his sister, Erin, would always be there to heal his injuries. He'd reminded me of my stepfather even before I'd found out that Alcais had been one of Asher's torturers. He was also the one Gabe had followed to find Asher when Erin told me he was still alive. The girl had been my only friend among Franc's people. If not for her, we would not have found Asher. My grandfather had known that she helped us, and I prayed that he hadn't hurt her for it. I'd wanted to call her so many times, but I worried it would make things worse for her.

As I washed my bowl and spoon, Lucy said, "I forgot to tell you. I called Lottie before I took a nap. She mentioned that she spoke to Gabe yesterday."

"Yeah?" I asked, feeling Asher's gaze on my back.

"Mm. He's in Europe somewhere. I guess he's been hanging out with old Protector friends, trying to see if any of them have heard of someone like you. He figures there has to be someone who knows something, and they're just not saying. He's going to stick around there a little longer to see what he can learn."

Or maybe Gabe was doing his best to stay away from Asher and me. He'd said as much the last time I saw him. Lucy didn't know that, though, so I said, "I hope he finds answers. We could use them."

After our dinner of cereal, we headed to the garage. Lottie had arranged for new transportation. Asher would continue to use the truck, and Lucy and I would take the black Mercedes that his sister had bought. She'd also arranged for new burner mobile phones for each of us, and we pocketed those.

Lucy climbed into the passenger seat of the Mercedes, toying with the controls. I hesitated to join her. If something happened, I might not see Asher again . . . He didn't seem to share my worry. He walked toward the truck, and I finally turned away.

*Enough, Remy. Let him go. Focus.*

I was about to open the car door when Asher whipped me around. His eyes clouded with worry, and he hugged me tight enough to steal my breath. I could only hold on, my heart pounding and my thoughts spinning. The embrace didn't last long enough.

Asher stepped back and tipped my chin up. "Be careful."

I nodded. "You, too."

We separated and got into our vehicles. It wasn't until I saw San Francisco disappearing in my rearview mirror that I realized we hadn't said "I love you." Would saying goodbye ever get any easier?

# CHAPTER FOUR

"*I*'m bored," Lucy said from the passenger seat when I hung up the phone.

"Don't even start," I told her.

I threw a cheeseburger wrapper at her. She didn't react, except to toss it over her shoulder into the backseat, where it landed with the other fast-food trash we'd collected. The interior of the car smelled like a menagerie of greasy take-out, spanning the range from tacos to French fries. We'd been watching Alcais and Erin's house for three days now and had nothing to show for it, except a list of times that their mother, Dorthea, had come and gone to work or to run errands. Erin, Alcais, and their friend, Delia, had been conspicuously absent, though I'd described them all to Lucy so she would know what to look out for.

Asher's luck hadn't been much better. Every day, he sneaked close to my grandfather's house in San Francisco, using the forest to hide his presence. Lights flipped on and off, and he'd noticed Franc passing by the windows a time or ten, but my grandfather never left the house. That in itself was unusual considering how he'd practically spent all his time in Pacifica when I'd lived with him.

The whole situation was anticlimactic, and if it went on much longer, I feared Asher would try to confront Franc. For all our worries, we'd sat around twiddling our thumbs, waiting for Alcais and my grandfather to show themselves. The inactivity was getting to all of us, and things hadn't gotten any better between Asher and me.

"What did Asher say?" Lucy asked, gesturing to the phone. "Any news?"

I shook my head, and the hopeful light in her eyes faded.

"Is he still acting like an ass?"

"Lucy!"

"What? It's true. He's being an ass."

I shrugged to avoid answering. Honestly, she was right. Asher was wound so tight these days that he snapped at Lucy—the person most likely to speak to him—more often than not. This morning, she'd threatened to join his stakeout if he snarled at her one more time. Very aware of her capacity to chatter, Asher had shut his mouth in a hurry. I'd found myself wishing that I'd sicced her on him sooner.

"Can I get out?" Lucy asked a few minutes later.

Once the sun had gone down, we had parked the car on a street facing the pier. We waited for dark when I could sneak closer. During the day we could blend in with all the people going to the beach, but at night we needed the shadows for cover before I could backtrack to Alcais's house. The Healers watched their neighborhood too closely for us to camp out on his street. In daylight hours, I stayed in the car, wearing a baseball cap to hide my hair and face, while Lucy scouted in the long brunette wig we'd picked up for her. Most Healers had never seen her, and she could explore without drawing attention.

The view of the pier brought back a lot of memories, a very few of them good. As the teenagers in the group, Erin, Alcais, Delia, and I had been thrown together often. Whenever we'd wanted to escape scrutiny, we'd wandered to the beach. I'd spent long hours there with Erin. She'd reminded me of my sister, and that had been a comfort for a time.

Beside me, Lucy grew increasingly impatient when I failed to answer her. She hated sitting in the car, but people would notice her now with the beach crowds gone for the night.

"No," I told her. The sun had set a short time ago. "You'll stand out too much."

She sighed dramatically, and I rolled my eyes.

"Can I call someone?" she asked.

"Who?" She'd already called Lottie an hour ago, and I'd just checked in with Asher.

"Nobody." She shrugged, faking nonchalance.

I scowled. "Lucy, you can't call Tim."

She missed her boyfriend. They'd begun dating about the time Asher and I had. It had been hard for her to leave him behind in Blackwell Falls.

Lucy's head whipped around, and her glare flayed me alive. "This sucks."

"I'm sorry." I meant it. I hated how trapped she must feel in this situation.

"No, you're not. This whole situation is perfect for you. Your boyfriend is here."

I tried not to react to her snide tone. "We're giving each other some space. Anyway, Tim doesn't know about Healers or Protectors. It wouldn't be fair to drag him into this world."

She turned away, but I heard her mutter, "Like you care."

"Hey! What is that supposed to mean?"

She crossed her arms and refused to meet my eyes. "You didn't exactly give me a choice."

I stared at her in disbelief. "I tried to protect you. I did everything I could to keep *this* from touching you." I waved a hand in the air so that "*this*" could be interpreted as me and Pacifica altogether. "I left home to keep you safe."

"But you didn't stay away, did you?" she accused.

A small dagger slid between my ribs, and the pain was sharp and swift. I sucked in a breath.

Lucy clapped a hand over her mouth, regret lighting her features. "I'm so sorry," she said. "I didn't mean that."

I looked out the driver's window to hide my expression. When I could control the tremble in my voice, I said, "It's okay. Don't worry about it."

She touched my right hand where it rested on the seat. "No, really, sis. I'm sorry."

She sounded so contrite that I repeated, "Don't worry about it. Just drop it, okay?"

I shoved the pain away. She'd hurt my feelings. So what? How could I blame her for resenting what I'd done to her life? It wasn't my fault that I was a freak, or that I'd come to Blackwell Falls to live. But I could have tried harder to move back to New York or, failing that, I could have moved somewhere else. The truth was that I had wanted to stay in Blackwell Falls. I'd needed the home and family that I'd discovered there. I loved them, and I hadn't been able to leave them. I'd made my choice and the fallout had affected everyone, from my family to the Blackwells. I might want to shove that thought away, but it always returned.

The ring of my phone broke the strained silence, and I answered it gratefully.

"Franc is finally on the move," Asher said without a greeting. "I'm in the truck following him. I think he's heading toward Pacifica."

I sat up straight. "Finally. Call us if you need us."

He agreed, and we signed off. In the rearview mirror, I glimpsed a familiar figure approaching behind us. Soon, she would pass us as she headed for the pier. I motioned to Lucy and we both crouched down until the girl passed. She crossed directly beneath a streetlight, and then settled at one of the cement benches that overlooked the beach a short distance from where we'd parked.

"Lucy, give me your wig."

She did, and I tugged my cap off to put the wig on. I checked my reflection in the rearview mirror.

"Remy?" My sister's voice trembled, our argument forgotten for the moment.

"That's Erin," I explained. "Stay here, okay? I'll be right there if you need me, and you know what to do if something happens."

I gestured to where Erin sat and glanced over to ensure Lucy understood. She nodded, tugging my cap over her hair. Her hands shook, and I wanted to comfort her, but there wasn't time.

I didn't make a beeline for Erin when I left the car. Instead, I took my time, going a circuitous route. My grandfather knew I liked Erin and that she'd helped me. If his people had spotted us in the area, he could have sent her out alone to draw me in. I sneaked glances in all directions, searching for anyone who stood out who might be a threat. It wasn't until I was sure we were alone that I approached the bench and sat next to Erin. She stared toward the ocean where the moon allowed a peek at dark waves curling toward the sand. Her blond hair hung in waves about her face and she looked like I remembered.

"Hey," I said nervously, wiping my sweaty palms on my jeans.

"Hey," she answered in the reserved voice she used with strangers. She glanced my way, and I knew the instant she saw past the wig and recognized me. Her body tensed, and her brows shot up. "Remy? Oh my God!"

Her arms stretched out to hug me, but I shook my head and she sank back into her seat. "Don't draw attention to us," I told her. "Stare forward, and pretend we're not talking."

She did as I said, her posture relaxing after a moment. "It's good to see you," she said softly, clasping her mittened hands together around one knee.

"You, too. I was worried about you. Did you get in trouble for helping me?"

She shrugged and tucked the ends of her red scarf inside her coat. "Not really. I lied and said you tricked me into giving you the info."

Relief rushed through me, followed by surprise. "You lied?" I asked. I had a hard time imagining her doing so. Erin was one of the few truly sweet people I'd ever met, though few saw past her shyness.

Her quiet laugh made me smile. "I *can* lie, you know. When I have a good reason to. And they definitely gave me good reason."

I hadn't realized how much I'd missed her until that moment. She'd been so gentle and kind when she welcomed me into the Healer community. She'd taught me about pure-blooded Healers like her who could heal without injury to themselves. The same age as Lucy, Erin had been one of the bright spots in Pacifica.

"There's so much to tell you," she said. Worry widened her eyes. "But first, are you out of your freaking mind? It's dangerous for you to be here."

Thirty yards ahead of us, the ocean barreled into the sand with a soothing rhythm and I inhaled the briny air as I evaluated how much to tell her without putting her in more danger. I pulled my knees up into my chest and wrapped my arms around them.

"It's Franc," I told her. "He's taken something of mine, and I have to get it back."

"Franc," she whispered on a gusty exhalation. "Everything comes back to him, doesn't it?"

"Yes. I—"

My phone rang in my pocket, and I checked the screen. It was Lucy's number.

I answered and she spoke in a panicked rush. "Alcais is coming! You have to hide! He'll be able to see you any second."

Fear pumped adrenaline through me in a mad wave. "Take the car and drive away," I ordered. "I'll meet you in thirty minutes at the spot we talked about."

I hung up and a car started in the distance. I prayed she would do as we'd discussed and head toward the McDonald's near the freeway entrance.

"It's Alcais," I whispered to Erin. "He's coming. I have to go."

She nodded, but grabbed my hand. My mental walls were up, but that monster that had always wanted to attack her rose up inside me. All Protectors felt this way around Healers. It was why they had mental walls and practiced using them as children. I shoved the beast back down.

"Meet me tomorrow," Erin said. "My mom is sending me to visit my aunt on the nine A.M. ferry from the Ferry Plaza to Tiburon. It's the only time I'll be alone for a while."

"I'll try," I said, not making any promises.

"Be safe, Remy."

I left her, crossing to the wall that separated the sidewalk and the beach several feet below. Then I launched my body over the ledge, dropping into a crouch in the shadows. I hid there, my heartbeat drowning out the rushing water. Soon, footsteps crunched through the grit near the bench.

"Erin, what are you doing out here alone?"

Alcais's arrogant voice hadn't changed a bit. Hate tasted

bitter on my tongue as I slid closer to the wall and crept toward the staircase that ascended from the beach to the walkway above where Erin sat.

"You're not my keeper," Erin replied to her brother with more spirit than I'd heard her use with him before.

"Franc told us to stay close to home at night. You're a fucking idiot. Can't you do what you're told?"

Luckily, the beach had emptied of strangers who might have noticed me crawling up the stairs. Near the top, I flattened my body, trying to glimpse Alcais as he yelled at Erin. I chanced popping my head up and my stomach roiled in revulsion when I saw him in profile, his right side to me as he faced a standing Erin with his back to the pier. The blond surfer boy with the cocky swagger and grin had been replaced by a man with a cruel expression and an aggressive stance. He wanted to intimidate his sister, and he was using his body to do it. If he hurt her, I would somehow make him sorry. I wasn't afraid of him. Once, I'd caught him holding her hand over a flame to force me to demonstrate my powers, and I'd warned him not to hurt her again. Only the threat of what Franc would do to my father kept me still.

Erin cried out softly, and I dared another glance.

That was when I saw Asher racing toward Alcais from the left, running parallel to the beach. Protectors moved at high speeds, and he should have been invisible, but I could see him approaching with his hands clenched like he intended to snap Alcais in half.

I dropped my mental walls and shouted, *Asher, don't!*

He ignored me.

Erin glanced toward my hiding spot, and our eyes met for one brief second. She must have seen my horror because her gaze flicked toward Asher, and she tensed. And then she abruptly sidestepped around Alcais and walked toward the street at a fast clip with him on her heels.

I didn't waste the gift she'd given me. As soon as they had turned their backs, I launched forward, using my own Protector speed to race toward Asher, hoping that Alcais wouldn't hear Asher or me. Asher was so focused on Alcais with a killing light in his eyes that he didn't see me. I intercepted him and put every last bit of strength I had into shoving him over the barrier wall. We flew over the ledge and landed in the sand with a jarring thud. I'd scarcely registered the pain when Asher rolled away and jumped to his feet. I did the same, trembling when he crouched in readiness to attack me, his face consumed with fury.

"Snap out of it!" I snarled at him.

Recognition dawned and replaced the blind rage, and he straightened. I shifted to listen for Alcais and Erin, but my attention never swerved from Asher in case he tried to go after Alcais again. The siblings' voices faded, and I didn't think Alcais even realized we'd been there. Because of Erin. She'd saved Asher a second time.

"Why did you stop me?" Asher bit off. "I could have taken him out!"

He sounded pissed, but I didn't care. I was every bit as angry. I invaded his space, forcing him to take a step back or bump into me.

"And then what?" I barely kept my voice from rising to a shout. "You get your revenge on him. What then? What happens to my dad if you take out one of the only leads we have?"

I wanted to hit him. The urge rose up in me, and I had to shove it down.

"I wasn't thinking about your dad," Asher admitted, his voice stiff.

I kicked at the sand, spraying it over his shoes. "You weren't thinking at all. What about Erin? She once risked her life to tell me you were alive. We found you because of her. You would repay her by putting her in danger?"

He could have hurt her when he attacked Alcais. He'd been out of control. I'd seen it in the way he moved and in his expression. The idea of my friend getting hurt sent another wave of rage through me, and I turned my back on Asher to contain it.

I counted to twenty. "Let's go," I said in a calmer voice. "Lucy is waiting at our meeting spot."

He fell into step beside me as we walked up the beach. I dialed Lucy to tell her we were on our way, and she sounded scared to death. Seeing Alcais had reminded her how very real the danger was, and I could tell she'd been crying. I spent a couple of minutes reassuring her before I hung up. Asher's struggle was almost palpable, his entire body tense with suppressed emotion. I pulled off the wig, shaking it to loosen the sand I'd gotten in it when I rolled on the beach.

"Remy," he said. He waited for me to face him. "I'm sorry."

His shoulders bent in shame, and my anger faded slightly. I was so damn disappointed and sad. "The only thing we have going for us is the element of surprise. You almost threw that away tonight."

He shifted, sliding his hands into the pockets of his jeans. "You're right," he admitted. "I saw Alcais and I lost it. Everything came back at once, and I wanted to . . ."

His voice trailed off. The unfinished thought hung in the air, and I shivered. He wanted to . . . hurt him? Kill him? Violence repaid with violence. Everything we'd done these last months heaped another helping of horror upon us.

The wind picked up, and I wrapped my arms around my waist. "What are you doing here? I thought you were following Franc."

"He drove here. By the time I found a place to park the truck and got back to the house, Franc had gone inside. I think he sent Alcais to find Erin."

We'd waited three days for my grandfather to leave his house. Even now, he could be with my father. We wouldn't know because Asher had abandoned him to follow Alcais. I didn't say what I was thinking, but I guessed Asher knew. He glanced away, the muscles in his sculpted face tensing. I thought about the look he'd worn earlier. Revenge had been his only goal. How was I supposed to trust that he wouldn't do something like this again? What if next time he put Lucy or me in danger?

Asher reached for me. The movement was so unexpected that I stiffened and stepped back. His eyes narrowed with pain, and he dropped his hand to his side. I wanted to shriek in frustration. For weeks, I'd practically begged him to touch me, waiting around for any scrap of attention he showed me. He was the one who had asked for space, but suddenly he wanted to touch me.

"I'm scared, Remy."

His jaw clenched. Fear was a weakness, and Asher hated being weak.

"Of what?" I asked.

He ran a hand through his hair, mussing the chocolate-brown strands. His mouth opened and closed as he tried to find the words to explain how he felt. Then his eyes lifted to some spot over my shoulder. The vulnerability I'd glimpsed in him blinked out, and once again, he'd shored up his defenses with me on the outside of his walls. The razor didn't cut as deep, dulled from overuse.

"This is one of those times when I wish I could read *your* mind," I told him in a soft voice. I stepped close to him. His breath touched my face, and I longed to sink into his heat. "Let me in, Asher. Let me help you. What are you afraid of?"

I dared to hold his hand. He allowed it, and I stretched out my other hand to trace his cheek. His head tilted like he savored the feel of my fingers brushing his lips. Flames leapt in the green depths of his eyes, sparking a familiar heat in me, and then his head lowered. He kissed me, his full lips parting mine. There was no hesitation in his embrace. He wrapped both arms around my waist and yanked me off balance as he pulled me into him. Instantly, I was lost in the feel, the smell, the taste of him.

He hadn't kissed me like this since Blackwell Falls, and all the pent-up longing I'd stored poured out of me and into our kiss. I dropped the wig to the sand. My hands explored his back, tracing his shoulder blades and following them down to his hips. I couldn't get close enough. It had been so cold without him. He smoldered, and I wanted to throw myself into the blaze.

Without warning, he shoved me away. I stumbled and would have fallen if he hadn't steadied me. I blinked at the pained grimace on his face, still lost in the haze.

"This," Asher bit out through gritted teeth.

I stared at him in confusion, and he lifted my hand. That's when I noticed the green sparks crackling where our skin touched. I'd forgotten how the air glowed so brilliantly when my body tried to heal his. I'd lost control of my powers, and I snapped my mental walls back into place. Reason returned by slow degrees, and I understood that he'd kissed me to make a point. I'd confused passion with manipulation, and I felt incredibly stupid.

"*This* is what I'm afraid of, Remy. Every time I touch you, the longer I'm with you, the more human I become." He dropped my arm and stepped back, taking his heat away. The sparks faded, along with any passion I'd felt. "Didn't you see me tonight? See how slowly I moved? How easily you overtook me? When have you ever been able to do that?"

Never. I'd tackled Gabe a couple of times, but he'd always overpowered me. Truly, I shouldn't have been able to take Asher down the way I had, but I hadn't hesitated.

The wind tossed my hair in my face, and I scraped it back, tying it into a knot at my nape as I tried to think of a response that didn't include slapping him.

Asher's hands disappeared into his pockets, and he rocked back on his heels. "I'm losing my powers, Remy," he said with despair weighing every syllable. "What good am I to you as a mortal?"

The despair broke through my hurt. My shoulders lifted in a helpless gesture. Once, Asher had longed to be mortal and prayed I could cure him. No longer. The man in front of me hated what he'd become and suffered constantly because of it. To see Asher brought so low made me want to weep.

He wouldn't meet my eyes when I insisted, "Your powers didn't make you a Protector, Asher. That was you. It's who you are and what you believe. Other Protectors would have killed me on sight, but not you. You're a good person, with or without your abilities."

His expression didn't change. I hadn't convinced him. Another breeze swirled sand into the air, and it stuck to my cheek. I swiped at it and felt the wetness of tears. I wished I'd never loosened that spigot. What was the point of crying? It didn't fix anything, and I never felt any better.

"I'm a liability," Asher insisted. "One day they're going to use me against you, and it's going to kill me."

I shook my head. "What do you want me to say? I can't predict the future. I don't know what will happen."

He bent at the knees to put our eyes on level and caught me with a determined stare. "Promise me that you won't sacrifice yourself to save me. Promise me that you'll walk away if they ever capture me."

*Never.* I would never abandon someone I loved. My mother had died because I'd left her alone with my stepfather. I wouldn't do that again. I didn't have to say a word.

Asher read my answer on my face. He straightened, his mouth turned down in disappointment. We always seemed to come back to this fight. He was willing to sacrifice himself to save me, but he couldn't accept that I would do the same.

"Where does that leave us?" I asked.

"I don't know. I really don't."

Later that night, I stood under the shower with hot water pelting my skin and washing sand down the drain. Lucy had gone to her bedroom as soon as we'd returned to the house. Asher hadn't joined us. Franc's car had left Alcais's house by the time we'd met up with Lucy and dropped Asher at his truck. He'd texted me that he was going to stake out my grandfather's house again and would call in the morning. I didn't argue with him, and that said more about our relationship than I wanted to admit.

Tonight it had become very clear that we were broken, possibly beyond repair. How could you be with someone who was afraid to touch you?

An ache expanded in my chest. Asher had admitted that his powers were disappearing, but that was only one problem. Tonight, I had felt stronger and faster than ever before when I tackled Asher. The two things had to be connected because that was the way our luck ran. I would bet anything that the energy I stole from him when I "healed" him had given my powers a boost. That was going to go over well when he figured it out.

I leaned against the shower wall, my thoughts tangled in what the changes in my body could mean. I was already losing Asher. What if I was losing myself, too?

# CHAPTER FIVE

*I* woke early the next morning with a nagging feeling that I'd forgotten something. I hadn't slept well, and it would take a crowbar to pry my eyes open. I'd waited up for Asher, and he hadn't come in until around three. I rubbed my feet together like a cricket and huddled under the covers to fight off the chill in the air. I started to drift off again when I remembered Erin. I was supposed to meet her on the ferry at nine.

I threw off the covers and checked the time on my phone. It was almost eight, and I would have just enough time to dress and head to the Embarcadero. Erin would be boarding the ferry at the Ferry Plaza. That meant someone would be seeing her off, and I couldn't risk running into them. But the same ferry would stop at Pier 41 to the west before crossing the bay to Tiburon. I could hop on at the second stop with less risk.

The problem was Asher and Lucy. I'd forgotten to tell them about the meeting the night before. I could tell them now, but they would argue with me and want to examine the meeting from every angle. By the time we decided on a strategy, the opportunity would have passed.

I dressed in jeans and a T-shirt in a hurry, considering my options: (a) tell Asher and Lucy and spend time we didn't have arguing, or (b) go without them and pay the price for it later. Either way, I intended to go because Erin could help us find my father. That fact was all it took for me to decide. I left a note on the table, grabbed the Mercedes keys, and tiptoed past Asher and Lucy's rooms on my way to the garage.

A half hour later I parked the car in a lot across the street from Pier 39, a famous tourist destination. Even this early in the morning, tourists swarmed the bright souvenir shops lining the wooden walkways. I bought a San Francisco sweatshirt for five bucks and pulled it on, along with my San Francisco baseball cap and Lucy's wig. I trailed behind the other tourists, blending in as I pretended to peruse the magnets, shot glasses, and key chains shaped like cable cars or the Golden Gate Bridge.

I bought a ticket for the ferry at Pier 41 and surreptitiously searched for Protectors or Healers. My spidey-sense didn't pick up on anything. The ferry was already boarding passengers, and I lined up with the others embarking the boat. Erin wasn't on the lower deck, so I headed up the stairs. Despite the amazing views of the Golden Gate Bridge and Alcatraz, few people had decided to brave the cold winds cutting across the open upper deck. I found Erin sitting alone on one of the wooden benches, wrapped in a peacoat, a knit cap, and a scarf. She gazed out at the gray-blue water and the painfully blue, cloudless sky.

"Hey," I said, sitting next to her.

She started. "Remy! I thought you couldn't make it."

"I wanted to be sure you were alone," I explained. "How were things last night? I was worried about you."

She shrugged. "No need. Alcais was just being Alcais."

An evil prick, then.

A smile curved her mouth as if she'd read my thoughts. "You really hate him, don't you?" My brows rose, and she added, "I saw your face last night. And your friend's."

I frowned. "I'm sorry about him. I think maybe there

are things you don't know about your brother. Things that he's done."

"Like what?"

Her brown eyes shone with an innocent light, and I debated how much to tell her. Would I be putting her in danger if I shared too much? Then again, if she knew what Franc and Alcais were capable of, maybe she would be willing to help.

She touched my hand, her pink knit mitten forming a barrier between her skin and mine. "It's okay. You can tell me. I know Alcais isn't a good person."

Of course she knew. As his sister, she was his most frequent victim. Despite that, I didn't think she understood exactly how cruel Alcais could be. Could I really tell her what a monster he was? With my father's life in the balance, I would do almost anything, and shattering her illusions was a small thing. We had a twenty-minute ride, and I used most of it.

Erin's face blanched white when I told her about the things my grandfather and Alcais had done to Asher and me. The kidnapping. The torture. The ways Franc had manipulated me. Then I told her about Yvette and the other Healers whom my grandfather had sacrificed to buy the cooperation of a few Protectors.

"Oh my God," she whispered, tears sliding down her cheeks and dripping into her scarf. "I knew her. Yvette was one of the kindest people you could meet. She helped as many people as she could."

I don't think Erin knew how she shook, and I wrapped an arm around her shoulder, ensuring my guard stayed up. Once I'd touched her with my defenses down, and I'd almost attacked her. That was the first time I'd learned that in some ways I was like other Protectors, and that I could steal a Healer's energy. I had to be careful around them, or risk hurting them.

"We trusted Franc," she said in a shattered voice.

"I'm sorry," I said.

The words seemed inadequate. I'd rocked the foundations of her world. The person Erin trusted to take care of her and her family had betrayed her. He'd betrayed me, too.

"If my mother knew . . ."

She didn't finish that thought. Perhaps she questioned exactly what her mother knew or what Dorthea would do with the knowledge. I didn't know, and I was so, so sorry that I'd planted a seed of doubt. Lost trust acted like a weed spreading through a garden.

"And Alcais . . ." she continued. "I thought I knew what he was capable of, but what he did to your friend. No wonder he looked like he wanted to kill my brother last night."

The boat bounced in the choppy water, and we slowed as we approached the dock at Tiburon. Time was running out.

"There's something else I need to tell you, and I really hope you don't freak out." I explained about my mother and father and my mixed blood and watched her eyes grow so wide they threatened to pop out of her skull. "I didn't know I was part Protector until I met Asher. Hell, I didn't even know what Healers or Protectors were. Since I found out last year, it seems like everyone is either trying to kill me or control me."

I thought Erin would be afraid of me after my admission. After all, she'd grown up fearing Protectors. She surprised me by giving me a crooked smile. "Well, that explains a lot, doesn't it? I wondered why Franc was experimenting on you, pushing you. The way he tricked you into healing Melinda was so cruel. I couldn't forgive him for that."

My grandfather had lured me into curing a stranger by pretending the woman was family. I'd almost died taking on her rare blood disease, and it turned out she wasn't a relative after all. The bastard had been testing the limits of what I could cure for his own purposes.

Erin shook her head. "People speculated about why you left. There have been a lot of whispers."

"What does Franc say?"

She pulled her hat down to cover the tips of her red ears. "Not much. Things haven't been the same. He's been disappearing more. He sends our men out on missions all the time, but they won't talk about where they've been or what they've been doing."

He'd sent them to follow me, I realized.

"People are nervous. I think they know Franc is keeping secrets, but everyone is afraid to question him after all he's done for us. But then, he has his own agenda, doesn't he?"

I grimaced. "He thinks he can use me to figure out how to make male Healers with powers. That or use me as a weapon against Protectors." I hesitated to tell her more, but I had to get it out. "Erin, he took my father. He's using him as bait. It's why I'm here. To find my dad."

Erin deflated and bent forward to brace her elbows on her knees. She was silent so long that I thought maybe she didn't believe me or that I'd gone too far, told her too much. Then she took a shaky breath and turned wounded eyes on me. "He really is a monster, isn't he?"

"Yes," I said simply.

The Protectors had turned him into one when they'd killed my grandmother in front of him. To them, she'd been one more Healer to use, but to my grandfather, she'd been everything. That didn't excuse the choices he'd made.

A voice squawked over the speakers, announcing that we should prepare to disembark the ferry. I rushed on. "I have no right to ask you for anything, but I—"

"Stop right there. I'll be sick to my stomach if you think

you have to ask me to help find your father." She sat up and took my hand. "That's what you were going to say, right? You don't even have to ask, friend. You once stood up for me when my brother hurt me. It's my turn to help you."

I swallowed, fighting a wave of emotion, and squeezed Erin's fingers in gratitude.

"We'll find your father, Remy."

For the first time in ages, I let myself believe it was true.

My phone blew up with text messages on the return ferry ride.

R U OK? That one was from Asher. Lucy's message was more to the point: WHERE THE HELL R U? I had known they would be angry and hurt that I had gone off on my own, and I braced myself for what was to come. I sent them a message of BE HOME SOON and tucked my phone away.

I retrieved my car from the Pier 39 lot and drove to the house, checking constantly to ensure I wasn't followed. Eventually, I pulled into the garage and sat in the unmoving car, gathering myself for the coming fight. My door opened, and I was yanked out of my seat. Furious was one way to describe Asher's expression. Apoplectic was another. Over his shoulder, Lucy appeared, and she didn't look much better.

"Where have you been?" Asher asked, his voice deep with rage.

"Meeting Erin. I left you a note."

I didn't mean to sound so defensive, but the words came out that way.

"A note? You go off alone, and you leave a fucking note." Lucy glared at me in disbelief. "I can't believe you."

I opened my mouth to answer her, but Asher shook me. "You do whatever you want with no regard for anyone

else. Do you know what we went through when we realized you'd left?"

Asher released me when I stepped back, and his hands
formed into fists at his sides. "I'm sorry I worried you, but
I had to go. I was careful."

"Oh, well, it's okay you scared us to death so long as
you were *careful.*" Sarcasm oozed from Lucy's words. She
looked ready to yell more, but suddenly turned on her
heel, heading for the stairs to the house. "You know what?
I can't even look at you right now."

That hurt like a bitch. I'd expected anger, but nothing
this extreme. "Erin is going to help us," I called out. Lucy
paused on the stairs, her body tensing. "I told her about
Dad, and she's going to see what she can find out."

After a few seconds, Lucy continued on without responding. That left Asher to deal with. I shut the car door
and leaned against it. He studied me, and I struggled not
to squirm under the intense perusal.

He shook his head. "You're not really sorry, are you?
Not really."

I lifted my chin. "I'm sorry I worried you," I repeated.

"But not that you went alone," he guessed, widening his
stance.

There was an odd acceptance in his words that unsettled me. It sounded too close to defeat. "What was I supposed to do, Asher? Lucy is in enough danger. If I could
keep her away from one meeting, why wouldn't I? And
you . . ."

I stopped, unwilling to admit that I hadn't trusted him.
Deep down, I had worried about how he would react if
we encountered Alcais or another Healer. I paced away
from Asher to hide my expression. How could I tell him
how alone I'd been since he'd shut me out? How abandoned I'd felt since we'd begun on this journey?

He'd been wrong about one thing. I was changing—

and I had nobody to confide in. The last time I'd felt safe had been with Gabe. Unbidden, I pictured Asher's brother as I'd last seen him in the Blackwells' kitchen. He'd said things that had terrified me. Things I'd tried to forget. I hadn't spoken to him in months, but a sudden yearning rose up in me to hear his voice.

I jumped when Asher laughed in a harsh voice. "What's so funny?" I asked, confused.

"Not a damn thing. Certainly not that you're standing in front of me and wishing my brother was here instead."

His words set my teeth on edge. "That's not true," I said stiffly.

"You care for Gabe," he accused, his jaw working.

I scowled. "I've told you that I care for Gabe. He's my friend."

Asher laughed again, and the bitter sound grated on my nerves. "Right. A friend. That's all you feel for him. Lie to me, but don't lie to yourself, Remy."

I was so sick of fighting this accusation. I'd chosen Asher. Even Gabe knew that. Asher was the one walking away, not me. "Are you really going there?" I asked, the words weighted with the anger I wanted to unleash.

"I don't know what you're talking about."

I stalked toward him and stopped with the toes of my shoes an inch from his. "Oh, it's okay for you to call me a liar, but what about you?" I was tired of stuffing everything down. Of pretending that I was okay when Asher ducked away from my touch or thought up a reason to avoid being alone with me. I wasn't okay, and he wasn't the only one hurting. My father had been taken. My stepmother was in a coma. I was suddenly taking care of my seventeen-year-old sister in an impossible situation. I'd lost everything, and he treated me like a diseased leper.

"What about me?" he asked, caution entering his voice too late.

I placed a hand on his chest and shoved. "This isn't about Gabe, and you know it. He's one more excuse to push me away. Just like you've been doing for weeks."

"That's not true."

"Lie to me, Asher, but don't lie to yourself," I mocked. "There's only one of us in this relationship. Let me give you a clue. It's not you."

Asher's jaw tensed the way it did when he ground his teeth. He wanted to yell at me, to strike out at me.

Hurt, I stared up at him. "Last night you said that you hated how mortal you've become because you can't protect me."

"And you think I lied?" he asked, outraged.

I shook my head. "No. But I don't think it was the whole truth. You won't admit it, but you're angry with me. Because of me, you were taken. And because of me, you felt everything they did to you."

Asher's eyes widened in fear. Something inside him had broken when my grandfather's men had tortured him. He couldn't get past it, and I understood. Hadn't I been tortured by Dean for years? Didn't I still have nightmares about it? Acting on instinct, I reached out to offer comfort. He took a big step back, and my hand hung in the air. *When will I learn?*

"You can deny it all you want, but your body tells the truth every time I reach for you." The words scraped out of my chest.

For one second, Asher's mouth softened like I'd reached him, but then a new determination lit his face. "This isn't working," he said, in a harsh voice. "I'll stay until we find your father, but this is over. We're over."

We had been since he'd suggested a break. Maybe even before that. I finally understood what it meant when people spoke of a broken heart, because mine splintered into a thousand tiny pieces. It was all I could do to stay standing when I lost my ability to do anything but absorb the raw, agonizing pain.

Asher's phone rang, and he answered it, eager to escape our conversation. I could tell it was Lottie, and I turned away. Asher suddenly gripped my arm, and his worried expression said it all.

My stepmother had taken a turn for the worse.

# CHAPTER SIX

*S*an Francisco was cold, but Chicago was a bitter, icy hell. Snow blanketed everything, and where there wasn't snow, there was ice. By contrast, the lobby of the Chicago Memorial Hospital was stifling. Asher hugged his sister like he wouldn't let her go, and I turned away from witnessing the easy way he touched another.

"How is my mom?" Lucy asked when they separated.

Lottie looked as pretty as she always had. Her chin-length bob, red lipstick, and angled bone structure made her look older than the sixteen she'd been when time froze her. She shared Asher and Gabe's green eyes, but not their height. Like Lucy, her head barely reached my shoulder.

Lottie grimaced. "Not good. I'm sorry. The doctors will be able to explain it better."

She walked us to the hospital elevator. Asher, Lucy, and I had caught a red-eye flight to Chicago, not an easy task when we had to sneak around and worry that Franc's men might catch us. We hadn't spotted anyone at the airport, but imagining them following us led to a sleepless night. It showed in our wrinkled clothes and the circles under our eyes. I'd hoped that my stepmother's condition might have changed for the better during the night, but Lottie's grim answer killed that idea. The sense of doom that had hovered since the call came wouldn't go away.

"Oh God," Lucy said.

She reached for Asher's hand, and I told myself it was a good thing. She should have somebody to comfort her, and in the last months he'd become a kind of brother figure to her. It was odd how a crisis could bring people together or rip them apart. The two of them hadn't exactly excluded me during the flight, but I hadn't been capable of offering much to the conversation. I wanted to crawl into a hole and shore up a wall behind me, but I couldn't do that now. So I focused on putting one foot in front of the other and taking the next breath, hoping I could survive this, too.

Lottie shot a confused glance at Lucy and Asher's joined hands and the good three feet of distance between them and me in the elevator. Clearly, Asher hadn't told her anything. I avoided her questioning gaze by staring at my feet and calling myself a coward.

"This way," she said, when the doors opened.

We exited the elevator on the floor marked Intensive Care Unit. The scents of sick people and the chemicals used to clean up after them wafted up my nose, and a panic attack threatened. That desire to run wouldn't go away. Nothing good had ever come of a visit to the hospital. Vivid memories assaulted me, and I tried to shove them away as I trailed after the others. There was no room for thoughts of my mother today. I would not remember how she had died from an injury like Laura's.

Lottie pointed us toward an empty waiting room and went to find a nurse. We took off our winter wear and stood around in awkward silence until she returned with Laura's doctor, a middle-aged Japanese man with a soothing baritone voice. Dr. Okada explained my stepmother's condition, using a lot of technical gibberish.

"I don't understand," Lucy asked, with a helpless gesture. "What does all of that mean?"

"I'm sorry," Dr. Okada said. "Her heart is weakening, and she's not eligible for a transplant. I'm afraid it's only a matter of time. A day, maybe less."

Lucy broke down. She fell against me, her body shaking with sobs that rattled out of her chest. Her tears dampened my shirt, and I rubbed her back in comforting circles. Through it all, I felt myself shutting down, all systems powering off. The pain floated away, and the apathy settled over me like an old companion. The way cleared for me to take care of business like I had all those years I'd taken care of my mother. There would be details to go over, plans to make, and my sister to watch over. The responsibility would be mine because there was nobody else.

Asher touched my hand, and I looked through him. He didn't figure into my plans for today. I couldn't deal with him, too. He swallowed, and his hand fell away.

"You can visit with her, one at a time," Dr. Okada said. Then he was gone, his white coat swishing behind him as he went off to save people who didn't have weak hearts.

Lucy's sobs didn't stop, but they quieted. She shuddered against me with great hiccups, sweating like an overwrought child. I pulled away to see her red eyes and shattered expression. "Lucy, do you want to see her first?"

She nodded.

"Come on," Lottie said, with unexpected gentleness. "I'll show you where she is."

She sent a sympathetic glance my way, and I remembered that she had lost both her parents and a brother on the same day. She took Lucy's arm to lead her away, and I was left alone with Asher. I retreated to a blue armchair. Happy striped wallpaper covered the walls, and a generic painting of a flower hung in front of me. Did anyone really believe that a picture of a flower would offer solace when all you could think about was how a loved one would never make it outside to see the real thing again? Idiots.

"Remy?" Asher repeated my name until I glanced at him. "Are you okay?"

He had probably read my mind, so what was the point of lying? "My stepmother is dying because of what I am. No, Asher. I'm not okay."

Despite my harsh words, my voice sounded flat. He didn't say anything else, and I was glad. Silence made it easier to sink into the nothingness. When Lucy returned, she wore a shocked expression as she chose a chair near Asher.

I rose to follow Lottie out of the room and jumped when Asher touched my arm. "Be careful. I know she's your mom, but . . . be careful."

I shifted so he had to drop his hand and walked away. Down the hall, Lottie had stopped in front of a door. I moved past her and the door *whoosh*ed closed behind me. It was just me, my stepmother, and the unnatural sounds of the machines keeping her alive. I looked at her in the bed and saw my mother instead. Laura's face was replaced by Anna's faded features, old bruises coloring her jaw and terror in her eyes.

*He'll come after you,* Anna had warned. *He knows. All my fault.*

Her last words had been a confession and a warning that my stepfather would try to kill me. She'd died, and I hadn't been able to do a damn thing about it.

I pinched the skin on my palms to stay anchored. "No," I whispered. "Laura's not Anna."

I took a tentative step closer to the bed with its white sheets and pink blanket. Laura's red curls had grown longer, and they framed her face, highlighting how pale her skin was. She'd lost so much weight. Already a petite woman, she now looked incredibly frail. I leaned closer and sniffed.

My stepmother's hugs had come with a cloud of floral perfume, but that was replaced by the slight odor of sweat and antiseptic.

The barrier I had erected around my heart teetered. This woman had welcomed me into her home. She had shown me more love in a few months than my mother had given me in a lifetime. Laura had given her affection without constraints, uncaring that I wasn't hers by blood. I grasped the bed frame to stay upright. What had I done? I should have stayed away from her.

"I'm so sorry, Mom."

My guttural whisper sounded loud in the room. I unfurled my energy into the air. The doctors could be wrong about her condition. I reached out to touch her arm, but I found myself bodily picked up and removed from the bed.

"Let me go!"

"No," Lottie said, locking steely arms around me.

She shook her head at me, her chin-length bob swaying. She looked sad as her gaze transferred to Laura, and that shocked me. She had only tolerated me because of Asher. Once she had tried to give me up to the Protectors to keep us apart. Now she almost seemed to hold me the way one friend might comfort another.

"She's too far gone, Remy," she said. "Not even you can save her."

My shoulders slumped. I could heal a complete stranger, but not this woman whom I dearly loved. What was the point of having these stupid powers? Bitterness surged, mixing with grief. Everything was so screwed up.

"She didn't deserve this. It's not fair," I said.

"No. It's not." She didn't offer words of comfort to make me feel better, but then, I wouldn't have believed them anyway. "Come on." She pulled me toward the door.

Without trying to be obvious about it, I freed my hand

from her grasp. All I needed was another Protector becoming mortal because of me. I followed her from the room, and she stopped in the hallway instead of returning to the waiting room.

Her green eyes narrowed on me as she leaned against the wall. "What's going on with you and Asher?"

"You should ask him," I said, focusing on a spot over her head.

I didn't want to be the one to tell her that Asher had ended things. I couldn't without falling apart, and there wasn't room for that right now.

"Have you heard from Gabe?" I asked to distract her.

She nodded with a speculative look in her eyes. "He asks about you."

"I'm sure he's worried about Asher."

"Yeah. Asher." Lottie smirked as if she knew I'd sidestepped her hint, and that look reminded me of how she used to hate me. I'd never mentioned that Gabe had feelings for me, but her brothers might have told her. It didn't mean anything that I missed him, and I wouldn't let Lottie make it mean more.

I bit the inside of my cheek and trained my gaze on the floor. She wore black high heels with her skinny jeans as if the snow outside didn't affect her. Knowing her powers, it probably didn't. I would never be able to repay her for what she'd done for my family.

"Lottie, thank you. You didn't have to do this. Stay here, I mean."

She tilted her chin in acknowledgment. "I know what it's like to lose a mom. I'm sorry, for what it's worth."

I nodded. "I'm sorry, too."

There was nothing else to say because we'd never been friends. Asher looked relieved to see me when we returned to the waiting room. He exchanged a glance with his sister, and I guessed he had sent her after me. I didn't know what I was supposed to think about that, so I set it aside for later. Lucy's face was pinched with grief, her black curls in disarray from running her hands through them. She'd go crazy sitting cooped up in the small, cheerful room. I grabbed my purse from where I'd left it on the floor.

"Come on, Luce. Let's go for a walk. There must be a coffee machine around here somewhere."

We followed a sign to an alcove that hid the vending machines. For once, I really didn't want coffee. I didn't think I'd be able to choke the hot liquid down, but I needed something to do with my hands. A nurse in pink scrubs rushed past the alcove as I dug through my wallet for quarters.

"Did you try to heal her?" Lucy asked in a tiny voice.

I froze. My hand shook, and I dropped a coin. It rolled across the tiled floor and disappeared under the machine. I waited until it was gone to raise my eyes to Lucy's. "I can't. I want to, but she's too far gone."

"Please, Remy," she begged. "You have to try."

I gripped my purse with clenched fingers. "Lucy, I can't. Her injuries . . . They're too much."

I didn't mention that I would absorb Laura's wounds: Lucy already knew that. She grabbed my arm and shook it with rising violence. I sensed the helpless rage in her and wanted to close my eyes against the lash of it.

"You have to," she insisted.

Her nails dug into my skin, but I didn't pull away. The inevitable door slammed closed, locking me into a fate that I'd sensed coming since Lottie had called.

"I've tried to heal a wound like hers before," I said. "It's impossible."

"You're talking about your mom, aren't you? The woman

was a shit mother, but you tried to save her. My mom has been nothing but good to you, while you've lied and gone behind her back. How can you refuse to help her?"

Her words battered at my control. "That's not fair," I whispered in a bleak voice. "I love Laura. I would do anything for her. But even if I set aside the danger and tried, it might not do any good. There are no guarantees with injuries like hers."

"You have to try! Please!"

I hesitated, torn between the desire to do what my sister asked and what I knew to be true. Lottie had stopped me from touching my stepmother for a reason. I would absorb Laura's injuries. Her failing heart. Her head wound. I could die, and even then, I might not be able to save her. And that assumed my attempts to heal her worked when I hadn't been able to heal her before now.

"Lucy . . ." I pleaded, reaching for her. *Don't ask me to do this.*

She shoved away from me in disgust, and my heart ached at the hatred in her narrowed eyes. "You did this," she accused. "They hurt her because of you, and you're going to let her die."

"That's enough, Lucy." We both started at Asher's harsh voice. He vibrated with anger as he stared at my sister. "Remy didn't make those men hurt your mother. She would die before she let harm come to any of you."

"I'm sure I'd believe you if my dad hadn't been taken, and my mother wasn't down the hall dying because of the people after *her*. Funny how everyone around her falls while she comes out standing every time. You should know that better than anyone."

Lucy pushed past Asher and disappeared around the corner, the sound of her sobs reaching us. Asher appeared torn between following her and staying with me.

I helped him decide by straightening my shoulders and

blanking my expression. "Go after her. She shouldn't be alone, and God knows she doesn't want me."

He hesitated for a second and then nodded. I watched him go, choking back despair. Lucy was right about everything. I imagined what my father would say if he was here. Somehow I couldn't get past the grief and blame that I knew would be carved into his face. I hadn't hurt Laura, but my choices had brought this upon us. Nobody had made me go to Franc. No, that had been all me. My grandfather wouldn't have known about my parents if I had kept my distance. Asher had warned me, but I'd rushed in, so sure I could handle things.

*My fault, my fault, my fault.*

My feet marched me to the door of Laura's room before I'd made a decision, except this had always been my destiny. The hardest choices sometimes boiled down to the most basic truths. I wanted Laura to live more than I feared pain or death. I would gladly pay the cost for her. I trembled, my hand shaking violently as I turned the doorknob.

The room was empty but for my too-still stepmother. I had to hurry before the others returned or fear took over. I touched my stepmother's hand and scanned her body. Laura's heart was shot. Worse, her head proved an impenetrable black fortress that my mind fought against entering. Perhaps it was my body's defense mechanism: I used my mind to focus my energy during a healing and taking on a head injury would cloud that and prevent me from healing myself. Whatever the reason, her injuries seemed impossible to take on. I battered against Laura's mind, trying to find a way in without success. I shoved my power at her, and nothing happened because my body instinctively fought against a death sentence.

*I can do this, Mom,* I thought, stroking her forehead. *I won't give up.*

I pictured my stepmom hugging me when I got home from school, and the joy she took from sharing her home and family with me. She'd been so proud at my graduation and enraged at the way I'd been treated by my mother. Stark love had shone out of her eyes when she helped pick up the pieces of me that had been left after my mother and stepfather had finished with me. She had accepted all of my rough edges and helped save me when I didn't think I was worth saving. Those were not gifts you could repay.

Something loosened inside me. I stopped fighting, and the tendrils of my power wound through her, healing her broken body. Her heart thudded triple-time like it would explode out of her chest. Her spine bent and bowed off the bed as she gasped around the tube in her mouth. Her mind . . . oh God, her mind unsnarled, the wound healing. Her eyes snapped open, and hope replaced despair. Then I saw how empty her brown eyes were. She was gone. The woman I'd known wasn't in there anymore.

Terror slammed through me as the machines blared warning alarms. I'd made things worse. Her body couldn't handle the energy I'd pushed at it. Her heart skipped, stuttered, stalled.

A door slammed open. Hands pushed and shoved me out of the room, breaking my connection with her skin. *Not again,* I thought, as my pulse raced and my heart worked overtime. *Please, God, no.*

Lucy appeared beside me in the hall with Asher, crying as she watched the doctors try to save Laura. Nobody noticed when I stumbled back and slammed into the opposite wall, crushed by the overwhelming pain.

*I'm having a heart attack,* I realized.

My vision blurred. From a million miles away, I heard Lucy sob and I knew Laura was dead.

# CHAPTER SEVEN

*N*obody noticed when I slumped on the floor. Laura's injuries had reverberated back onto me. The strong *thump* of my heart pulsed in slow, thready beats, and pain streaked up my left side. The center of my chest felt like a vise had been wrapped around it, and the pressure tightened until I struggled to breathe. Knives stabbed the inside of my skull, undermining my ability to think. There was a reason my body had fought against this.

Instinct kicked in when I began to lose consciousness. Time froze and the hospital hallway faded when energy surged at my heart. The muscle seized for ten of the longest seconds of my life before it kick-started to life. Beat by beat, my pulse picked up the pace. Adrenaline stormed my system, and my world narrowed to getting my breathing under control while the icy aftermath of healing spread through me. *Inhale. Exhale. Inhale. Exhale.*

"Remy?" Lottie spoke from somewhere above me. She crouched beside me and patted my arm awkwardly. "I'm so sorry."

She watched Asher holding Lucy, and I realized that she didn't know. None of them had a clue about what I'd done. She thought me bowed with grief, but that wouldn't last when my post-healing hypothermia kicked in. Using the wall as a crutch, I rose to my feet, thinking to get help.

Asher could help me. My heart skipped a beat, stuttering like it would stop again. My legs almost gave out under me, and I leaned against the wall to stay upright. Every breath hurt, and my head throbbed with a pain so intense I gritted my teeth. Even the light hurt, the fluorescent rays burning the back of my skull.

My movements drew Lucy's gaze. She swung around, an avenging angel pointing a finger at me. "This is your fault!" she screamed.

In that instant, I knew it would be useless to tell her that I'd tried my best to save our mother.

She shoved me, and I slammed into the wall, almost losing my footing. "You brought this on us. I hate you. Do you hear me? I hate you!"

Her shouting drew attention that we couldn't afford, and Asher tried to hush her. He couldn't even look at me. Lottie stepped toward Lucy, too, and I used the distraction to stumble away from them. My shaky limbs threatened to give out, but through sheer force of will, I kept going, even as my teeth chattered and chills racked my body. I didn't stop moving until I saw a sign for the hospital chapel. The wooden door opened with a slight shove, and I entered the dim room, grateful to find myself alone. Powers depleted, I collapsed on a pew in the darkened back corner, curling into myself as a cold sweat broke out on my skin. I fought off a wave of nausea.

I should have been crying. I wanted to cry, but I couldn't. Everything hurt too much.

Growing up with Dean and my mother had taught me about pain, though. I'd learned ways of dealing with it when I'd understood how my fear had excited Dean. My stepfather had used my emotions like weapons against me, and so I'd buried them. I set about doing that now. By the time the last of the shivers faded, I had dug a hole so deep that I could almost pretend I felt nothing. Almost.

*   *   *

At the funeral, I hid behind oversized sunglasses and watched my stepmother be buried far from her home with only the Blackwells, my sister, and me at her graveside. It shouldn't have been this way. My stepmother had been loved by so many people, and she'd deserved to have all those people present to celebrate her life and mourn her death. My father should have been there to grieve for his wife, but he didn't even know she was gone.

*My fault, my fault, my fault.* My heart almost seemed to beat to the words now.

After the service, we drove back to Lottie's apartment. She'd rented a small one-bedroom to stay in while she watched over Laura. The place felt crowded with four people occupying a space meant for one. Sadness stifled the air, making every breath a workout even before you factored my weakness into things. Despite the cold outside, I slipped through the sliding glass door off the living room. Lottie had a couple of lounge chairs on the enclosed balcony, and I curled up on one, tucking my legs under the skirt of my black dress. Even the gray skies seemed to mourn my stepmom, crying tears that I couldn't. The rain poured down a few feet away, creating an invisible wall around the balcony and making a mess of the snow on the ground. Nobody could see me, and I let my guard down for a minute.

The second I stopped trying to hide the pain, it engulfed me. A sharp, constant ache bashed the inside of my skull like the mother of all migraines, making the sunglasses a necessity to block out the light. Sometimes my heart beat erratically like it would explode out of my chest. The damage was serious, and it took the little energy I had to stay upright and moving. I could have asked Asher to help me heal myself, but that option had been taken off the table. I would rather deal with the pain than see him hate me for making him weaker. The same was true of Lottie.

It turned out it wasn't too difficult to hide my injuries when everyone avoided me. Lottie kept her distance, not wanting to be human. My sister could hardly look at me. She had no idea I'd tried to heal our mother. I could have told her, but what was the point? I'd failed. And Asher . . . Things had changed between us so completely that a piece of my soul had been severed and then cauterized.

The sliding glass door opened, and Asher stepped out like my thoughts had called him. Maybe they had because my mental guard was down. He carried a plate of food, which he put on the ground by my chair. He'd changed out of his dark suit and into jeans and a light blue T-shirt that molded to his muscles. He looked strong and the desire to lean on him was so tempting. Whatever nightmares he might be having, he was hiding it well.

"You should eat," he said with worry in his voice.

If he suspected how close I'd come to dying, he didn't say. I nodded. I wouldn't eat, but I wanted him to go away. His presence and the ever-growing distance between us magnified the pain, and I couldn't take much more. Instead of leaving like I wanted, he sat across from me in the other chair. His perusal ate at me. I knew what I looked like. The injuries had taken their toll even in a few days. I'd lost weight I couldn't spare, and without the sunglasses to hide them, my eyes had taken on a sunken quality.

"Are you okay?" he asked in a quiet voice. "You've hardly said a word in days."

"I'm dealing," I said with no emotion. I changed the subject. "How's Lucy?"

She'd disappeared into Lottie's bedroom when we'd returned to the apartment. Her sobs had echoed through the rooms until I'd had to retreat to the balcony.

"Not good. She needs you."

My mouth curved in a humorless smile. "She hates me. I'm the last person she needs."

"It wasn't your fault. She knows that."

*Lies. Don't lie to me, Asher.* It hurt how much I wanted to believe him. I rubbed a hand against my chest when it tightened. "You don't have to take care of me, Asher. It's not your job anymore, remember?"

*Please go away.* I just wanted to be alone. It was easier that way.

Asher didn't hear my thought or chose to ignore it. "You can't let her grieve alone."

I swung my legs to the side of the chair and faced him. "She has you."

He shook his head. "I'm not you."

I had been thinking about this since I'd left the chapel. Lucy needed someone, but she didn't want me. Asher didn't want to be around me because of how my powers changed him. The three of us were stuck together, but we'd often paired off for surveillance. Usually, I'd taken care of Lucy, but I didn't see how that could work anymore.

"She needs a friend, but it can't be me." My lip quivered, and I bit down on it hard enough to break the skin. "Lottie certainly isn't going to do it."

I couldn't bring myself to ask him, but he understood anyway. "You want me to watch out for her."

It wasn't a question. "Please," I begged. "She won't be alone, and you won't have to be near me. Problem solved."

His jaw clenched in frustration. "Don't do that. I care about you, Remy. I know you're hurting, even if you won't admit it."

For a moment, I thought he was acknowledging my injuries, but the emotion on his face didn't fit. Something wasn't right, and I couldn't put my finger on it. I spread my hands. "I'll say whatever you want. Do whatever you want. Just please do this. I don't want her to feel alone."

"But it's okay for you to be alone?" he asked.

My breath hissed out. "I *am* alone. You broke up with me, remember?"

He glanced away, his cheeks flushing pink in guilt. He rested his elbows on his knees, his white-knuckled hands clasped between them. He was so close, mere inches away. My defenses shook, and I thought, *Please touch me, Asher. Make me feel something other than the pain.*

The rain continued to fall, and Asher's expression didn't change.

"I didn't mean for things to happen like this," he said.

That statement encompassed so many things. He hadn't meant to become mortal. He hadn't meant to be taken hostage. He hadn't meant to attack me in the middle of a nightmare. He hadn't meant to break up with me the night before my stepmother died. He hadn't meant to fall out of love with me. None of this was his fault.

"I know. I'm sorry." I hooked my hair behind my ear and stared at my feet. "I don't know what you want from me."

His toe almost touched mine, and I shifted away. I couldn't let him touch me. Not now, when I was hanging on by an unraveling thread.

"I want to know you're okay," he said.

*I'm far from it,* I thought. I shrugged. "Of course. Aren't I always?"

He stared into my eyes like he was trying to read my mind. *I need you, Asher,* I thought. *I'm right here.* He rose, putting his hands in his pockets, the way he often did around me. The better to avoid touching me.

"I'll watch out for Lucy," he promised. "You have my word."

"Then everybody wins."

Asher didn't answer, and I couldn't blame him. Even I didn't believe that lie. He disappeared into the apartment, and I turned away, clutching my stomach. The tears almost came then, as I mourned one more death. I'd figured out what wasn't right. My defenses had been down, and he hadn't known. He hadn't been able to read my thoughts.

Our bond was broken.

Lady Gaga's "Poker Face" blared out and snapped me out of a dreamless sleep. It had taken me ages to fall asleep on the couch, and I didn't appreciate being woken. I opened one eye to glance at the clock on Lottie's wall. Six P.M. I groaned. Lottie had left her phone on the coffee table. I would have to kill her or make her taste pickles later, at the very least. Beside the phone was a note in Asher's handwriting. *Took Lucy and Lottie to grab dinner. Didn't want to wake you. Be back by 7.*

It didn't escape me that they'd probably wanted to get away from me. The phone rang again, and I glanced at the screen out of habit. The caller ID read *Gabe,* and I snapped up the phone without another thought.

"Gabe?"

There was a moment of silence and his deep voice came over the line. "Remy? Where's Lottie?"

He didn't sound upset exactly, but I could hear the confusion in his clipped British accent. "Out to dinner with Asher and Lucy. I was asleep."

"Ah . . . I'm sorry I woke you." Another awkward pause. "How are you?"

"Fine." *Awful.* "What about you? Where are you?"

"Europe. Paris, to be exact. I've been meeting up with old friends, other Protectors. There's an old story about someone like you, born of both bloodlines sometime in the sixteen hundreds. I've been asking around, but so far it seems to be more fairy tale than truth."

That sounded about right. I wouldn't have believed stories about someone like me, either.

He continued. "I've been asking about Franc, too, but

if people know the Protectors who are helping your grandfather, they're not talking."

I'd hurt Gabe when I chose Asher. He'd told me that he loved me, and I'd rejected him. Gabe could have washed his hands of me, but he was out there searching for answers.

"Thanks for trying," I said in a husky voice. "It means a lot."

"Remy, what's wrong?" he demanded. "Why are you with Lottie?"

I sighed. "You haven't spoken to her? Or Asher?"

"Not for a few weeks. I've been around Protectors, and there's been too much gossip about us. I didn't want to take any chances until I was clear. What's going on?"

His voice dropped, and the sound of it rumbled over me. The throbbing started behind my eyes, and I let my head fall back against the pillow.

"Aren't we friends still? Come on, Remington."

That old nickname cracked off a piece of the iceberg that had taken up residence inside me. "It's Laura," I blurted out. "She died." My voice cracked, and I threw an arm up to cover my eyes.

His breath gusted out in a weighty sigh. "Oh man. I'm so sorry, sweetheart. How are you holding up?"

"Lucy's devastated," I said. "She blames me. I . . . Well, I'm sure she just needs time."

A lifetime should about do it.

"I didn't ask about Lucy. I asked about you. How are you?"

I never could fool him. "As well as can be expected, I guess. My heart is broken."

"Did you try to heal her?"

He asked the question without blame, but I felt guilty anyway.

"She was too far gone," I said. He would assume that meant I didn't try to heal her, and I was okay with that. What could Gabe do if he knew? My chest constricted and I rubbed a circle on it with my fist. "It doesn't matter. Listen, I think you should know . . ."

I hesitated. If I told Gabe that Asher was losing his powers, Asher might be angry. Maybe it would be better for him to tell his brother in his own time. Except we were headed back to San Francisco tomorrow. What if Asher got hurt?

"Yeah?" Gabe prompted. "What should I know?"

"Call Asher," I said. It was my compromise. Gabe would know something was up, but I wouldn't have to betray Asher. "Soon," I added to be safe.

There was a moment of silence. "There you go taking care of other people again," he said, and I knew he understood. "Who's taking care of you, Remington?" he asked in a softer voice.

I almost came undone, but I steeled myself against the emotions. Gabe would join us if I asked him to, but I wouldn't ask. I might feel less alone if he was around to share the burden, but I would be using him and his feelings for me. I hadn't fallen far enough to do that to him. Suddenly, I was overcome by how much I'd missed him. It shouldn't have been so difficult to hear his voice again after all these months, but I hadn't known how we would slip back into the easy friendship we'd shared before everything had gone to hell. I had to get off the phone before I weakened.

"I'm okay, Gabe. I'm a survivor, remember?" Before he could answer, I added, "I should go. If Lottie finds me on her phone, she's going to lose it. You know how she is."

The forced humor in my voice fell flat. I said good-bye, and Gabe echoed me without argument. Perhaps he had finally remembered that he wasn't supposed to care about me anymore. And who knew? After all this time, he probably didn't love me anymore. Everyone moved on.

It was hours before I realized that Gabe had no idea Asher had broken up with me. Relief sighed through me. His pity might have put me over the edge.

# CHAPTER EIGHT

*O*ne morning, about a week after we'd returned to San Francisco, I poured myself a cup of coffee in a travel mug and slipped out of the house on quiet feet with my phone in my coat pocket. I'd left a note, but I'm not sure it would have mattered.

Somewhere between Chicago and San Francisco, I'd discovered a well of anger. My life had gone to hell in the last months. I had been dumped by a man who had promised me the world, and then walked away when that world wasn't what he wanted after all. My sister hated me for not saving our mother, and she snarled at me, acting like she was the only one who had suffered a loss. Sometimes, I wanted to lash out at both of them, and the urge had almost become uncontrollable. That's why I'd suggested scouting on my own this last week. I hadn't wanted to cause more pain when they both looked edgy and brittle. The others had only put up a temporary resistance to my idea. Rather, Asher had argued for all of a day, but I hadn't backed down. They had hurt me, and I needed some distance from them so that I could lick my wounds.

I covered the couple of blocks to the beach in minutes. All my life, I'd lived near some body of water, and I wondered how people got by without an ocean to remind them how small they were.

At the water's edge, I sat on the sand, propping my elbows on my bent knees. I sipped my coffee and let the roar of the water and the soft sunrise work their magic. A few surfers in full body suits straddled their boards, riding the gentle lift and fall of the swells. They called out to each other every once in a while, though the words weren't intelligible. Burnished rose-gold light brushed everything, and the tightness in my chest eased a bit. I propped my sunglasses on my head and closed my eyes to soak up the rays, pretending they were warm like the light.

"Hello, Lottie," I said, not looking around. I eased my mental walls up to protect her.

I slid my sunglasses back over my eyes to avoid the migraine the light could cause. She dropped into the sand a few feet away, always careful to keep her distance. For once, she'd abandoned her heels and wore running shoes like me. She couldn't feel the cold like I could, but her angled face had colored a ruddy red from it just the same.

"How did you know I was there?" she asked.

I tossed her a small smile. "You always are. Asher asked you to follow me. Again."

I'd suspected that I hadn't really been patrolling on my own. I'd sensed her presence more than once, though Lottie had done a good job of remaining hidden.

"You knew," she accused.

The laces on my shoes gave when I untied them, and I took them off to shake the sand out. "He gave up the argument too easily. He knew I wouldn't cave so he went around me."

Lottie kicked off her own shoes and shook them out, too, gazing at the grains in disgust. She hadn't felt them. "You guys are so mental. He sends me after you and he watches over Lucy. Why don't you do us all a favor and watch over each other?"

"You know why," I said, observing her. "It's the same

reason you're practically sitting in Nevada." Mortality terrified Lottie, and she wanted nothing to do with my healing powers.

She flushed and didn't say anything.

"Can I ask you something?" I prodded.

Her eyes flashed annoyance, but she nodded.

"Why are you here, Lottie? In San Francisco, I mean."

It had bothered me when she had returned with us. She'd
been very clear on her decision to stay away from me.

She lifted a pile of sand in her hand and let it sift through
her fingers. I did the same, savoring the silky feel of it falling
away. The brine of the ocean filled my nostrils, coating my
soul with memories of sand castles and ice cream. So many
of my favorite moments could be revisited when I experienced certain sensations, but that wouldn't happen for
Lottie. I could help her senses return, but she rejected the
idea.

She wiped her hands on her designer jeans and considered her words. "My brothers. I would do anything for
them. They're the only family I have left, so if they need
me here, then here is where I'll be."

I respected her choice, one that I'd made before. "I get
that, but you have to know what you're risking." I waved
a hand between us. "You should stay away."

Lottie made a face. "Okay, Mom." I must have looked
stricken because she winced and muttered, "Sorry."

The wind tossed her neat sleek bob into a mess of brunette waves, and I remembered a photo I'd seen of her in
Asher's island house. She'd looked like a 1920s gangster
moll. Even at this time in the morning, she wore her trade-
mark red lipstick. I couldn't help asking, "Were you a flap-
per?"

Her mouth quirked in a mysterious smile that gave
nothing away. "I'm not a stranger to the Charleston." She
gave me a sly sideways look as she put her shoes back on.

"Does this mean we're sharing now? Because I've been dying to ask you when you decided to go Bono. I like the sunnies, but you never take them off anymore."

I snorted and rubbed my chest when that set off a new ache. My powers were returning a little more each day, but I hadn't been able to heal myself yet. I'd come out to the beach to try. Her eyes fell to my hand, and I dropped it to my side. My ringing phone saved me from answering.

"Hello," I said.

"Remy, it's Erin. We need to meet."

Erin wouldn't share her news over the phone. She insisted we meet in person, and I suggested Muir Woods. The woods consisted of six miles of trails with multiple loops and access points that would be too much ground for our enemy to cover in case this turned out to be a trap. Plus, it was always full of tourists and locals, and an attack in the open would be too conspicuous.

I drove the truck to the woods, while Lottie, Asher, and Lucy followed in the Mercedes. As we drove over the orange-red Golden Gate Bridge, I was reminded of my grandfather's promise to take me to Muir Woods once. Instead, he'd taken me to Melinda's house and tricked me into healing her. It was the last time I'd believed in him. Now, I couldn't help but wonder if he was behind this call from Erin.

The windy drive through the hills to Muir Woods ended at a crowded parking lot. I found a spot near the entrance and shut off the truck's ancient engine. I hopped out, pocketing the keys in my jacket and fingering the handle of the knife I'd hidden there. I'd dressed warmly in jeans, hiking boots, a scarf, a thick navy blue sweater, and a black waist-length jacket. The Mercedes approached, and the others drove by. They would find a parking spot and follow me into the woods at a distance with Lucy and Asher acting like any couple on a date, while Lottie scouted the hiking trails. As they passed, Lucy's gaze flicked to mine. Worry sparked in her eyes for just a second and was gone.

After Lottie and I had returned from the beach and shared the news of the meeting with Asher and Lucy, there hadn't been a lot of time for discussion. We'd only had a couple of hours to gather our things and make the drive across the bay. Asher had looked like he wanted to suggest we skip the meeting, but I'd stared him down. He could come with or stay behind, but I was going as long as there was a chance Erin knew something about my father. Lucy agreed with me. With Lottie acting as a neutral party, two were pitted against one, though my alliance with Lucy was shaky at best.

I walked toward the entrance with a bounce in my step. I shouldn't have been so happy to be walking into danger, but I was. Anything—even walking into a trap—had to be better than feeling cornered in a house with the others. Other girls could wear ratty sweats and holey T-shirts, eat Ben & Jerry's, listen to crappy breakup music, and cry to their friends when their boyfriends trampled on their hearts. I had to continue to live with him, watching him comfort my sister and making her smile. It didn't help that I'd asked him to do it.

After buying my ticket and a map, I entered the park, glancing around with curiosity. The main canyon floor had been designed to be accessible to everyone with various semi-flat loops that people could wander on. Thousands of redwoods, the tallest type of tree in the world, stretched high into the sky. Fog clung to the treetops, blocking out most of the sunlight, and I was able to remove my sunglasses. Asphalt paths and boardwalks curved around the centuries-old giant trees, one hollowed trunk large enough for people to walk inside. Green ferns and moss sprouted from the damp red-brown earth, clinging to tree trunks and branches. Birds chirped. Children laughed and ran down the path. The Redwood Creek trickled nearby. Hikers called to each other on the trails that spoked off into the hills. It would have been idyllic on any other day.

I strolled through the park, letting my mental walls down to sense any Protectors who might be near. The hair rose on the back of my neck as I felt something, but I couldn't pinpoint any threat. My footsteps echoed on the winding boardwalk, and my eyes scanned from side to side. Ten minutes later, I spotted Erin waiting for me near the bridge at Cathedral Grove as we'd discussed. The spot was far enough into the park to be secluded, but not so far that others wouldn't be around. Nobody appeared to be lurking in the foliage.

"Erin," I called when I was a few feet away.

She started and swung toward me on the path, her features locked in momentary panic until she recognized me. "Remy!"

Erin leaned against the fence that bordered the trail, and I followed her lead. She'd dressed warmly, too, bundled up in clothes similar to mine. Her eyes flitted about, never seeming to land on any object for long.

"Were you followed?" I asked.

She shook her head, her blond ponytail swinging behind her. "No. They think I'm over at Delia's." She focused on me again and her mouth opened in surprise. "Wow. You look awful."

"I have a cold," I lied. I'd been feeling better today, but then I usually did at the start of the day before I'd tired myself out. By the evening, I would be fading and forced to rest whether I wanted to or not.

"Are you sure?" Before I could step back, she touched my hand. I jerked away, but too late. Her eyes widened with horror and sympathy. "Remy, it's bad. You could die if you don't see to that."

Apparently, I could hide my injuries from the Protectors I lived with, but not this Healer. I smiled to reassure her. "I'm working on it."

Her brow wrinkled. "I'd help you if I could, but I don't have your power. I can't heal things this serious."

I tugged on her ponytail. "Don't worry. I need a little time to rest up and I'll be able to heal myself." Before she could question me more about the injuries, I asked, "You said you had news?"

I gestured for us to move, and we strolled along the path. A whisper of someone's energy floated in the air, and my head shot up. Anyone could have hidden on the hillside with all the foliage. We'd counted on the huge number of pedestrians walking the paths to keep them at bay. A flash of light caught my eye as I studied the hill above us, and I recognized the hair. Lottie tracked through the woods, keeping pace with us. That was who I'd sensed.

Beside me, Erin didn't seem to notice my unease. Her brown eyes shone with excitement. "It's your dad. I don't think he's in California."

My legs jolted to a stop, unable to carry me forward. "Are you sure?" My hands fisted so that I wouldn't reach for Erin.

Her head bobbed in an excited nod. Over her shoulder, I glimpsed Asher and Lucy approaching from the opposite direction. They played their part, holding hands as they explored the woods. They stood a mere fifteen feet away. I met Asher's eyes and he tensed when he saw my face. He raised a brow.

"Where—"

My question cut off when two things happened: Lottie whistled a warning from her lookout and two men approached from behind Asher and Lucy. The boardwalk clattered behind me, and I threw a glance over my shoulder and saw another man approaching. All three of them gave off Protector vibes as they boxed us in. It was a trap.

Asher and I snapped into motion, working in unison. We whipped Lucy and Erin about so they stood between our backs, as we faced the oncoming threat from either side. We'd never be able to take out three of them with Asher's weaker powers and my rotten health. Where was Lottie?

The tall thirty-something man in front of me had the same thought. "Where's the other one?" he snapped to his friends. His cultured British accent made him sound like he should be in a smoking jacket drinking cognac between seducing women like some second-rate James Bond. Black hair formed a deep V at his forehead where the hairline retreated at the temples. Dark whiskers shadowed his thin face, and dark blue eyes offset a narrow nose.

"Didn't see anyone else," one of the others answered in a Cockney accent. In the brief glance I sent his way, I noticed he had a big birthmark on his forehead. His shorter partner wore a newsboy cap and shiny loafers. In fact, they were all dressed for a business luncheon, not a walk in the woods.

*Good,* I thought. They hadn't found Lottie. I fingered the knife in my pocket and pulled it out, wondering if I would be forced to use it again.

Knockoff Bond dropped his gaze to the weapon. He stopped abruptly and held up both hands. "You don't have to do that," he said. His blue eyes wrinkled like I'd amused him.

My eyes narrowed. "Something funny?" I asked.

"You," he said. "You actually think you can take down three of us?"

I let my energy unwind in the air for a second and drawled, "Well, it wouldn't be the first time. Do you remember what pain feels like? Because I would love to remind you."

A hand gripped the sweater at my lower back. Asher didn't want me to push the stranger too far. He was probably right, but dealing with Dean had taught me never to back down. If you showed a predator a weakness, they would take advantage of it. He turned again to face the two men who had paused a few yards away. They seemed cautious but not poised to attack.

Knockoff Bond had stepped closer while my attention was divided. "You don't want to do that," I told him.

The knife didn't scare him. That was obvious from the amusement still on his face. He said, "A cut wouldn't be enough to stop me if I decided to put an end to this."

I trembled. Either rumors of my abilities were making the rounds of the Protectors, or these men worked for my grandfather. It made sense that Franc had sent them after Erin, guessing she would make contact with me again.

"Maybe not," I told him. "But that's not the only injury I'd transfer."

His questioning gaze roved over me. I dared him to attack, almost wanted him to. My injuries would weaken these men at best, but it would feel good to use my abilities again. I let my energy swirl in the air longer than before. His face tensed with the pain that the hum of my power caused Protectors.

He straightened and backed off a little. His entire demeanor changed from threatening to charming. "I'm not going to hurt you or your friends," he said. "I'm here to talk, Miss O'Malley. Just talk."

He lied. Protectors wouldn't let me go. My mind raced for a way to keep my friends safe, and I saw only one path. "Great. Let my friends go, and we can have a nice chat."

That hand at my back twisted my sweater harder, and I ignored it, widening my stance to stay balanced. Asher didn't want to leave me on my own. Noted. Too bad. He'd promised to watch over my sister. If he could get away with her, he'd better damn well go.

It was a moot point anyway. Knockoff Bond *tsk*ed and folded his arms. "I'm sorry. I can't do that."

"Then we really don't have anything to talk about, do we?"

A movement behind him distracted me. My eyes couldn't quite pinpoint what the blur was, and my first thought was that Lottie had arrived to rescue us. Knockoff Bond noticed my inattention and twisted toward the new threat. I launched forward, using my Protector speed. The blur swept past us, and I hoped Lottie rushed to help the others.

All the hours of training I'd done with Gabe kicked in. I slammed my flattened hand into Knockoff Bond's throat in a textbook throat strike, cutting off his ability to breathe. His hands shot to his neck, and I ducked down, sweeping ·my leg out to knock him off his feet. My next move would be to use the knife, but my fingers jerked open, the muscles refusing to grip the weapon. A wave of dizziness had me swaying like the trees as the knife clattered to the ground.

My heart seized and beat erratically.

*Not now. Please, God. Not now.*

My vision blurred, and I landed flat on my back staring up at a canopy of green. I waited for the attack to come, completely helpless to protect myself. Shouting sounded from a distance, and I heard the thud of fists pounding skin and bones. I whimpered.

Knockoff Bond's face appeared over me, and for a second, he reminded me of someone. His fingers gripped my shoulder in a painful grasp, and the image faded before I could catch hold of it. He gasped for air and his eyes narrowed with rage as he glared down at me. "You should have listened to me. Come with me now."

"Never," I choked out. I would never enslave myself to a bunch of Protectors. I pushed against him, but my hand fell to my side uselessly.

"You don't understand. We—"

"Get away from her!" Gabe shouted.

That couldn't be right. Gabe was in Europe. It had to have been Asher. Knockoff Bond disappeared as if he'd been ejected through the air, and the sounds of fighting resumed. A steel band tightened around my chest when I tried to breathe. Lucy appeared beside me. I groaned when she forced me to sit up, the pain ripping through me. One of her arms slipped under my armpit, and she heaved me up to my feet with Erin's help. We stumbled along the path with the two of them propping me up. Asher limped beside us, cradling an arm. From the angle it hung and the way his face blanched white with pain, I guessed it was broken.

"Where's Lottie?" I asked. We couldn't leave her behind. She'd just saved my life.

"Right here."

I glanced back, and there she was a few steps behind us. I frowned and would have stopped if Erin and Lucy hadn't kept me going. "I don't understand. Where did those Protectors go?"

No way would they have let us go. Not with only one Protector left standing. The odds had been in their favor when I went down. Suddenly, the last of my strength disappeared. My entire body went limp, and I felt myself falling into a face-plant when Erin and Lucy lost their grip on me. I was yanked up at the last second and bodily lifted into the air.

Gabe's chiseled, grim features hovered over me. The

most inane thought popped into my head; I'd forgotten how beautiful he was. "They took off after I bashed their leader's face," he said. "Be still, Remy. We'll take care of you. You can rest now."

He cradled me against his chest, his strength obvious in the easy way he carried me. I believed him when he said I could rest. For the first time in ages, I entrusted myself to another and let go, drifting into the abyss of unconsciousness where the pain didn't exist.

# CHAPTER NINE

*W*e broke into another house. I heard snatches of conversation. The consensus was that we shouldn't return to our house until we understood how they'd found us. Lottie had apparently collected a list of empty residences in the vicinity that we could use as safe houses, and we headed to the closest one in Sausalito, a small artsy community that faced San Francisco across the bay.

I didn't notice much about the house, except that it was furnished. Gabe lowered me to the overstuffed brown suede couch, and the others sprawled on the floor or in chairs in the living room. Lottie shut the blinds in the front window, cutting off the sunlight. I closed my eyes in relief. My sunglasses had been lost in the fight, and my head was killing me. I focused my energy enough to steady my heart again. The ache between my eyes didn't go away, but the room was dark enough that I could deal.

I sat up slowly and took stock of our group. Lottie, Gabe, and Erin had apparently come through the fight without a scrape. Lucy had a cut on her forehead, and Erin knelt before her chair, already healing the minor injury. I wondered what she would think when she realized she was in a room with three Protectors. Most likely, she'd run home screaming, and the best we could hope for was that we would be long gone by then.

Asher sat in an armchair by the fireplace, his long legs stretched out in front of him. His head rested against the chair's back and he stared at me with an unreadable expression. Gabe sat beside me on the couch, his hip against mine. His deep brown hair had grown out to his nape, and long waves fell over his forehead. He shared Asher's green eyes, angled bone structure, and proper accent, but he was larger and more muscular. His size used to scare me, but I'd gotten past that. His beauty, not so much. The man was sinfully handsome. I couldn't look at him for more than a second. If I did, I would blush and there was no reason to. I didn't think about him like that.

Gabe refused to be ignored. "What the hell happened to you back there?"

The room stilled as all attention swiveled to me. Dammit. Gabe never could let anything go.

I stuck my chin in the air. "I'm fine."

"Bullshit," he answered emphatically. "You went down before he laid a finger on you."

Erin shifted uncomfortably, and I glared at her with a silent warning to keep her mouth shut. She couldn't help me, and I wouldn't ask any of the others to give up their powers for me. Gabe wouldn't let this go, though. I had to prove I was okay. I rose and locked my knees when I began to sway. I put one foot in front of the other and tossed a triumphant look at the group when I made it to Asher without stumbling. I sat at his feet, suddenly glad that the distance had been so short. I felt like a weak kitten.

I reached for Asher, but Erin slid between us. "Let me," she whispered in my ear.

I didn't argue with her. If I was honest with myself, I didn't know if I could have healed Asher. It had been foolish to think I could. I moved back to give her room and listened to her soft voice telling Asher to put his guard down so she could heal him. A minute later, he groaned when the bone in his arm snapped into place. Erin moved away, her features tight with exhaustion. Unlike me, using her powers only wore her out. She didn't have to take on the injuries she healed.

A finger tipped my chin up. Asher had pressed forward in his chair, and I found myself staring up at him. "Are you really okay?" I opened my mouth and he added, "Please don't lie."

My cheeks burned with embarrassment because I'd been caught. His gaze wouldn't let me go, and I gave up. I shook my head.

He grimaced, a muscle working in his cheek. "Since when?" he bit out.

*Since I tried to heal Laura.* "A while," I whispered. *I almost died.*

I closed my eyes to escape him. He couldn't hear me, and it made the ache in me spread. My heart tripped again, and I concentrated on getting it back to normal. Why couldn't I heal this already? I was so sick of the headaches and the mini heart attacks. Lately, I used up all my energy acting like a freaking pacemaker.

"What's wrong with you?" Asher asked.

"She just told you, man."

Gabe's angry voice spoke from over me, and my eyes popped open. He wasn't facing me, though. He was glaring at his brother, and he looked ready to thrash him. "It's been two weeks since Laura died. You've been letting her walk around with her heart about to implode anytime. What the fuck is wrong with you? Why didn't you help her? Any of you."

"Gabe . . ." I warned.

He didn't seem to hear me.

"You tried to heal Mom?" Lucy asked. She stood by the coffee table, her mouth twisted with anguish.

A sigh rattled through me. At last the truth was out

there, but I didn't feel the satisfaction I'd daydreamed about. Lucy's shock added to the pain I'd been trying to shove down. As my sister, she should have known the answer to her question.

My tone was bitter when I said, "Of course I did, Lucy. I loved her."

She stumbled back until her calves hit the coffee table and she abruptly sat on it. She crushed a hand to her mouth, obviously shaken, and her misery saddened me. I hadn't wanted this. I hadn't wanted to feel again.

"How could you not help her?" Gabe repeated to Asher.

He didn't understand the expression that had come over Asher's face, or the reason behind it. I did, and the bleak sorrow was too much for me to take.

*He didn't know, Gabe.*

My thoughts finally broke through to Gabe. He crouched by me. "How could he not know?" he asked, confused. "Your pain is flashing all over your thoughts like a damned neon sign."

Five beats of my heart went by before realization swept over Gabe's face.

Asher pressed a hand to my cheek. It wasn't an affectionate gesture, but a purposeful one. I sensed that he was testing me. Testing our bond. His eyes searched mine. *I'm so sorry.* The hope that he'd guessed wrong died, and his hand dropped to his side.

"I can't read your mind anymore," Asher said with a heavy voice.

# CHAPTER TEN

"Guys, can we focus?" Erin suggested, breaking through the tension that coated the room like an oily film. Blank stares met her announcement. "Remy," she prompted. "Her injuries are serious. I sensed it in the woods."

Asher almost shook himself. "Erin's right. How bad are things, Remy?" He tossed an unreadable look at Gabe and added, "For those of us who can't read your mind."

I spoke haltingly with a worried glance at Lucy. "Laura's brain injury was severe. I tried to heal her, but it was like nothing was there. She wasn't there." Lucy moaned, and my voice faded to a whisper. "Something happened. She had a heart attack while I was healing her. I've been having migraines since, and my heart . . . It's damaged." I'd tried to downplay my injuries, but it sounded awful to say them out loud. "My powers haven't fully returned, and I haven't been able to heal myself."

"You almost died," Lottie said with dismay. "In the hall at the hospital. You were having a heart attack."

I nodded. I'd tried to tell them, but then Lucy had turned on me and I'd only thought about hiding to lick my wounds.

Lucy jerked to her feet. "I think I'm going to be sick." She ran out of the room clutching her stomach.

In another surprising act of kindness, Lottie rose to go after her. "I'm sorry," Lottie told me, her mouth pulled down in a grimace. "I wouldn't have wished that on you."

"You couldn't have known. I was in shock, and then I was too hurt to tell any of you what was happening."

She gave a tight nod before leaving, and I wrung my hands, the knuckles turning white. I'd felt so alone the last two weeks. Longer than that. A hand covered mine.

Gabe tugged until he'd pried my fingers apart. "Come on," he coaxed, raising our hands to brush a tear off my cheek. "Your injuries aren't so bad. We've taken on far worse than that before." He loosened his hold and backed away.

Asher met his expectant look with despair. "You have to do it, Gabe."

Asher didn't explain why he couldn't help me, and Gabe didn't insist. He returned to crouch in front of me. Asher rose and crossed the room to the window. He stood silhouetted against the closed blinds with his back to us, closed off and miserable.

Gabe touched my cheek again. "Focus, Remington. You can make up with him later."

Gabe's energy flowed toward me, and I had to focus or be overwhelmed by his power. How could I have forgotten the heat of it? It scorched through me, and I grabbed hold. The pain had been constant and terrifying, worse so because I'd tried to hide it. My inability to heal myself had eaten away at me, and I'd begun to lose hope that I would ever feel okay again. But with Gabe's power, the impossible became surmountable. I focused on my heart first. Scar tissue had begun to form, and I attacked the cells. I pictured a perfect heart, thumping away at a rapid, steady beat, and the muscle healed, pumping blood in a beautifully normal rhythm. My head took longer, but eventually that injury healed, too.

When I'd finished, I loosened the hold I had on Gabe's wrist—when had I reached for him?—and felt his energy receding. His skin had grayed with exhaustion, and I realized a lot of time had passed. The room had emptied out of everyone but Gabe and me. Someone had turned on lamps when night fell, and I could see the lines of weariness around his green eyes.

"It's gone, Gabe. The pain is gone." A relieved laugh burst out of me, and I dropped my head on his chest. "Thank you," I whispered, overcome.

"Anytime," he said into my hair. "Anytime."

I waited for everyone to fall asleep before I left through the back door of our "borrowed" house. It had been a long evening, full of searching glances and questions that I couldn't answer. The whole day had sent me spiraling, and all of my carefully crafted walls showed cracks. I had retreated to one of the bedrooms soon after Gabe helped me heal myself. Now, with everyone crashed out, I could be alone, the way I wanted.

The backyard faced the hillside, and there was no view. In one corner of the yard, the wooden fence butted up against the side of the house. I gripped the top and pulled myself up. I stood on the upper ledge and used it to climb onto the gabled roof. Once I'd gauged where the best view would be, I stepped lightly across and over the highest point to the side that faced the ocean. I sat on the slant, planting my feet so my butt wouldn't slide down, and then I laid back to stare up at the sky. Nobody could see me up here.

Sometime tonight, as I'd pretended to sleep, I'd realized that whatever happened, I was going to have to leave. As I'd stared around the room of people I'd loved, it had struck me that they all could have been killed. My presence put their lives in danger, and I couldn't keep on like this indefinitely. It wasn't exactly my fault, but people got hurt around me like collateral damage in a war I didn't want to fight. It might kill me to do it a second time, but I was going to let my family go once we found my father. And if it kept the Blackwells safe, I would let them go, too. For good. When I left them behind, I would not return.

"Mind if I join you?" Gabe said.

I rolled my head to the side to see him coming over the top of the roof like I had. I sighed, not the least bit surprised. "I do if you're going to yell at me for being on the roof."

He mirrored my position a foot away from me. His teeth flashed white in the dark. "I promise not to yell at you."

"How did you know I was up here?" I asked.

"Easy. Whenever you're upset, you go outside," he said, staring up at the sky.

I frowned. "I do not."

He put his hands behind his head and smiled. "You do. Forests, oceans. It doesn't seem to matter as long as you're outside."

I thought about his words. My brows rose when I realized he was right. In Blackwell Falls, I raced to the beach or the forest. Same with San Francisco. Somehow the sky acted like a balm. Maybe because I'd been raised in New York's steel and concrete forest with the views hemmed in by skyscrapers. It was odd that Gabe had noticed my habit when I hadn't.

"I notice everything about you," he said softly.

*Whoa. Can't go there.* I snapped my mental walls into place, sorry when it caused him to grimace in pain. I didn't want anyone reading my mind tonight. The silence went on, but it wasn't uncomfortable.

I studied the constellations and let my mind go. The pain had kept so much at bay since Laura's death. How could I grieve for her when it hurt to think, breathe, be?

But now, with the pain erased, the sadness consumed me in a tsunami that wiped out all illusion of control. A tear escaped. Then two. I sniffed and lowered my arm over my face.

Gabe slid closer, his body heating mine from shoulder to thigh. His arm tucked under my neck, and he pulled me into his side despite my pathetic protest. One large hand curved around my head and tucked my face into his chest. His actions confused me, but then I hiccupped and realized that I'd been crying louder than I'd realized.

"Go ahead and fall apart a little, Remington. Nobody is here to see it, and I won't judge."

His fingers drifted through my hair, stroking the strands from my neck to my back. His other hand stayed behind his neck, as if to prove that he wasn't making a move on me. This was about offering comfort and nothing else.

"Let me be your friend," he said.

His offer unhinged me. My fingers clutched at the lapel of his jacket, and I sobbed into his neck, the first real cry I'd had since Laura passed. I thought of my stepmom's smile and the way she'd loved me, even when I was sure I didn't deserve it. I remembered her laugh, and the fierce look she'd used to admonish me even though she'd hated to do it. She was a mother who preferred hugs over discipline, and I had soaked up every ounce of her affection. I missed her desperately, and I couldn't believe that I would never see her again.

My throat ached when the tears faded. I hiccupped so hard that I shuddered with it. I sucked in a breath and it sounded squelchy. *Oh, frick. I probably have snot coming out of my nose, and do I have a tissue? No. Of course not.*

Gabe laughed, and my head bounced on his chest with the movement. *Damn it.* When I felt strongly, he could read my mind even with my defenses up. He tucked his hand in the sleeve of his coat and swiped it across my face, wiping up the whole mess.

I covered my face with my hands, dying with mortification. "I can't believe you just did that. Tell me you did not just wipe my snot like I was six."

My head bounced some more as he snickered. "I had to. You were obsessing about it."

*I'm going to die,* I thought. *Melt into a puddle and slide right off the roof.*

Gabe squeezed my waist. "Chill out, Remington. You're missing out on an amazing sky."

I considered obsessing some more, but if Gabe wasn't embarrassed, why should I be? I settled against him and gazed up.

"Is this weird?" I asked a while later. "Us being here like this after everything?"

Gabe hesitated, his hand pausing mid-stroke through my hair. "Does it feel weird?"

"No," I said after thinking about it. "It feels like us. Like we were in San Francisco."

Gabe pointed at a constellation. "Big Dipper."

I moved my head to follow the line of his hand. "No way. That's the Little Dipper."

"Bullshit. I know my constellations, and that is the Big Dipper."

"Just because you were around when Copernicus lived doesn't mean you know your stars," I said.

Gabe stilled under me. "You think you're so funny, Remington. I'm not that old, you know."

I tilted my head to smirk up at him. His face was closer than I expected, a mere inch separating our lips. I jerked back and sat up, brushing my hair from my face. "I should go in," I said, casually. "We need to get some sleep before we go for Round Two tomorrow with the gang."

I stood and held out a hand to him. He let me pull him to his feet and followed me back to the edge of the roof. He climbed down first and waited while I stretched a foot off the roof, reaching for the fence. Gabe's hand wrapped around my ankle and guided me to the ledge. When I would have jumped down, his hands encircled my waist and he lifted me into the air with my feet dangling. A gravity-less second later, he set me on the ground and stepped back. He rocked on his heels and stared at me until I squirmed.

I used to think that Gabe was a more beautiful, slightly older version of Asher. But Gabe had seemed too perfect, too handsome, too much. I'd thought him incredibly arrogant, and I'd disliked him for a long time. Then I'd thought Asher dead, and somehow Gabe had become my friend as we grieved together. As I reacquainted myself with his features, I grasped how wrong I'd been. Gabe looked beautiful, but he was too human to be perfect. How odd to realize that now on a day when he'd displayed all his Protector strengths. I shifted from foot to foot, uncomfortable under his perusal, and reinforced my defenses.

"What's going on with you and Asher?" he asked.

I had been dreading that question. It had too many layers to it. Layers I couldn't deal with. I sidestepped it, wiping my mind of every thought. "What do you mean?"

His eyes narrowed thoughtfully. "Things are different between you two. Tense."

Something told me he'd know if I lied, and I wasn't ready to tell the truth. I gave him a frank stare. "Look, I don't really want to talk about it. Okay?"

I hoped I hadn't offended him. He looked frustrated by my answer, but didn't push. He nodded, and we started toward the house. "Did you call him after Chicago?" I asked.

"No. I decided to show up here instead."

Did that mean he knew how much Asher had changed? He'd opened the door when I remembered.

"Give me your jacket. I'll wash it."

He laughed again and bumped his fist under my chin. "Head case."

I ducked away and ran into the house.

# CHAPTER ELEVEN

*I*t was Lottie who called everyone to the kitchen the next morning. We gathered around the island with its tiled countertop, standing because there were no seats. The rumpled state of everyone's clothing showed that we'd all slept in the clothes on our backs. Someone had a made a coffee run. To-go cups and pastry bags were set on one counter. I sniffed the air, wishing I could inhale the coffee and the much-needed caffeine. Gabe pushed one of the paper cups in front of me.

"Thanks," I said.

It was sure to be black, my least favorite way to drink the brew. I resolved to make do, but when I took a sip, it tasted sweet and creamy, already doctored to my preference. I glanced up in surprise, but Gabe had turned away. My attention switched back to the room. To say things were tense was an understatement.

Across the island, Asher held himself apart from everyone, his muscles tight and his green eyes defeated. I'd expected him to appear angry but not resigned. He looked like someone who'd given up.

*Oh Asher. Please don't close yourself off.*

Lucy stood to his right, looking petite beside him. If last night had changed things between us, I couldn't tell. She'd shifted from outright anger to avoidance, dancing away from me whenever I got within two steps of her. Her black curls were flattened to her head on one side, and black smudges ringed her brown eyes like she'd had a restless night.

Only Lottie wore an immovable mask, from her place between her brothers. She had a take-charge attitude that I appreciated. Someone needed to step up and lead us, and I was glad to take a backseat. To my right, Gabe watched Asher with confusion, his brow cocked like he was trying to puzzle something out. I reinforced my mental walls to ensure he couldn't read my mind. He slid me an arrogant, amused look out of the corner of his eye to let me know he'd felt it, and I ignored him.

Erin stood to my left, shifting her weight back and forth. Her eyes darted from person to person, her smile nervous and more than a little shaky. She had to be wondering what the hell she'd gotten herself into. She leaned against the counter, gripping the edge like a lifeline. I hugged her waist to offer some measure of comfort.

"It's okay," I whispered low so the others wouldn't hear. "Nobody will hurt you."

"But don't their kind lose control around Healers?" she whispered back.

Her body shook under my hand, and I felt like an ass for not looking after her the previous night. She probably hadn't slept, waiting for one of the Blackwells to attack her. She'd been raised to believe they were all monsters. Just because she'd helped me find Asher and healed him last night didn't mean that she'd forgotten everything she'd been taught.

"Erin, they aren't like the others. They can control it. Right this minute, they all have their guards up." Well, Gabe and Lottie did. I couldn't tell with Asher anymore. I didn't know if that was because he no longer used it or if he was too human to have one. "Trust me. They would never hurt you."

"We're all too afraid of Remington to chance it," Gabe observed in a wry tone.

*Damned Protector hearing.* His breath *whoosh*ed out when I smacked him in the stomach. "Shut up, Gabriela."

The old nickname shot out of my mouth before I realized. Lottie choked and threw a hand over her mouth to cover a smile.

"Gabriela?" she asked Gabe with a raised brow.

He lifted a shoulder, completely unbothered. "I'm not afraid of my feminine side."

I laughed. The sound startled me, and I coughed. I hadn't really laughed since my father had been taken. Obviously I'd shocked the others in the room, too. My cheeks heated under their appraisals, and Asher's stare was the worst of all. He looked at me like I'd betrayed him, his eyes wounded. My first instinct was to bow my head in guilt. *Screw that.* I raised my chin instead. There were a lot of things I was guilty of, but I had never cheated on him with Gabe or anyone else. He didn't get to judge me.

I deliberately faced Erin. "He's kidding. You're safe here."

She nodded, her eyes huge. I suppose from her viewpoint it would be weird to see Healers and Protectors interacting like we did.

"Yesterday you were about to tell me about my dad . . ." I prompted. I'd wanted to push her last night, but she'd disappeared from the living room while Gabe helped me heal myself.

The shy girl hooked her blond hair behind an ear and spoke to me as if the others didn't exist. "Since you and I met up on the ferry, I've been paying more attention to things. Calls, comings and goings. Fat lot of good it did.

Franc used to come to our house all the time, but lately, he's stayed away."

We knew that to be true from the surveillance we'd done. Asher had only seen him leaving his house the one time he'd gone to Pacifica.

"What about Alcais?" I asked.

"My brother used to disappear for hours at a time, but he's been sticking to home. Staying close to me. It's why I couldn't call or get away until yesterday. Maybe I'm paranoid, but it felt like . . . he was waiting for something. Watching."

I nodded. "It makes sense. Franc knew you and I were friends. That you're the one who told us about Asher."

Asher spoke up. "That explains how those Protectors found us yesterday. If they were watching you, they might have followed you, hoping you'd lead them to Remy."

"Oh no! I'm so sorry!" Erin said, pulling away from me. "You must all hate me."

I tugged her back to the counter. "Don't be silly. You've risked your life more than once to help us. Nobody here hates you."

She didn't look convinced. I understood why, considering the way Lucy and Lottie glared at her. I hugged Erin and shot them both warning stares over her shoulder. Erin was nervous enough and didn't need them making it worse.

"So what happened?" I stepped back and downed a too-hot sip of coffee.

"It's stupid, but Alcais lost his mobile phone with a little help from me. Anyway, whenever someone called the house phone, I listened in from my room." She shuddered, and her nose twitched in distaste. "By the way, my brother and Delia are dating now. I won't be recovering from their conversations anytime soon."

I imagined what they might have said and had to hold

back my own shudder. Delia, another teen Healer, had been in love with Alcais forever. The two of them had bickered incessantly, and Alcais had used Delia's powers, taking stupid risks because she would drop everything to heal him. Delia hadn't liked me, but I'd thought she'd moved beyond her crush on Alcais after he'd hurt Erin. Guess not.

"There's no accounting for taste," I said with a grimace.

"Right?" Erin asked. "Day before yesterday, Franc finally called Alcais. They mostly talked about our patrols, but at the end of the conversation, my brother asked about a package. He wondered if it had been moved yet, and Franc said Alcais didn't need to worry about it anymore. That Morrissey was looking after it now. I didn't know what they were talking about, but then Alcais said, 'I'd love to see Remy's face when she finds out it's gone.' Franc yelled at him for using your name, and then they hung up soon after." She glanced around the silent group. "I'm assuming that your father is the package."

"Son of a bitch," Gabe cursed under his breath.

Disappointment twisted my stomach in a knot. I'd hoped that Erin might actually know where my father was, or at least have some clue that would lead us to him. Now, we were back to zero. If he was the package, then he was most likely no longer in the area.

"It had to be the Morrisseys," Asher said, slamming a fist on the counter. His jaw worked the way it did when he was angry. Normally, I would have comforted him, but I held myself in place on my side of the counter.

"Guys, confused here. Who are the Morrisseys?" I asked.

"The Morrisseys are an old Protector family. They used to be friends of ours," Lottie explained with a frown.

"Why is that such bad news?" Lucy asked, twisting her black curls into a clip at the back of her head. A few instantly sprang free, making her look vulnerable. "If they're friends, maybe they'll help us. Can't you try calling them?"

Asher shook his head. "I'm sorry, but no. They're not like us. In fact, they're the opposite."

"You mean they hunt Healers?"

The others remained quiet, reluctant to answer, and it was Gabe who answered my question. "He means they make a sport of hunting Healers, and they're vicious when they do catch them. Last I saw Bram, he kept a tally of his hunts with hair he'd cut off the women." Gabe sounded disgusted. He shook his head like he was shaking off a nightmare image he couldn't get rid of. "We didn't want to be like them, so we cut off contact. They weren't happy about it."

I didn't ask who Bram was. It was enough for now to know the bastard had a scoring system for Healers he'd murdered. I tried to think of something else, some other advantage. "My dad is a Protector. Is there any way to use that?" The Blackwells exchanged hopeless glances, and I let out a frustrated sigh.

Erin wrapped her hands around her cup and asked, "If this family hates Healers so much, why are they working with Franc?"

The Blackwell siblings shifted, all three of them staring at me. "What?" I asked.

Asher's green eyes burned with regret as he rounded the counter to stand in front of me. I frowned in confusion when he brushed my hair away from my face. Whatever he had to say would be awful if he felt the need to touch me while he said it.

He laid a warm palm against my cheek. "It's you, Remy. Remember what I told you would happen when our kind learned that you could take their immortality? Some Protectors would come after you because they want to be human again. Others would want you dead because they don't want things to change and they don't want you to be used as a weapon to make them mortal."

*And others wouldn't want me at all because they hated how my power changed them.* I pressed Asher's warm hand to my skin, wishing we could rewind things to a time before I wrote my grandfather. Asher's eyes reflected the same sorrow that I felt.

I cleared my throat. "Let me guess. The Morrisseys are door number two."

He acknowledged my guess with a dip of his chin, and his hand rubbed my back in comfort. Like you would do for a friend or a sibling.

"I'm sorry," he said. "They'll use your dad against you."

"Great." I took a deep breath and stepped back. Asher's hand trailed down my arm until he held my hand, his grip light and friendly. It hurt to be this close to him and not be able to have more. He still cared, though, and that mattered. I squeezed his fingers. "Do you know where the Morrisseys might keep him?"

The Blackwells shared another look and answered at the same time. "London."

I picked up my coffee to occupy my hands and faked a smile. "I guess we're going to London, then."

It took all of a day for Lottie Blackwell to arrange for fake passports for the group, and I was afraid to ask how she'd worked that miracle. By the next night, we were watching a terrible in-flight movie on a red-eye flight to London. Once again, we'd had to go through the process of ensuring that we weren't followed, and the fear didn't ever seem to really fade anymore. I'd ended up seated next to Asher—was Lottie trying to punish me?—while Gabe sat next to Lucy three rows in front of us. Erin and Lottie were on the other side of the plane, a row back.

I still couldn't believe that Erin had decided to come

with us. I'd brought up the whole kidnapping charge her
mother would slam us with, but she'd argued that she was
safer with us. Franc's men had followed her into Muir
Woods, and she didn't feel safe going home when they had
proof that she was helping me. This time, she wouldn't be
able to convince them that I'd tricked her. After three seconds of imagining what Alcais would do to her if she returned home, I caved. Anyway, as she'd told me, it wasn't
my decision to make.

"Not everyone is your responsibility," she'd said in the
kitchen. It wasn't meant unkindly, but I'd taken the hint
especially when Gabe muttered, "Hear, hear," under his
breath.

Well, then.

Most people on the plane had fallen asleep, but I
couldn't rest with Asher next to me. It would have been
so easy to let myself lean on him, so I worked that much
harder to stay away. I'd folded myself into the window as
much as I could to give him space. I'd never been part of
a couple or summarily uncoupled. How was I supposed to
act around him? I was too tense to sleep, worried that I
would crash out and slobber on him. Did my powers work
in my sleep? With my luck, he'd be entirely human by
morning.

"It's weird."

I started at Asher's low voice and raised my brows.

"Not hearing you anymore," he said, tapping the side of
his head. "I can tell you're upset right now, and normally,
I would have been able to hear you. I'd gotten so used to
it that it was like your thoughts were a part of me."

He rested his cheek on the headrest to study me, and I
did the same. He looked sad and tired, and I missed how
we used to be. Once upon a time, I would have kissed him
and held him to make that expression go away.

"Why didn't you notice that you couldn't hear me anymore?" That had bothered me a lot. Had he distanced himself from me so much that he didn't care by the time our bond broke?

"I thought it was your doing. That you were blocking me all the time. When did you know?" he asked. "That our bond was broken?"

"Since the day of the funeral," I admitted. "I guess that subconsciously I wanted you to know that I was hurt. I left my guard down, but you acted like you couldn't hear me. Even with everything that's happened, you never would've been that uncaring."

"Thanks for that, at least." He shook his head, the disappointment and anger plain on his face. I made to turn toward the window, but he gripped my chin, forcing me to meet his hurt gaze. "You know I would've helped you if you'd asked, *mo cridhe*. You know that. So why didn't you ask?"

My eyes flickered closed at the old endearment, but that didn't stop the tears from leaking out. "I couldn't," I said in a halting voice, jerking my chin away from him. "You broke up with me because my powers are making you human. To heal me, you would have had to open yourself up to more of that. I couldn't ask you to do that when you made your feelings about it clear. We shouldn't even be sitting together like this." I gestured to how close we were, and Asher grabbed my hand out of the air, refusing to let me go when I fought against him.

"Remy, don't," he said, touching a thumb to my cheek. He used it to wipe away a tear, but more fell to replace it. "I'm so sorry."

I stilled. "For what? Breaking my heart? Protecting yourself?"

He didn't answer my question, but placed his hand on my thigh, palm up, to twine our fingers together. The warmth of his hand reminded me of better times, and I relaxed, unable to fight him. Chaos and confusion flooded through me. Was this his way of trying to show he still cared? Did he want me back?

"You haven't told Gabe about us."

The statement came from left field and added to my confusion. "It didn't seem to be my place to tell him. Why does it matter?"

He gave me a sad half smile. "It matters. Don't you wonder why he came back?"

I frowned. When Gabe had called, I'd told him to check in with Asher. I'd assumed it had to do with that. "Because of you. He was worried about you. And with Lottie joining us, he probably wanted to be back with his family."

Asher tilted his head to the side. "I'm sure he's happy to see us, but his being here has everything to do with you."

He sounded angry, and this whole scene began to make sense. Lottie knew we'd broken up and wouldn't have put Asher next to me on this plane unless he'd asked. Not out of kindness to me, but to protect Asher. And now Asher held my hand when he'd made it clear that he hated touching me. This was about jealousy, not love or wanting me back or missing me. He didn't want me, but hell if he'd let his brother be my friend without staking some kind of claim. My stomach twisted. I should have been angry, but mostly I felt stupid for thinking he might want me back.

I took a deep breath and let him see that he'd hurt me. "This isn't fair of you," I told him in a wounded voice. "Don't make me out to be the cheating girlfriend. You pulled away from me months ago." He wanted to deny it, but I needed to have my say. "Do you understand what that did to me to have you disappear on me like that? I tried to be patient and understanding because I know better than anyone what you went through. I swallowed my pride every time you pulled away, and I can take a lot from you because I do get it. But this"—I looked down at our joined hands—"it's unkind, Asher. Don't give me hope where there is none. Because if you haven't changed your mind about us, and this is about competing with Gabe, it's mean and I don't deserve that from you."

He had the good grace to look ashamed, and he didn't protest when I gently pulled my hand from his.

"Remy . . ." he started, his voice thick with apology. "I didn't mean—"

"Let it go," I interrupted. "Really." *Let me go. If you don't want me, stop making me care.*

I turned away, crying, and he passed me his drink napkin without a word.

The silence became awkward after that, and sleep more impossible than before. At one point, Gabe passed down the aisle on his way to the bathroom. I frowned at the grim smile on his face, but he moved on without saying anything. Asher thought Gabe had returned because of me, and I didn't know what to think of that. This wasn't exactly the time or place to figure it out, either. With the Morrisseys out to murder me and . . . Something about that day in the woods had been bugging me, and I hadn't been able to pinpoint it.

I frowned. "Asher, how did Gabe know where to find us?"

Asher set aside his phone, abandoning whatever he'd been doing. "He called Lottie. In fact, he beat us to Muir Woods. He was already scouting the place when we arrived."

I shifted in my seat, running the day through my mind. Something didn't sit right.

"Why?" Asher asked.

"No reason." I hesitated, but the nagging feeling wouldn't go away. "It just doesn't make sense."

"What?"

"You all described the Morrisseys as brutal killers out to get me."

"Right."

"Did you recognize those Protectors in Muir Woods?"

He shook his head. "No. I'd never seen them before. Listen, I see where you're going with this. Those men weren't part of the Morrissey family, but that doesn't mean they weren't working with them."

"Then why didn't they attack us?"

"They did. I was there, remember?"

I thought back to the confrontation. "Not really. I attacked first when they wouldn't let you go. Before that, the leader said he wasn't there to hurt us. He wanted to talk. That doesn't sound like the Morrisseys you described. If those men worked for them, they would have tried harder to take me out." I leaned forward. "Asher, that man had me. Before Gabe showed, my heart blew. That man knew I was down, and he didn't act on it."

Asher looked up, lost in thought. "Come to think of it, I don't think they meant to break my arm. I went after one of them, and he defended himself. I think he expected me to be using full strength." His smile was wry. "I'm guessing he didn't know what to make of the new, weaker version of me."

I thought back to the group in the living room yesterday. "And besides you and a minor cut for Lucy, nobody was hurt, right? That doesn't seem off to you, considering how vicious the Morrisseys are?"

His jaw tightened. "It does now."

I tried to understand what this meant. If those men in the woods hadn't been working with the Morrisseys, who were they? Was Franc working with different Protector factions now? To do that, he chanced bringing hell down upon his community. A few Protectors might be willing to deal with my grandfather for access to a limited supply of Healers. Add more Protectors into the mix, though, and the supply diminished. Simple economics. Franc would have a disaster on his hands working with different groups, not to mention his people would find out and hang him.

I glanced over at Erin, making out her blond ponytail over the seats. Suddenly, I was glad that she had decided to come with us. I didn't trust her brother to look out for her if the Protectors got tired of scraps. And Franc was perfectly capable of feeding her to the Protectors when he decided she was no longer useful to catch me. Once we found my father, I'd have to help her find a safe place to stay. Then I'd have to find my own haven. I sighed, pushing thoughts of the future away.

"I hate this," I said. "Not knowing who is after us. Are we going to be safe in London?"

"As much as we ever can be. We've never told anyone about this house. We wanted a little hideaway in case anything happened."

I almost moaned at the word *little*. How were the six of us going to get along crammed into a tiny house?

# CHAPTER TWELVE

*I* was going to have to talk to Asher about his sense of proportions. His family's "little" hideaway turned out to be a huge terraced Victorian house on Chapel Street, situated at the heart of London in Knightsbridge. It didn't take a genius to figure out that the neighborhood was affluent. We passed exclusive shops that I would never dare to enter and fancy homes that looked more suited to the movies than real life. I didn't know people who could afford to live like this. Except somehow I'd become part of this world when I'd met Asher.

He'd gone ahead in another car with Gabe so they could check things out in advance. Once they secured the house, they'd let Lottie know it was safe for us to approach. The house didn't have a garage, so Lottie instructed our driver to pull over on the tree-lined street to let us out. One tall bricked home butted up against another here, giving the appearance of a solid wall of buildings. A black wrought-iron fence and gate lined the sidewalk, blocking off the front doors and what appeared to be a staircase that led to a basement-level courtyard.

I stared at the house in shock, counting four floors aboveground, plus the basement. The second floor up from ground level had balconies opening off floor-to-ceiling windows, and neat planters decorated every window. I had the absurd thought to wonder who looked after those plants when the Blackwells weren't home. Geez. They probably had staff.

I followed the others into a bright entranceway. Morning sunlight lit the whole area, sending prisms of light through the giant chandelier hanging above us. We went up the staircase directly in front of us, and I peeked through a doorway into another room. Walnut floors shone from a recent waxing. Nutmeg brown walls blended well with expensive tan furniture that invited a person to sit by the fireplace. I took one step into the room and glimpsed a grand piano.

That was enough for me. I'd never felt so out of place, and I'd been comfortable at the Blackwells' home in Blackwell Falls. If that place had seemed a mansion, this place was pure decadence. I wouldn't be able to sit on the furniture without freaking out that I'd break something. Someone bumped into me.

Lucy stumbled to a stop beside me, her eyes bigger than mine. "Toto, I don't think we're in Kansas anymore."

Our eyes met and we both giggled. Lucy sobered a second later and wandered away, and I was sorry the moment had ended. At least I wasn't the only one feeling like I'd walked onto a movie set. Erin disappeared into the next room to explore, looking just as shell-shocked.

Lottie opened the curtains over the windows that faced the balconies. She'd never been more Queen of the Manor.

"How many rooms do you have here?" I asked.

"Well, you saw the entrance hall downstairs, but that's not really a room. On the ground floor, we also have the dining room, kitchen, library, and toilet. This is the drawing room we're in now, and back there is a conservatory and roof terrace. One floor up is Gabe's room and his bathroom, and the top floor has two more bedrooms and a bathroom. There's also a lower floor with a wine vault, family room, and another bedroom and bath."

She moved about, describing corniced ceilings and marble bathrooms, but she'd lost me back at drawing room. I'd grown up in a five-room crappy apartment that could have fit onto one floor of this house. Twice.

I shook my head to clear it. I needed a nap before I tackled more of the house. "Lottie, where are we sleeping?"

"I thought the Healer and the mortal might want to share a room."

"Gee, thanks," Lucy said, with a wry twist of her mouth.

Lottie shrugged. "I thought the Healer girl might feel more comfortable in a room without a Protector."

"The Healer girl has a name," Erin snapped, returning to the room.

I winced. This was going to be fun if we couldn't get along for five minutes.

Lottie simply shrugged again. "Whatever. You two will take Asher's room on the top floor near mine. Gabe and Asher will share his room. And Remy will take the basement room."

They were hiding me in the basement, with a whole floor separating me from the others. Awesome. Had that been Asher's choice? When would his rejection lose its sting?

Lottie saw my expression and added, "It was Gabe's idea. Yell at him."

I held up both hands. "I'm too tired to argue. I think I'll head down and take a nap. Where did Asher and Gabe go?"

"Not sure. I think they're upstairs arranging rooms."

*Good answer,* I thought, dragging myself to the staircase with a wave at the others. I hadn't slept at all on the flight, and I was so tired that I was stumbling into walls. Between the scene with Asher on the plane and the weird glances Gabe had tossed me at the airport, I couldn't wait to be alone for a while.

I took myself down two flights of stairs, happy to let my mental walls relax once I was away from the others. Keeping my defenses constantly up took energy I didn't have. At the bottom of the stairs, I hesitated, unsure which way to go. With a shrug, I went toward the direction that faced the street. I passed through the family room Lottie had mentioned and ended up in the wine vault. Dozens of bottles were slotted into the wall in front of me and lined the wooden counters on both sides.

"This place is like the Met," I muttered. I'd once gotten lost in the huge New York museum, and I felt the same way now.

"It's easy once you know your way around."

I whipped around to find Gabe standing in the doorway blocking my exit. He didn't seem inclined to move aside, either, crossing his ankles and bracing a lean hip against the doorjamb. He watched me, his mouth quirked with another of those odd smiles he'd worn on the plane and at the airport. He reminded me of a cat who had found a mouse to toy with.

"Oh, I think you're more the cat than the mouse," he said in a silky voice. "Like a cat, you're crafty and hard to pin down."

I narrowed my eyes. "Very funny. Does that make you the mouse?"

"Catch me and find out," he challenged, his green eyes darkening.

I sucked in a breath as unwanted awareness scorched through me. Embarrassment burned my cheeks. He couldn't have meant that how it sounded. Because it sounded like the kind of thing a guy told a girl he liked.

"In case you're confused, Remington, that was me flirting with you. And I more than like you."

My systems went on red alert, shrieking warnings to my brain. My hands went damp with nerves, and my heart raced like I'd chased a Red Bull with a gallon of espresso.

"Uh, Gabe. I don't think . . ." I stumbled to a stop as realization hit. Gabe was flirting with me. If Gabe was flirting with me, then he knew . . .

His full lips curled into a satisfied smile, making them look more sensuous than usual. "That you and Asher broke up? Hell, yes."

And damn it if he didn't look happy about it.

"How?" I said, reduced to a one-word response.

"Lucy. She let it slip on the plane. And before you get angry at her, she had no clue that I didn't know." Gabe straightened, taller and bigger than I'd remembered. More everything than I'd remembered. I took a quick step back and he matched it with one forward. "What I find really interesting, Remington, is that you didn't tell me in all the times we've talked."

It was ridiculous to feel stalked, right? I knew Gabe. He was my friend. And yet I glanced both ways, looking for a way to escape. "Don't read into it. Asher's reasons for breaking up with me are tied to what's happening to him. I thought it wasn't my place to tell you about that."

"No," Gabe answered emphatically, taking another sure step when I stumbled back. "That's not it."

Affronted, I came to an abrupt halt. "Excuse me? Are you calling me a liar?"

"About this?" He stopped, too, and tilted his head to one side like he was considering it. Then he said, "Yes." I gathered myself up to yell at him, but he stalled me by pressing a finger to my lips. "Before you argue, let me add that I don't think you're doing it intentionally."

"What are you talking about?" I mumbled against his skin.

He dropped his arm. "I think maybe you know that you and I could have something, and it scares the hell out of you. You didn't tell me about Asher ending things because you're afraid to give us a chance."

I glared at him. "Nice theory, but I've told you that we're just friends. It's been two weeks since Asher and I broke up, and my feelings haven't suddenly changed because we're not together."

I thought maybe I'd gone too far, that maybe I'd hurt his feelings, but Gabe raised one brow and leaned forward to say, "I agree. You've had feelings for me since San Francisco."

Denial rose up fast and furious, and I shook my head. He was insane. He'd gone completely mental. I opened my mouth to tell him, and that's when he took two giant steps forward, invading my space with all his muscles. I tripped away until my back hit the wall. I had nowhere to go, and Gabe was practically plastered to my front. I threw a panicked gaze his way and slid to one side to duck past him. He planted a hand on the wall by my shoulder, ending that plan. He did the same on the other side, before the thought occurred to me to change direction.

I was caught between his body and the wall. I stared up at him, helplessly confused. "Gabe . . ."

"Have I ever told you what it was like when my parents died?" I shook my head, thrown by the non sequitur. The last thing I'd expected him to talk about was his parents. "Asher was eighteen and Lottie sixteen. We had suddenly become immortal in a battle that we didn't intend to fight. Our parents and older brother were dead. And I'd become responsible for keeping my family together."

"I'm sorry," I whispered, trying to concentrate on his

words. It became more difficult when our breaths syn-
chronized and our bodies brushed with each inhalation.

"We got by. Everything I've done since that day has
been about keeping my family safe. All of my choices have
been about them. Where we lived. How we lived. What
was best for them, even when it meant giving up what I
wanted. Because I was the oldest. And I was okay with
that."

I got that. Hadn't my life changed when Lucy had become my responsibility? Gabe's breath brushed my face,
and I trembled. *Duh, it's cold in here,* I told myself.

"And then you came along. Tradition and history say
the Healer bonds to the oldest brother, but then you're not
like other Healers." He shook his head ruefully. "No, you
fall for my brother and bond to him. I wanted you for myself, but I stepped aside. Because I love Asher. And I hated
watching you together, but I tried to be okay with that,
too."

He took an extra deep breath, touching me from chest
to waist in an action I suspected was deliberate. I held my
breath for all of two seconds and then gasped for air. *Because I'm dying from lack of oxygen. Obviously.*

"Why are you telling me this?" I asked, jumping when
his hands landed on my shoulders.

"When you chose Asher in September, I left to give
you both space. But now my brother has made his choice.
I love him, but he had his chance, and I'm not leaving
again."

Gabe's fingers traced my shoulders and stroked upward
to cup my neck. His thumbs tipped my chin up. The heat
in his eyes weakened my knees, and I would have fallen if
my hands weren't braced against the wall behind me.

"I'm rushing you, and I'm confusing the hell out of
you. This isn't the right time. I know that. But I heard
your thoughts on that roof, Remington. You're planning

on leaving when we find your dad. I can't let you go without giving us a try. This time I'm going after what I want."

He bent his knees and leaned in to press his lips to my neck. His mouth kissed a damp path to my ear, and I shuddered at the steam, hotter than fire, curling under my skin. His words tickled my hair when he whispered, "This is me giving you fair warning that I'm going to chase you with everything I have, and when you decide to let me catch you, you'll never doubt how much I love you. Even when I become a weak human and you can kick my ass six ways to Sunday."

My eyes filled with tears. "Don't say that. You can't know that." Asher had promised the same thing.

"Yes, I do. Don't make the mistake of thinking my brother and me are alike. We're not. I'm not going to play fair."

He already wasn't. His tongue touched my ear, and I lit up. He began to trace a path to my chin, and the idea of him kissing me was too much. I panicked, shoving against his shoulders until he stepped back. I stayed leaning against the wall as he retreated. When I dared to meet his eyes, he'd put on the calm, arrogant mask he always used to wear when I first met him. Except now I saw how his eyes burned like a banked fire and his chest lifted in fast breaths. How much had I missed because he didn't want me to see it or I hadn't dared to look?

"I can't do this right now," I pleaded.

Disappointment flashed across his face so quickly I thought I'd imagined it, and then the mask returned. "Okay. It's been a long day. Your room is that way," he said, pointing in the opposite direction. "There's a small, private courtyard connected to it, and I thought you would appreciate being able to go outside when you liked."

His change in gears had given me whiplash. "Thank you," I said. I winced at how out of breath I sounded.

He nodded and turned to go.

"Gabe?" He paused in the doorway when I said his name. The more distance he put between us, the more my brain seemed to recover its higher functions. I had to stop this before it went any further. "This can't happen. You have to know that. I don't think I can trust somebody again after Asher."

"Hm."

My announcement didn't seem to affect him, and I glared at him, irrationally irritated by his indifference. "What does that mean?" I asked.

He smiled, bracing an arm against the jamb. "You trust me more than you realize. Think about it."

He left, and I heard him humming some song as he disappeared and started up the stairs. The second he was gone, my legs gave out and I slid down the wall until my butt hit the floor.

*What in the hell was that? I've been ambushed.*

I stared vacantly into space, trying to jump-start my senses back to normal. A normal that wasn't filled with the scent and feel of Gabe's skin. It was a good five minutes before it occurred to me what Gabe meant about trust. My walls had been down, and I hadn't bothered to put them back up when Gabe walked in. He'd heard every overheated thought I'd had about him.

*I'm so dead.*

# CHAPTER THIRTEEN

*I*'*m a ho.*

The thought popped into my head before I'd even opened my eyes the next morning. It was the same thought I had when I tried to wear red lipstick. On other women, I found red lipstick beautiful. Daring and sexy, like Lottie wore it. My stepmom had made it look classy when she wore it on special occasions. But the second I painted it across my lips, I morphed into somebody's judgmental, prudish grandmother with dentures and the morals of a Victorian miss. The red-lipped girl in the reflection was a hussy, and that was that. Of course, the truth was that I lacked confidence. Women who wore red lipstick looked so bold, and I . . . wasn't. Enter Gabe and suddenly my inner grandmother was raising her head and shrieking at me like a bloody banshee.

This morning was definitely a red-lipstick morning.

I moaned and pulled the covers over my head. This wasn't like me. I had almost kissed Asher's brother. How could this have happened? It wasn't right to feel . . . attracted . . . to Gabe when I'd hardly begun to accept that things were over with Asher. What kind of girl was attracted to two brothers at the same time?

*A ho,* my inner grandmother accused, and I wanted to punch her in the face.

What was Gabe thinking? We had enough to deal with to find my father and keep everyone safe in the meantime. Why did he have to go and confuse everything by declaring his intention to chase after me? Whatever that meant. I shivered, thinking about yesterday and the way he'd leaned into me. If that was "chasing," I was toast.

I clambered out of the oversized bed, tripping over the blanket that I tucked around my shoulders. In bare feet, I padded across the wood floor to the glass doors on the wall opposite the bed. I peered outside at the courtyard. About eighteen by seven feet, the small enclosed garden had ivy climbing the far brick wall and potted trees spaced here and there on a wooden deck. It wasn't much to look at in the dead of winter with the rain pouring down on everything, but Gabe had been right: I wanted to be outside where I could clear my mind.

*Stupid Gabe. He doesn't know everything.*

I turned my back on the garden and focused on the room that I'd hardly noticed yesterday. The bed had a giant, black leather-paneled headboard. Instead of a closet, the room featured a black wardrobe. On the other side of the bed, a giant TV had been mounted to the gray wall. This room had been done up in grays, black, and chrome, all modern and shiny.

The decadence blew my mind, and I decided to see what the bathroom might hold. I flipped on the bathroom light and jumped back at the reflection of myself in the floor-to-ceiling mirror that comprised one entire wall. *Oh, heck no. If I can't even bring myself to wear red lipstick, how am I going to strip down naked in front of that to shower?* I shuddered and flipped another switch, but couldn't figure out what it did.

Then, as I brushed my teeth, I felt the floor beneath my feet begin to warm. My bare toes curled into the tiles, as I considered a world in which floors could be heated. A world that I did not belong in. This was ridiculous. I had to tell Gabe to back off. Honestly, I cared for Asher. Even if you took that out of the equation—and how could you?—I couldn't watch another person grow to hate me when I made them human again. I wouldn't survive another beating like that, and no matter what Gabe said, I didn't trust him. Last night, everything had gotten complicated and messy, but the simple truth was that I had been right when I decided to leave when I found my father.

I would not risk my heart on another Blackwell.

After showering, I went hunting for Gabe only to have Erin explain that he and Lottie had gone out hours ago.

"What time is it?" I asked.

"Noon. We were all getting a little worried, but Asher said to let you rest."

I'd slept over twenty-four hours. Between the pain and Asher, I hadn't been sleeping well lately. I guess my body had finally decided to take what it needed.

"Where did Gabe and Lottie go?" I asked.

"They said something about trying to reconnect with their friends to see what they could find out about the Morrisseys," she said. "They might be gone for a few days. They didn't want to chance leading anyone back here."

Oh. I felt deflated. I'd been ready to lay down the law with Gabe, and he'd left without saying anything. I was not going to be upset about that, either, because that would be ridiculous.

Erin sat at the dining room table with seating for eight. Sometime between yesterday and this morning she had accepted this place as her temporary home. She looked completely relaxed with a bowl of cereal and a laptop cracked open in front of her.

"What are you doing?" I asked, coming around the table to peer at the screen over her shoulder.

"Ordering clothes. Gabe gave me a credit card and told me to pick some things out since we can't leave the house and we didn't bring anything with us."

I scowled. *Bastard. Why did he have to be so thoughtful?*

Erin misinterpreted my expression. "He had Lucy order some things for you, too. He said you didn't like shopping, but I don't think he'd care if you picked out a few things."

"Thanks. I'm good with whatever Lucy picked out. She has better taste than I do." Unless she picked out a bunch of skirts and dresses, which was possible considering how she felt toward me at the moment. I went off to the kitchen to scrounge for food.

That's where Asher found me, standing perplexed in front of two ovens. From his expression I guessed he didn't know that Gabe had confronted me, and I didn't feel ready to talk about it. Asher appeared tired, and I wondered if nightmares still plagued him.

"Why do three people need two ovens?" I asked in desperation.

He grabbed a container of milk out of the fridge. "I think one is a convection oven."

"Convect . . . You know what? I'm not even going to ask." He took two glasses down from a cabinet and offered to pour me some milk. I nodded and ducked into the pantry. "Do you want soup? I think I can manage soup." I reappeared with a can of tomato soup and headed in search of a pan.

Asher took the can from me and set me bodily to one side of the kitchen. "I'll do that. You scare me in the kitchen. Do you want a grilled cheese sandwich?"

I sighed happily. "Have I told you lately that I love you?" The words landed in the room like a gas bomb, and I smacked a hand over my mouth. For a minute, we'd been like our old selves, working together as a team. Asher shot me a wry smile, as he buttered slices of bread, and I dropped my hand. There were two ways to deal with the weirdness between us: wallow or make the best of it. I chose to make the best of it. "Well, that wasn't awkward at all."

He stared at the ceiling. "Ah, a good night's rest and she's found her sarcasm bone."

I hopped up on the counter to keep him company as he cooked us lunch. I ran a hand over the surface. "Should I be up here? This isn't cut gold-veined marble, is it? Or some kind of other precious material that would cost more than my right arm?"

"No. It's made from the tears of a thousand crushed dreams. Since when are you upset by nice things?"

"Since it became apparent that you're absurdly wealthy, which is a step beyond the sickeningly wealthy I thought you were." I used my hands to show him the levels in the air.

"Snob," he accused as he flipped the toasting sandwiches in the frying pan.

"Am not," I said, affronted.

"Yes, you are. You're a reverse snob. Our money freaks you out."

The house had sent me reeling. "True. I never had much growing up. This is beyond decadent."

He plated both sandwiches and poured the soup into two bowls. "So why don't you just enjoy it?"

I grabbed the glasses of milk and followed him into the dining room. "I'll try. I have to admit a special fondness for the heated floor in my bathroom."

Erin's head snapped up from where she still sat at the table. "The bathroom floors heat up? Are you kidding me?" I nodded, and she ran out of the room saying, "I have to check this out."

Asher handed me my plate with a laugh. We managed to

eat a meal in companionable silence. Maybe we'd reached a turning point on the plane. He didn't want to be with me, and I could accept that. We didn't have to be enemies.

I pushed my plate away. "So what's the plan? Erin said Lottie and Gabe have gone visiting old friends for a few days."

"Yeah. They can't just show up and start asking questions. They're going to hang out at Spencer and Miranda's, let it be known they're in town, and see what they can find out."

Spencer and Miranda were two Protector friends of the Blackwells who had once come to Blackwell Falls for a visit. Then, we'd been afraid of what they'd do if they discovered me. What about now?

I toyed with my spoon. "What about you? Why didn't you go?" Erin and I couldn't go for obvious reasons. Hello, Healers. And Lucy couldn't protect herself. But these people had been Asher's friends.

He ran a hand through his hair. "They'd know I'm different. Gabe and Lottie sensed it and so would they."

Asher tried not to show how this upset him, but I knew him. The frustration would eat at him. He would want to be doing something, but if the Protectors sensed that he'd lost his powers, there would be questions. Questions that would lead straight to me, which meant he was stuck here with us.

"Well, this is going to be fun." At his questioning look, I added, "You and three chicks on lockdown. Too bad there aren't more rooms so we could get away from each other."

I put on an exaggerated sad expression. Asher didn't laugh, but he smiled, and that was progress. His empty plate and bowl reminded me of how he took his ability to taste everything in stride now. At first, every new flavor had delighted him. "Is it really that bad, Asher? Being human? Is there nothing to love about it?"

I wanted to take the words back as soon as I said them. The amusement on his face disappeared and he looked trapped. His eyes flicked about the room like he sought escape. So I cleared my throat and pretended that I'd been teasing. "How can you not be willing to give up everything for a great grilled cheese sandwich?"

I didn't fool him, but he latched on to my bad joke. "I thought you were mad for macaroni and cheese."

I picked up our dishes to clear the table. "I'm crazy about cheese in general." He followed me back into the kitchen with Erin's cereal bowl. "Hey, where's Lucy?"

"I think she's in the study. Next room over. She had that book you took from Alcais. She mentioned wanting to read it."

I'd stolen the volume on my last visit to his house. It had been full of fear and hatred toward Healers and Protectors who would dare to have children together.

He handed me the bowl, and I said, "You cooked, I clean. Go on. I've got this." I smiled and shooed him away with a wave.

After a brief searching look, Asher left the room, and I heard his footsteps on the stairs. I let the false smile fall from my face. We'd managed to get through an encounter without fighting or hurting each other. That had to mean something. I settled in to wash the dishes, wondering if it also meant something that I hadn't told him about Gabe and yesterday's almost-kiss.

In my mind, my inner grandmother reared her head again, and I sighed, wondering if she was right.

Three days. Three freaking long days had passed with no news from Gabe or Lottie. Lucy hid in the study, poring over Alcais's book like it held the key to unlocking the mystery of Stonehenge, while otherwise ignoring me. She'd made a couple of snide comments in passing that warned me she was still angry with me. The waiting made things worse, and I had to stuff my own anger down when she took her frustration out on me.

Asher also tended to disappear to the room he shared with Gabe or to the family room to watch TV. We'd had a couple more run-ins that had been tense but not completely unpleasant. It got a little easier each time. Erin's presence helped a lot. She was the same girl I had grown to like in Pacifica, sweet and caring, and I loved spending time with her.

On the fourth day with no news, I thought I might go crazy. The rain wouldn't let up, so I couldn't even go on the rooftop terrace or into the courtyard to get some air. I went in search of company—even Lucy's snippiness would be better than my thoughts—and found Erin in the family room. She was pushing the coffee table against the couch and clearing a space in front of the TV.

"Hey, Erin. Whatcha doing?" I drawled. "I thought I was bored, but you're taking it to a new level if you're re-arranging furniture."

She laughed and flipped her ponytail. "Nah. Asher mentioned that he and Gabe have trained you to defend yourself. My plan was to corner you and promise to cook you something cheesy if you helped me learn a few things."

"Something cheesy? I sense Asher's influence here." I moved to help her shift a ceramic vase out of harm's way. Our clothes had arrived two days ago, and we both wore jeans and T-shirts.

"Whatever works. Will you do it?"

"Why not? I could use the exercise. I'm going stir-crazy." Plus, this would get my mind off Gabe. I couldn't decide if I was more worried or irritated at him for not sending us some sign that he and Lottie were okay.

We set about pushing the rest of the furniture back, and I pulled my hair into a ponytail at the back of my neck. We sat on the ground to stretch our muscles.

"Remy, can I ask you something?" At my nod, she continued, "When those men found us in the woods, you never once suggested that I might have been helping them. Why didn't you suspect me?"

"Are you confessing?" I teased her, reaching for my toes.

She shook her head. "I'm serious. Most people would have at least thought it was a possibility that I led them to you."

Her brown eyes had widened with confusion. I sat up. "A couple of reasons, I guess. First, you didn't have to help me find Asher. You knew it was risky and you did it anyway. That says a lot about you."

She thought about that and nodded. "And the other reason?"

I hesitated. "It was the way your brother treated you. He hurt you, didn't he?"

"You were there. You saw it for yourself."

Her forehead wrinkled in confusion, and I had to hand it to her. She was almost as good at covering up for Alcais as I had been for Dean.

I shook my head. "No. I mean, he hurt you before that. And probably since."

Erin's face drained of color, and her gaze dropped to the floor. I'd worn that look of shame often. "You knew?" she asked.

Alcais had abused her in front of Delia and me. I had wondered what else he might have done to her when nobody was looking. Alcais had a streak of cruelty in him, and Erin had been an easy victim, since she could heal the injuries he inflicted on her. I'd never had proof of that, but something in me had recognized a likeness in her, a shared history that we didn't like to talk about. I'd been sure when she didn't think twice about running away with us. She'd been escaping her brother.

I shrugged. "I recognized the signs. I know what it's like to live with somebody like that. I had a feeling that you were looking for a chance to fight back in your own way. Say, like when you helped me."

"You stood up to him. I couldn't do nothing." Erin's fingers twisted together, as she admitted, "Nobody at home knows about this. Well, maybe Delia, but he does the same thing to her."

I crawled across the floor to sit beside her, our shoulders touching. "Erin, your brother is a psychotic douche. Please, please, tell me you know that you're not to blame for how he treated you."

There should be a special place in hell for people who abused Healers. Our ability to heal our injuries over time seemed to bring out the worst in sadistic people, as if they considered it a challenge. How far could they go before they broke us? Unfortunately, our abilities meant they could go far.

Erin's mouth pressed into a thin line, and then she laughed. "I can't believe I'm laughing. I've never told any-one about this. Why am I laughing?"

"You're not," I said softly. I reached for the box of tis-sues on the table and passed them to her so she could wipe the tears on her face. "Listen, you don't ever have to go back there. We'll figure something out."

"That's the problem. I will go back." She lifted one shoulder. "I can't leave my mom back there with what Franc is doing to our people. That's why I want to learn how to defend myself. So I can protect her."

The rage and determination in her voice reminded me

of the girl I'd been not so long ago. I hadn't been able to save my mom or stepmom. Maybe Erin would have a better chance, and maybe I could help her.

I rose to my feet and pulled her up. "Okay, there are some things you need to know."

# CHAPTER FOURTEEN

*E*rin was a fireball once we'd run through some moves. I knew from experience that the worst part of the training wasn't the pain: it was those moments when your opponent beat you, and your own sense of helplessness threatened to swallow you whole. I didn't have a man's build, but it didn't matter. The first time I pinned her to the rug she burst into tears and then shook for the next ten minutes. I suggested we start again later, but she stood up and insisted we try the move once more. I was filled with admiration for her and disgust for Alcais for hurting her.

"That's enough for today," I said after a couple of hours.

Erin lay on her back on the floor where I'd tossed her, and I helped her up.

"She's hesitating when you grab her."

I spun around to find Asher watching us from the doorway. I acknowledged his comment with a nod as I wiped sweat from my forehead with my forearm. "I know. We're working on it."

He hesitated and then asked, "How are your defenses doing?"

His gaze touched on Erin, and I guessed he referred to her. "I still feel the urge to attack, but it's controllable. I kind of understand what you meant about how it got easier for you to be near me over time."

He'd once said that the urge to attack me had lessened after a while. Then, the problem had been my body's instinct to cure him.

Erin listened to us, her head swinging back and forth like a fan at a spectator sport. She frowned in confusion. "Wait. You feel the urge to attack me?"

"Part Protector, remember? It's like my body senses an immortal cake, and it can't have just one slice. Luckily, I don't like immortal cake."

Erin blinked. "Am I the immortal cake in that image?"

Asher grinned. "Nice analogy." He turned to Erin. "Remy has mental walls like Protectors do. She's learned to keep them up around Healers."

I started moving furniture back and the others jumped in to help. "I wouldn't hurt you, Erin. I'm careful."

"Oh, please. If you were going to hurt me, you would have done it by now." She collapsed on the floor, and I sat beside her. "All those questions you asked in Pacifica, you really didn't know, did you? How our powers worked? It's because yours are so different."

I explained to her how my abilities differed, including the bonding and how my powers affected Protectors. She'd never heard of a Protector who had regained their senses to the extent Asher had, and her face lit with curiosity.

"So you're more human now?" she asked Asher with narrowed eyes, studying him like a lab rat in a maze. She suddenly reached over and pinched him. "Did you feel that?"

He rubbed the red mark on his arm, his mouth twisting in amusement. "Yes. I can also taste the food that you're about to cook us."

Erin groaned. "Have I told you that I hate cheese? It's so yellow."

I smiled, so glad this girl had become my friend. "It

comes in orange and white, too. I prefer the Day-Glo orange powder variety myself."

We started up the stairs, Asher leading the way and me trailing after Erin. I missed whatever she did, but I suspected she'd kicked Asher when I heard him trip and yelp.

"Did you feel that?" she asked him.

He muttered, "You two have been hanging out too much. Remy is rubbing off on you," and I burst out laughing.

After lunch, I headed into the library to find a book to read. Downstairs, Asher's family had every episode of *Doctor Who* on Blu-ray and not much else in the way of movies or TV shows. I wouldn't have minded watching it, except after three days cooped up in the house, I was already halfway through series two and onto the Tenth Doctor.

The library consisted of two walls lined with bookshelves from floor to ceiling and two cozy armchairs with footrests by a hearth. Huge windows on the fourth wall invited natural light into the room. It still rained outside, and the room might have been gloomy but for the fire that blazed in the fireplace. What the family room lacked in movies, the library made up for with books. I browsed the shelves, reading the spines. Most of the books were classics, and I had a sneaking suspicion many of them were first editions. I pulled down a copy of *The Great Gatsby*. On the inside cover, Lottie had scrawled her name in cursive along with the date of 1925. I shook my head and put the book back. I would never get over the lives the Blackwells had led. I strolled to another shelf, and there sat one book that looked older than the rest. It had a cracked leather spine and no title on the cover.

"Oh, you're in here!" Lucy said.

I almost dropped the book and spun around to find her standing in the doorway with a teacup. She glanced at the chair by the fire where a book lay open on the table between the chairs. It was the book I'd stolen from Alcais.

"I'll leave," she said with a scowl and turned to do that.

"Lucy!" She paused and I tried to think of a way to get her to stay. I missed my sister, and I wanted to spend time with her before it was too late. Before we found our father, and I had to leave them. My gaze landed on the book again. "Anything interesting in there?"

I'd scanned it when we first went on the run. It had been full of inflammatory lies about Healers and Protectors. The book had been meant to incite people to rage and instill them with fear about the offspring of the union between the two groups. It had made me more than a little sick to my stomach.

Lucy shrugged. "It's interesting."

"What is?" It was like pulling teeth to get her to talk to me.

She sighed. "Does it matter? Look, are you going to stay in here? Because I'm happy to find another room."

"Lucy, please," I pleaded. I was so tired of us walking around each other.

"Please, what?" she snapped, advancing into the room. The teacup clattered when she slammed it on the table. "Did you think that everything would be okay between us because you tried to save Mom? Tried and failed, by the way."

That hurt. My sister had a mean verbal hook when she wanted to. Along with the pain, though, anger rose in me, and I didn't try to stem the tide.

"Tried and almost died, by the way. Would you be pleased if I had?" I asked.

Lucy's hands landed on her hips. "No, because that

would make you happy. You're so quick to die for everyone around you, it probably would have given you a thrill."

I stared at her in shock. "That's what you think of me?"

She walked to the fire and threw a log on it from the pile nearby. Sparks flew up when she shoved at them with a poker. She didn't say anything, and I stalked over to her.

"Come on, Lucy. Don't be a coward now. You've been bitching at me for weeks, blaming me for everything that's happened. Why don't you just spit out whatever you have to say?"

She dropped the poker, stood, and shoved me with both hands on my shoulders. "You ruined everything!" she screamed, pushing me again. "Everything was fine before you came along. We were happy. And now my mom is dead and my dad is probably being tortured somewhere and I'm stuck here with you. Don't you see? You're poison! You destroy everything around you. I hate you!"

A switch flipped inside me the second time she pushed me. When she tried to shove me again, I calmly stepped out of her reach, cradling the book I still held against my chest. She stumbled, and I let her catch herself. I was so sick of blaming myself for everything that had happened. Dean, Franc, and yes, Asher and Lucy, they all had opinions on my powers. Save this person. Don't save that person. Use your powers. Don't use your powers. Dean wanted to use me for money. Franc wanted to use me as a weapon. Asher and Lucy had wanted me to only use my powers when there was no risk involved. Now, Asher wanted me to keep my powers to myself, and Lucy wanted me to throw the risk out the window when she decided the person mattered. And even then, she punished me. They all had opinions about something they couldn't possibly understand. And suddenly, I was sick to death of feeling guilty for what I was.

Lucy was breathing hard from her outburst, and I'd never felt calmer, fueled by a cold anger. My voice sounded steady and firm when I spoke. "You're acting like a brat. You were pissed at me when I wouldn't heal Mom and now you're pissed because I tried. You can't have it both ways, Lucy. Either I'm a monster for letting her die, or I'm a martyr for trying to save her. Pick one, and have a little conviction if you're going to punish me for it."

I'd never spoken to her so harshly. Her mouth fell open and she stepped back, her muscles rigid.

I continued. "I didn't ask for this any more than you did. I've made mistakes, but I'm doing the best I can. I'm sorry if that's not good enough for you. And I'm sorry that you've lost everything and that you're sad and hurt and angry. But look around—you're not the only one."

I left her standing in front of the fireplace, but I turned back when I reached the door. Three times now she'd called our parents *hers,* as if I hadn't belonged.

"One more thing . . . They're *my* parents, too. Whatever you may think about me, they saved my life when they brought me home and made me their daughter. You don't get to take that away because you're mad at me."

With that, I left the room and ran smack into Asher. He gripped my shoulders and squeezed. In a low voice, he said, "Good for you, *mo cridhe*."

I used the book as a shield to push him away. "And you. Stop calling me your heart when you don't mean it."

He stepped back like I'd slapped him, and I shoved past him without looking back.

I couldn't go outside, so I went to the next best place. The conservatory had a glass ceiling and walls, offering a view of the rooftop terrace through the double doors on one end. Rain fell on the roof, creating a musical cacophony before drizzling down the sides. Two wicker chairs and a table had been positioned in one corner to make the most of the tranquil room.

Dropping the book on the table, I sank into the chair near the doors, tracing a drop of condensation on the glass. I probably shouldn't have said what I had to Lucy, but I couldn't keep sucking it up and turning the other cheek. That would make me the martyr she thought I was, and I didn't want to be that person. I had always tried to heal people when I could. What Asher and Lucy had always failed to grasp was that my decision to do this wasn't about a death wish or being impulsive. I healed people because I knew what it was like to hurt and feel like nobody would be there to help you. I understood what it was like to be weak and at the mercy of fate. My friends and family all seemed to think that I didn't value my life, but the opposite was true. I healed people *because* I valued life. To be able to cure someone's suffering, to save a life, that was power. And I was good at it.

What would I do, though, when we found my father and I moved on alone? I could try to set down roots somewhere. Except every time I used my abilities, I chanced being found by one of my enemies. Did that mean that I should stop using them? Could I watch someone hurt when I knew I could help them? The idea of it made me sick. It reminded me of all the people who had turned a blind eye to the bruises and burns I hadn't been able to hide or heal as a child. Dean had tortured my mother and me, and nobody had stepped in to help us. Alcais had been hurting Erin and nobody had helped her, either. I didn't think that I could be someone who sat on the fence. Not when all those years of healing my mother had made me feel like Dean's collaborator. I couldn't go back to living like that.

Maybe it would be better to live on the run, moving from place to place. If I never tied myself down, then I would never bind myself to someone who could be hurt. Suddenly, I wished that I could confess everything to my father. He had a way of looking at all the sides of a thing and cutting to its heart. I wanted to be able to talk to him and hear his voice so much that I ached with it. I wouldn't believe for a second that he was gone forever. We'd find him, and he'd be okay. But if he wasn't, I would heal him, and then anyone who had hurt him would pay for what they'd done. Hell hath no fury like a Protector whose family has been threatened.

Gabe and Lottie had better come back soon because I wasn't going to wait around for much longer. Soon, I was going to look for them, even if I had to go through Protectors to do it. I picked up the book I'd brought with me for no other reason than I'd forgotten I held it. The book fell open on my lap, the pages worn and well-read. All of the entries were handwritten in an old script that was difficult to read. I flipped through a couple of pages, trying to understand what I was looking at. It appeared to be some kind of genealogy book tracing Healer and Protector bloodlines.

Names had been entered onto the pages, and marriages had been indicated with small equal signs. Dates were listed next to names, and I thought they might indicate births and deaths. Healers had been marked with an *H* and the Protectors with a *P*, and the two never mixed under a surname. A birdlike symbol appeared next to a very few names.

I scanned page after page of dates. Some of the births dated back to the 1300s, and it was odd to see how many Healers' names had death dates listed, while the Protectors stopped dying after the late 1800s. The last update to the book that I could find had been the year the war started. Death dates had been added to three Protector names: Sam, Helene, and Angus Blackwell. Asher's parents. I traced the entry and wondered who had made the addition. Not Asher, because I would know his handwriting. Lottie had been sixteen at the time. It must have been Gabe. I imagined them all near my age, having lost their parents and their brother on the same day they lost their senses, and my heart ached for them.

I flipped back through the pages, scanning names this time. Twenty-six pages in I gasped when I saw the name O'Malley with a crest beside it. The crest showed a ship, a horse, a wild boar, armor, swords, and bows and arrows in a complex design. Under the design, three words appeared in what I guessed was Latin: *TERRA MARIQUE POTENS*. Then a column of names appeared, but it was a shorter column than under other surnames because the last O'Malley entry was in 1629.

I stared at the page. It could be a coincidence. I mean, did I really think this was my family? What were the odds that my father was descended from this group? It was a common Irish surname, after all. *But how many O'Malley families are also Protectors, Remy?* I shook myself. Did it matter? After all, the O'Malleys in this book had disappeared long ago.

I was about to close the cover when another name caught my eye. A Healer named Camille Lovellette had married Martin Dubois in 1853. I'd heard both names before, for very different reasons.

My mother hadn't talked about her parents often when I was growing up, but a couple of times she'd mentioned how she'd loved my grandmother's maiden name. Lovellette sounded like love letter, and the romance of it had appealed to her when she was a child. I doubted there were many Healer families with that last name. It would have been dangerous for my grandmother's family to use such a unique last name once they went into hiding, unless they thought the name had disappeared from people's memories when the last Healer named Lovellette married and became a Dubois in 1853, years before the war.

It wouldn't have mattered, except Camille had given birth to a daughter: Elizabeth. I was 99.9 percent sure I was a descendant of Elizabeth Dubois, the woman responsible for killing Sam, Helene, and Angus Blackwell. The woman whom Asher had killed while defending Lottie and the reason he'd become immortal in the first place.

The book fell to the floor, and I gazed into space. *It can't be. This can't be happening.* My ancestor had started the war between the Healers and Protectors. I rocked back in my seat, dropped my head on my knees, and huddled into a ball. Fate had a screwed-up sense of humor. The Blackwells were going to freak. *Right when we'd begun to settle our differences and get along so well. Ha!* I laughed and it had a hysterical edge.

*Son of a bitch.*

"That wasn't quite the welcome I was expecting, Remington."

# CHAPTER FIFTEEN

*M*y mental walls snapped into place before I'd sat up straight, and Gabe frowned at me. He'd obviously just come up the stairs; he still carried his bag in one hand and his damp brown hair looked almost black. He dropped the duffel at his feet and shook his head, sending little droplets of water everywhere. I squeaked and dove for the book to protect it.

He stared at it with curiosity. "Why are you reading that? It has to be the most boring book in our library. Man, I haven't seen that thing in decades."

"I was in the middle of a fight with Lucy when I picked it up. I didn't plan to read it. It caught my attention because it was so old."

He took another step into the room and flipped on an overhead light. I hadn't even noticed that it was getting dark, but now all I could see was how the light created a kind of halo around his body, outlining his broad shoulders and narrow hips. I licked my suddenly dry lips. My thoughts dipped in a direction they shouldn't, and I yanked them back.

"Have you ever heard of such a thing as a phone?" I snapped. "You could have called so we knew you weren't dead."

My anger bounced off him. "I see my diabolical plan has worked," he observed.

"What plan?" I asked with narrowed eyes.

"Absence makes the heart grow fonder. Tone down the outpouring of affection, Remington, or I might get the wrong idea and kiss you."

My mouth dropped open. I regained control of my jaw with effort and snapped it closed again. "Try it," I dared with a vicious smile. "I'm in a mean mood, and I'm likely to bite your tongue off."

"Promises, promises," he said in a low voice that whispered along my nerves. My mind raced through escape scenarios, and Gabe laughed. "I'm teasing you. Come on. Lottie and I brought dinner and news. We're all gathering downstairs in the dining room."

He swept a hand toward the door and waited for me. I rose and made to walk by him when he snagged my waist and pulled me behind the door where nobody would see us. I gasped and looked up. His green eyes had focused on my lips, and his head lowered toward mine. This close, he mesmerized me, and it took the closing of a distant door to snap me out of it.

I smacked a hand against his mouth. "Don't even think about it."

"Oh, I'll think about it," he said against my fingers. It tickled and I dropped my hand in a hurry. "But I won't push you. Just tell me you thought about what I said and that you missed me like crazy."

I pressed against his shoulders and he let me back away. A whole inch. I sighed. "Of course I did, but that doesn't mean anything. I'm not doing this."

"This?"

I waved a hand in the whole six inches that separated our chests. "This. It's too complicated." *And I'm not a ho. Take that, inner grandmother.*

"Why are you thinking about red lipstick?"

This time, he let me go when I gave him a hard shove. "Damn it, Gabe. Stay out of my head."

He held up both hands in a gesture of innocence. "Hey, I'm not the one who feels so strongly about cosmetics that my thoughts are practically shrieking about it."

"Whatever," I muttered. I retrieved the book from the floor and followed him down the stairs. I praised myself for handling that well. After all, I'd avoided a kiss. So what if I admired his butt as we took the stairs? And who could blame me for wishing there were more stairs when he moved the way he did? It occurred to me that he was moving at a snail's pace, and I suddenly realized why. I reinforced my walls to look like a fortress in hopes of keeping stray, lecherous thoughts from sneaking out.

He threw a satisfied smile over his shoulder and said, "You're no fun, Remington."

"And you're eavesdropping."

He shrugged, and I knew he didn't care a bit.

We finally reached the dining room, where the others had already gathered. To-go containers were scattered around the table, and everyone was helping themselves to a plate like any other family eating together on a Friday night. The scent of curry thickened the air, and I inhaled happily. I hadn't eaten Indian food since I'd moved to Maine. I was fixing myself a plate when I felt Gabe watching me. With a smug smile, I doubled up on the garlic rice and garlic naan bread, the smelliest foods on the table. He merely raised his brows in challenge and added a triple helping of garlic-laden dishes to his plate.

*I'm not kissing you.*

He smiled as if this didn't concern him. Maybe he hadn't heard me, though. His gaze dropped to my lips. Then again, maybe he had.

"Can you pass me the samosas?" Erin asked Gabe.

His attention shifted, and I was finally able to focus on the others in the room. We settled into our seats. I sensed Gabe sitting next to me and ignored him. At one end of the table, Lucy studiously avoided making eye contact with me by staring at her plate.

It was Asher who finally called us to attention. "Don't keep us in suspense. What did you guys learn?"

I didn't expect them to say they'd found my father. Gabe would have told me immediately. That didn't mean I wasn't disappointed when he said as much.

"We weren't able to get near the Morrisseys. They've closed ranks, and it would have looked suspicious if we suddenly showed up. But we did do some asking around to see if the others knew anything." His face took on a grim bent, and I steeled myself for more bad news. "Remember our friend Xavier?"

Like I could forget the bastard who had shot Asher and tortured me. He'd also helped kidnap my father and run Laura down. My hands fisted in my lap. If I could get my hands on him, I would break every bone in his body. "Is he here?" I asked, sounding almost hopeful.

Across the table, Asher gritted his teeth. He looked as bloodthirsty as I felt, and I didn't blame him.

Gabe shook his head, his expression unchanging. Under the table, his warm hand covered my fist. He stroked my fingers until my hand relaxed, and then he retreated. He picked up his fork again and continued. "He's not here, but he was. Spencer knows him. Xavier bragged about the setup he had going with Franc." He turned to me. "Your grandfather is a real sweetheart. He's promised you to the Protectors if they catch you. Apparently, he's given up on the idea of using you and just wants revenge."

"More likely, he plans to double-cross them."

I'd seen the crazy light in Franc's eyes. Somebody as fanatical as he was wouldn't give up so easily. Not when he was sure that he was right and that the ends justified the means. His moral code had been compromised long ago, and he wouldn't think twice about betraying a Protector.

"What a bastard," Erin muttered.

I snorted. That was putting it mildly.

Lucy asked, "Did Spencer and Miranda suspect that you knew Remy?"

The question surprised me. Was she asking because she was worried about me? I couldn't tell from her expression. She tucked her hair behind her ear and watched Gabe's face. Her attention switched to Lottie when she spoke.

"No. We were careful. They did wonder why Asher wasn't with us, but we told them you'd decided to make a side trip to Paris. I'm not sure they believed us."

Considering how long they'd been gone, I was disappointed that they didn't have more news. I guess I'd hoped they'd have some kind of clue that would lead us to my father. How much longer could we sit around without doing something? They'd already had him for too long. Look what they had done to Asher in a matter of weeks. They'd had my father for months.

Lottie stood to begin clearing plates, and I said, "Can you wait a second? I have something to tell you, too."

Gabe tensed beside me like he thought it was about him. I waited for Lottie to retake her seat before I told them what I'd found in their book about the O'Malleys. It hadn't occurred to me to keep it a secret when we all had too many things left unsaid already. Lucy's eyes lit up when I described the crest in the book. I opened it to that page and pushed it toward her. She read the three words below the crest out loud.

"Mighty of the land and sea," Asher translated.

"The crest has a ship in it," Lucy said, touching it. "Do you suppose sailing has always been in our blood?" she asked me with wonder in her voice.

I smiled. "I think Dad would insist it is." He'd made his living building ships and spent every weekend he could on a sailboat.

Gabe tapped the table, lost in thought. "You know, it's weird. I don't remember any Protectors named O'Malley. How does a family just disappear? We might not have known every Protector in existence, but we knew of every family name. Do you guys remember the O'Malleys?"

Asher and Lottie both shook their heads. My gaze landed on the page opposite the O'Malley page. "Hey, Gabe. Do you know what these markings mean?" I pointed at the small birdlike symbol that appeared next to some names in the 1600s.

He studied it. "Never seen it before."

"There's more. I think I found my mother's ancestors, too." I explained what I knew about the name Lovellette, and how I suspected my grandmother's family had taken that name back.

"It makes sense," Lottie said. "I could see your family wanting some connection to their heritage when they'd been forced to cut themselves off from everything. Most Protectors don't have a record like our family kept in that book, so they were probably safe using the surname. Does it say what name Camille married into? Maybe we knew your mother's family."

"Oh, you knew them." Dread made me wish I hadn't eaten that last piece of naan bread. I took the book back from Asher and found the page with Camille's name. I pointed to it. "Read it, Gabe."

He leaned over. His entire body tensed a second later and his eyes shot to mine. He whispered, "Son of a bitch," echoing my earlier sentiment in the conservatory.

"Who is it?" Asher asked.

"The Duboises," I said. "And Camille and Martin Dubois gave birth to a daughter, Elizabeth Dubois."

I braced myself, waiting for the uproar and the explosion of outrage. Nothing happened. The room fell into total silence. I shifted in my seat, lifted my fork up, and then set it back down again. This wasn't what I'd expected.

"Okay, I'll bite. Who the heck is Elizabeth Dubois?" Erin asked, confused.

"Only one of the most powerful Healers we've ever heard about," Asher said.

He left out all of the important details about Elizabeth's very direct impact on his family. I dared to lift my eyes to his. Blame, anger, disappointment: any of those emotions I would have expected, but I saw evidence of none of them. Asher's gaze was calm and clear.

"Don't look like that," he told me. I realized I must have looked terrified. "Remy, it's okay. To be honest, it makes sense. Your powers are off the charts. You could only be descended from a powerful Healer, and Elizabeth was one of the most powerful that we knew of."

"Aren't you at all creeped out by the coincidence?" I asked them. Because I was.

"No," Gabe said. "There are only so many families. We were bound to know your ancestors. And it's not like we're going to hold you responsible for what some relative of yours did a hundred years ago."

I'd pumped myself up for their outburst, and their non-reaction left me nonplussed.

"I don't know. I kind of want to kill her now," Lottie said. Every head turned, and she laughed, her green eyes crinkling at the corners. "I'm kidding, people. I think we're past that."

She began clearing the table, and that signaled the end of the conversation.

After dinner, everyone but Asher and Lucy headed to the basement to watch—wait for it—more *Doctor Who*. I sank into one corner of the couch and could have hugged Erin when she planted herself beside me, effectively blocking Gabe. My smile of relief came too soon, though, because he sat on the floor by me, using the couch arm as a backrest.

His shoulder bumped my knee more than once, and it could have been an accident. I believed that right up until his hand slid over the top of my bare foot, his thumb brushing my instep. I nearly jumped out of my skin, and Erin sent me an odd look. I tucked my legs under me, putting my feet well out of Gabe's reach. The second Erin's attention returned to the TV, I shoved Gabe's shoulder. He glanced at me with a wicked smile, and I scowled.

Then his phone rang. He reached into his pocket and pulled it out to check the screen. Lottie silenced the TV when he held up a finger. He gave a warning glance around the room and answered the phone on speaker.

"Miranda, hi."

"Gabriel," a female voice drawled. "I hope I didn't pull you away from anything."

The Protector's tone was loaded with innuendo. I raised my brows when Gabe's cheeks flushed pink.

"Not a thing. Everything's okay, I hope?" he asked.

"Spencer and I are fine. It's you we worry about. Are you in trouble, dear?" she asked.

Gabe paused. "Now, why would you ask that?"

"Well, you and Lottie show up here without Asher, you won't tell us where you're staying, and there are rumors. Rumors about the Blackwells and a Healer girl. You're keeping things from me, Gabriel. I'm hurt," she said in a pouty voice.

Was this woman for real? Of course, they'd heard about me. That wasn't really a surprise at this point. But how would Gabe handle direct questioning from a longtime family friend?

He laughed. "No, you're not. We all have our secrets. It comes with the territory of who we are."

"Yes, but your secrets have landed at my doorstep."

Lottie pressed forward in her armchair. Erin leaned over to whisper to her, but Lottie's green eyes narrowed. She pressed a finger to her lips and watched Gabe.

He sounded less calm than before. "What do you mean?"

"A package was delivered to the house for you. The messenger was that fellow Xavier that we told you about. You never mentioned that you knew him."

She didn't sound accusatory, but Miranda didn't sound trusting, either.

"We only met in passing," Gabe told her. "I wouldn't say I know him."

That wasn't exactly true. He had once pretended to be Xavier's ally in order to rescue me from the torture the Protector was inflicting on me at my grandfather's request. Another of Franc's tests, though I hadn't known it at the time.

"Well, he knows you. Word has gotten around that you were at our house, and he asked where you'd gone."

"And you told him . . . ?" Gabe's voice tapered off with a dangerous note.

"I told him the truth. We had no idea where you'd gotten to." Silence stretched on for a moment, and she added, "I know you're not suspecting us of betraying you. That would be an insult among friends, and we are friends, are we not?"

"We are," Gabe said in a soft tone that matched hers. "I'm sorry, Miranda."

"Never mind, dear. Spencer thought it best he meet you somewhere to deliver the package. It might not be a good idea for you to come 'round the house anytime soon. There seem to be a lot of eyes on us all of a sudden."

Lottie grabbed a piece of paper and wrote something on

it before shoving it across the coffee table toward Gabe. He read it and nodded.

"Have him meet me at the police call box outside the Earl's Court Tube Station. I'll be there in two hours."

Miranda agreed, and they hung up. Lottie and Gabe wasted no time. They both rose and started for the stairs, talking at a million miles an hour.

"Stop." I didn't raise my voice, but Gabe looked at me. "I'm going with you, Gabe."

I thought he would argue, but it was Lottie who spoke up. "Is that wise, Remy?"

I gave her a half smile as I stood. "We all know that package is meant for me. I'm not going to let you both walk into danger while I sit on my hands."

She considered me for a moment and seemed to make a decision. "In that case, I'll stay here and keep the Healer company."

"My name is Erin," Erin muttered.

Lottie smiled, and I guessed she'd purposely teased Erin to put the girl at ease. Both girls moved to the sofa, and Lottie picked up the remote as they argued about Lottie's manners. That was the last I heard as I ran to my room to grab shoes, a knit cap, and a jacket. I was shoving my hair under the cap when I met Gabe in the entrance hall.

"Is that your idea of a disguise?" he asked, tugging on an escaped strand at my cheek. "Come on. Let's get this over with," he said grimly, taking my hand and opening the front door. He wore the same jeans and T-shirt he'd had on downstairs, plus a black jacket.

I stared at his back and trailed him down the street. Rather than walk to a car, we continued on to an entrance with a blue and red sign that said UNDERGROUND. "We're taking the Tube?" I asked.

He nodded. "It'll be faster that way."

It turned out that the London Underground wasn't that

different from New York's subway system. If anything, the London system was easier to navigate, and Gabe obviously knew what he was doing. The other difference was the polite voice telling people to "mind the gap" as they stepped on and off the train.

On the crowded train, Gabe grasped a blue pole that ran from ceiling to floor in order to stay balanced while standing. He pulled me into his side, wrapping an arm around my shoulder to shelter me from a rowdy group out to have fun on Friday night. I didn't fight him, and we didn't speak. My mind had begun to spin possibilities about what could be in that package. Franc had sent it, obviously, with Xavier as his messenger. It would contain a warning of some kind, I was sure, but what kind? My stomach lurched when the train stopped twenty minutes later.

Gabe held my hand again as we climbed the stairs. At some point, we stopped and he said, "Spencer is a good friend, but don't give him any info that we don't have to. We want to keep him out of this, and while he might not hunt Healers, I want you to be on your toes. Guard up, okay?"

I realized I'd forgotten to raise my mental walls, a common occurrence around Gabe. I took care of that, and we exited the station. Like Gabe, I glanced around, staring into the shadows to see if someone lurked there. Everyone seemed to be going about their normal day, not paying any attention to us. Then my gaze lit on the police call box that sat a short distance from the station entrance: a blue police box like the one that was used as a time machine in *Doctor Who*.

"Did Lottie really pick the Doctor's Tardis as our meeting place?" I asked in a wry voice, watching a tourist in a *Doctor Who* T-shirt pose for a picture in front of the structure.

Gabe sent me a quick smile as he continued to scan the

area. "I thought the choice was inspired, myself." He straightened with sudden awareness. "There's Spencer. He's alone."

Spencer looked up as we approached and smiled at Gabe, huge dimples forming on either cheek. A tall man who appeared to be in his thirties, Spencer had blond hair and hazel eyes. Neither handsome nor unattractive, he would not stand out in a crowd, except for those awesome dimples. Gabe didn't let go of me when Spencer hugged him, and I shifted my weight awkwardly until they stepped away from each other.

"So you're the one causing all this trouble," Spencer said to me with a quizzical smile. His accent sounded straight out of *Pride and Prejudice*. I felt a hint of energy that wasn't Gabe's drifting in the air, but I kept my face expressionless.

"Spencer . . ." Gabe warned him.

The Protector held up both hands. "Can't blame me for being curious. I've never known the Blackwell boys to act so secretive."

"I'm sorry for your trouble," I said sincerely. It had never been my intention to come between the Blackwell family and their friends. "You mentioned there was a package?"

He slipped a small, white jewelry box out of his coat pocket and passed it to me. He gave me a quizzical look. "The man who dropped this off isn't the type to mess with. I don't know what you all are mixed up in, but you need to be careful."

"We will," Gabe promised.

Spencer waved at us. "Go on now. As curious as I am about you, Healer, it's not safe out here in the open. No doubt they were using that box to draw you out."

My head whipped up when he called me Healer, but Spencer was already walking away. He climbed into a waiting black cab. When the car passed us, I saw a woman was with him in the backseat. A stunning woman with red hair, high cheekbones, and full lips. She waggled her fingers in a wave, and then the car drove off. Gabe gripped my elbow and pulled me back into the Underground station.

"Was that Miranda?" I asked.

He nodded. "I should have figured she'd be here. They never go anywhere if they aren't together. Most likely, she was acting as backup in case there was trouble. They have always been very protective of us."

I thought about that, running my fingers over the box that I'd slipped in my jacket pocket. I was glad that the Blackwells had Spencer and Miranda to watch out for them. I wished that my presence hadn't affected their relationship.

We didn't take a train straight back to Chapel Street. Gabe wanted to take a circuitous route in case someone had managed to follow us from the meeting. I went along with his plan in silence, relieved to have him with me while I was lost in my thoughts.

Three trains later, Gabe guided me to a seat and finally prodded me. "Is not opening the box worse than opening it?" I stared up at him, and he tilted his head. "You're torturing yourself, Remy, with what might be in it. Just open it, and get it over with."

I glanced around. We were alone in the train car. Dread filled me as I took the box from my pocket. With a quick intake of breath, I pulled the lid off and then promptly wanted to throw up when I saw the contents. It was the bloody tip of a finger.

Gabe took the box from me as I doubled over, choking on tears. Was my father dead? What had they done to him?

"Remy, it's fake, sweetheart. It's fake."

His voice finally penetrated the horror that consumed

me. I sat up straight, staring at him blankly. He brushed the hair from my face, his expression worried.

"It's not my father's?" I whispered.

He shook his head. "No. It's a very real-looking prop that was meant to scare you."

I laughed without humor. "It worked." I breathed for a second, trying to calm myself. Franc was a total bastard to do that to me. "Is there a note?"

"Here."

He handed me a folded slip of paper. I opened it and read the short message.

*This is the last warning you get, granddaughter. Give yourself up.*

# CHAPTER SIXTEEN

$\mathscr{T}$ he next morning rage still flowed through my veins. My grandfather had left a phone number on the note, as if I would immediately call him and turn myself in. *Hold your breath, Franc. Please.* Gabe and I had shared the contents of the package with the others when we returned. Lottie had alerted Asher and Lucy by then, and they had all waited up until we got back. I'd made sure that Lucy hadn't seen the fake fingertip, not wanting her to be more upset than she had to be. The group had gone to bed unsettled and oddly quiet, each of us lost in our own thoughts about the escalated violence that the note seemed to warn was ahead.

After a quick breakfast of cereal, I headed into the kitchen to wash my dishes. Like a coward, I considered running to my room and hiding out there because I had a feeling that Gabe wanted to talk. There were things to be said after how we'd left things five days ago, and last night hadn't been the time to go into them. Honestly, I didn't know what to do about him. Until that scene in the wine vault I'd never thought of him in *that* way.

*Liar.*

I scrubbed my bowl in frustration and used my shoulder to shove back a piece of hair that had fallen out of my

French braid. Okay, maybe I'd always noticed Gabe—how could I not when he looked the way he did?—but that hadn't meant anything. I'd admired him in a distant kind of way, the way I'd notice a pretty statue. Yeah. He was *David* or some other Greek statue. In fact, I hadn't liked him all that much, and then he'd gone and become a good friend. The kind of friend who held your hand during a crisis. I scrubbed the dish a little harder. Everything had changed, and this was his fault. Gabe had started me down this path with his talk of wanting me for himself. What was a girl supposed to say to that?

"I think that dish is clean."

I dropped the bowl and splashed water up the front of my shirt. "Damn it, Gabe." I shoved my elbow into his side as he appeared at my side.

He reached around me to shut off the faucet, wearing an unrepentant smile. "You should practice using your Protector senses more often. If you'd had your walls down, you would have heard me coming."

He handed me a towel, and I wiped my hands dry. "If I had my walls down, you would hear what I was thinking."

"It'll be rough, but for you, I'm willing to take that risk." He put a hand on his heart, looking the picture of piety.

I snorted. "I'm sure you are."

We worked together to dry the clean dishes and put them away. Our hips bumped as we moved, and my pulse kicked into gear as if a gun had gone off at a race.

"Nothing has changed for me." His low voice tripped along my nerves, and I stilled at his sudden gravity. "I meant what I said five days ago."

Yet, he'd said what he had and then left for days without a phone call. It shouldn't have bothered me, but it did.

"Because I wanted to give you time," he said.

The way he answered my thoughts so easily, shoving through my barriers, unnerved me, and I jumped when he shoved away from the counter to face me. My head spun when he reached for my hand and tugged me in his wake. A door opened off the kitchen to a room that I hadn't been in before. He pushed me in ahead of him and shut the door behind us, closing us in. I had two seconds to glance around and see that we were in some kind of utility room before Gabe's hands landed on my waist and he lifted me off my feet, planting me on a counter. He hadn't turned on a light, and the room had no window, but I could see his face, half-hidden in shadows. His hands landed on my knees, and a shiver started there and worked its way up.

"Gabe . . ."

"Do you remember the last time we were like this?"

I nodded, feeling towed under by a wave of emotions that I didn't understand. Last September, we'd been together like this in the Blackwells' kitchen, the night before Gabe left. That night, he'd pushed me. He'd wanted to know if I could have loved him instead of Asher if I'd met him first. Now Gabe said, "Tell me you've thought about what I asked. Tell me you're willing to give me a chance."

I sucked in a breath when his hands slid up my thighs to grip my hips, his fingers pressing into my skin through my jeans. I'd been so sure that I could avoid this, that I could shove these emotions down. I'd been wrong. My hands latched on to his forearms, and my knees pressed into his waist. If my intention had been to push him away, I failed miserably, and it terrified me how easily I found myself giving in to whatever this was between us. I stared into Gabe's eyes, utterly caught, but when he tipped his head to kiss me, I stopped him at the last second.

"We can't do this." It hurt to say the words with his lips

hovering so close. Gabe's eyes took on a tortured look, and I touched his cheek, feeling the rasp of whiskers under my palm. "This isn't right. We're not these people who sneak around."

"You feel something, Remy. I can hear it in your thoughts."

I didn't answer. His jaw worked as he stared over my head, and it was a long moment before he seemed to give in. His head dropped to my shoulder, and I couldn't resist the urge to wrap my arms around him. My fingers slid into his hair, and I sighed at how soft the strands felt. A moment later, his arms wrapped around me, and my thighs slid open so he could stand between them. My chin rested on his shoulder and it felt so good to be held. It went no further as we stood there leaning on each other with our breathing the only sound in the room. I wasn't ready for more than this, and Gabe didn't push me. Every time I'd asked him, he'd been there for me. Sometimes, he'd been there even when I'd fought needing anyone. He'd given me so much without asking for anything in return.

The way he treated me demanded honesty. "I feel something for you, Gabe. I'm confused and scared and this seems all wrong, but I feel something."

He pulled away, enough to see my face. "It's Asher, isn't it?"

"Yes," I said with regret. "So many people have been hurt since this all began. Asher more than most. I won't go behind his back like this. He and I may not be together, but it feels wrong to sneak off with his brother."

"So we tell him," Gabe said.

I brushed a strand of hair off his forehead. "Do you think this is the time to do it? With everything that's happened? I can't hurt him like this."

"So that's it? We give up and walk away?"

"Yes," I whispered around the ache in my throat. "It's

the right thing to do. And you're a good man, Gabriel Blackwell."

"You don't fight fair. If I push, I'm a bastard." He stepped back, his hands falling from me. "Go, okay? Before I prove I'm not good at all and try to convince you to change your mind."

I slid off the counter to stand on shaky legs. He turned his back on me as I walked to the door and reached for the doorknob. I didn't want to go. I thought again of the way he'd supported me last night, never arguing with my need to go, but holding me when I reaped the aftermath of opening that stupid package. A small voice warned me that I would be missing out on the possibility of something amazing if I walked away.

My eyes squeezed shut, and I took a chance, throwing myself into the wind. "I'll stay."

"What?"

"After we find my father, I'll stay." Gabe spun me around to face him, and his eyes were lit with so much hope that the ache in me eased. This decision felt right.

"Do you mean it?" he asked.

I nodded. "We'll find my father, and then we'll have time to figure out what this is. But we have to tell Asher when the time is right. And we don't do this." I gestured to us and the room. "Okay?"

Gabe ran his hand down the length of my braid, looping the end around his finger. "Okay. I've waited this long. I'm not going anywhere."

His hand fell away, and we stood there, staring at each other with silly grins while our world shifted. It wasn't until later, when I'd crawled under the covers in my bed alone, that I realized what had changed. I was exchanging a future on the run for something entirely unknown. It should have scared me, but all I felt was hope.

★   ★   ★

Gabe and Lottie had told their Protector friends that they were taking the weekend to visit Asher in Paris. That gave them Saturday and Sunday to relax at home before diving back into the Protector scene. This whole process moved so slowly, and the arrival of that package had changed things. My grandfather knew he could get to me through the Blackwells, and we needed to figure out what to do next. Plus, there were other Protectors to consider. If we weren't careful, we could set the whole lot of them on us, and there were too few of us to fight back.

On Saturday, we decided to eat lunch on the rooftop terrace to celebrate a small break in the rain. After being locked up in the house, it almost felt like a party with everyone pitching in to help. Nobody mentioned my grandfather's latest threat, as if we'd all agreed to leave it alone and enjoy the moment. Asher and Gabe had dragged a table and chairs out of storage, and Erin and Lucy had teamed up to make lunch for everyone. I set the table with china—old and expensive, I suspected—and silverware— made of real silver—that Lottie had brought out. No one seemed to care that our party food consisted of small bites of sandwiches and piles of crudely cut up fruits and veg- etables. The girls had tried their hand at tea sandwiches, small finger sandwiches stuffed with cucumbers and fancy cheeses. Rather than looking dainty, the ragged edges of the crust-less bread looked like they'd been hacked at with a butter knife, and the flattened centers showed the inden- tations of fingertips where the chefs had held the sandwich for slicing. Nobody teased Erin and Lucy, though. Our group had finally begun to gel together, and I studied everyone with quiet satisfaction. We almost seemed like a family.

Asher helped Erin carry the food out, and he managed to save a bowl of fruit when he stumbled. I heard Erin mutter, "Did you feel that?" followed by Asher's, "Yes.

I've never hit a girl, but I suspect I'd feel that, too." She just laughed, and I gazed at her in surprise. How far had she come to laugh in the face of a threat from a Protector? She trusted him, I realized. It hadn't taken him long to affect her. Asher had that way about him, as I knew from experience.

We all took our seats, with Lucy and Lottie at the heads of the table. Erin and Asher sat on one side, and Gabe and I sat on the other. Gabe was careful to keep his distance, true to his word of the night before. There would be time for us to figure out how we felt, but that time wasn't now.

"What have you all been doing while we've been gone?" Gabe asked.

"Remy has been training me," Erin said.

He glanced over at me in surprise, and I smiled. "She should be able to defend herself."

"Of course she should," he agreed. His gaze turned thoughtful. "In fact, we should work on your training, too."

I groaned. It was one thing to work with Erin, but training with Gabe was different. I spent more time flat on my back on the mat. My ears burned when that thought replayed in my mind. At least, Gabe seemed to have missed one of my embarrassing mind hiccups. He passed me a plate of sandwiches and smiled with a hint of naughtiness. *Or not.*

I cleared my throat and tried to stem the urge to hide under the table.

"He's right, Remy," Asher said, distracting me. "What you're doing with Erin is great, but it doesn't test your skills. You need to train against a Protector."

I glanced around. "What do you say, Lottie? Here's your chance to take me down. Want to brawl?"

Her narrow shoulders shuddered in distaste. "Um, no. My luck, I'd end up bonded to you and be stuck listening to your thoughts for the next decade. Thanks but no thanks."

A snort sounded from the opposite end of the table. Lucy grinned at Lottie. "Not likely," she told her. "That's not how things work for Remy's kind."

A sense of unease crawled up my back. Lucy knew that I'd bonded to Asher, then Gabe, and that my bond with Asher had broken, but I hadn't told her that I differed from other Healers in that way. Before me, the Blackwells had never heard of a Healer bonding with more than one person.

"How do you know?" Asher asked her in a quiet voice.

She chewed on the end of a slightly smashed sandwich before answering. "That book I've been reading, the one Remy stole from Alcais—it talks about it."

Erin's brows shot up, and I winced. Awesome way for my friend to find out that I'd stolen from her brother. "I'm sorry," I told her. "He was acting suspicious and . . ." My voice trailed off when she laughed.

"Can I call you Captain Klepto? Pretty please?" To Lucy, she asked, "Can I see it?"

My sister ran into the house to get the book and returned a moment later. She handed it over, and Erin studied it, flipping the leather-bound volume over in her hand. Her smile faded into a thoughtful frown.

"I remember this from Franc's library. If I recall right, a Protector wrote this, though I have no idea how Franc ended up with it."

She passed the book back to Lucy. "I'm not sure why Alcais would have had this. It's full of extremist crap. Protectors advocating killing off babies born with both Healer and Protector blood. I couldn't get through it. When I first saw it in the library, I remember thinking it was total mythology. We had never heard of anyone like you, Remy, except in stories."

"The book is about a lot more than that," Lucy said. "It says there were others like Remy. Listen . . ." She flipped to a page and read out loud. *"Children born with the blood of both Healers and Protectors should be feared. These half breeds have shown a propensity to grow in power as they age. More to the point, we suspect they will grow into a power that could endanger all of our kind and should therefore be exterminated before they destroy us."* She looked up at me. "Do you think that power they're talking about is the way you can hurt people?"

"No idea," I said.

That passage had made my stomach knot when I read it, imagining babies being killed because some bastards were afraid of what might be—the mythical power of the half breeds. In my mind, I gave the author the finger for referring to my kind like livestock. The book hadn't described what our power was, and I'd been unable to continue reading after it described myriad ways to dispose of the "half-breed babies." That my grandfather had owned such a book made me sick, and I wondered how much of it he believed.

"It could be talking about how she can heal immortality. But that would assume they knew that Protectors could become immortal. Does the book mention that?" Asher asked.

Lucy shook her head.

"What does this have to do with the way Remy bonds?" Erin asked.

"There's a section in here that describes it," Lucy said.

Asher and Gabe both looked at me and I grimaced helplessly. I didn't remember reading anything about that. Maybe it had been in the part of the book I'd skimmed.

"What does it say?" Asher prompted Lucy. "You know, female Healers and Protectors used to bond all the time. What made you think Remy couldn't bond with Lottie?"

That sense of unease returned, and I set my fork down.

"Well, they don't exactly love each other. Sorry, Lottie. No offense."

"None taken," Lottie said.

"What does that have to do with it?" Gabe asked. "Bonds aren't about emotions. They're about compatible power, each person's energy helping the other's to strengthen."

Tension radiated from Gabe and Asher. Both men had leaned forward in their seats and stared at her with intense expressions. Lucy finally picked up on it, her confusion palpable as she tried to understand why this mattered to them so much. I swallowed around a lump of dread and folded my hands in my lap, waiting for what I guessed was coming.

She spoke in a halting voice, her eyes flicking to me with worry. "Um, Remy's bonds are. About feelings, I mean. The book says full-blooded Healers and Protectors bonded against their will, but Remy's kind are different. Some never bonded at all, and others bonded more than once, but always their emotions were involved. Let me see if I can remember exactly what it said . . ."

*No, Lucy. Please don't say it.*

She paused, thinking, and then snapped her fingers. "Right! I remember now. The book says that they seemed to form bonds 'according to their hearts.' "

Lucy's announcement met with a weighed kind of silence. Her gaze bounced from Asher to Gabe to me. A flush of realization swept over her face when she saw my face and the sorrow I couldn't hide. Too late she understood why this mattered, finally connecting my circumstances with Gabe and Asher to the state of our bonds. Our eyes met and hers were filled with apology.

The table shook when Asher rose in a hurry and bumped it. A glass tipped over, spilling water everywhere. Everyone stared at him in shock, but his entire focus was on me. His enraged action had even surprised him, and he breathed in quick gasps. I'd never seen so much pain in his eyes, and it killed me to be the one causing it.

"I don't know why I'm surprised," he said. "I knew it. From the moment I saw the two of you together in Blackwell Falls last September, I knew you cared about him more than you wanted to admit."

I shook my head in denial. I hadn't known. Not then. My hands clenched in a painful grip. Asher and Gabe had said that I was controlling the bond somehow, but I hadn't believed them. It had been one more thing I hadn't understood and shoved away into a box because I couldn't deal with what it might mean. My heart betrayed me, becoming a reckless thing that did whatever the hell it wanted and hurting others in the process. It didn't matter that I'd been honorable. No, my damned bonds behaved like a lie detector telling everyone around me what I felt before I even understood it myself. It wasn't fair. I bit the inside of my cheek to fight back the tears.

"Asher, calm down," Gabe said in a soothing voice, placing a hand on my shoulder. "Remy has always been true to you. You know that."

Asher laughed and the sound of it grated my heart. "Except when she bonded to you. And now she's yours. The proof is written all over you two." His gaze fell to Gabe's hand like he knew that his brother had offered comfort after hearing my thoughts. "I'm outta here. I'm not going to stick around here to watch you two getting together."

He shoved his chair away from the table. He made it as far as the conservatory before Gabe stopped him by gripping the lapels of Asher's jacket. "No, it's not safe. We have to talk."

Asher didn't struggle. He looked at Gabe's hands and then at his face. "You know you can keep me here against my will. I'm too weak to fight you now. I'm asking you to let me go. Don't do this to me in front of her," he said in a proud voice.

He wouldn't look at me. Clearly, he considered Gabe the victor, and the humiliation changed the way he carried himself. His shoulders slumped, and his movements were jerky. Gabe struggled for a long minute, a muscle working in his cheek, and then he stepped back, letting his brother go. Without another word, Asher walked away, disappearing down the stairs. A moment later, the front door slammed.

This was everything I hadn't wanted to happen. I loved Asher, and I'd never wanted to hurt him. Instead, I'd devastated him.

I shoved back my chair and rose, ignoring the stares of Lottie, Lucy, and Erin. Gabe stood in the conservatory, looking torn between crying and punching something when I approached him.

"You're going after him," he said.

"I have to. I can't let him go like this, imagining that we . . ." I gulped.

My mind shut down on the possibilities of what Asher might be imagining. The things he thought Gabe and I might have done while I'd still been with Asher.

Gabe nodded. "Be careful. I'll be here when you need me."

I took off at a run, hoping I'd know what to say when I found Asher.

# CHAPTER SEVENTEEN

*O*utside, cars and people surged down the busy street. I shoved past a man in a suit to catch up with Asher halfway down the block.

He spun around when I said his name. "Damn it, Remy. Get the hell away from me!"

He turned on his heel and charged ahead.

I ignored his command and spoke to his back. "You know I was never unfaithful to you. You were everything to me."

The muscles in his shoulders tensed, but he didn't slow. "I mean it. I don't want to talk to you," he said.

That hurt, but I didn't let it sway me. I couldn't let him go off on his own like this. Aside from the danger, I couldn't stand that he doubted how I felt about him. "When my grandfather's men shot you, and I thought I watched you die, I wanted to die, too. And when they tortured me, I hoped they would kill me because it hurt too much to be alive without you."

He stopped so abruptly that I almost ran into him. The glare on his face threatened to burn me alive when he did an about-face. "How long did you feel that way before you bonded to Gabe?"

"You can't blame me for this. I didn't plan it. Gabe was my friend and nothing more."

Asher's eyes darkened. "*Was* your friend," he repeated in a dangerous voice. "You admit something's happened?"

"The day we arrived in London. Gabe found out that we broke up and he asked me to give him a chance," I admitted.

"And what did you tell him?"

"That I couldn't hurt you like that." Asher's expression lightened infinitesimally. Honesty compelled me to barrel forward. "But I do have feelings for him. I realized it while he was gone these last few days. I told him as much last night."

Asher threw back his head like he would shout at the sky, but he merely gritted his teeth.

I continued. "I asked him to give me time. To give you time, Asher. Neither of us wanted to hurt you."

"Bang-up job you did, Remy. Finding out like this made everything better." I cringed at the hate in his voice. "Go back to him, and stay the fuck away from me."

He struck out at me with his words and then walked away. Walked away like he had been doing for months, while I begged him to love me like a pathetic girl. The injustice of it made it difficult to swallow his rage.

I yelled at his retreating back. "Right. I forgot that you were the honorable one in our relationship. The one who never lied. You said we were forever, Asher, but that wasn't true, was it? Who lied first? Did you ever care for me, or was I just your ticket to feeling human again? Lucky for you, you hate it so much, and you can blame me for that, too!"

A woman pushing a stroller on the opposite side of the street eyed me, and I flushed with embarrassment. I'd been reduced to screaming at Asher on a London street when he wanted nothing to do with me. For months, he'd had all the control, while I reacted to whatever he did. You could only run after a thing for so long before you tired of never reaching it.

Tears blinded me as I strode back to the house. This had gotten so out of hand, and I couldn't fix things. Feet pounded on the pavement behind me, and I whipped around. Asher's body slammed into mine, and he lifted me off my feet. He kissed me hard, his hold on me fierce. I didn't fight him, but I couldn't kiss him back. We'd gone too far past that. Asher lifted his head when he realized I wasn't responding, and we stared at each other at a loss for words. What did you say to someone you'd fallen out of love with?

"I ruined everything," he whispered, his breath sweet on my lips. "You accused me of wanting you to be the type of girl who needed a hero, and you were right. I wanted you to need me that way."

But I couldn't. I would never be that girl. Too many years, I'd been alone and waiting for someone to save me from the brutality that my stepfather had inflicted on me. Somewhere along the way, I'd stopped waiting and learned to fight. That wasn't something I could undo for him. I didn't want to be that fearful, angry girl anymore. I'd worked too hard to change.

"I'm sorry," I said, and I meant it. I was sorry I couldn't be the girl he needed.

"You tried to tell me, but I kept pushing you. Last June, you almost went to San Francisco alone because I wanted you to do things my way on my time."

We'd fought about me going to see my grandfather. At the time, I'd hoped that Franc would have answers, some way for Asher and me to have a future together. Asher had only seen the danger in my going, and in the end, he'd been right.

He shook his head, and then touched a thumb to the corner of my mouth. "I tried to keep you hidden, but that was never going to be a possibility for you. You were always going to leave."

"You got hurt," I whispered. "I'm so sorry. I don't blame you for hating me for what they did to you."

He frowned down at me. "What are you talking about?"

"It was my fault. I insisted we go there, and you got caught. And because of me, you felt everything they did to you."

"Is that what you think? That I pushed you away because of that?" He swore and loosened his hold on me to pace away a few steps. He rocked on his heels, staring off into space across the street.

"Asher?" I asked in confusion.

He threw me a sad smile over his shoulder. "It was shame, Remy. I pushed you away because I was ashamed."

"I don't understand . . ." I said, circling around him.

"The day I became immortal, I hated it. Without my senses, I felt half-alive, and not a day passed that I didn't wish for my old life."

My fingers found the scar on his brow. Protectors couldn't age, but there were ways for them to die. He'd once thought about ending things, and that scar had been a reminder of a day he'd come too close to acting on the impulse.

Asher reached for my hand, lowering it to my side. "I wanted to be human again, to feel again, more than anything. But when you came along, none of that mattered. You have to believe me. I love you."

I nodded slowly. Despite what I'd accused him of earlier, I'd never doubted his love.

He closed his eyes as if in relief. "I would've done anything for you, but loving you changed me. The idea that I might become too human, too powerless to protect you, terrified me." His eyes opened. "But if I'm honest, I still wanted to be human."

He said this like it was a shameful thing, but I'd never

blamed him for loving the return of his senses. I'd been grateful that I could give that to him.

"Then we were captured. Your grandfather's men beat me, burned me, drowned me, suffocated me. When I couldn't take it anymore, they'd bring in a Healer to take care of my injuries just enough to keep me alive, and then they'd start all over again."

My breath hitched at the pain in his words. He'd said so little about how they'd hurt him. I'd known it was horrific because I'd seen the damage to his body firsthand. The damage to a spirit was harder to grasp, though. He'd gone so many years without feeling anything, and they'd shown him only the ugly side of mortality.

Asher didn't cry. He looked into the distance and saw nothing but the past. "They took me to the edge of death so many times that I prayed for it. And I realized that I'd been wrong all those years that I'd wished for mortality— I don't want to be human."

He squeezed my hand, his fingers unconsciously clenching and unclenching. "You saved me, and I tried to convince myself that I could go back to the way things were. Love conquers all, right?" Bleak eyes met mine. "But the feeling didn't go away, Remy. I'm a coward for thinking it, but I don't want to be this . . . breakable thing. I'm sorry I let you down."

"Oh Asher . . ." This was what he'd been holding on to all these months. The reason he'd pushed me away. He'd didn't blame me for making him more human. He blamed himself for not wanting it anymore.

"I didn't keep my promise. I told you I would do anything to be with you, but . . . it's too much. They used me against you, and there was nothing I could do about it."

I tugged my hand and pressed my palms to his cheeks so he would see me. We'd put so much effort into not talking and hiding how we truly felt that it hurt to see him with the blinders off. He'd given me so much, and he had no clue.

"It wasn't your fault. Don't you see? Loving you was never about your strength or how you could defend me. After Dean, I was so broken that I thought of myself as damaged goods. I didn't think I could love anyone or be loved by anyone. You changed all that. You with your big heart and your patience. You're my hero, Asher. I'm stronger because of you. I have a family because of you."

The expression on his face was half-hope and half-disbelief. His arms surrounded me and his hands clutched my jacket, gripping me so tight that I couldn't breathe.

"I still love you, but I can't be what you need, Remy," he said. "I'm sorry."

"Me, too."

I held him as he shuddered in my arms, crying without noise. And I cried, too, because I realized what this was. It was good-bye. What we'd had was over. Really and truly over.

Eventually, he pulled away, his hand tangling in my hair. "I think you've known that I wasn't the right one for you for longer than you want to admit," he said sadly.

I didn't want to talk about our broken bond or my bond with Gabe. Asher didn't seem to want to, either.

"Kiss me," he said.

I nodded, and this time, I returned his gentle kiss. My blood didn't burn, and I didn't light on fire. Instead, I re-membered what had been with open eyes and a bruised heart. He lifted his head, and we looked at each other, feeling the bittersweet sadness of something ending.

Then Asher's gaze shifted over my shoulder. His eyes widened, but it was too late. Someone grabbed me from behind.

# CHAPTER EIGHTEEN

*T*wo men held me, and I struggled to free myself. One of them muttered when Asher punched him in the stomach, and I almost got away. The man retaliated with a swift blow to Asher's head that laid him out on the sidewalk. They left him there as they heaved me into the trunk of a waiting car, throwing a black hood over my face and binding my wrists together with a zip tie before they locked me in. Through all of this, the men never said a word.

They hadn't taken Asher, and that knowledge consoled me as my body swayed with the motion of the car. The others would find him soon, and he would be okay. The pungent scent of gasoline and oil burned my nose. The hood they'd thrown over my head was stifling, and I fought off the sensation that I was suffocating. I really, really hated small spaces. I couldn't get my hands free so I rubbed my face against my shoulder, using my teeth to work the hood off. At last, it slid off, but I could only see the black interior of the trunk.

I considered my options. Sadly, they were few and it didn't take long. The men had been careful not to hurt me. In fact, they'd almost been gentle, which led me to believe that they knew how my powers worked. I had no injuries to inflict on them. The element of surprise could work in my favor if they didn't know about my speed. Then again, I was pretty sure they were Protectors, which meant they were as fast, if not faster than me.

*Super. I just have to wait for a chance to escape.*

Gabe's face flashed into my mind, and I knew that Asher and Gabe had both been right about my feelings. Gabe would do anything to save me, even put his life at risk for mine. He would do all that for a girl who'd never kissed him, or been brave enough to take a chance on him. Suddenly, I regretted that immensely. My life had never looked to be long, and putting things off until tomorrow suddenly seemed like a stupid strategy. If I made it through this, I was going to kiss Gabe and throw myself into finding out what we might have together. I hoped that Asher would forgive me.

The car's brakes squealed as we arrived at our destination, and I braced myself against the jarring impact as I rolled. I thought I heard the motorized sound of a gate opening, and then the car started again. Less than a minute later, the engine shut off and car doors opened and slammed. I blinked when the trunk opened and sunlight blinded me. One of the men—had I seen him before?—grunted and pulled the hood back over my face before I could get a good look.

Gentle hands lifted me from the trunk, ignoring my attempts to struggle. Strong, impersonal arms carried me, and I gave up fighting for the moment. That tactic obviously wasn't going to work right now, and I concentrated on memorizing the turns the man took as he walked. That might have worked in movies, but I ended up dizzy.

"Where are you taking me?" I asked.

Silence.

I sighed. "Can you at least take the hood off? I can't breathe."

"If you can talk, you can breathe," the man carrying me

said. His accent sounded Irish with softer vowels and a lilting rhythm to the words.

Triumph flashed through me because I'd gotten him to respond. "So you can talk."

He grunted again and merely shifted his hold on me. We must have reached our destination because he plunked me down in a hard chair and backed away. I let my mental walls down enough to try to sense how many bodies were in the room. I thought I felt at least three Protectors before I raised my defenses again.

"That hurts something fierce, girl," a voice said in a thick Irish brogue.

He'd confirmed my suspicion that I was surrounded by Protectors. Only they could feel the pain caused by the hum of my powers. Someone whipped the hood off my head, and I found myself sitting at one end of a large table that could easily seat twenty people. The grand dining room had cloth-covered walls, ornate molding, and a sideboard that could have probably paid for my college education. Beside me, at the head of the table, sat the man from Muir Woods that I'd dubbed Knockoff Bond.

"What happened to the accent?" I asked him. He'd sounded British before. Now he sounded like Jonathan Rhys Myers, pronouncing his "th" as a hard "t."

He smiled and didn't answer. He gestured to the bowl in front of me. It contained some kind of rich, meaty stew. "Are you hungry?"

"No, thanks. I've never mastered the art of eating without my hands."

I pulled up my arms to show him they were still bound behind my back. He signaled to one of the other men in the room and a moment later my hands were free. I rubbed my wrist to ease the blood flow back into it and sighed in relief as the ache in my shoulders eased.

"I remember you," I said to the man who'd cut my tie.

He was the same man who'd carried me into the house. I bared my teeth at him. "You broke my friend's arm."

I'd only had the briefest glance at him in Muir Woods since I'd been occupied by Knockoff Bond, but I recognized the birthmark on his forehead. The oversized man had tree trunks for arms. I sounded dangerous to my own ears, and I wondered at my daring. Who was I to threaten these men when they had me outnumbered? Despite his advantage, the man looked suddenly cautious.

Knockoff Bond laughed, breaking my concentration. "Quit threatening Sean. The man is terrified of you."

"And you're not?" I asked, narrowing my eyes.

He lifted a glass of red wine to his mouth and sipped. "I am not your enemy, Miss O'Malley."

I crossed my arms over my chest. "I beg to differ. You're working with Franc Marche, and that most definitely makes you my enemy."

The wine sloshed in his glass when he slammed it down on the table. "I am not working with that man, and I would thank you not to accuse me of it," he spat out, his dark blue eyes pinched in a glare.

I leaned forward in my seat, and my hair fell over my shoulder. I shoved it out of my face and scowled. "Then why did you follow Erin into the woods? How could you have known we'd be there if you weren't working for my grandfather?"

He raised a brow, appearing bemused. "You are mistaken. I wasn't following your little Healer friend. We tracked Gabriel Blackwell from Paris, and he led us to you."

*Crap.* Hadn't I thought the whole setup was odd? We'd escaped with few injuries when the Morrisseys were touted as sadistic. And this man had let me go when I'd been vulnerable. In the forest, he'd asked his cohorts where "the other one" was. At the time, I'd thought he'd meant Lottie, but my grandfather's men hadn't known about her. No, this man had been referring to Gabe, wondering what happened to the man they'd followed into the woods.

Just to be sure I demanded, "Are you working with the Morrisseys?"

Knockoff Bond paused in the act of dipping a fork into his stew, his black eyebrows lowering in menace. "First Marche and now the Morrisseys. If you are trying to insult me, you have succeeded."

Fear tickled at the back of my neck. Who the hell was this guy if he wasn't working with my grandfather or the men who had my father? And what did he want from me? The unknown suddenly seemed a much worse fate than facing the enemies I knew. I glanced around the room, looking for the exit and calculating my chance of making it out of the house alive.

"Look, Miss O'Malley. I think we have gotten off to a bad start . . ."

I interrupted him, pushing my chair back from the table. "You kidnapped me off the street and you hurt my friends. No shit."

The men behind me started toward me, and I prepared myself to fight them. But Knockoff Bond gestured for them to back off. He rose and held out an arm, offering to seat me again. "Let me explain. Please . . ."

Charm rolled off the man in waves. He exuded it, and I didn't trust him a bit. I sat anyway because I didn't really have another choice. He retook his own seat and motioned for me to eat. I picked up a fork, but didn't take a bite. I wouldn't put it past him to drug me, and I wasn't going to chance it.

He sighed. "Lord, you are stubborn. My name is Seamus, and the two men behind you are Sean and Alec. We had been tracking reports of a Healer in New York City for months. Stories were cropping up of serious illnesses suddenly healed. A woman with cancer whose disease disappeared one day."

"And you make a habit of tracking Healers?" I asked. That wasn't a comforting thought. Protectors had one reason for hunting Healers.

"When they can cure cancer? Yes."

Erin and the others had told me that I was curing things that only the most experienced and powerful Healers could. Using my powers had triggered their hunting like I'd been warned it would.

"We thought we'd found the Healer in Brooklyn when a story got back to us of a man who claimed his daughter had attacked him with her mind and that she'd given him injuries like hers. He spoke of a scary, flashing light that went off when she attacked him. The officer who wrote that in his report thought the man was crazy, but we pay attention to things like that."

*Dean.* I'd never thought he would tell anyone what really happened because it made him look crazy. That bastard had led these men to me.

Seamus paused to eat a bite of his stew before continuing. "But the Healer and her parents had disappeared before we arrived. The mother had died, and the father had skipped parole. We found no record of the mother in our Healer lineage and so we thought the matter closed. It was a fluke, a crazy man telling tales to cover up how he'd abused his daughter."

"Stepdaughter," I snapped. I heard my breathing and realized that I was close to hyperventilating. I focused on calming myself as he continued his story.

Seamus didn't give me the pitying look that others often did when they found out about how Dean had treated me. His face revealed nothing about his thoughts, and I almost wished for the pity so I would know he had some kind of compassion.

"As you wish. Stepfather. Soon after that we heard a rumor that the Blackwells were harboring a Healer in Blackwell Falls."

Freaking Lottie. She'd set that fiasco in motion when she told Spencer and Miranda that a Healer had moved to town. She'd hated my relationship with Asher and how my powers had begun to affect her, so she'd sicced the Protectors on me, hoping that would take care of things. Except Asher and Gabe had found out in time and arranged to hide me while Spencer and Miranda came to investigate.

"So?" I asked Seamus.

"We followed up on the rumors, but the Blackwells said they had killed the Healer. By the time we figured out they had lied, it was too late. You had disappeared from Blackwell Falls, along with your family and the Blackwells. It was not until Gabriel Blackwell surfaced in Europe that we had a lead."

I'd never stood a chance. They'd been on to me before I'd ever moved to Maine and met Asher. It had only been a matter of time before they discovered me. Everything that had happened had served as a delay tactic putting off this inevitable moment.

"So you've found me," I bit off in helpless anger. "What exactly do you want from me? Because if you think I'm going to let you use me, think again. I'd rather die and take you down with me."

"We have no intention of hurting you. If we had, you'd already be dead. I could have taken you in California, but I didn't." His gaze challenged me. He spoke the truth, and we both knew it. "You belong here with us, Miss O'Malley, where we can keep you safe."

*Never.* I shook my head and felt my lip curl in disgust. What was it about me that made these bastards think they could control me? They would keep me safe. Right. Did they think I was stupid? I placed both hands flat on the table on either side of my untouched bowl. He didn't seem to notice when my fingers curled around my fork.

"And if I don't want to stay?" I asked.

Seamus sipped his wine, eying me thoughtfully. "Really, I'm surprised at you. We're doing you a favor. The sooner you reconcile yourself to that, the easier things will be for you."

He said I was safe in one breath and threatened to lock me away in the next. The rage slammed into me like a train, obliterating reason. I'd been a prisoner most of my life. *Never again.* I snapped to my feet, all reaction and no thought, and stabbed my fork into Seamus's hand. It crunched through bones and skin before it hit the hard table on the other side with enough force to puncture the wood. Seamus grabbed for his hand to free it, while I lifted his knife off the table. His two guards launched forward, but I'd already spun behind Seamus, pressing the knife against his throat.

I lowered my shield, letting the hum of my energy stream through the air. "Feel that, Seamus? Imagine what it will feel like when I slice your throat open. I can make you feel it all."

"Stop! Don't touch her!" Seamus yelled to the men, and they stopped moving. To me, he said, "Remy, I don't think you understand."

A noise gurgled in his throat when I let the knife slice his skin a little. "Understand what? That you want to make me your puppet?"

Seamus didn't answer. He exploded upward, knocking my arm away. His head slammed into my chin, and I saw stars as I twisted around, reaching for my shoulder. I kicked his chair forward with enough force to knock him off balance and then yanked on his outstretched arm. His weight acted against him, and I only had to move out of his way as he crashed to the floor. Then I was on him, straddling his chest, as I placed the knife once more to his throat.

Blood seeped out of a thin cut at his neck, and I stared into his widened eyes. His mental wall tumbled down, and I sensed him readying to attack me, poised to steal my energy to weaken or kill me like Protectors had done to Healers for the last century. A haze of fury surged through me. My mind snapped wide open, and I attacked first.

The monster inside me tasted Seamus's power and it roared, wanting more. Heat flashed inside me as my energy lashed to his, taking, taking, taking. My heart thudded at twice its normal speed, and red sparks exploded in the air as I stole his energy.

"Stop, girl!"

The voice broke through my concentration, and I glanced over at the man who'd spoken. Sean stared at me in horror. Beneath me, Seamus's blue eyes were wide with fear and agony. I could kill him, but if I did, I would become like him. Immortal and unable to feel a simple touch. That, more than anything, enabled me to break free and pull myself back from the edge. The monster, denied what it wanted, snarled inside me, and I shoved it back in its cage.

Slowly, I lifted the knife from Seamus's throat and eased away from him, rising to my feet. He didn't move, hardly dared to breathe. I backed away from his prostrate body, circling the table to steer clear of his men. They seemed as eager to avoid me, watching me with wary expressions. I reached the doorway as Seamus sat up with Sean's help, holding a hand to his bloody throat.

He shouted, "Stop! We're not who you think we are."

I didn't have to be told twice to run.

Panic placed my heart squarely in my throat, and I gasped for air as my head swung both ways, looking for an exit. I tried to remember which way Sean had carried me through the house, but the memory had faded. Making a decision, I turned left, running down the hall while footsteps gave chase behind me. I pushed myself hard, and my feet slid, looking for purchase when I rounded a corner faster than I'd expected. I steadied myself against a table, and the knife went spinning through the air.

I had reached some kind of entrance hall with a grand staircase leading to an upper floor. I dove for the front door and gave one last look over my shoulder before turning the doorknob. And what I saw stopped me in my tracks.

Seamus entered the hall with several men on his heels. He backed off when he saw where my gaze had latched on to and threw out his arm to stop his men.

"It can't be," I whispered. "This can't be."

A large tapestry hung at the top of the stairs. The art depicted a family crest with a ship, a horse, a wild boar, armor, swords, and bows and arrows woven into the design. I moved closer, trying to make out the words under the design.

"It's an old O'Dugan quote from the fourteenth century," Seamus said softly, pointing at the words I tried to read. "It says, 'A good man yet there never was, of the O'Malleys, who was not a mariner; of every weather, ye are prophets; a tribe of brotherly affection and of friendship.' "

*O'Malley.* It couldn't be a coincidence.

"Who are you?" I asked.

He approached within reaching distance. "I am Seamus O'Malley, and you are my kin, Remy O'Malley."

# CHAPTER NINETEEN

$\mathcal{H}$e held out a hand like we'd met in polite company without the kidnapping and the threats. In Muir Woods, I'd thought him vaguely familiar, and I understood why now. His features, the black hair and blue eyes, they echoed my father. Seamus wasn't an exact copy, but rather a duplicate of a duplicate of a duplicate. Hints of the original existed, but the lines had blurred between the generations.

"What do you want with me?" I demanded.

"I mean you no harm."

That wasn't an answer. I avoided his outstretched hand, the one I hadn't stabbed. "I don't believe you. You kidnapped me," I accused.

He winced a little, finally dropping his hand to his side. "And you put a fork through my hand and tried to kill me. I'd say we're even, cousin."

I started, backing away a step. "Cousin?"

"As far as we can tell. And let's just say there are a lot of greats in front of cousin."

"Did you know I was an O'Malley when you began tracking me in New York?"

He shook his head. "No. The Healers have done too good a job hiding their bloodlines."

"You say you're not like the Morrisseys, but you track Healers. Why? To give them friendship bracelets?"

Heavy sarcasm dripped from my words, and Seamus seemed to be biting back a smile. "We don't track Healers. We track Healers like you whom we suspect might be something more."

Imagine that. Protectors hunting me for my mixed blood. "And my father? Did you know about him?"

"No. The O'Malleys . . . disbanded a long time ago. We didn't know what family you belonged to until we tracked you to Blackwell Falls. You can imagine our surprise when we realized the girl we sought was a daughter of O'Malley."

One of his men shifted, drawing my attention. They had spanned out into a half circle to surround me. Sean spoke into a radio, and I guessed others waited on the other side of the front door. I balanced on the balls of my feet. If any of them made a move, I would run and chance facing what waited outside. I cursed myself for letting that stupid tapestry distract me. Sure, I'd taken Seamus down while riding high on his energy. Could I do it again with five Protectors ready to take me? Not likely.

"So now what?" I asked Seamus. "You expect me to fall in line because we're family? No, thank you. My grandfather already tried that tactic, and I showed him what I thought of his plans."

"Remy, look at me." I did and Seamus spoke in a low voice full of sincerity. "I'm not going to hurt you. I swear it. We brought you here to keep you safe."

My eyes narrowed in distrust, and I waited for my bullshit meter to go off. It didn't. Something told me that Seamus spoke the truth. Yet, he'd threatened people I loved. I took one step back toward the door, reaching behind me for the handle.

"You kidnapped me for my own good? That's your story?" I scoffed.

A guard handed Seamus a cloth and he wrapped it around his bloody hand, his mouth tilting in a rueful smile. "I can see I've handled this all wrong. I expected you to be grateful when we rescued you from the Blackwells."

Rescue? I stared at him in confusion. "The Blackwells are my friends."

He grimaced. "No wonder you attacked me. We thought you were their hostage. Obviously, I was mistaken. Give me a chance to explain who we are, and if you still want to leave, I'll let you go."

He sounded like he meant it, but people lied all the time to get what they wanted. Unless I wanted to battle it out with these men, though, I had to play along.

"Fine," I said. "We talk, and then I leave."

"Let's go upstairs," Seamus said. "I need a first aid kit to take care of this."

He lifted his crudely bandaged hand, and I flushed. "Don't expect an apology," I warned him.

"Wouldn't dream of it," he said in an amused tone. "This way."

The four guards backed up to allow me to follow Seamus to the staircase. I walked past them, almost tiptoeing with caution and sure I was making a huge mistake. What if I was following him into my prison? A bead of sweat dripped down my back. I hesitated halfway up the stairs when Sean climbed after me. Outnumbered and cornered? No way.

I crossed my arms. "I'm not going another step until you tell your friends to go play elsewhere."

Sean actually looked affronted at the idea that I found him suspect, but I didn't care.

Seamus sighed. "You do realize that it's me who has come out of both of our encounters wounded?"

I didn't budge and he caved, telling Sean, "Wait here. I'll yell if she tries to kill me again. Happy?" he snapped at me.

I nodded and climbed the stairs to reach him. "Delighted. It's not every day I get kidnapped by a distant cousin."

He snorted but didn't answer. We rounded a corner and entered a long hallway with portraits of dead people hanging high up on the walls. There was no furniture in the hall, and the sensation that the painted eyes followed me creeped me out.

"Why don't the other Protectors know you exist?" I asked.

Seamus paused in the long hallway, his expression curious. "What makes you think they don't?"

"Asher said that a lot of the Protector families know each other, but the Blackwells didn't know about the O'Malleys." I thought of the genealogy book I'd found. The O'Malley bloodline had seemed to drop off after the last entry in 1629.

"Good. That's exactly what we wanted." We reached a doorway, and Seamus said, "Wait here a moment."

He returned a second later with a first aid kit, and we continued on to some kind of sitting room with fancy wallpaper and enormous framed portraits of women from different time periods. Seriously, who needed this many paintings of people from past centuries?

Seamus set the first aid kit on a low table and motioned for me to join him on a sofa of brocade cushions and carved wooden details. I left a cushion between us, and watched him attempt to open the first aid kit one-handed. My conscience pricked at me, but I ignored it. I was not going to help this man. We might share a last name, but we weren't family.

"What did you mean when you said you wanted to keep me safe?"

Seamus grimaced. "You have a lot of people after you, cousin. The Morrisseys have put the word out that they're willing to pay a lot of money to the Protector who finds you. We thought the Blackwells were controlling you. And you know your grandfather is here in London looking for you, don't you?"

My hand shook when I pushed my hair out of my face, and I sat on it to hide how that last statement had affected me. "And you expect me to believe that you're trying to keep me safe from all of the bad men?"

"It's what we do," he responded in a voice that vibrated with pride and sincerity. "Or rather, what we used to do when there were more of you."

My attention had latched on to a drop of blood pooling in the hollow of his throat, but my gaze snapped to his in shock. "There are more people like me?" I choked out.

"There used to be."

He glanced toward a portrait on the far wall. The woman's blond hair had been parted down the middle and hung down her back in long, looping curls. Her green gown had huge puffy sleeves that attached to the dress with ties at the shoulders. The clothing reminded me of something from the 1500s. She wore some kind of gold necklace around her neck. The painter had caught a sad expression in her blue eyes. I found myself wanting to see the necklace up close, but Seamus continued speaking.

"You thought you were the first?" he asked.

He didn't sound amused, so I answered honestly. "Every Protector or Healer whom I've met has sworn they've never heard of anyone like me before."

He nodded, and I thought I glimpsed a hint of satisfaction. "Then we did our job. You know I'm a Protector, but it's more complicated than that. Once, I was a Protector of the Phoenix."

"Phoenix?" I asked. "Like the bird?"

"It's what our family called them," he said with a shrug. "The phoenix is a symbol of new life."

"If there were more like me, what happened to them?" I asked in desperation.

"The Healers happened," Seamus said with a fierce grimace. "They had all the power almost from the beginning, but it was a tenuous kind of power. We are stronger and faster, and they knew it. For a time, though, we existed in harmony, helping others and ourselves. But as children, we were taught that our races did not mix. It was almost a religious taboo, and you did not go against the church and live back in that day." He shifted in his seat, finally unlatching the plastic kit. "Things changed with time. People are people, and they fall in love even when the odds are against them."

My cheeks heated as I thought of Asher and Gabe. *Especially when the odds are against them.*

"A few Healers and Protectors broke the rules, and people looked the other way. It was still a taboo, but one few spoke of. Until the first children were born. The boys became Protectors, but the girls . . . The daughters of those unions changed everything."

"Why only girls?" I asked.

"Because only girls are born Healers. Your friends must have told you that."

I frowned. Franc wanted to change that. He'd thought he could use me, experiment on me to understand why there were only female Healers. It was part of his plan to create male Healers to increase his numbers and take down the Protectors. Of course, he'd told me all of that before I understood what kind of man he was. Who knew what degree of truth had been in his words?

"So what happened when the girls were born?"

Seamus set supplies on the table, gauze, tape, and packets of antiseptic lined up like soldiers. "They grew up, and they grew into their powers. And as you know, that is no small thing. The Healers recognized a threat to their power. If they couldn't control it, then the threat had to be destroyed."

Destroyed. He meant murder. The hair rose on my arms. "You mean they killed them?"

"Every last one they could find. They slaughtered women, girls, babies."

I shuddered and swallowed back my fear.

Seamus's scowl darkened his face, and I guessed what he'd like to do to those Healers who had killed my kind. "That wasn't enough for them, though. They wanted to be sure it could never happen again. So they killed all Healers and Protectors who dared break the taboo to set an example for others. Within a year, the Phoenix had disappeared, and after several decades, they were just a memory. A few centuries passed, and the Phoenix became a myth. A tall tale that the Protectors and Healers told their children."

Seamus paused in the act of unwrapping his hand to face me. "And now there's you," he said in a soft voice.

I couldn't decide if that sounded ominous or hopeful on his part. He finished pulling the towel from his hand and fumbled with an antiseptic wipe packet. When he dropped it for the second time, I couldn't take it anymore.

"Give me that," I said, shifting closer to him. Irritated, I yanked the packet from his fingers, opened it, and applied it to the cut on his neck. He hissed, and I reached into the kit to find a gauze pad to sop up the blood on his hand. I couldn't hide my grimace as I cleaned the injury. The fork had gone all the way through his hand, and the mess of it was disgusting, the smell of iron strong in the air. It reminded me of the fake fingertip in the package from the night before.

"I'm going to be sick. Here, hold this." I pressed his free hand to the gauze pad to hold it in place, while I leaned away and breathed through my nose.

"You're a shite nurse," he observed.

"Oh, please. I've taken care of far worse." Except I'd never stabbed anyone's fleshy palm with a utensil. I suppressed a heartfelt "ew" and reached for a roll of white bandages. "What do you want with me?" I asked.

I felt his eyes on me as I bandaged his hand, winding the gauze around and around the injury.

"The first Phoenixes were born O'Malleys. Many of our ancestors died trying to protect them, to save them when the killing began. We failed, and the Healers targeted us, forcing the few of us who remained into hiding. Ever since then, we've been following the stories, waiting for another Phoenix to be born. We won't fail you again."

That explained why their bloodline had disappeared from the book. The family had been a victim of Healer greed as much as the Phoenix had.

"You expect me to hide out here with you," I said. "You took me from my family and friends."

I finished taping off his hand a little rougher than necessary. He felt it, if his grimace was anything to go by. Already my nearness was affecting him.

"As I mentioned, I handled things wrong. Your situation is not what we thought. You are not who we expected. I thought to find a mere child, but you are not that, are you?"

I'd never been given the chance to be a child. Dean and my mother had seen to that. I studied Seamus's features.

The way he met my gaze made me think he was holding something back. Perhaps he wasn't lying, but he wasn't telling me the whole truth, either. And I'd learned not to trust somebody who hid their motives.

"You said I could choose to go after I heard you out. Did you mean it?"

He didn't want to agree. That was plain on his face and in the tense way he held himself. He nodded anyway. "Yes. You're making a mistake, but we won't force you."

I stood and walked across the room to the portrait of the blond woman. "I don't know you, Seamus. My grandfather is trying to kill me. The Morrisseys have my father. The only people who have stood by me are the Blackwells." I glanced over at Seamus with raised brows. "Call me crazy, but I'd rather stick with the people who've had my back since this began."

Seamus rose and joined me in front of the painting. He touched a finger to the charm that hung at the woman's neck, a golden phoenix with ruby eyes. The action was tender, as if he'd known her. I inhaled, realizing this woman had been like me—a Phoenix.

"Who was she?" I breathed.

"My wife," he said.

There was a finality to his tone that defied more questions. He dropped his hand and turned to face me, the tender expression gone as he propped one shoulder against the wall. "Tell me how I can earn your trust."

My mind ran through possibilities, calculating how this man could be used to help me. Others had been using me for ages. Why shouldn't I work their desires against them?

I leaned forward at the waist. "Find my father. You help me get him back, and then we'll talk."

Seamus shook his head. "You couldn't ask for something easy like stealing the Crown Jewels, could you?" He waved when I opened my mouth to snap at him. "No.

You've got yourself a deal. Come on. I'll have Sean and the boys return you to your friends."

I followed him to the door. "I think Sean and I can manage without the boys."

He understood my meaning in an instant. I didn't want to go anywhere with a crowd of Protectors who could turn on me. "You really don't trust anyone, do you?"

I didn't answer. Let him believe what he wanted. We went downstairs, and he instructed Sean to take me back to the Blackwells. He took a phone from one of his men and handed it to me. "We'll call when we find him." Just before I walked out the front door he called to me, "You know we would have gone after your father anyway. He's an O'Malley, and we look out for our kin."

"Prove it," I challenged, and then I closed the door behind me.

# CHAPTER TWENTY

*S*ean wasn't much of a conversationalist, and I was okay with that. At Seamus's, the big man had opened the back door of the Mercedes for me, and I couldn't decide if he was acting as a chauffeur or if he didn't want me in the front seat within reaching distance. I wanted to be relieved that Seamus had let me go, but until I reached my friends, I wouldn't relax. Instead, my mind spun with everything I'd learned.

I wasn't a half breed like Alcais's book called me, a term that reduced me to an animal with a poor pedigree. I was a Phoenix: a creature that rose from its own ashes. The name felt truer than anything I'd learned. My life had mostly been ashes, and I'd been trying so hard to raise myself up out of the grime, to be more than people expected. The Phoenix was also a fiery thing, and I wondered if the name hadn't been christened in part because of the red sparks that went hand in hand with our unique ability to inflict our pain on others.

Two hours ago, I'd thought my life over. I'd thought the Protectors had me with no possibility of escape, but I hadn't given up. I hadn't cowered or waited to be rescued or thought I deserved what had happened to me. I'd changed this last year. You didn't hide in a hole when you had something worth fighting for, and I had more than a lot of people.

Sean stopped the car, and I realized we'd arrived at the Blackwells' home. "Are you sure we weren't followed?" I asked.

He looked insulted and grunted like that was an answer.

"It was super meeting you, Sean," I exaggerated. "Bye, now."

I reached for the handle, but the door didn't open. Hiding the start of fear that made my palms damp, I met Sean's eyes in the rearview mirror.

"We'll be near," he said in his gruff voice. "Don't be stupid, girl."

The locks disengaged, and I opened the door, grasping that I'd been given the guard's version of a reassurance/warning. In other circumstances, I might have reacted with sarcasm, but now, giddy relief flooded through me. Seamus had been true to his word so far. I was home.

I launched toward the front door. It opened before I touched the handle, and I was yanked off my feet by Asher, swarmed by my friends as multiple arms tried to hug me at once. Behind me, I heard Sean's car pulling away, but I guessed he wouldn't be going far. I had Protectors now. Lottie, Gabe, and Asher stared at me with worry and relief, and I thought, *More Protectors, then*.

"Are you okay?" Gabe asked, his voice rough. A muscle in his jaw jumped and he remained on the staircase, his hand clenching the banister. "We've been going insane trying to figure out who took you. Lottie and I were leaving for Spencer and Miranda's to see what they might know."

Aside from Lucy, Gabe was the only one who hadn't embraced me, and I tried not to be hurt.

"It's a long story," I said. "But I'm okay."

Lottie patted me on the back with an awkward thump. "I'm glad you're not dead," she said.

Erin raised a hand and bit her lip. "Shouldn't we be packing up and running if those guys know where we live?"

I'd thought about that on the way here. Seamus could be gathering his people to attack, but my gut said he wouldn't. He wanted something from me, and he needed my cooperation. Attacking my friends ensured I would never cooperate, and he knew that now. It would be a leap of faith to trust him, but it was one that I would take. The others had to make their own choices, though. I wouldn't decide for them.

We headed to the dining room as I explained everything that had happened since I'd been taken. Someone placed a plate of food in front of me. Lucy leaned over me, wearing an expression I recognized. It was the same one I saw in the mirror when my heart ached and I tried to hide it behind stoicism. I touched her hand, and she squeezed my fingers before pulling away. I sighed and let her go.

Between bites, I finished telling them what Seamus had shared, leaving out the part where I attacked him with a fork. It didn't take long for everyone to explode in reaction.

"I can't believe they killed all of those people," Erin said, her voice heavy with sadness.

"They're going to find Dad?" Lucy breathed.

"A Phoenix. Fitting," Asher said.

We shared a smile. I'd thought the same thing. A movement caught my eye when Gabe shifted, staring at the table when a moment before he'd watched me.

I focused on the whole group. "What do you want to do? We can run, though I don't know what good it will do. They've tracked us this far."

"Do you believe he's going to search for Ben?" Gabe

asked, his gaze locked on something over my right shoulder.

I nodded, swallowing my hurt. For some reason, he couldn't even look at me. "I do. I'm not sure his motives are as altruistic as he'd have me believe, but I think Seamus wants something from me and he's willing to find my father to get it."

"Then we stay," Gabe said in an even voice.

His quick support surprised me, but I was glad to have it.

"I vote for staying," Erin said. "The whole point of coming here was to find your father. If this is the best way to do it, then we give Seamus some room to help us."

"I agree," Lottie said, with a shrug. "To be honest, we've hit a dead end. We couldn't have dug much deeper without making everyone suspicious. In fact, I think they already are. I was worried about returning to Spencer and Miranda."

That didn't sound good. Spencer and Miranda had been like family to the Blackwells, helping them to get out of Italy when their parents were killed and the war began. To hear that Lottie didn't feel safe with them sent a wave of unease through me that grew when Gabe frowned. They had been worried, but they would have returned. For me and for Lucy. My eyes burned. A year ago, I couldn't have imagined anyone risking their lives for mine. I loved these people.

Gabe's eyes flickered with momentary heat as if he'd heard that thought, but the spark disappeared.

"You all know where I stand," Lucy added.

"So we wait for Seamus," Asher said, and a round of agreeable murmurs sounded around the table.

After that, the group kicked around ideas of stepping up our vigilance in case Seamus proved an enemy. Gabe used this as an excuse to slip away, saying he wanted to do a quick patrol of the neighborhood to be sure the O'Malleys were the only ones watching us and that they weren't surrounding us. He left the room without once meeting my eyes or looking in Asher's direction, and I wondered what had been said in my absence. Had they fought?

Eventually, the long day caught up with everyone. Erin was the first to say good night, with Lucy and Lottie minutes behind her. They disappeared one at a time until Asher and I were left alone. He avoided my gaze with the same old guilt, and I guessed he was upset that I'd been taken on his watch. He hadn't been able to stop them, exactly as he'd feared. I was sorry that happened, mostly because we'd finally reached an understanding in those moments before Seamus's men showed up.

I toyed with the edge of my napkin. "How's your head?" I asked.

He touched his forehead with a scowl. They must have hit him pretty hard, though no mark remained. "Fine now. Erin healed me when they found me on the sidewalk."

I smiled with a trace of meanness. "If it makes you feel any better, I showed Seamus exactly what I thought of him hurting you."

Asher asked suspiciously, "What did you do?"

"Let's just say that Seamus and his men are a little nervous around me and silverware."

My statement confused him, but he laughed. "You always surprise me. Whenever I think I know you, you do something that convinces me that I don't know a damned thing. I think I'm going to head off to bed." He rose and pushed in his chair, while I cleared the table.

"Remy?"

I glanced up to find Asher staring at me with a pained expression. He gripped the back of his chair tight enough that his knuckles drained of color.

"You should know . . ." His jaw worked like he struggled to get the words out. "I saw Gabe's face when he realized they'd taken you. I've never seen him so . . ." He cut off, breathing hard. "Not since Sam and our parents died." Asher pinned me with a furious glare when I tried to speak, and I snapped my mouth shut. I subsided, and he cleared his throat. "My brother is the best man I know. The only person worthy of you. I love you, and it's going to kill me to see you together, but I'm not going to stand between you. If he's what you want, you should be with him. Be happy, *mo cridhe*. You deserve it."

With that, Asher turned on his heel and left the room.

I don't know how long I sat there alone and crying before I dragged myself to my bedroom. I couldn't decipher the myriad emotions battering my heart. Asher was my first love, and I grieved for us and what we might have been. Our friendship had to change, and that made me sad. I worried about how things would be between Asher and Gabe. I was sorry to cause Asher pain when I still loved him, even if that love had changed. And overlaying all of that, I hoped that this thing between Gabe and me could be something real and worth all the pain we were causing his brother. Maybe Gabe wondered the same thing, and that was why he'd avoided me tonight. What I knew was that I wanted to move forward, to give us a try. Life was short, and I didn't want to wait anymore.

I showered and readied for bed in a daze, worn out from everything that had happened. I thought I might not be able to fall asleep, but I was exhausted. Just before I drifted off it occurred to me that something seemed odd about my darkened room, but I was too tired to investigate.

The opening and closing of my bedroom door woke me. The footsteps sounded light and hesitant as bare feet tiptoed across the floor. I heard familiar breathing, and knew it was Lucy. There was no moonlight to light her way tonight, and she cursed in a whisper when she stubbed her toe on the nightstand. I watched her approach, her features clear as she blindly made her way to me. And I remembered what had bothered me as I was falling asleep.

*I can see in the dark.*

I bolted straight up, scaring a scream out of my sister as she knelt on the bed beside me.

"Sh!" I whispered. "It's just me."

"You scared me!" she said.

"I noticed," I told her. "My ears are still ringing. You scream like a girl, Lucy."

She shoved my leg. "Shut up." She didn't try to hide how nervous she felt, but then, she didn't realize I could see her. "Can I talk to you?" she asked.

I nodded to test her. Maybe the room was brighter than I thought. Except she didn't seem to notice my gesture. Out loud, I said, "Of course," and her expression flooded with relief. She couldn't see me, but I could see her. This had to be because of what I'd done to Seamus. Hadn't I been moving more quickly than usual when racing down the hall, too? I'd almost crashed when I underestimated my speed. Was I becoming more of a Protector? I hadn't healed anyone in a while. What if those powers were drying up? I didn't even know if such a thing was possible.

"I'm sorry," Lucy said, and my attention swung back to her.

"What?" I asked in confusion, torn from my thoughts.

She began crying, sniffling. "When they took you today, I thought I might not see you again. I was so scared and I've been a jerk, blaming you for everything. Do you hate me?"

*As if.* I'd missed talking to her.

"Oh Lucy." I tugged my sister into my arms. "I love you, sis. I could never hate you." She cried harder into my shoulder, and I added, "Be frustrated with you, yes. Want to pull your hair? Most definitely. But I don't hate you."

She choked. "You should. I was so awful to you. What I said when Mom died . . . You almost died, and I was cruel. I didn't mean it. Any of it."

Her body shook in my arms, and I hugged her tighter. "You were hurting. We both were. I'm sorry that you ever got involved in this. All I wanted was to keep you safe."

"It doesn't matter. Like Seamus said, they would have found us anyway."

They would have. It had only been a matter of time. I could have stayed away, and they still would have come. After a time, Lucy quieted in my arms, and I reached for my purse that sat on the nightstand to give her a tissue. She sniffed and blew her nose, the small sound marking her vulnerability.

"Want to have a sleepover?" I asked.

"Can I?" she asked shyly.

In answer, I slid over in the bed and lifted the covers for her. It reminded me of all the times she'd sneaked into my room at home after she'd had a nightmare. She settled beside me and reached for my hand. Love for my sister stole my breath. I'd missed her so much. We lay there for some time, each of us lost in our thoughts.

"Do you ever wonder why I don't have powers?" Lucy asked. "I mean, I'm an O'Malley and Dad is a Protector and you're you. Why did it skip me?"

I had asked myself the same question. "I don't know. I guess when I wondered I was always glad that you didn't have powers. I thought you would be safer if you were normal. In fact, I was jealous of you."

"Of how normal I am? Gee, thanks," Lucy said with a laugh.

"I mean it. All I've wanted was to be normal. I didn't

ask for any of this. But I've decided something. I'm not going to hide from it anymore. I'm tired of running, and it doesn't do any good. Can I tell you something I didn't tell the others?"

I flopped on my back and described how enraged I'd been when Seamus threatened to keep me a prisoner.

"What an ass! What did you do?"

"I stabbed his hand with a fork and then I attacked him with his knife." I could feel my sister's shock, even though I stared at the ceiling. "His men are kind of afraid of me, and it felt good to stand up for myself. Seamus knows that he can't push me around like that again."

"You've changed," Lucy said quietly.

"Yeah. I think I have. For the better, I hope."

"Be careful. I'm not saying don't use your powers, but you're all the family I have," she said in a broken voice. "Please don't let anything happen to you."

My sister was losing faith. I could hear it in her voice. "Hey! We're going to get Dad back," I said.

She squeezed my fingers, but I wasn't sure I'd convinced her. So much time had passed and it was difficult to hold on to hope. We hadn't seen our father in almost six months. I closed my eyes to imagine his face, his blue eyes and black hair. My father could be gentle and stern. He'd turned to mush when I'd stopped calling him Ben and started calling him Dad. He adored fast cars and fast boats and his town. And he loved Lucy and me. Tears filled my eyes, but I didn't want to cry. I wanted a happy memory to hang on to.

"Lucy, did I ever tell you about my first driving lesson with Dad?"

We rolled over to face each other in the dark, and I told her about how I'd jumped a curb and nearly taken out a tree. She giggled so hard she snorted.

"He acted like he was calm, but you should have seen how hard his foot was reaching for the brakes."

I kicked the covers like I was trying to stop a car, and we both lost it. It felt so good to laugh that I told another funny story, this time about Laura. Then Lucy told one. For hours, we talked about our parents and we laughed uproariously, trying to outdo each other. We didn't fall asleep until the sun had begun to come up, lighting the room in soft pinks and yellows. For once, we both wore smiles as we drifted into dreams.

# CHAPTER TWENTY-ONE

*I* woke up sometime after lunch and took my clothes into the bathroom to dress so I wouldn't wake Lucy. I wanted to see Gabe, and I threw on jeans and one of the prettier tops Lucy had picked out for me, but when I caught my reflection in the mirror, I stopped. I'd gone to bed with wet hair, and it showed. The mass of the dark blond waves had frizzed out around my head. Add to that the circles under my eyes from lack of sleep, and I looked awful. Gabe might have seen me at my worst, but that didn't mean I had to put extra effort into it. Sighing, I turned on the shower so I could start over. At least my hair was redeemable.

Twenty minutes later, the wet strands hung to my waist, way longer than I liked to wear it. It had been so long since I'd thought of my appearance that it hadn't occurred to me to cut it, except when the tangles had made me crazy. Eying the mass of it, I had an idea and went to drag Lucy out of bed.

She groaned when I bounced on the bed beside her. "Go away," she mumbled.

I laughed. "Oh, the shoe is on the other foot. Now you know what it's like to be woken up." More than once, she'd bounced into my room, all cheer and smiles before I'd opened my eyes. "Payback is a bitch. Come on, Luce.

I need your help." She pulled the blanket over her head and didn't move. I leaned over her and lowered my voice. "Please . . . I want to cut my hair before I see Gabe."

That did it. She threw off the covers and squealed so high that I slapped my hands over my ears. "You do like Gabe!" she shouted.

I slapped a hand over her mouth, peeking at the doorway. Nobody appeared, but that didn't mean a Protector hadn't heard. "Pipe down! We're trying to figure things out."

"Does Asher know?" she mumbled.

Her scandalized expression showed above my fingers. "Yes. We talked about it yesterday." I dropped my hand.

She frowned. "He must be so sad."

I nodded. "He is. Things have been ending between us for a long time, but it still hurts."

She must have seen some of my grief because she touched my cheek. "I'm sorry. You've been going through a lot, and I haven't been there for you."

I smiled. "You can make it up to me now. I need a haircut. My split ends have split ends."

She launched out of bed with more excitement than I'd seen from her in ages. My sister loved projects, and I was one of her favorites. She ran upstairs to hunt down scissors, and I prayed I wasn't going to end up with a lopsided Mohawk.

I sat on a chair we'd dragged into the bathroom, gulping every time six-inch hanks of hair fell to the floor. Once Lucy had finished trimming my hair, it hadn't needed much else. With all of the weight taken off (and the help of a little product), the strands almost curled to the middle of my back. I felt like a new person.

After we'd cleaned up the evidence, I went on a Gabe hunt only to find he'd gone out to patrol the neighborhood again. I felt let down, and then guilty for feeling let down. It probably only seemed like he was avoiding me when he was out there trying to keep us safe. Besides, how would he know that I wanted to see him when I'd done more pushing away than anything else?

I wandered through the house, bored out of my mind. Lucy had disappeared into the library. Asher and Lottie had ventured out of the house for a change, and Erin watched TV in her room. I ended up in the kitchen looking for a snack in the pantry. I grabbed a granola bar and flipped off the pantry light. The darkness sparked an idea, and I closed myself in the small closet, checking to ensure it was pitch dark. With the lights off, I turned to the rows of cans and boxed goods lining the shelves and read the labels: baked beans, tomato soup, and mushy peas (ew). I flipped the light switch and stared at the cans. The labels appeared exactly as I'd seen. I could read in the dark.

What had Asher once said about his abilities? When the Protectors had lost their senses of touch, taste, and smell, their other senses had been strengthened. They could see in the dark, hear better than humans, plus they were faster and stronger. Aside from my speed and an extra helping of strength, I'd never exhibited any Protector powers. And the speed and strength hadn't happened until I'd stolen Asher's energy back when Dean had shot him. This new ability to see in the dark had come after I'd done the same to Seamus. Fear mingled with excitement skittered along my nerves. What else might I be able to do?

I shoved my way out of the pantry and ran to my bedroom. I grabbed my phone, planting myself on the bed. Lucy picked up on the second ring.

"Lucy, when I hang up I want you to read something from your book."

"I was doing that until you called," she answered in a dry tone.

"Out loud. I'm testing something. Come on. Just do it."

She agreed and we hung up. I closed my eyes, concentrating. At first nothing happened. I heard traffic on the street above, and water rushing through pipes somewhere in the house. The same noises as usual. I dropped my mental walls in frustration and that's when it happened.

". . . *was Mr. Rochester now ugly in my eyes? No, reader: gratitude and many associates, all pleasurable and genial, made his face the object I best liked to see; his presence in a room was more cheering than the brightest fire . . .*"

I called Lucy back.

"What?" she asked.

"You're reading *Jane Eyre.*"

"You don't have to sound so shocked. I can read."

My laugh had an edge of hysteria.

"Are you okay?" she asked.

"Sure. You go back to your book."

I hung up and stared at the wall. An entire floor separated Lucy and me, but I'd been able to hear her as if she sat beside me. Luckily, I had to concentrate to make that sense come alive. I couldn't imagine being bombarded by noise constantly. It was enough to adjust to my changed vision and hearing. What else had changed?

Eager to do another test, I jumped up. I glanced around, looking for something heavy that I normally wouldn't be able to lift. Nothing that wasn't a huge piece of furniture. Too much. I ran into the family room and slammed into Gabe. He threw out his arms to brace us as we tumbled to the floor in a pile of arms and legs.

His breath rushed out of him when I pancaked his lungs. Awesome. I couldn't be a petite girl who wouldn't cause damage, could I? Beneath me, Gabe stilled. His green eyes narrowed, and I smiled, though it felt a bit wobbly. I couldn't help it. I was nervous. *He* made me nervous.

"Gab—"

He lifted me off him with gentle hands and sat up. I watched in bewilderment as he stood and proceeded to leave without saying a word. Either it was my imagination or he was pissed at me. I'd spent the last several hours anxious about seeing him, and he ditched me the second we bumped into each other. My emotions whipped from confusion to hurt in a matter of seconds.

"Wow," I said to his back. "I knew you were a player, but you do move on fast, don't you?"

Gabe froze. His icy "Excuse me?" cooled the air around me by ten degrees.

I stood, too, putting my hands in my pockets like I hadn't a care in the world. Screw him. I wasn't like the girls who had chased after him begging for his attention. "Oh, I'm pretty sure you heard me. But just in case . . ." I lowered my mental guard and called him a few names in my mind.

He definitely heard me that time. He spun on his heel, and his mouth twisted in a grim smile. "Take that back," he said slowly.

"No."

"Remy, I'm not in a good mood, and you are pushing it."

His eyes had almost narrowed to slits. Maybe I shouldn't push him . . . I remembered how excited I'd been to show him my haircut and my eyes narrowed, too. Then again, sometimes it felt good to give someone a shove.

"Oh, I'm scared!" I mocked. "Why don't you man up and tell me what your problem is?"

"My problem?" he asked in an incredulous voice. His brows shot up, and he took a step toward me. I rocked on my heels, ready to spring away. "*You* are my problem," he added in a low voice that thrummed through me. "You said you'd give us a chance." He took another step. "And that you cared about me." Another step. "And then you kissed my brother. Who's the player now?"

I blinked at him. "What are you talking about?"

"I saw you yesterday! Look, I'll do my best to stay out of your way. Congratulations on patching things up with him."

He sounded more tormented than happy for me. I considered his once-more retreating back. He wasn't jealous so much as hurt. I could see that in the creases around his eyes before he turned away. He thought Asher and I had made up, and it was time to set him straight.

"For your information, that was a good-bye kiss, Gabe. He knows about us and he wants us to be happy," I called to him.

I'd stunned him. He'd gone still as a statue halfway up the stairs. I could only see the bottom half of his legs, but when I opened my senses, I could hear how fast his heart beat, thumping against his rib cage with passion or excitement. He was so good at hiding how he felt because he'd gotten used to putting others before himself. Until me. I liked being the one that he wanted enough to grab hold of, the one person who made him lose his control.

The thought of Gabe losing control excited me. I shoved harder, hoping it would incite him to riot. "You know, for someone who said he was going to chase me with everything he had, I have to say this act is total weak sauce. I expected more of you."

*Whoa.* He launched off the stairs in an explosion of speed that would have been impossible to dodge without my new abilities. By the time Gabe reached the spot I'd been standing, I'd spun out of his way and stood on the staircase. We'd reversed positions, and he hadn't seen me.

Gabe swung around, shock widening his eyes. "How did you do that?"

I'd never been faster than him. He had always been able to overpower me until I used my "special" violent abilities. A giddy bubble of excitement rose up in me. This was going to be fun. *Game on.*

"Do you know what I thought of when they took me yesterday?" I asked in a conversational tone.

He shook his head, studying me like he sought a weakness. I could almost hear him thinking, *Challenge accepted.* I loved that about him, the way he stood toe-to-toe with me, and made me laugh while doing it.

"I realized that I might not see you again, and it hurt imagining that. You know what my next thought was?"

He devoured me with his eyes and didn't say a word.

"I regretted that I hadn't kissed you," I told him. "I've thought about it. A lot. What it will be like with you."

Gabe's face lit up with a smile, and his muscles tensed. I could swear I saw steam rising from him. Any second now he would pounce. "Come here, Remington, and we'll find out," he said in a low voice that sent shivers along my spine.

I backed up a stair. "I don't think so. You said you were going to chase me." I breathed a little harder, remembering that moment in the wine vault. "Chase me, Gabe, and I promise to let you catch me."

I stayed still long enough to see the fire catch in his eyes and then the game began.

# CHAPTER TWENTY-TWO

*I* shot up the stairs with him hot on my heels. It didn't help that I really, really wanted to be caught. I hadn't understood how I felt about Gabe until confronted by him, but now it seemed like the emotions had been there forever, growing steady and sure over time. Still, when his fingers brushed my waist in the entrance hall, the challenge of the play lit in me, and I surged up the next flight of stairs, escaping him.

He gasped and rested with his foot on the bottom stair, while I hesitated on the top landing. I could feel the satisfied smile on my lips. This was a game we would both win, and the anticipation heightened every sense. I could inhale his scent from where I stood, the spice of him, and I wondered what he would taste like.

"Giving up?" I taunted.

"Not a chance," he promised, his features sharpened by emotion. "You're faster than before."

"And I can hear better. Your heart is pounding."

He seemed to listen to the silence. Then he smiled with a heat that curled into me. "So is yours," he said, and we were off again.

On the next floor up, I managed to lose him. Many of the rooms had multiple entrances so I could enter through one door and leave through another. I hid behind a door on the third floor, but he sneaked up on me. I had a feeling he let me go; the escape was too easy and he had more experience with our powerful senses.

I made it to the fourth-floor storage closet, peeking around the edge of the cracked door. Gabe tiptoed down the hall, checking rooms with a smile on his face, and I wanted to laugh.

"Am I hot or cold, Remington?" he asked, tipping his head to listen for me.

I pictured him with his shirt off, a mile of muscles rippling from his wide shoulders to his lean hips. *Hot, Gabe. Definitely hot.*

He paused mid-step in the hall, seeing the image in my mind, and his jaw clenched. The intensity upped another notch, and some of the playfulness dissipated. He stalked forward, slow and sure. "Have I told you about the first time I saw you?"

*At the Underground. The first time Lucy brought me there.*

"No, I saw you before then."

Confused, I almost gave away my hiding place when my hand slipped, knocking into a broom that leaned against one wall. I caught the handle just before it clattered into the door. I paused, but Gabe passed my hiding spot, striding down the hall. He reappeared a moment later, and his low voice mesmerized me.

"Before you arrived in town, things had become unbearable. Asher was lost. Lottie was . . . well, Lottie. Something had to change, but I didn't know how to help them. Maybe after what I'd done in Italy, how I became immortal, I didn't deserve to be happy, but I couldn't accept that for Asher and Lottie. I thought to go out of town, to clear my head, figure things out . . . That night, I sat at the airport in Portland, desperately wanting some kind of sign. And the doors opened at the gate, and you walked off the plane."

I pressed my forehead to the door, feeling him on the other side, a disembodied voice. Gabe had been there the night I'd first arrived in Blackwell Falls, broken and battered by Dean. I'd been covered in bruises and soul-weary from years of his abuse and my mother's neglect. Thank God, I'd changed since then.

"I saw you that night, Remy. I don't know where your dad was, but you stood there for a while waiting for him. Do you remember?"

*Yes.* My dad had been worried that people would jostle me. He'd asked the flight attendant to let me off the plane first so I wouldn't be hurt further. It was one of the first times he'd shown me that he cared, and the memory was bittersweet.

"You didn't have your guard up," Gabe said.

I almost gasped. He was right. I hadn't heard of Protectors then or understood that I should guard against them. I'd usually kept my mental walls up in crowds to protect myself from sick people, but I'd been waiting alone in a mostly empty airport, and I'd been so tired from the flight and my injuries and dealing with the father who'd abandoned me.

*You knew. You knew I was a Healer.*

"Yes. The first I'd seen since the war began. I almost went up to you, but you looked so angry and hurt. Then your dad joined you and I recognized him from town. I waited a whole fifteen seconds after you left before I grabbed my bags and went home. I don't believe in love at first sight, but my gut said you would change everything."

I placed a shaking hand over my stomach. *But when I saw you two days later at the Underground, you ignored me.*

"You're a Healer, and I'm a Protector, and our kind had hated each other for a century. I thought you would run the second you knew what I was, and I wanted to give you space so you wouldn't feel threatened. I didn't know that you'd met Asher at the beach that morning, and that I was already too late. I'd waited too long."

*I didn't know. I thought you hated me then.* Something about Gabe's power had always unnerved me, but I think it was because I'd sensed the intensity behind it. I'd thought the danger came from his desire to protect his family from a naïve Healer, but I'd been wrong.

"Back then you were afraid of me, but you're not any-more. I've been waiting a long time for you, Remington." I could almost feel him on the other side of the door, his heart pounding as he leaned close to whisper, "Don't make me wait anymore."

I took a deep breath, no longer caring if he heard me. I wanted to be found. The door opened the rest of the way when I gave it a slight shove. I stepped into the empty hall and glanced both ways, but Gabe had disappeared. I lis-tened with my other senses.

"Chase me," he said, from a distance.

The game had ended. I walked to the stairs and fol-lowed the sound of his heart. A minute later, I found him in the wine vault, leaning against the far wall where he'd held me less than a week ago.

"Gotcha," I told him.

"For as long as you want me," he said, his eyes smiling.

I stepped inside the room and kicked the door closed behind me. There was something about Gabe, about Gabe and me, that negated my nerves in this moment. Once I'd realized that he wasn't scary, something had shifted in our relationship. It had happened so slowly that I hadn't been aware of it. Maybe because I hadn't liked him in the be-ginning, I'd never tempered my actions around him or tried to be someone else for him. He'd been treated to the undiluted, imperfect real me, and that was whom he'd waited for.

I twisted the door's lock behind me, and then I walked up to Gabe, stopping only when my feet tangled with his. He didn't move, and I glimpsed a small amount of doubt on his face. He'd chased me for so long with no reciprocation from me. This time, he needed me to make the choice to move us forward.

His chest lifted in a heady sigh when I finally laid a hand over his heart.

His eyelids lowered. "Remington, kiss me alre—"

I cut him off by pressing my lips to his. For a moment, he went completely still against me, my breath entangling with his. Then his arms wrapped around me and he whipped me around so that my back was to the wall. All hesitation evaporated the second he had his hands on me. And there the hurrying ended.

It was if the waiting had built a patience in Gabe, a desire to make our first kiss something lasting and infinite. His lips brushed mine, back and forth, asking me for an invitation, and I gave it. His hands gathered up the weight of my hair and let it fall through his fingers, testing the way it felt. His body leaned into mine, so that the wall propped us both up when gravity tugged me down. Then those fingers slid under my shirt to discover the small of my back, and my skin wanted to throw a party.

I stopped thinking and did what I'd imagined so there would be no regrets. My hands met at his neck, traced across his shoulders, and explored the muscles and skin between there and down to his hips. I flattened my fingers against his shoulder blades to pull him closer. I tasted his mouth, and I fell deeper into him. And when we came up for air, our eyes met, naked with emotion. Then he smiled and I had to see what that tasted like, and we dove back into each other to find out how our second kiss would be.

It was during our fourth kiss that green fireworks ignited against my eyelids. Neither of us had bothered with our mental defenses, and I stole his immortality—healing it.

"Gabe," I warned, as his mouth slid to my jaw. "My powers . . ."

The panic rose in me, but he soothed a hand down my back. "I know." I thought he would ignore what was happening, but he eased away in stages, his lips finding a new patch of exposed skin between retreats. He rested his forehead against mine, his green eyes burning with fires that I wanted to throw myself in. "It doesn't matter."

Our ragged breathing sounded loud in the small room, and I stared back at him. I couldn't help it if this scared me. Being with him felt natural—necessary—but what if I hurt him? The first time I'd kissed Asher, I'd thought I was going to kill him when I'd lost control of my abilities. That hadn't occurred with Gabe, and I didn't understand why when I burned everywhere we touched.

"Gabe, something is happening to me. I think . . ." I licked my lips, hesitating. "I'm changing. Can't you sense it? It's like I'm siphoning off your energy. The more I take, the more powerful I'm becoming."

Trust Gabe to stay calm with a tornado bearing down us. The timbre of his voice soothed some nerves, while sparking others. "You're faster. You're hearing things you shouldn't. What else?" he asked.

"I can see in the dark. I'm stronger, too."

"Are you sure it's not that we're growing weaker?"

Gabe didn't sound upset about the possibility, but I shook my head. "The thing is . . . I may have left out a bit about my visit with Seamus."

I explained about what happened when I'd attacked Seamus. He listened in silence, his hands never losing their place on my back. When I finished, I dropped my gaze to his Adam's apple and waited for the explosion, the lecture about the dangerous chances that I took. Asher had hated that, and we'd argued about it all the time, especially when I didn't tell him about things that I knew would upset him.

"Hey." Gabe bent to see my face. "I'm not Asher. I trust you, Remy." I must have looked shocked, because he laughed and dropped a solid kiss on my mouth. "Look, you're used to taking care of other people. Bad things happen, and you either process it or you put it away until you can deal with it later. I get it. I get you."

That was exactly how I worked. I had needed time to think about what I'd done to Seamus before I told the others. The violence I'd displayed hadn't surprised me, but the way I'd devoured his energy had. I had liked it too much and that scared me. I hadn't imagined that Gabe would get that I needed to figure out how I felt before I could tell someone else about it.

"You see a lot, Gabriel Blackwell," I said, brushing a lock of hair off his forehead.

He tilted his head into my caress. "I see you. You're fierce when you love someone. It's how you tick, and I think it's obvious that I like the way you tick." I bit my lip and Gabe grinned. "I also know when you're biting back the sarcasm. Go ahead and mock me. You know you want to."

"Who me? No way. That was one of the sweetest things anyone has ever said to me." Then because I couldn't leave things alone, I walked my fingers up his chest in a blatant come-on and added in a deep voice, "Baby, are you a clock? Because I like the way you tick."

Gabe lost it, throwing his head back and laughing. "You are impossible to romance."

I tilted my head to the side so I could kiss his neck, and his laugh disappeared. "I don't know. You seem to be doing just fine."

"Yeah?" he breathed.

"Yeah."

His head dropped, and I lost my ability to count somewhere after kiss number six.

# CHAPTER TWENTY-THREE

*G*abe and I tried not to be obvious around the others out of consideration for Asher. We acted as we always had, never touching and making an effort to keep our eyes off each other. We hid our impatience to be alone, and then practiced holding our breath whenever we managed to sneak away. The green sparks kept on, but Gabe didn't care. It had taken months to change Asher, and I prayed we'd find my father before that happened to Gabe. If Asher noticed that things had shifted between Gabe and me, he didn't give anything away. Three days of waiting for Seamus to call with news, and we thought we'd succeeded in keeping our relationship a secret.

On the fourth morning, I sat in the dining room eating cereal when I heard Gabe roar upstairs. A minute later, Lottie came speeding through the dining room, almost cackling with glee. That was enough to snap me awake, but then Gabe ran into the dining room looking like he'd just rolled out of bed. His brown hair stood on end, and he looked deliciously sleepy. He spied me and drew to an abrupt halt.

My nerve endings stood up and did cartwheels when I saw he wore sweats and nothing else. Well, almost nothing else. I blinked at his chest. Someone had taken a black

Sharpie to the skin over his heart and written PROP-
ERTY OF REMINGTON. Flowers and vines bordered
the words in fancy curlicues. Under my perusal, Gabe's
skin flushed a bright shade of red, and I raised both brows
when the color spread.

"Sound sleeper?" I asked. He had to have been out for
Lottie to do that.

"I was up late," he reminded me.

My fault. I'd insisted I couldn't sleep until he kissed me
one last time. That had turned into a lot of last times by
the time he went to his room.

"I regret nothing," I quipped.

Behind him, Lucy and Erin appeared. "What's the
ruckus?" Lucy said. She circled Gabe, saw his chest, and
clapped a hand over her mouth to smother her laugh. Erin
peered around him to see what had caused the reaction,
and they both collapsed into giggles.

Gabe's stare dared me to join in. Instead, I motioned
him forward with a sweet smile. He narrowed his eyes at
me, but he did as I asked. When he stood in front of me,
I touched his hand and "healed" his skin, restoring the
cells. The marks disappeared from his chest, and his hooded
gaze dropped to my shirt like he wanted to see how they'd
transferred to my skin. I felt myself turning red, and his
lips finally quirked in a smile.

"Lottie?" he asked calmly.

I pointed toward the kitchen and he leaned down to lay
a kiss on me that would have wrecked my ability to stand
if I hadn't been sitting. "Good morning," he whispered in
a husky voice.

Then he was gone, and his shout of "I'm going to kill
you, Lottie!" echoed through the house.

As soon as he disappeared, I glanced over at Lucy and
Erin, who watched me with huge eyes. I peeked inside my
shirt, and the evidence of Lottie's prank stripped the last of

my control. I laughed so hard I cried, and I couldn't remember the last time I'd felt so happy.

If not for Gabe, the waiting would have been inter-
minable. As it was, I wanted to call Seamus a thousand
times a day to see what kind of progress he was making. I
still wasn't sure if I could trust him, but I didn't know what
other choice I had. We'd exhausted our other options for
finding my father, and there was no way we would give
up on him. So we waited, and I tried not to lose my mind.
Later that day, Gabe went off to patrol with Lottie, and
Erin and I made a bowl of popcorn to take down to the
family room. We'd developed a *Doctor Who* addiction to
fill the time. Erin loved the Eleventh Doctor, Matt Smith,
but I was a die-hard fan of David Tennant, the Tenth
Doctor. We settled on the couch with feet propped on the
table to watch our favorite episode, where Sally Sparrow
took on the creepy Weeping Angels with a little help from
the Doctor. Halfway through the episode, I realized that
Erin wasn't paying attention. She'd drifted off into her
thoughts, and they weren't happy ones judging by the expression on her face.
I touched her leg, careful to keep my guard up. Since
my run-in with Seamus, I'd noticed that I had to be more
careful around her. That monster inside me woke whenever I was around her now, and I didn't want to chance
hurting her. In fact, Asher had taken over training with her
to make things easier. She excelled at it, sparring with him
and Lucy with a determination that I understood. I think
she imagined Alcais as her opponent and it lit a fire in her.
"Popcorn for your thoughts," I said.
She smiled. "No pennies?"
I shook my head at her. "The popcorn has butter and
salt. I was offering you gold, woman." She ignored the
bowl, and I said, "Seriously, are you okay?"

She sighed and the sound was heavy with sadness. "I was thinking about home. I miss my mom."

She'd been so agreeable since she joined us that sometimes I forgot how she'd been ripped from her life and everyone she loved.

"I'm sorry, Erin."

"Are you sure I can't call them?" I frowned, and she rushed on. "You said it yourself. Seamus followed Gabe into the woods that day. Franc didn't send them."

My feet hit the floor, and apprehension wound its way around my spine. "You can't call home. Franc has already shown that he's tracing our calls, and even though it wasn't him in Muir Woods, he knows that you're with us now. I'm sorry. We have to be careful."

The apology sounded weak to my ears. I wondered if it would have consoled me if I was in her place, and I knew it wouldn't have. She missed her family and her community, and I couldn't blame her.

"Tell you what. Why don't you write her a letter? We'll figure out a way to get it to her."

It wasn't enough to remove the sadness from her eyes, but Erin nodded. "Okay."

We turned back to the show, but I could tell Erin's heart wasn't in it. Maybe Gabe would have a way for her to call home without it tracing back to us. I resolved to ask him about it.

Gabe let himself into my room after everyone had gone to bed that night. It was difficult to date someone when you couldn't actually leave the house to go on dates. The newness of Gabe and me was something I wanted to savor, and we couldn't do that in the open where it might cause Asher pain. These late-night visits were a compromise. Our way of spending time alone.

I laughed when I saw what he was wearing. Gray sweats and a white T-shirt.

"Nice," he said, eying my matching outfit. "We're already dressing alike. Imagine how in sync we'll be a year from now."

He carried a book with him and dropped it on the nightstand. His gaze followed me as I put my clothes away in the wardrobe. The hungry look on his face said there would be a lot of kissing in my near future. He sat on my bed on top of the covers with his back against the headboard and his legs stretched out in front of him. His size ensured he took up a lot of space, more than his share of the bed, and he never apologized for it. I liked how confident he was and the way his confidence infected me. If I wanted more of the bed, he trusted that I would tell him so or shove him over. Gabe didn't play head games. I would always know where I stood with him.

"What?" he said. "You have an odd look on your face."

"Nothing," I answered. "Hey, do you think you could find a way for Erin to call home?"

I told him about my talk with her, and he frowned. "She's so even-keeled that I didn't realize she was upset."

I took my earrings off and walked to the dresser to put them in a dish for safekeeping. "That's how she gets by. Where I used anger to deflect things, she uses smiles. She might have me beat in the strength department."

"Alcais really did a number on her, didn't he?"

I nodded and gritted my teeth. "It makes me wish I'd known when we were in Pacifica that first time. I would have found a way to make him sorry."

"Remington the Fierce. Woe to those who screw with her loved ones."

He smiled with understanding when I turned to face him. "It really doesn't bother you, does it? That I would fight to keep the people I cared about safe, even if it means endangering myself?"

His answer meant a lot to me, and he seemed to sense it. He considered my question for a moment before saying, "Not even a little. It's who you are. I suppose it would worry me if you were always risking your life to save mine, but you wouldn't do that."

"I wouldn't?" I asked, bemused by his certainty.

He shook his head. "No, you wouldn't. Just like I trust you to take care of yourself, you trust me in the same way. And I know you would ask for help if you needed it, the same as I would."

That was the second time he'd brought up trust. Who knew the word was such a turn-on? I smiled and stalked toward the bed, crawling across it until I could reach him. I straddled his thighs, and his hands landed on my waist.

"May I?" he asked, one of his hands tugging on my French braid. I nodded and he pulled the rubber band off. His fingers loosened my hair, separating the strands so that it hung over one shoulder. The intent look on his face made me shiver, and the backs of his hands brushed my collarbone.

"What's that?" I asked in a shaky voice, tipping my head to the book.

He shrugged. "I found it in the library. It's a book on Greek mythology. There's a section about the phoenix that I thought you might like."

"Read it to me?" I asked, touched by the thoughtful gesture.

He nodded, and I moved to lie beside him, our heads sharing a pillow. That didn't feel close enough, and he agreed because he slid an arm under my head and pulled me half on top of him with my leg over his and my arm across his chest. I tucked my face into his neck to breathe him in. I loved the scent of him. It reminded me of running beside him in the moonlight in San Francisco. We settled together like we'd always known each other. No awkwardness or hesitation.

"It's so easy." I tilted my head up to see his face. "Being with you. I didn't expect it."

"I did." His fingers tangled in my hair, always in my hair, and I sighed with pleasure.

"But how could you know?" I asked, touching his jaw. He'd shaved, and I savored the feel of the smooth skin.

Gabe kissed my hand, and placed it against his heart so I could feel the steady beat of it under my hand. "Because we fit," he said simply.

His low voice washed over me as he propped open the book and began to read about the phoenix. Only one phoenix could exist at a time, and every five hundred years, the bird would die in flames only to be reborn in the ashes. A symbol of immortality, the phoenix would always resurrect itself. One story told of how the creature could heal itself when wounded by an enemy. *An immortal Healer,* I thought, with a shudder. I didn't think I would want that life, especially when I watched the people I cared about die.

What could my future with Gabe hold? He said we fit, and he was right. We were alike in so many ways. Fierce protectors of our families. Survivors.

Gabe's voice dropped off, and I looked up expecting him to be asleep. Instead I found him staring down at me. "Where are you tonight?" he asked.

"Do you know when my feelings for you changed?"

Gabe shifted, rolling onto his side so that we faced each other. He tugged a blanket over us and reached for my hand. "I suspect it was when we bonded, but I could be off about that."

I shoved him and he gave a quiet laugh. "Smart-ass. But do you know why my feelings shifted?"

He was quiet for a moment and then he said, "In the beginning, I worried it was because you had mistaken me for Asher."

I reeled away from him, though our joined hands didn't let me go far. "You're not interchangeable, you know."

"I know," he said. "But you love us both."

Sometimes the truth hurt, but I wouldn't lie to Gabe. "You're right. It shredded me to feel something for both of you, so I pretended that I could never care about you. But you wouldn't stay in the box where I'd put you."

He didn't judge me, but then he'd known how I felt. "The one marked enemy?"

"No. The one marked friend, idiot."

"I'm stubborn that way." He kissed my nose, and then gave me an expectant look. "So tell me about how great I am and how you couldn't resist me."

I laughed. "It wasn't like that. Do you remember the night you rescued me in San Francisco? We thought Asher had died, and I wanted to die, too. You wouldn't let me."

"I yelled at you when you wouldn't heal yourself," he said with a grimace.

I laid a hand over his heart. "You also sang to me and helped me heal myself and nursed me and held me while I cried for your brother. You were there for me before I even knew I needed you. You always have been."

His heart jumped under my fingertips, skipping a beat.

"I didn't want to care about you then, Gabe, but you're pushy. Every time I turned around you were there, and now I can't imagine it any other way. You make me happy. I've laughed more with you than I ever have."

There hadn't been a lot of joy in my life. I hadn't played or laughed freely, but Gabe gave that to me. It felt like I betrayed Asher to admit that.

His features softened. "You love him, Remy. I know that. I'm not asking you to stop." He tugged me closer, his lips touching mine. And then he pulled back to say, "But if you could maybe arrange to not kiss him and promise to love me a little more, I would be okay with that."

I suppressed another laugh, shaking my head. "I do love you, Gabe."

"I know, Remington. I've just been waiting for you to figure it out."

The certainty in his voice bound me to him a little more. He'd been so sure of me, and it warmed me to my toes to know someone had that much faith in me. That he'd loved me enough to wait for me to come around to my feelings only made it sweeter.

Gabe rolled to his back, taking me with him. "Is it too soon to ask for a favor?"

I lifted my head to give him a suspicious look.

He tugged the neck of his T-shirt slightly askew so I could see the edge of Lottie's latest artwork. "She used permanent marker. It's not washing off."

He looked sheepish, and I grinned. I laid my hand over his heart and "healed" the latest marker tattoo. Then I pointed at my lips and said, "I expect payment in kisses. At least seven or eig—"

Later, much, much later, he held me while I tilted into sleep. I was almost disappearing into a dream when he whispered, "Psst. Read the marker."

I blinked and pulled away enough to peek inside my shirt. The writing wasn't Lottie's. It was Gabe's. He'd penned a heart, and inside the heart it said GABRIELA LOVES REMINGTON.

I dissolved into giggles that grew louder when Gabe insisted that he should probably check his artwork.

# CHAPTER TWENTY-FOUR

*I*n the morning, Gabe and Asher set out together. It had been Gabe's idea. The two of them had been avoiding each other, but it would be difficult to continue that in a house with so many people. Gabe had given up his room to Asher to stay on the couch in the family room, but I don't think anyone was fooled when he could never be found there. He had convinced Asher that they should get away from all the girls and go do manly stuff. Gabe had mentioned the gym, but I suspected they'd probably sneaked off to a pub for a Guinness.

Lottie had griped about not getting to go with them, but she'd given up when Gabe produced a Sharpie and brandished it in her direction with a scowl. After lunch, Lucy, Erin, and I decided to spend the time training. Apparently, Asher had been working with Lucy for a while.

"I'm tired of being the powerless one," she said as we moved furniture in the family room. "Whenever the fighting breaks out, everyone scrambles to cover me because I'm so freaking helpless. After what happened in Muir Woods, I couldn't stand it anymore. I asked Asher to teach me a few things, and we've been working together when we can."

It surprised me, but I was glad. Maybe a little hurt that

Lucy hadn't included me, but then she'd hardly been speaking to me then. "I should have suggested it sooner, Lucy. I know how it sucks to feel like you can't fight back. I'm sorry I made you feel that way."

She shrugged off my apology. "You didn't make me feel anything. I let you take care of me because I was scared. I want to pull my own weight now. I don't want you to have to risk your life to save me. I want to save myself." She turned around and saw the look on my face. "What?" she asked.

I shook my head with a smile. "Nothing. It seems we've both been doing a lot of growing up."

Erin shoved a table to the side. She straightened and her eyes latched on to my chest. "Lottie strike again?" she asked.

I glanced down and saw the edge of Gabe's drawing showing above my tank top. The blush started at my chest and worked its way up to my ears. That was like waving a red flag at Erin and Lucy. They tackled me at once, tugging the neck of my shirt aside. They shared knowing glances.

"Ahem. That doesn't look like Lottie's handwriting," Lucy said.

Erin suggested, "Need a hand healing that?"

*No way.* I stuck my tongue out at them and zipped up my hoodie. "Shut up. Let's get to work."

Since Erin and Lucy had begun working around the same time—and both lacked Protector blood—they were fairly matched in a fight. I stood to the side, instructing them as Asher or Gabe would. Lucy turned out to be a pretty great fighter. She had good instincts and could guess what her opponent would do next. When she'd thrown Erin for the third time, I stepped in.

I took Erin's place and dropped into a crouch. "Come

on, Lucy. Try that with me. I want you to see what it will
be like against someone bigger and stronger. You wouldn't
be able to throw a man off balance in the same way."

Lucy's eyes took on a speculative glint. She gave too
much away, and I guessed she planned to come at me with
everything she had. I readied myself and waited. A second
later, she swung out with her arm. She tipped forward too
far, losing her center of balance. I used her weight against
her, grabbing her arm and tugging her toward me. Instead
of meeting resistance, she fell forward and I used her arm
to flip her through the air. Too late, I realized that I'd put
too much force into the move and I cursed. What might
have tipped her over before sent her flying with the help
of my newfound strength. I sped forward to keep her from
hitting the wall, but her chin smacked into my head. We
collapsed in a heap on the ground, both of us moaning.

"Sorry, Lucy. I didn't mean to throw you like that."

"I guessed that when you yelled 'shit' in my ear." She
touched her bloody mouth. "Ow. I bit my tongue when I
headbutted you."

I scowled at the ceiling from where I sprawled. "I think
I'm about to have the mother of all headaches."

Erin stepped forward, and I waved her over to Lucy.
"Can you help her, Erin?"

She nodded and knelt on the ground by my sister. I
winced, rubbing my eyes. How was I going to know the
limits of my abilities if the line kept moving? A week ago
I couldn't have thrown Lucy like that, but I hadn't been so
strong. My head throbbed, and I squinted, letting my energy unwind through me to see if I could heal the goose
egg already forming on my scalp. I sensed Erin's energy in
the air, even though I wasn't touching her. The monster
perked up, and I thought, *Quiet, beast. Nothing for you here.*

"Damn," Erin said.

I rolled my head toward her. She had a hand on Lucy's arm, and she frowned at the blood seeping from my sister's cut lip. "What's wrong?"

"My powers don't seem to be working."

"What happened here?" Asher said, coming down the stairs. He walked over to Lucy, tipping her head up so he could examine the cut.

Gabe entered the room behind him and crouched over me. "What's up, Buttercup?"

I narrowed my eyes. "Call me Buttercup again, and I break a finger."

He tapped my nose. "Violent today, aren't we?"

I stuck my tongue out at him, and his gaze dropped to my mouth. I snapped my mental wall in place so he wouldn't hear what that did to me, while we were surrounded by others. His mouth curved in a promise that we'd talk about it later.

"There!" Erin said. "Finally!"

Purple sparks lit the air between Lucy and Erin and the cut on Lucy's lip disappeared. Asher helped them both up. His gaze slid to his brother and me for a second, and his mouth compressed into a tight line. He saw me looking at him, and he forced a smile that didn't quite reach his eyes. A pain in my chest throbbed, and I stared after him as he climbed the stairs with the girls.

Fingers snapped in front of my face. Gabe gave me an understanding look, and I shrugged off the ache. It was what it was. Everyone had made their choices, and we would have to live with them.

"Up with you!" Gabe said, pulling me to my feet. "Obviously you need training. If you're on your back, you're not doing it right."

I snickered at his unintentional innuendo.

He shook his head. "Get your mind out of the gutter,

Remington. We have work to do." He stripped off his T-shirt and kicked off his shoes. His jeans rode low on his hips, and my mouth watered like I'd discovered a dessert buffet. He smirked, and I guessed he'd done it on purpose.

I smiled and unzipped my hoodie, throwing it toward the couch. His eyes latched on to the edge of his artwork on my chest above the tank top and his breath caught. I used his inattention to knock his feet out from under him. He landed on the floor staring up at the ceiling.

"If you're on your back, you're not doing it right," I observed.

I danced out of his reach when he made a grab for me, and the game was on.

"How did things go with Asher today?" I asked Gabe.

We were in the kitchen. The two of us had been volunteered for kitchen duty for the night, which meant Gabe did the cooking and I would do the cleanup so that everyone would survive the meal without food poisoning. While he buzzed about the kitchen, pulling together something he'd called shepherd's pie (which looked like Hamburger Helper topped with mashed potatoes), I sat on the kitchen counter to keep him company.

"Awkward and painful," he said, stirring vegetables into the ground beef and gravy. He shrugged. "So basically what I expected."

I felt for him. I wasn't sure how to behave around Asher yet. While I wasn't ashamed of Gabe, I didn't want to flaunt things in front of Asher. We were stuck together and that meant we had to figure out a way to get past this.

Gabe touched my hand. "We're going to be okay. Give it time."

I smiled. "Did you put lima beans in that?" I asked, changing the subject.

He set aside his spoon and walked over to cage me in

between his arms. "Why? Have you got a beef with lima beans?"

I smacked a kiss on his nose. "No. I like the way they pop in my mouth. They don't taste great, but they have an awesome texture so they pass inspection."

He grinned. "You have a rating system for food?"

"Of course."

"And which foods pass both the texture and taste inspection?"

"There's really only one. Pop Rocks," I lied, imagining the candy that exploded on your tongue.

He shook his head. "That's not a food. I'm realizing that most of your favorite meals can be classified as Fair Food."

I pondered that. "What do you mean?"

"Fair Food. Foods that one would eat at a fair. I bet you love funnel cake."

A laugh burst out of me. "It's like you can see into my soul."

His attention caught on my mouth, and I gripped the front of his T-shirt to tug him closer. We both groaned when my cell phone sounded off in my pocket. He took a step back so I could retrieve the phone.

My heart stopped when I saw which number was on the screen. "It's Seamus."

I answered and he wasted no time replying, "We have located your father."

My breath heaved on an involuntary sob, and Gabe rested a hand on my thigh to offer strength. "Please tell me he's okay."

"He's alive," Seamus said in his thick Irish brogue.

That could mean that my dad was really hurt. I couldn't think about that, though. I had to focus on the fact that he was alive. "What now, Seamus?"

I expected him to tell me the location and demand that

I live up to my end of the bargain. After all, he'd found my father as promised. Retrieving him hadn't been part of the deal.

"The Morriseys are keeping him at their home just outside of the city. Tomorrow half the Morrissey family is going to be in London for a meeting with your grandfather. We go in then."

"We?" I asked.

"Is your father not my kin, too?" he asked in a defensive tone. "We should plan to meet in the morning to make a plan."

"Gabe will come, too," I said.

"Fine," he grumbled. "But your human friends stay behind. They're a liability we can't afford. Sean will be around to pick you up at nine."

He agreed so quickly that I guessed he'd known all along that I would be going in with at least one of the Blackwells. Asher and Lottie would stay behind to watch over my sister and Lucy. Everything would be set in motion tomorrow, and Gabe and I would have to be ready for them to pick us up in the morning.

We hung up, and I turned to Gabe. "Tomorrow. We go get him tomorrow. Sean's going to pick us up in the morning so we can figure things out."

Gabe slipped his arms around me. I'd thought I would feel happy or excited, something more than the numbness settling over me. We'd waited so long for some kind of news, and now that we had it, I didn't know how to react. Tomorrow would change everything. We would find my father, whatever condition he was in, and then we'd decide where to go from there. Would he hate me? What had they told him about me? How would he react when he found out about Laura? Dread formed a pit in my stomach at what was to come when he found out she'd died.

"Remy?" Gabe touched my chin. "Focus on the rescue. We can handle the rest later."

I nodded. He was right, of course. What was the point of jumping ahead six steps? It could get me killed if I wasn't paying attention to the here and now. I pushed off the counter and Gabe stepped back to let me. "Let's go tell the others."

"I want to go," Lucy said.

We sat in the family room. Erin, Asher, and she had been playing *Call of Duty* when I found them. Gabe had gone to find Lottie so I was on my own. I understood Lucy's desire to be there when we found our father, but I couldn't let her go.

"You can't," Asher told her before I could. I looked over at him in surprise. His mouth had tightened into an angry line. "None of us can," he added, taking in Lucy and Erin. "The three of us would be in the way."

He expelled a frustrated breath and dropped his head back against the couch.

Lucy cried, and I knelt in front of her chair. "I'm sorry, sis, but he's right. These men are dangerous, and you wouldn't be able to defend yourself."

"But the training," she protested.

I shook my head. "Think about how I hurt you today. I wasn't even using all of my strength. And the Protectors are faster and stronger. You can't go. Dad would never forgive me if you were hurt, too."

She squeezed my fingers. "Promise you'll bring him back."

"I'll do my best," I promised.

Gabe and Lottie appeared, coming down the stairs together. She walked to the couch and perched on the arm next to Asher, while Gabe stood near me.

"I have to admit, I'm excited," Lottie said, flipping her

hair. We all stared at her like she was crazy, and she added, "I'm sick of waiting around for something to happen. I want to be *doing* something."

Asher's jaw tightened another degree, but he didn't say anything.

"Excited isn't exactly what I'm feeling, but I get what you mean," I said in a wry voice. "Erin? Are you okay?"

She hadn't said a word. In fact, she'd been quiet most of the day. Her gaze didn't quite meet mine and she flushed as if she felt guilty. I wanted to tell her that it was okay to be relieved that she didn't have to go. I wouldn't have if I could have avoided it.

She smiled, but it didn't reach her eyes. "Sure. I'm good. What can I do here to help?"

The discussion turned to preparations and what had to be done by the morning. Weapons would be needed, and we wanted to have a backup plan in case Seamus and his men let us down. An hour later, we called it quits, deciding the best thing we could do was try to get a good night's sleep—a thing I feared would be impossible.

Lucy and Erin hugged me before following Lottie up the stairs. Gabe looked at me, and I motioned for him to go on. I needed to talk to Asher. He gave a small nod and went upstairs.

"Is this where you tell me you're sorry that I have to stay behind, too?" Asher said, his voice bitter.

I sat on the couch beside him. "No. This is where I beg you to keep my sister and Erin safe." My answer surprised him, and his eyes searched my face. "I'm afraid. If I don't make it back . . ." I choked on the words and had to begin again. "If I don't make it back, I need you to promise you'll look after them."

Asher cursed under his breath, and the use of another language almost made me smile. "Don't talk like that. You're going to make it out just fine."

He turned away, but I grabbed his hand, pressing it between mine. "Promise," I begged. "I can't go if there's a chance something will happen to my sister."

I didn't say what we both knew. If I didn't make it back, most likely Gabe wouldn't, either. He would never leave me behind. The gravity of what I asked didn't escape me. It wasn't fair to ask this of Asher, but there was no one else I trusted.

"Please," I said again.

His hand moved to grip mine. "You have my word. Nothing will happen to them."

"Thank you," I breathed.

"I wish I could save your father for you," Asher said.

"I know," I whispered.

The silence grew awkward, and he waved me on, a sad look in his eyes. "Go on. I'm fine. You need to rest."

I left him there, knowing that no matter what I said, he would beat himself up because he wasn't strong enough to protect me like he wanted.

# CHAPTER TWENTY-FIVE

*A* sound woke me out of a deep sleep. Before I could move, Gabe pressed a hand to my arm. He touched a finger to his lips in warning. Someone was breaking into my room from the courtyard, and they were being very quiet about jiggling the sliding glass door. The room was oddly still and silent.

I hesitated to drop my guard to discover if the stranger was a Protector. If I did, he or she would be able to sense me and know that I was different from other Protectors. The person—a man, I could see now—pushed the door open in micro movements. Any second now he would be inside the room. We could wait for him to enter and attack, or we could attack first. Indecision held me hostage. Then the man entered, and I could see a face.

Xavier. I would never forget his features. Black hair, olive skin, the lean build. He'd tortured me for two days, suffocating me and cutting me. He'd fired the gun that I thought killed Asher, and he'd been one of his torturers, too. Xavier had been there the day my father was kidnapped, and he'd been in the car that had struck my stepmother.

The Protector had destroyed everything, and a bloodlust rose up in me unlike anything I'd known before. I rolled out of the bed, and Gabe did the same on his side, as another man followed Xavier into the room. I'd kept a knife handy in the nightstand, and I palmed it as I stood. Then I was launching across the room intercepting Xavier as he took his second step into the room, while Gabe went after his friend.

Xavier grunted when I stabbed at him with the knife. He managed to block the blow I'd aimed for his stomach, and the knife sliced into the skin and tendons of his arm. Warm, wet liquid splashed on my tank top. Xavier didn't feel pain, and the cut had only surprised him. I lowered my guard, letting my energy sift into the air.

"Feel that? That's only the beginning, Xavier," I said with satisfaction when he grimaced.

"Bitch," he said through his teeth.

From across the room, I registered that Gabe was fighting the other man, their movements a blurred symphony punctuated by groans and exhalations as my energy enabled them to feel the pain of the brutal punches they landed on each other's bodies. Xavier took advantage of my distraction and swung at me. He didn't expect my speed, though. I spun sideways, and his fingers only caught a strand of my hair. He gave it a tug, and I cried out when the hair ripped from my scalp. But I was loose, and I ducked low, swinging the knife. The blade caught Xavier across the back of his knee, and he tumbled to the ground.

I rose and stood over him as he crawled forward on his stomach, trying to escape me. He gripped handfuls of the bedspread, pulling himself up so that he could twist about to prop his back against the foot of the bed. A few feet away, Gabe ended the fight with the other Protector by throwing him into the wardrobe. The wood splintered and broke beneath the man's weight. My clothes tumbled out and fell over him. Before he could recover, Gabe smashed his head against the ground, ensuring he wouldn't wake anytime soon.

"It's been a while, Xavier," Gabe said evenly, joining me.

As calm as his voice sounded, his body language told another story. He wanted to kill the man almost as badly as I had. Why, then, had I hesitated?

"What do you want to do with him?" Gabe asked me.

He left the decision to me, trusting I would know what to do. The problem was that I couldn't kill a man in cold blood, even if he would hurt me. *You're not like them, Remy. That's a good thing.*

"Can you hand me my phone?" I asked Gabe.

He picked it up from the nightstand and tossed it to me. "Watch him for me," I said, dialing a number.

Seamus answered on the second ring. "Everything okay?" he asked in a sleepy voice.

"There are two Protectors in my bedroom right now, and there might be more on the way."

"Morrisseys?" he asked, more alert.

"No, these are my grandfather's men. How fast can you get here?"

"Twenty minutes," he said, and I could hear the sounds of clothes rustling as if he was dressing. "If you can get out of the house, you should run now."

"That's the plan," I said. As soon as we found my sister and the others. "Hurry."

I clicked the phone off and crouched near Xavier. There wasn't time, but I needed answers.

"How did you find us?" I asked.

Xavier laughed. "You think I'm actually going to tell you?"

"Yes. You have no sense of loyalty." I pressed the knife against his throat, letting him feel the sting of it cutting into his skin. "You only care about yourself. You can tell me what I want to know, or I can do to you what you did to me in California. Do you remember?"

His brown eyes gleamed when Gabe flipped on a light,

but Xavier pressed his lips together. We could play this game all night, but I wouldn't let that happen. He wouldn't believe my threat if I didn't back it up with action. My stomach twisted, and I took a deep breath. A cry escaped his mouth when I jerked the knife down and slid it across his thigh, slicing through black cotton and skin.

"How many times did you cut me?" I studied him with cold eyes. "Do you know that I counted every injury I healed? I think we made it to thirty-eight before Gabe rescued me. You're at three. Do you think you can last another thirty-five?"

A tinge of fear crossed Xavier's face, and I knew I had him. "How did you find us?" I repeated.

Drops of sweat appeared on his forehead, and he pressed a hand to his thigh to stanch the bleeding. "The little Healer," he finally bit off. "She called home to talk to her mother, and we traced the call here."

Instant denial had me jerking away from him. Erin had brought them on us. She'd been homesick and lost patience. *Oh Erin. You should have waited.*

"Is it just the two of you?" Gabe asked.

Before Xavier could answer, a shrill scream sounded upstairs. He smiled with grim satisfaction, and I turned the knife in my hand so I could grip the blade. Then I smashed the handle into his head and watched his eyes roll back into his head. He tipped sideways, smacking his head on the wood floor with enough force to open a cut on his forehead. The bastard was lucky that I wasn't like him, because I could have done so much worse.

Gabe was already racing into the family room, and I hit the stairs a few feet behind him. The scream had come from one of the upper floors, and feet pounded up the stairs somewhere above us. We bypassed the first floor and continued up to the next floor. The door to Gabe and Asher's bedroom stood open, but nobody was in there.

We continued up another flight to the top floor, and the sounds of the fighting reached us before we entered the chaos.

Three doors opened off the landing: one to the right for Lottie's room, one a little farther down that opened onto a shared bath, and one more directly in front of us that was Erin and Lucy's bedroom. Lights were on in each of the bedrooms. My grandfather's men had divided to conquer us, and they were winning up here. Lottie fought three men in her bedroom, and Gabe peeled off to help her. I ran on to the other bedroom, where two men and a woman cornered Asher. Behind him, Lucy pressed to the wall, her face wet with tears.

My mind processed the scene in an instant. Asher's mouth bled, and he already had an eye swelling shut. He could hardly stand, but he refused to move from his spot defending my sister. And I recognized two of his attackers. Goatee Man from Maple, Alabama. The other man was Xavier's partner, Mark. White-blond hair shone on his head, and I guessed Asher recognized him, too, because his face had twisted with hatred.

I had one moment to wonder where Erin was, and then glass shattered when Asher threw a lamp at Mark's head. The woman cursed when a shard of glass hit her cheek, and I watched as the fresh cut began to close. She was a Healer. I must have made a noise of surprise because heads whipped toward me, and Mark sprang forward.

Shorter than me, he had more muscles, wider shoulders, and outweighed me by a good seventy-five pounds. His momentum and strength sent me flying into the wall on the landing, and somewhere along the way I dropped the knife. I slid to the floor, catching my breath. Mark sprinted toward me again, and I rolled away, jumping to my feet to face him. We circled each other in silence, and I was ready when his fist flew at my head. At the last moment, I ducked to the side to avoid him, and I brought my foot up between his legs. He doubled over, probably feeling the first intense pain he'd experienced in months. Maybe since the last time we'd met when a truck put in motion by Gabe had rammed into him and broken his legs.

As he was distracted, I dove for the knife where it had fallen on the floor. From the bedroom, I heard a shrill scream—was it Lucy?—and I scrambled to the doorway. Asher fought Goatee Man, fists pummeling bodies in a fair fight since neither of them had powers. The Healer appeared to be trying to reach my sister, but Lucy managed to punch the woman in the jaw.

An arm lashed around my neck from behind and pulled me back onto the landing. I jerked against the hold, scratching and pulling at the hairy forearm that pressed against my windpipe and cut off my air supply. Mark's muscles bunched as he tensed and yanked me off my feet. I gripped the handle of the knife and drove it backward into his meaty thigh. His hold on me loosened, and he fell, taking me with him. I sucked in a breath and fought against his arms. Mark grunted when I freed an elbow and shoved it in his gut, but he wouldn't let me go. Finally, I reached for the knife sticking out of his leg and twisted it. The Protector shrieked and shoved me off him as he pulled at the weapon.

"I'm going to kill you," he hissed at me.

I answered by unleashing my energy in preparation to lash out at him.

"Enough!" a male voice shouted from behind me.

I twisted around to find Alcais pointing a gun at my chest. Behind him, Erin cowered, a bruise coloring her cheek. Worse was the way she stared at the floor, her spirit gone. Her time away from him had been so short, and it was too easy to fall into a lifetime of training. It had taken me months to stop ducking for cover when voices were raised.

"Hiding in the bathroom, Alcais? That sounds just like you," I said with barely restrained anger.

"Shut up!" he yelled.

"Send the Healer to me," Mark told Alcais. "I need her."

Franc thought he controlled these Protectors, but he was wrong. The hunger pervading the man's features belied anything but a vicious motive. Mark had no use for Erin as a person, and once she healed him, he could steal her energy. And unlike the Healer they'd brought with them—a traitor my grandfather probably tricked into helping his Protectors—Erin would not be under Franc's protection. No, she would be considered the enemy for siding with me.

Over his shoulder, Alcais told Erin, "Get over there and heal him."

Erin's eyes widened as she looked from her brother to Mark. "I can't heal a wound like that. You know that."

He reached backward, grabbed her wrist, and yanked her forward. She stumbled and fell to her knees near me, sobbing. The Protector would kill her. Over my dead body.

"I'm not letting her near him," I told Alcais.

The sounds of fighting continued in both bedrooms, and I knew I was on my own. Erin had trained, but she was too distraught to fight. So this fight was on me.

"It's not up to you," Alcais said, waving the gun. "Erin? Do what I said."

The "or else" at the end of that statement was implied, and Erin shuddered. She crawled forward, until I blocked her path to Mark. The Protector worked to tie off his injury and sat up. I stood just out of his reach, but he could change that at any time. Terror filled me imagining what he could do to my friend.

"No, Erin. You don't have to listen to him." I met her shattered gaze without judgment.

"It's my fault they're here," she whispered with shame. "I'm so sorry."

I slashed a hand through the air to make her stop. "It's okay. I don't blame you." She started to drop her eyes and I insisted, "Erin! I don't blame you, okay? Now, please get up."

Behind her, Alcais scowled and took a step forward. I glared at him and he stopped, rethinking approaching me. At my feet, Erin fought her fear and rose in wavering degrees. As soon as she stood, I saw that she'd found some of her strength. She would need it.

"Erin, go to the stairs and walk down them. Leave the house and run until you can't run anymore." She froze, a wild flush coloring her cheeks. I snapped my fingers. "Move! Now!"

She took one hesitant step and then another.

Alcais cursed. "I swear if you go another step, I'm going to shoot you."

She stopped, a lifetime of fear giving her pause, and I told her, "He's lying. He won't do it. Keep going."

Her body shook, and my heart broke a little more for her. "I'm scared," she said, her voice trembling.

"It's okay to be afraid, but you have to keep moving." Fear for her injected urgency into my words when I shouted, "Go, damn it!"

My yell startled her into a run. Alcais aimed the gun at her, but as I'd suspected, he didn't shoot. It was one thing to beat his sister, and another to murder her outright. Still, once she'd disappeared down the stairs, he spun on me, fury mottling his skin shades of red and pink. I knew men like him. He wanted to be a leader, to be the one everyone looked up to with respect, but he would never be that person because he was small. Small of heart, small of courage, and small of character.

"Why did you do that? She'll tell everyone."

I hoped she would. Maybe then Franc would lose his hold over the Healers, and they could find another way to keep their people safe.

Hands up to placate Alcais, I said, "Put the gun down. This is over."

"You're right. It is." The despair on his face looked real, but I felt nothing for him as he paced a few feet back and forth, the gun waving about. "She'll poison everyone against me. I'll never be able to go back."

He raised his head and let off a shout of frustration, and then he fired a shot into the ceiling. The sound reverberated in the small space, deafening me. The scent of gun powder burned my nostrils, and my eyes watered. I heard a roar from nearby that sounded like Gabe calling my name, but I didn't dare turn my attention from Alcais.

"This is your fault," he told me, almost in tears. "Why couldn't you do what we wanted?"

The gun aimed at my chest, and I believed he would pull the trigger this time. "What about Franc? He wants me alive."

Determination set his face in hard lines. "I don't care anymore."

Suddenly, from the stairs, Erin shouted, "Alcais, stop!"

I swore under my breath. "Erin . . ."

She ignored me, rushing onto the landing. "Franc started this, but you don't have to be like him. Please, let's leave. I want to see Mom and Delia. We can still go home." As she spoke, she walked toward her brother, her hand out as she pleaded with him. "Please, Alcais. Let's go home," she said, weeping.

She meant it. Whatever he'd done to her, she loved her brother. That sincerity that had drawn me to her convinced her brother. He wavered a moment, longing in his eyes. But then his hand steadied again.

"Franc won't stop while she lives. This won't end until she's gone."

He squeezed the trigger. I prepared to jump sideways, and Erin did the same. Directly into the path of the bullet. It slammed her backward into my arms, and I stumbled.

"No!" The word ripped out of me in an agonized shriek. I lowered her to the ground, and the monster in me roared where we touched. I slammed my guard up to protect her, surveying the damage. Blood blossomed over her belly where the bullet hit her, and her eyes flickered closed.

"Give her to me!" Mark said, clambering to his feet.

The eagerness in his voice made me sick. Alcais surprised me when he stopped Mark from reaching his sister. "No. Leave her alone."

"You think you can stop me, child?" Mark scoffed.

He proved his words true by knocking Alcais off his feet with his fist. I huddled my body over Erin, awaiting the Protector's blow, but Gabe was there, fighting him off.

Erin didn't make a sound in my arms. She was bleeding out, and this was the type of injury you didn't recover from. If I tried to save her, I would die. The knowledge of it flooded through me, and a sob ripped out of me. Could I save her, even if I tried? Could I control the monster that even now fought to get out?

"Why did you come back?" I asked her, blinded by tears. "You could have escaped."

Erin didn't move. Her muscles slackened, and her weight settled against me more. "No . . ." I wailed. "Please, don't go, Erin!"

*No! Oh God, please no.*

The life faded out of her brown eyes by degrees, and I sobbed, rocking her in my arms. Without thinking, I touched my fingers against her pale cheek, skin to skin, and it didn't matter that I had my guard up. A surge of power erupted between us, and pain like I'd never known tore me apart.

# CHAPTER TWENTY-SIX

*I*n the moment before she died, Erin's energy invaded my body like an arctic blizzard. Every frozen molecule rammed the pain up another increment, and the torment made me want to claw at my skin frantically. Even my blood seemed to solidify, and my breath froze, shards of it cutting my lungs as I inhaled in desperation. I couldn't even shiver, and time stretched on while I begged for the numbness that would surely come before death.

My grip on Erin loosened, and I crumpled to the ground next to her still body, sprawling on my back. Her empty eyes stared into mine with accusation, and another sobbing moan escaped my parted lips. My hand fell from hers, and the frigid pain snapped away. An avalanche of energy surged through me driving out the bitter frost, and I moaned at the burn of heating all at once. Fiery ice— that was what it felt like inside me. Was this what the Blackwells experienced when they became immortal, or was it different for me because of my mixed blood?

Gabe and Mark fought to one side of me, and I wanted to help. My body wouldn't listen. I rolled my head the other direction to avoid Erin's gaze. And I saw the Healer woman stab Asher in the shoulder while he fought Goatee Man. Another moan burst from my lips when I watched him fall. But in the confusion, somehow the woman fell, too, landing on top of Asher's back. Perhaps Lucy had struck her. That left my sister and Goatee Man.

"Lucy," I whispered.

*Get up, Remy!* Agony speared through me, but I turned over and managed to get my feet beneath me. I rose and stumbled in dragging steps toward the bedroom. Goatee Man had cornered my sister, though she looked ready to fight back. The vase weighed a thousand pounds when I took it off the dresser and hefted it over my head. Goatee Man went down like a rock dropped off a cliff, hitting the ground with a thud after I struck him in the head. I teetered and barely managed to stay on my feet.

Lucy rushed forward, and we both turned to Asher, where he lay on the floor with the Healer sprawled over him. My sister knelt by them and pushed the woman off him. I took one step back and sank down on the bed, while Lucy cried out. The Healer had fallen on her knife when she landed on Asher, and it was buried to the hilt in her chest.

I lowered my guard for one moment, and I knew. Asher's energy buzzed in the air, the vital power reminding me of the day I'd first met him. Intentional or not, he'd absorbed the dying Healer's energy. Asher had gained his greatest wish—he was immortal once more. And stealing that woman's energy didn't seem to affect him the way stealing Erin's had done to me. His eyes opened, and I sensed the stretching of his powers, along with his muscles, as he sat up with little care for his injuries. And why should he care? He could no longer feel them. I guessed the instant he felt my energy, though, because he winced with the first hint of pain. Slowly, I put up my walls to block him out like I had that first day on the beach. We stared at each other, and it was as if everything that had happened between us had been deleted, along with his senses.

Gabe and Lottie appeared in the doorway, and the five

of us surveyed each other. Bruises and cuts (everyone), one broken limb (Asher), a knife wound (also Asher), and Gabe wheezed like he couldn't catch his breath. I guessed broken ribs.

"Mark?" I asked.

"Ran away," Gabe answered matter-of-factly.

I swallowed. "And Alcais?"

"Gone. He ran down the stairs while I was fighting Mark."

Lottie pushed past Gabe to help Asher. She ripped the sheet in strips and wound one around his shoulder to stem the blood flow. Another looped around his neck to create a makeshift brace for his broken arm.

"We should get out of here before they have a chance to regroup," she said.

Then Lucy asked, "Where's Erin?"

I shook my head at her, unable to speak past the boulder in my throat.

My sister's face drained of color.

From downstairs, we heard the slamming of doors before I could explain. Enemy or friend? I gritted my teeth and stood. Wordlessly, the five of us arranged ourselves into some kind of formation with Gabe and Lottie at the forefront. We waited to see what kind of hell would be unleashed on us next. I pressed a hand to Gabe's back, and he reached back to touch my waist. The momentary connection made my pounding heart settle and my mind still. *One fight at a time.*

Feet thudded up the stairs, and three women appeared on the landing. Immediately, I sensed it. I could feel Gabe, Lottie, and Asher, but this energy was different. Familiar. And there were three sources.

I stared at them in shock. The scowling blonde with the miniskirt and combat boots. The curvy vixen with fire-engine-red hair and a nose ring. The tall, elegant brunette with dark brown skin and gentle black-brown eyes. They were all different and similar at the same time. They stared at me with just as much curiosity, somehow able to divine that I was like them in a room full of people.

*Phoenix*, I guessed. Seamus had lied about me being the first one born in centuries.

Lottie sensed something about them, too, but she interpreted it as a threat. She crouched, ready to attack, and I laid a hand on her shoulder. "No, Lottie. They're like me."

The brunette spoke up in a French accent. "We're here with Seamus. We need to go. The Morrisseys could be on their way, and we don't have the numbers to fight them."

"There were two men in a bedroom on the bottom floor," I said.

"They are gone," the woman answered. "We found no others."

She left the room, heading for the stairs with the other two women. I pushed Lottie ahead of me and told her, "Help me with Erin." Lottie appeared the least hurt out of the group, and I wouldn't leave my friend's body here for the Protectors to find, even if she was beyond caring about such things. We left the room with the others behind us. With each step, I could feel my strength returning.

"Where is Er—"

Lucy's words cut off when she stepped onto the landing and saw Erin's lifeless body. "No," she whispered. "How?"

"Alcais shot her," I said in a dead voice. *And I stole her energy as she was dying.*

My sister approached Erin. She leaned down, grief tightening her mouth into a flat line. Though she crouched close, she didn't touch Erin, but gazed at her with pained eyes. Lucy disappeared somewhere inside herself where none of this world existed.

I bent down to touch my sister's cheek. "Lucy, we have to go."

She didn't respond. Her blank eyes looked right through me when I tugged her to her feet. Lottie lifted Erin, carrying her like a sleeping child. The sight of it loosened the sob I'd buried, and I shoved it back down again. I wouldn't cry again. Not until we were safe. The four of us limped to the stairs after Lottie.

Seamus met us in the entrance hall, a newsboy hat pulled low over his forehead. His gaze roved over us, from our injuries to Erin, and I shook my head when he appeared about to offer sympathy. He gave one short nod of understanding. "Sean is waiting for you in the Land Rover out front. A few of you can join him, and the others can come with me in my car. Let's go."

He strode forward, unconcerned that we might not follow his lead. The street outside looked the same as it always had. Nobody seemed the wiser for what had happened in our house. The neighbors had never heard of Erin and would not mourn her passing. The thought of it knotted my gut. My throat closed, and I looked up at the black sky, feeling just as empty as it appeared. Fingers twined with mine, strengthening me, and I gripped Gabe so tightly that it hurt.

He led me to the Land Rover, and we climbed in with Lucy between us. Sean slammed on the gas as soon as my door closed, and the house blurred and disappeared.

The blank expression on my sister's face worried me, and I leaned forward.

"Lucy?"

Her eyes finally focused on my face, and she shattered into pieces. I wrapped an arm around her, and she fell across my lap, her fingers clutching at my sweats helplessly. She shuddered in my arms, and I stroked a hand down her back. I wanted to cry with her, but I was afraid of what that would unleash.

*Keep it together, Remy.*

Gabe laid a hand over mine, and I looked up, meeting his watery gaze. We didn't say a word for the entire ride. It was enough that we held on to each other, the three of us grieving for another lost member of our family.

They took us to Seamus's place. I hadn't realized how large the house was until we pulled through the gates and onto the property. The cobblestone drive had probably stood up to hooves and carriages back in the day, and I spared a thought for the O'Malleys that had ridden in them.

Lucy had managed to fall asleep on the short drive, and I shook her when Sean stopped the SUV. She opened dull, swollen eyes, and I brushed the hair from her face. "We're here."

Sean opened the door on my side, and we all clambered out. Lucy glanced around, looking more lost than curious. Another car pulled up behind us, and Seamus, Lottie, and Asher joined us. I frowned when I got a good look at Lottie limping toward the house. Though hurt the least, she wore the badges of her fight with the Protectors. Cuts, scrapes, and bloody bruises darkened her skin, and she had a black eye forming.

Seamus paused in front of me, and I asked, "Erin?"

"We will take care of your friend. We can make arrangements to get her back to her family."

I nodded gratefully.

Seamus held out an arm to usher all of us through the front door. He and Sean led us upstairs to the sitting room I'd been in before.

"First aid kit?" I asked, but Seamus shook his head.

"You won't need one."

I glanced around the room, assessing the injuries as everyone collapsed in whatever was available, from armchairs to the couch. Asher's broken arm needed attending, and so did the wound at his back. Lottie's limp would need to be checked. My sister appeared physically unscathed but her eyes said something else.

We all wore the evidence of battle, but we weren't soldiers. A crack formed in my shield, and I tried to patch it up. *There's work to be done. Fall apart later.*

Gabe drew my attention with his stillness, and I studied him with a frown. I'd thought his ribs might be broken, but now I wondered if it was something worse. His skin had a gray tone to it, and his expression had turned stony the way it did when he was being stoic in the face of pain. Like me, he would wait for the others to be tended to before he asked for help.

I dropped to my knees in front of his chair. "Gabe? What is it?"

He tried to smile and failed miserably. "That bastard Mark managed to stick me in the back with a blade before he got away."

I tore at Gabe's T-shirt looking for the wound. "Damn it, why didn't you say something? Seamus, help me!"

Seamus joined me, helping Gabe out of his T-shirt. Asher approached, too, watching the process with a grimace. Gabe leaned forward so I could pull his arms from the sleeves and he grimaced in pain. I rose and gasped when I saw his back. Mark had been aiming for Gabe's spinal cord, and Gabe had managed to veer so that the injury landed an inch to the right. Blood oozed out of the cut, seeping into his sweats and shirt. And he could feel it. Asher couldn't feel his injuries anymore, but Gabe could. Because of me.

"Remy?" Gabe said faintly.

I couldn't see his face, and he couldn't see mine bent over like he was. I swallowed, glad I didn't have to hide my horror. "Yeah?"

"If you dare try to blame yourself for any of this bullshit, I'm going to be pissed. It hurts like a son of a bitch, but I can handle it. Got me?"

The challenge in his voice steeled my faltering courage, and I laid a hand over his neck to warm him. "Got you," I answered. "Hold on, okay?"

He nodded under my hand, and I motioned to Asher to move away. The last thing I needed was for his energy to jack with mine. Who knew how our powers would interact now that he'd gone back to his old self? Asher's mouth tightened into a straight line, but he stepped back.

"I hate that this will hurt you," Gabe whispered. "That's why I didn't tell you."

"Sh. It's like a Band-Aid. It will only hurt for a second because you'll help me heal myself. Ready?"

Gabe gripped my fingers in answer, and I lowered my guard to unleash my energy. I almost recoiled in shock when it leapt out of me and green sparks struck Gabe. He jumped as if I'd jolted him with an electric current, and the wound on his back disappeared like it had never been.

Never had my powers worked so quickly or been so out of my control.

Terrified, I yanked my hand from Gabe's, and the pain was instant and furious when a similar wound ripped open on my back, and bruises and cuts scattered over my body. Relief filled me because this was normal. Now Gabe could help me heal. I winced, imagining the ugly wound at my back. More power coursed through me, slamming into my injuries in a flash of pain. I cried out as everything healed at once, including the wounds Mark had inflicted.

*What's happening to me?*

"What was that?" Gabe asked. He shifted, the muscles in his back rolling, and then he sat up, his expression full of confusion. "How did you do that?" he asked me in wonder.

I had healed Gabe without having to envision the injury

or the mending. That had never happened before. I sank back on my heels, almost falling. Gabe's hands clamped on my forearms to keep me upright. Asher circled us to peer at my back. I twisted around, studying my shirt, the material hardly damp with blood at all because the wound had healed so quickly. I lifted the hem and saw the evidence of what I'd done. Aside from a small stain of blood, the injury might never have existed. My mouth dropped open in wordless shock.

"What the hell?" Asher asked in bewilderment.

I shrugged, entirely at a loss.

"Are you okay?" Gabe asked, running a finger down my cheek.

I shook my head, unable to keep it together another second.

Gabe pulled me onto his lap. Hot tears threatened, and I pressed my face into his neck to hide from everyone. I could feel their stares, and for once, I didn't care what they thought about seeing me with Gabe. I needed him. The change had to be because of what had happened when Erin died. Gabe's arms wrapped around my back and one leg, tucking me closer and securing me against him.

*I should heal the others,* I thought. The idea of it terrified me. How else might my powers have changed?

"No," Gabe said. "They're already being looked after."

I dropped my defenses enough to sense the presence of the women I'd met at the house. *The women are Phoenix, aren't they?*

Gabe nodded. Any other time, I would have been full of a thousand questions, but the night had caught up with me. I'd been running on adrenaline and denial and the fierce desire to see my family safe. Warm and in Gabe's arms, I could no longer hide from what had happened.

*Get me out of here, Gabe. Please.*

He stood, lifting me in his arms, and I looped my arms

around his neck, blocking everyone out. Gabe asked Seamus a question and the man's voice rumbled in answer, and then Gabe was carrying me from the room. I didn't care where we went, except I didn't want to see anyone else. The air changed and I finally lifted my head. We were on a stone balcony that faced a private garden. Gabe had brought me outside without leaving the safety of the house. The sweet gesture unraveled me. Losing Erin had hollowed out a section of my heart, and the ache of all the death that happened around me felt permanent. Fixed grief that would never go away or heal.

There were no chairs on the balcony, but Gabe sat on the cold stone, curling me around him again. He tucked my feet into his hand so they wouldn't touch the ground, and I realized I had no shoes on. I still wore the tank top and sweatpants that I'd worn to bed. I shuddered, my body jerking so hard it was painful. Reaction had set in, and I couldn't stop it.

"I've got you, Remington."

And he did. Gabe held me while I cried, murmuring nonsense. Later, when the air became too cold, he carried me back into the house and tucked me into bed. I fell asleep in his arms while he sang me a song that I remembered from a long-ago night when he'd carried me in the darkness. It seemed Gabe had always been there for me, and I vowed to hold tight to him.

# CHAPTER TWENTY-SEVEN

*D*awn lit the room in golden tones when I woke in Gabe's arms. I shifted a little, and his hold tightened.

"Stay," he said in a gravelly morning voice that I'd come to love.

I relaxed again, trying not to think about anything but Gabe. His eyes were still closed, and I traced a finger over the lids and the long dark lashes. His lips tilted in the barest smile, and I traced that, too, feeling the rasp of his morning beard under my fingertips. This was something to be grateful for on a morning when my soul ached with loss. I loved this man, and he loved me. We had a future worth fighting for.

Gabe kissed my fingers, and his eyes opened, the green so bright and luminous that I could lose myself in them. How could one person make you feel so much? "I love you," I told him, and the words didn't seem enough.

A muscle in his cheek jumped under my hand. "Why do I feel like you're about to say 'but I need to leave you for your own good'?"

I propped myself up on an elbow and shook my head. "No. You're stuck with me now."

His fingers tangled in the fall of my hair, letting the curls brush his bare chest. "That's a relief," he said. "I've been chasing you for so long that I'm ready to kick back and chill for a while."

"Wimp!" I scoffed. "I thought you had stamina."

His eyes lit with a playfulness I loved. "Was that a dare? Because it sounded like a dare." Gabe shoved me to my back and rose up on his knees to straddle my hips, his hands holding mine hostage by my head. "Prepare to be awed by my stamina," he threatened.

He bent forward, and I lost my breath when I thought he might kiss me. His breath brushed my collarbone, and I shivered when his lips touched my skin. Then I froze in shock when he blew a raspberry on my neck. This was promptly followed by his hands loosening their grip on mine in order to begin an all-out tickle war.

"Uncle!" I shrieked, laughing breathlessly.

He finally let up and sat back, looking far too pleased with himself. "That will teach you to mock my stamina. Have you learned your lesson?"

I nodded solemnly and crooked a finger at him.

A wary expression crossed his face. "You're up to something."

"I just want to kiss the victor."

His eyes flared with heat and he placed a hand on either side of my head. He bent closer, muttering, "I know this is a trap, but I can't stop myself. You're my Fair Food."

The mischief I'd planned faded from my mind. "You say the sweetest things." I wrapped my arms around him and tugged him down to kiss him.

He was out of breath when he raised his head. "I love running in the forest with you. I love how you savor the good things in life because you know they matter. I love how you love people with two hundred percent of your heart, and I love how your mind works and that I get to hear it. Most of all, I love your laugh because your entire body lights up with it and it's like holding a mirror up to

your soul so the rest of the world can see it. I could spend
the rest of my life listening to that laugh."

I stared up at him wordlessly. My heart belonged to
him, and I felt the *click* of the lock as I tossed the key away.
Nobody had ever known me so well and loved me so
much. Gabe had never asked me to change, and he never
would.

"Hey, what's this?" he asked, brushing his thumb over
my cheek.

"You overwhelm me sometimes," I said, sniffing. "In
the best kind of way."

I pulled him close again, and his weight rested heavy on
me, but I didn't care. He laid his head on my chest, and I
ran my fingers through his hair. Outside our room, people were waking and moving about, but in here it was just
us and this moment when I felt safe and adored.

"Your heartbeat is changing," Gabe said, listening with
his ear pressed against it. "It sounds more like ours every
day."

In Gabe's embrace, I could finally admit what had happened. "Erin died in my arms, Gabe." I hesitated and then
confessed the rest. "I stole her energy like the Protectors
do to Healers they hunt. I didn't mean to do it, but it happened."

"I know," Gabe whispered. "I can feel how your power
has changed." He didn't add to that, and I knew it didn't
matter to him, except that he worried with me about what
this might mean. "Can you feel me?" he asked, and I heard
the fear in that.

My fingers traced his shoulder blades and back, explor-
ing the muscles. "Feel you and smell you and taste you. All
senses accounted for." I opened my mind so he could hear
how I savored him and wanted him. "Do you doubt it?"

His arms tensed around me in a convulsive, relieved
hug. If this had been any other moment, I would have

found myself thoroughly kissed. "No. I'd say we're safe on that count." He sucked in a breath, obviously digging for control.

"I didn't lose my senses, but is it possible that I'm becoming immortal?" The thought of it terrified me. What if I healed Gabe's mortality only to become immortal myself?

"I don't know what you are, sweetheart. You defy definition."

We settled into silence again until I said, "Last night, I thought about killing Xavier and Alcais."

"You were defending yourself."

"No, I wanted revenge for what they did to me. To all of us." The hate that had poured through me terrified me. "I don't want to be like Franc, but that's what I'm becoming. Protectors killed my grandmother, and his bitterness changed him. I'm changing, too, Gabe, and sometimes I don't like what I see."

Gabe rolled to the side, easing his weight off me. "Remington, you could never be like him. You're angry at the hand that has been dealt to you, but I would be more worried about you if you weren't. Don't you think that I was pissed off when the Healers killed Sam and my parents?"

I lifted my head to see his expression. His eyes drooped with worry and sadness. "How did you get past that?" I asked, stroking a finger over his forehead to smooth the creases.

"Asher and Lottie. I had to take care of them. If I'd gone off and gotten myself killed, who would have looked after them?"

My thoughts turned to Lucy. Last night, I'd abandoned my sister with the others.

"She's fine. In fact, she was worried about you." I raised

my brows, and he admitted, "I checked on everyone after you fell asleep. It's not all on your shoulders. Don't you see? We're a family, the five of us. You're allowed to take a turn being the weak one, especially after what happened last night."

Last night, our family had lost another member. My mind spun with scenarios, trying to figure out if I could have done anything differently that might have saved her. No matter how I worked it, though, the end came out the same. Erin had made a choice to help her community and to help us, and she'd died saving my life. Maybe it had been out of guilt for bringing my grandfather's men to our house, but I didn't think that was it. Sometimes you made sacrifices for people you loved, and she'd been my friend. If things had been reversed, I would have made the same choice.

I sighed, the weary sound pulled out of me. "I'm sad, Gabe. I don't think I can stand losing anyone else, and I don't want this life for us. I don't want to spend my entire life looking over my shoulder."

"So we fight back," he said. "We put an end to this, once and for all."

He was right. There had to be a way to finish this, and get my father back. We couldn't do it alone, though. Thank God, we had the Phoenix and Seamus on our side. The thought of what we could do together energized me, and I tucked the grief away to be dealt with later.

I jumped out of bed, startling Gabe when I smacked him on the butt. "Get a move on, Gabriela. There are plans to be made."

"What plans?" he asked, sitting up.

I paused in the bathroom doorway. "I'm tired of my grandfather winning all the time. He's going to be sorry that he ever messed with me."

★　★　★

After showering, I left the bedroom on a mission. Last night I had been too overwhelmed to register much about the Phoenix, but it was time to get some questions answered. I thought about going to Seamus, but I didn't completely trust him. He wanted something from me, and people lied and manipulated to get what they wanted. His truth would always be colored by his desires. So I decided to go to the source instead.

In the hallway outside the bedroom, I paused, dropping my walls and listening with all of my senses. Gabe showered in the bathroom off our bedroom. Seamus and Sean were talking somewhere downstairs. Some of his men were scattered about the house, their tense voices indicating they were on alert. Lottie was in my sister's room, nagging her about sleeping in too late when she really was just checking on her. My sister argued back, but it sounded like she was grateful for the company because she didn't put a lot of effort into it. Another few seconds of listening, and I finally heard three women speaking in various accents. They had to be the Phoenix.

I entered the sitting room without knocking first. I thought they would have heard me coming, but all three women looked up in surprise at my noisy entrance.

"Hi," I said. I gave a small wave, and then felt like an idiot when they stared at me in silence. I tried again. "We didn't exactly get introduced last night. I'm Remy O'Malley."

The woman with the fire-engine-red hair rose from her seat on the sofa. She'd pulled her hair back in a retro bouffant ponytail that had a lot of height and about a can of hair spray holding it together.

"I'm Ursula Hitzig," she said.

"You're German?" I asked with surprise. For some rea-

son, I'd assumed that all of these women lived here. Hadn't
Seamus said he wanted me to join them? Ursula's thick accent reminded me of an exchange student I had gone to
school with in New York. Ursula was also younger than I
had expected. They all were. I thought they might be in
their early to mid-twenties.

Ursula smiled. "*Ja*. Yes." She pointed to the blond
woman who had exchanged last night's miniskirt and
combat boots with tight jeans and an oversized sweatshirt.
"That is Brita." She turned to the brunette woman in the
chic emerald-green silk dress. "And this is Edith."

She pronounced the last woman's name like *ai-ditt,* the
way my French teacher had once pronounced the famous
French singer's name.

"As in Edith Piaf?" I asked.

"Exactly," Edith answered. "My mother was a fan."

All three women approached me, but none of them
shook the hand I held out. I dropped it to my side, sens-
ing they all had their guards up. If they had mental walls,
we were alike in a lot of ways. After another round of awkward staring that threatened to turn it into an Olympic
sport, Ursula suggested we all sit. She and Brita almost
rushed the sofa, leaving Edith and me to take the armchairs. I was beginning to wonder if these women thought
I had the plague with the way they avoided contact.

"Thanks for the clothes," I said, with a wry smile.

When Gabe had carried me to our room last night,
clothes had been waiting for us on the bed. It hadn't occurred to me to ask, but I'd been grateful since my pajamas had been stained with my blood and Erin's. Likewise
Gabe's clothes had been stained, too. The jeans left for me
were a tad too short, leading me to believe they were Ursula's, and I'd rolled the cuffs to hide that fact. The T-shirt,
on the other hand, had to be Brita's. She seemed to be the

most likely candidate for the blue T-shirt with the rainy cloud that proclaimed, *"I'm peeing."* Gabe had busted a gut laughing when I'd come out of the bathroom wearing it.

Ursula nodded, and Brita's lip curled, confirming my suspicion.

I crossed my legs and clasped my fingers around my raised knee. "So. You're all Phoenix."

*Subtle, Remy. Really freaking subtle.*

"Not exactly," Ursula said, but she didn't elaborate.

*I'll never learn anything at this rate.* Frustrated, I rocked in my seat and tossed around for an opening.

"We are very sorry about your friend." Edith pinned me with a pitying look that made me want to cry all over again. "She was a Healer, *non?*"

"No. I mean, yes. Erin saved my life. And Asher's. She was a good friend. Do you know . . ." I gulped. I wanted to ask if they'd ever experienced what I had with Erin at the end, but I struggled to find the words.

Brita propped her legs on the table, displaying the scuffed-up combat boots she wore with her torn-up jeans. Her loud, exaggerated sigh sliced through the tension in the room. "Somebody kill me already," she muttered in an American accent that I couldn't place.

"Brita!" Ursula admonished her.

The woman scowled, tossing her blond hair. "What? Like you don't have a thousand questions for her? And you know she's dying to interrogate us. Aren't you?" she challenged me.

I nodded.

"So spit it out," Brita said. "Interrogate away."

My words gushed out, tumbling over each other. "How do your powers work? Do you absorb the injuries you heal? How do you affect the Protectors here? Do you feel anything around other Healers? Are you immor—"

"Whoa," Brita said, holding up a hand with short black

fingernails. "How about we take it one question at a time?"

Ursula shoved Brita's legs off the table and ignored the other woman's glare. "We can heal people with our touch, and we do absorb their injuries. You, too?"

I nodded with relief, glad to hear of another similarity. I'd always thought of myself as a freak, but here were three women like me.

Edith crossed her long, elegant legs. "It's unpleasant at best, painful at worst. Brita refuses to heal broken bones."

Brita scowled. "It freaks me out when my bones break, and it takes too long to heal them. Not to mention how brutal the pain is. I'd rather take on cancer any day."

A sigh hissed out of me. They could cure cancer. The Healers in Franc's community had been stunned that I could heal serious diseases and illnesses, but these women could do it, too.

"Do you have to imagine the injuries to heal them?" I asked. "I have to . . . picture them. I don't know . . . see them in my mind somehow."

Ursula shook her head. "No. The ones like us that came before taught us how to direct our power. Think of the power like an electric current."

Brita sat forward. "Yeah. The Protectors pull the current toward them, which is why they can steal energy from Healers. The Healers push the energy away, usually into another body, where it can be used to heal what is broken. Give-and-take. Ebb-and-flow. The energy never goes away. It's just handled differently."

My mother had given a similar explanation once about Healers and Protectors. "Which one are we more like?" I asked.

Edith smiled and held up her hands. "We are neither and both. We push and pull power. It is chaotic and beautiful."

Chaos described last night perfectly. I'd had no control over my abilities, and being out of control scared the hell out of me. I ran a hand through my hair, gathering my thoughts. "But, Edith, what about the people around us? Aren't we a danger to them?"

"Ah! You worry about your man and the pain you cause him," she guessed. "Don't worry so much. We use our shields, they use their shields, and they are safe."

"But don't they become mortal around you?" I asked.

Brita crossed her arms. "Only if we're not careful with our shields. Or if one of our kind is careless enough to bond with one of them." She noticed my expression, and her face lit up with a delighted smile. "Don't tell me you've gone and bonded to that beautiful man you brought here?"

I winced. "Both of the beautiful men actually, though my bond with Asher is broken."

Brita's mouth dropped open. "No freaking way. Those boys are hot. I don't know if I should be jealous or pity you." She smacked her lips with a dreamy look on her face.

I scowled, wondering if she was imagining Gabe. "Frankly, it hasn't been a lot of fun. They could both read my mind at one point." I decided to change the subject because I did not want to dig into that history. "Haven't any of you bonded? Could they read your mind?" I asked.

Ursula pointed at Edith. "She's the only one. Brita and I have not met someone we cared about like that. Most of the men here are like family. Brothers, uncles. The idea of kissing them . . ." She shuddered.

Well then. If I'd needed more proof that my emotions had controlled my bonds with Gabe and Asher, here it was. Not that I had doubted it, but it would have been nice to have another reason behind all the pain I'd caused.

Edith's brown eyes shone. "My husband, Sean, is somewhere in the house. I believe you have met him. He spoke highly of you."

I almost jumped out of my seat at that revelation. "Sean? Yea high?" I waved a hand way above my head. "Sean the Protector?"

"*Oui*. My teddy bear."

Brita made a gagging sound, and I almost wanted to join her. If Gabe tried a pet name like that on me, I'd have to kneecap him. I'd take "Remington" any day over "teddy bear" or "schnookums."

"Edith, is he becoming mortal?"

She hesitated a moment and then nodded with some regret. "He does not care." Her elegant shrug said that she still worried. "We keep our guard up to slow it, but eventually that won't matter. We knew it would happen, and he is content."

"What about you? Do his powers change you?" Really I wanted to know if she was becoming immortal. The question had hovered over my head like an ax since my proximity to the Protectors had begun to change me. What could come of a relationship where one person would never age?

Edith reached over and almost touched my hand before she pulled back, seeming to think better of the gesture. "We are not immortal. We grow old like every other human."

I closed my eyes, grateful for that at least. Gabe would become mortal, but we would age together.

Then Edith added, "But, Remy, you are no longer like us."

My eyes flew open, and I stared at her in confusion.

She sighed, the sound of it heavy with regret. "Last night, the way you healed your man, that is a gift that few of us have. It only happens when one of us takes the life force of a Healer. Your friend, *non*?"

I nodded, my heart thudding with dread as I tried to decipher what she was telling me. "It was an accident. She died while I was trying to save her." I swiped a hand over eyes that felt as dry and gritty as a desert. Maybe I'd finally run out of tears, because this latest revelation threatened to break me but I didn't cry. "If I'm not a Healer or a Protector, then what am I?"

She shrugged. "You are none of those things and all of them. My dear, you are a Phoenix."

"But you just said that I'm not like you . . ." I said in confusion.

"We are not Phoenix."

Her short answer frustrated me, and it must have shown on my face.

Brita snorted. "Stop speaking in riddles, Edith, and give the girl a damned answer. Can't you see you're making it worse?"

Edith glared at Brita before she continued. "We are born a balance of Healer and Protector. When we bond with a Protector, the balance is thrown off. Our powers increase because of what we take from them. But you . . . you have taken from another—a Healer. You must find balance again."

Her words made no sense to me. How could you balance what you couldn't control?

"Does this mean I'll become immortal?" I asked, fear dropping my voice low.

Edith shook her head. "I wish I could help you, but I've never met a Phoenix."

"Ah, Remy! I have been looking for you."

Seamus had entered the room, cutting my interrogation short. I rose to meet him, and his grave look warned me that more storms were ahead. Lucy, Lottie, Gabe, and Asher followed him into the room with Sean bringing up the rear, and I could see that he'd gathered them, either to give us the bad news at once or in hopes that the others would temper my reaction to whatever he had to say. Seamus avoided my gaze when he spoke again, and I guessed it was the latter.

"I am sorry about your father, but you understand we can't possibly go forward with our plans to retrieve him now after last night. In truth, we think it best if we leave London immediately."

His words didn't surprise me exactly. I'd had some time to think through things in the shower this morning, and I'd guessed this might be his tactic. Still, I asked, "Why?"

He met my gaze with conviction. "These women must be protected. The O'Malleys are sworn to watch over them. Watch over you, if you would allow it. One man's life is not more important than that."

Once, I might have wished for someone to save me and keep me safe. But these last months had tested me, and now things had reversed. Others depended on me, and I wouldn't let them down.

I speared Seamus with a direct look. "It is to me when that man is my father." I let my gaze encompass the rest of the people in the room. Edith, Brita, and Ursula watched me with varying degrees of curiosity. "We were given these powers for a reason. I will not hide or cower from men like my grandfather. Please help me."

Sean wore a tiny smile as he wrapped an arm around Edith's waist. Gabe, Asher, Lottie, and Lucy surrounded me in a half moon at my back, each of them offering silent support. That said a lot about how far we'd come together. Gabe's fingers twined with mine, and I felt that surge of love grounding me again. He smiled to encourage me, and I squeezed his fingers.

My attention returned to Seamus, and the grim look on his face somehow calmed me further. He'd kept the O'Malleys and these women hidden for years because they had the potential to become Phoenix. I respected him for that, but there was a difference between regrouping in the trenches and hiding in them like a coward.

"It would be senseless to fight them," he insisted. "You must see that. Tell her," he said to Gabe and the others.

My friends didn't say a word, and Seamus cursed.

"I'm sorry," I told him in a softer voice. "I get that you went into hiding to save what was left of the O'Malleys and to protect women like us." I gestured from me to Edith, Brita, and Ursula. "But there comes a point when you have to take a stand. Last night, they attacked my family, and they killed another person we cared about. We will not walk away from that. I hope you'll join us, and God knows we could use the help. But if you can't get on board, well, then . . . get out of our way. We *are* going to get my father back, and we're going to show Franc and the Morrisseys and anyone else who's watching that we'll fight back if they try to destroy us."

Lucy found my free hand and gripped it. Asher had his arm around Lottie's shoulder, and she touched Gabe's arm. His fingers pressed mine again. We were all connected somehow, the five of us. My found family stood together as a united front, willing to climb deeper into hell if it meant putting an end to the fear and agony of these last months. And we would do it together, watching each other's backs the whole way.

Silence stretched on as if Seamus hoped the ticking of the seconds would change our minds. When a full minute had gone by, I turned on my heel, and our group moved as one toward the door.

"Wait!" Seamus shouted. I paused and glanced back over my shoulder to find him studying me with grudging respect. "Have it your way then. I cannot speak for all of my men, but you have my aid if you wish it."

"And mine." Sean stepped forward, his smile wider and almost proud.

One by one, Brita, Edith, and Ursula volunteered, too. A lump formed in my throat that these people I didn't know would fight alongside us.

Seamus's blue eyes blazed at me with challenge. "You have us, but I still say we cannot go forward with our original plan. I don't suppose you have a Plan B."

I shared a quick glance with Gabe, and he gave me an encouraging nod. "As a matter of fact, we do."

# CHAPTER TWENTY-EIGHT

"*H*ello." My grandfather answered his phone on the third ring.

I took a deep breath. "Hello, Franc."

"Remy? This is a happy surprise," he said.

He didn't sound warm or jovial like he had the last time I'd called, but his calm voice gave nothing away about his true feelings. My heart fluttered in a little shock of fear, and sweat broke out on my forehead. A cowardly part of me had hoped that I would get a recording, but it was too late for that now. The only way forward was through it. I pictured Laura and Erin, both of them gone because of my grandfather's ambition. That was enough to refortify my waning courage.

"Is it a surprise?" I asked, my voice caustic with bitter sadness. "I would have thought this is what you wanted."

"What exactly is *this*?" he asked. "The last time you called you had an ulterior motive."

*There*, I thought. He sounded angry, the edge of it cutting through his calm manner. Anger clouded things, and that was a good thing for our side. "*This* is me giving up," I said.

I heard him breathing over the line and nothing else for several long seconds. "Why now?" he finally asked.

"I'm tired, Franc. Tired of running and watching the

people I care about die. Last night with Erin . . ." My voice broke, and the grief was real, clogging my throat and making it ache with the pressure of what I held back. "I can't watch another person die for me. I'm through fighting you."

"What do you want?" he asked. He tried to hide excitement behind skepticism, but I could hear it anyway.

"I'll give myself up on two conditions. You let my father go, and you don't bother my friends or family again."

"I can't promise that," he said immediately.

My palms had grown damp with sweat, and I rubbed them on my jeans. Franc thought he had all the power and would push me as far as I would let him. I had to make him believe that I wouldn't bend on this. I imagined Gabe calling me Remington the Fierce, and that's who I was when I said, "Then we have nothing to discuss. Good luck finding me the next time."

I waited, pretending I would hang it up. A few seconds later, Franc called my name. "What?" I asked.

"I'll see what I can do. The Morrisseys may not agree to this."

My grandfather's voice sounded sincere, but I didn't believe him. "Not good enough. If I'm going to turn myself over to you, then I want guarantees. You bring my father, and I'll bring my sister. I'll go home with you, and you let my father go with Lucy."

"You're more powerful than I am. You don't honestly believe that I'm going to come alone?" he asked.

I'd known this would be a sticking point and was prepared to counter. "So bring Xavier and Mark, but that's it. Think about it, Franc. If you bring the Morrisseys, what's to stop them from keeping me for themselves?"

There was another pause as he considered his options, but my grandfather knew I was right. The rumor was that Franc had promised to give me to the Morrisseys in exchange for their help, but I'd guessed all along that he intended to double-cross them. He hated them, and my grandfather had no compunction about betraying the people he loved let alone those he loathed.

Eventually, Franc caved. "Fine. Shall we come to you?"

"No," I said. "We meet in public."

"It sounds like you don't trust me, granddaughter." He sounded amused by that, and bile sloshed in my stomach.

I struggled to tamp my emotions down. *Stay on plan, girl.* "Let's meet in the Reading Room at the British Museum. Tonight at six."

"Okay," he agreed. He waited one, two beats and then added in a dangerous voice, "But Remy, I have a condition of my own."

I closed my eyes and waited.

"You won't fight me anymore." His whisper slid over me, promising and threatening at the same time. "You will do everything that is asked of you. If I give you to a Protector, you will give him what he wants. Do you understand?"

He would let them use me over and over again. The horror of what I imagined was there in my voice. "You're a monster, Franc. My mother would be sick if she knew what you'd become."

"Your mother was weak," he snapped in a rage. "You will do what I ask, or I will kill your father. I'm tired of these games."

"Okay," I said, sounding beaten. "You have my word. As long as my father is there, I'll do whatever you tell me."

"Good. It's not going to be so bad, granddaughter. You'll be helping us win the war."

A war that existed only in his mind. "Good-bye, Franc."

"No. Not good-bye. I'll be seeing you, Remy."

He hung up, and I struggled to control my emotions. His soul had twisted into something that was hardly human anymore. What would my grandmother think of what he'd become in her name?

"Remy?" Asher asked from the seat beside me.

My stomach knotted and heaved.

"Stop the car!" I shouted.

Sean abruptly pulled over on the bridge, ignoring the horns sounding behind him. I jumped out, running to the ledge that kept foot traffic from falling into the water below. I gripped the stone with my free hand, feeling the weather-smoothed edge of it beneath my fingers as I bent over to stare at the water below. I thought I would be sick, but nothing came out when I heaved. When I could breathe normally, I pulled back my arm and pitched the phone as far as I could into the river below. Then I climbed back into the car, and Sean pulled away from the curb as if nothing had happened. Except I'd had the phone on speaker, and Seamus, Sean, and Asher had all heard how willing my grandfather was to use me.

"You okay?" Asher asked.

I nodded. Sean had driven us around the city while I spoke to my grandfather. It had been part of the plan to get rid of the phone since we expected Franc to trace the call, but Asher knew our stop had been about more than that. I fought back a fresh wave of tears. The car fell silent again.

We passed the Wobbly Bridge, and I wished I could toss my pain away as easily as I had the phone. I knew what my grandfather was and it still hurt that he could plan to use me so callously. I sniffed, and a handkerchief suddenly appeared in front of me.

Sean held it out behind his head, and I met his eyes in the rearview mirror. "Well and now, I have to say that your grandfather is an arsehole," he announced.

"Jesus, Mary, and Joseph, Sean. Do you have no tact?" Seamus said.

I laughed and took the handkerchief. "No, he's right. Franc is an arsehole."

In the front passenger seat, Seamus twisted around to ask, "Do you really think he'll leave the Morriseys behind?"

"Yes," I said. "They don't fit with his plans, but he's not coming alone. Mark and Xavier will be the least of our worries."

Seamus nodded. "We'll be ready for that."

He turned around, and Asher said under his breath, "Are you sure this plan is going to work?"

Gabe had looked surprised when I'd asked if Asher could accompany me on this ride, but he'd agreed without asking any questions. He trusted me, and that was enough for him. Asher had seemed surprised, too, but explanations would come soon enough.

To answer his question, I whispered, "Well, it's better than the plan Gabe and I had when we rescued you, and we made it out of that okay, didn't we?"

He smiled down at me. "Does that mean you plan to crash a car through the museum?"

Sean overheard that, and his eyes met mine in the rearview mirror again. I smiled innocently. To Asher, I said, "Ha, ha."

Sometime later we arrived back at the O'Malley house. Sean and Seamus exited the car, but I stopped Asher before he could follow them.

"Can I talk to you for a minute?"

A brief flicker of pain whispered through his eyes, but he hid it quickly. "Sure. What is it?"

I hadn't told Gabe about this, but it was the reason that I'd wanted Asher to go in his place.

I hitched a leg up on the seat so I could turn to face him. "I need to ask you something and you're going to hate it and it's completely unfair to you and I'm so sorry, but there's nobody else I could trust with this."

"What, Remy?" he asked with a concerned frown. "You know you can tell me anything."

The idea had come to me after I'd left the Phoenix in the sitting room this morning. It might not work, but it was all I had to cling to. I met Asher's green eyes, letting him see all the hope in mine and then I leapt. "I need your help. I think I know how I can be free of all of this, but I can't do it alone."

"Whatever you need. I'm in," he said without hesitation.

Relief flooded through me that I wouldn't have to convince him to do this. "Okay, here's what we're going to do."

At exactly 5:46 P.M. that night, I walked into the Great Court at the British Museum with Lucy at my side. My sister's head tipped back as she stared upward, and I followed her gaze. I had never been to the museum, but it had been Lottie's idea to meet here. It was public, but it would offer places for our people to blend in and avenues for escape. We'd walked through the floor plans, but that wasn't the same as seeing it in person. The Great Court had a glass and steel roof, and in the center of the court was a round, cream-colored building. Two large staircases wound up each side to gain entrance to the Reading Room.

"We're all in place, Remy," Gabe said. Seamus had given us tiny earpieces to communicate with each other. It was the next best thing to having Gabe beside me. He injected a note of humor in his voice as he asked, "Why did I agree to this plan again?"

I turned my head, acting as if I spoke to my sister as we

walked across the Great Court. "Because you think it's brilliant."

"Right," he said. "That must have been it."

Lucy shook her head at our nervous banter, and I led the way to the staircase on the right.

"I wish you didn't have to be here, Lucy." We'd tried to think of another way to show Franc that I was naïve, but this had been the biggest gesture I could have made. At the very least, Franc would believe he could use her against me.

"I know," she answered. Her voice only shook a little, and I wished I could hug her.

Swarms of people surrounded us as we climbed, and it was difficult to pick out one face in the crowd. My heart skipped along at an urgent pace, and I gripped Lucy's arm, reminding myself that we weren't alone. Somewhere behind us, Sean and another man followed at a distance in case Franc had decided to overtake us on our way in. I didn't look for them, but I was relieved to know they were there.

Inside the Reading Room, my gaze was once more drawn upward to the blue, cream, and gold papier-mâché-domed ceiling. Bookshelves lined the curved walls on three floors of the round building. On the bottom floor, tables and desks had been arranged for visitors to read at their leisure. The grandeur of it was at odds with our purpose for being here.

We made our way to the bottom floor, where tourists took pictures and some locals sat at the tables with books propped open in front of them. Right away I spotted Franc sitting alone on one side of a long table. Stationed mere feet behind him, Xavier and Mark sat like two vultures waiting to pick apart a carcass. They had chosen a spot well away from anyone who might overhear our conversation.

My father was nowhere in sight, but then we'd expected that. I just prayed he was still alive. With one last shared glance with Lucy, I pushed her toward the front desk, well away from my grandfather and his men. Then I touched the phone in my pocket, hitting the speed dial for a number that would be our insurance. That was when Franc spotted me. A satisfied smile slanted across his face, and I could see his thoughts flashing across his face. *Poor naïve Remy, falling for my tricks again. See how I'm going to use her.* He thought he had me trapped. Duped.

And that was going to be his downfall.

# CHAPTER TWENTY-NINE

*I* squared my shoulders and strode forward. My grandfather watched my approach, and something new
flared in his eyes when he studied my face. Caution,
maybe.

Through the earpiece, Gabe warned, "Remy, pull back
on the ferocity. You look like you're going to kill the man
as soon as you're close enough to wrap your hands around
his neck."

That was the opposite of what we wanted Franc to
think. A little anger would fly and would even be believ-
able, but my grandfather had to see me as beaten. So worn
out and out of options that I would deal with him. I lowered my gaze to the floor and slumped my shoulders. My
gait slowed as if I dreaded nearing him. It helped that I
wasn't alone in this confrontation. We hadn't known how
many people Franc would bring, and his group could easily outnumber our reinforcements: Gabe, Asher, Lottie,
Lucy, Seamus, Sean, Edith, Brita, Ursula, and Seamus's
Protectors. Some of Seamus's Protectors occupied nearby
tables or blended with the crowd. Franc had no idea because he didn't know the O'Malleys or the potential
Phoenix existed.

Gabe, Asher, and Lottie hid out of sight since they could
be identified, but I could feel them watching over me and

that gave me courage. Still, when I looked up, all traces of emotion had been smoothed away except defeat. My heart beat frantically in my chest when I slid into the seat across from my grandfather.

We stared at each other, taking in the differences that the last months had made. Franc's shock of white hair had been trimmed close to his head, and he'd grown a beard. The white and gray whiskers loaned him a doting grandfather kind of appeal, and his brown eyes reminded me of my mother for one painful moment. It was his wide shoulders and hulking height that prompted me to remember that he was a threat and not the gentle giant he appeared. Words like *gentle* and *doting* didn't describe the kind of man he was. For a moment, my anger threatened to resurface. *Remember the plan, Remy. First, get proof of life. The whole plan is pointless if my father is dead.*

It hurt to even think that word, and that pain echoed in my voice. "Where's my father, Franc? You agreed to bring him."

My grandfather paused in his examination of my features, and I wondered what changes he'd noticed in me. Grief had acted like waves smoothing glass; sometimes I felt worn down to nothing. Other times, anger made me feel like glass before the water could soften the jagged edges. I threw one quick glance at Lucy to check on her. My sister looked scared but sturdy as she watched us, and I'd never been more proud of her.

Franc raised one gray brow, silently mocking me. He thought that he could push me around and I wouldn't fight back.

I stood. "You didn't keep up your end of the bargain. Deal's off. We're out of here."

He laughed with a twisted kind of affection. "You haven't changed, I see. Sit down." I ignored his command. All amusement fled from his face, and my pulse sped up at the dangerous look in his eyes. He repeated, "Sit down," in a soft voice.

Despite myself, I dropped into my chair with a thud that shuddered up my backbone.

"Remy, let's get a few things straight. You're not in a position to bargain here. You will walk out of this place with us, and you're going to do it without calling any attention to us. Do you know why?"

A trickle of sweat slid down my back, my terror palpable as I shook my head.

My grandfather produced a phone from his coat pocket, pressed a few buttons on the screen, and then pushed it across the table. The phone's screen showed a video feed. The camera tilted, panning indiscriminate shadows and light in a dizzying manner. Then Franc said, "Show Remy's father," and the camera moved up and stilled on a face.

My heart crashed to my stomach when I glimpsed my father for the first time in six months. I choked and reached for the phone to get a closer view, but Franc gripped my wrist.

"Calm down, or I take the phone away," Franc warned, glancing around to ensure I hadn't drawn attention to us. Nobody seemed to have noticed my outburst.

I bit my lip and nodded. Franc removed his hand, and my gaze slammed back to my father. They had tortured him. Both of his eyes had swollen shut, blood crusted at the corner of his mouth, and bruises of varying colors mottled the skin that I could see. Yellow, green, purple, red, pink. The colors meant he had been beaten so often that new bruises layered over the old ones. What kind of pain had he endured? Acid swished in my stomach, and I swallowed.

"Dad," I said, my voice cracking on the word.

My father's head turned in different directions as if to determine where my voice came from. "Remy? Is that you?"

"It's me, Dad. I'm here."

"Thank God you're alive," he said hoarsely. "Is your sister with you? And Laura?"

That last question almost stole my ability to speak, but I pushed the words out of lips that felt swollen. "We're safe, Dad."

I couldn't tell him about Laura. Not like this. I glanced over my shoulder and met my sister's worried stare. My lips trembled, and I wanted to run to her and celebrate because our father really was alive.

A hand touched my cheek, and I flinched. Franc tugged my face back toward him, and I wanted to punish him for putting his hands on me. He assumed that I wouldn't use my powers, and the arrogance made me want to show him how wrong he was. My father's battered face flashed in my mind, and I shoved my rage down.

"I know you won't believe me, but I never intended to hurt you," Franc said. "I want us to be a family. I love you, Remy."

He swiped a thumb across my wet cheek, and his brows lowered in sorrow. I could almost believe he meant it if I didn't know the truth about him. Except I knew what he was capable of. One quick glance at my father's face proved it.

"Can you tell where they're keeping Ben?" Asher asked over the com.

There were no clues in the small amount of background I could see behind my father. I snatched the phone off the table. "Where are you, Dad?" I asked in a rush.

My grandfather eyes narrowed, and he spoke to the person on the other end of the line. "Hang up the phone, Alcais."

*Alcais.* We'd been sure he would appear.

Before Erin's brother could comply, my father said, "A parking garage. Franc left here about thirty minutes ag—"

The call disconnected. I shivered at the promise of retribution that crossed my grandfather's face.

"The Bloomsbury Square Car Park is the closest public garage," Gabe said. He sounded like he was running. "We're on our way there now. Seamus says there are seven levels, and this may take a while. You need to stall your grandfather."

"I'm not going anywhere until you tell me where my father is," I said in a shaky voice.

Gabe understood the double message. "Got it. Hang in there. Asher is there if you need him."

"Do what I ask, and I'll take you to him," Franc said.

"If you didn't plan to keep up your end of the deal, why bring my father with you?"

Franc shrugged, and I guessed, "It's the Morrisseys. You promised them they could have me. You plan to betray them, and you can't go back there now."

At least, that was what I'd thought would happen. It had been the biggest gamble in this plan, but I'd been sure that Franc wouldn't hand me over to the Morrisseys. It would be giving up his greatest asset, and he would never do that. Once he had me, he would have to get the hell out of London, and what better way to control me than to threaten my father?

"You're afraid of the Morrisseys," I said. "You're afraid of what they'll do to you when they find out that you've double-crossed them."

Franc folded his hands, and he almost looked tired. "Stop fighting me, Remy. You'll only make things worse for you and your sister. Mark, go get the girl," he ordered.

Mark started forward, and then drew to a halt. "Where is she?"

Franc's gaze flicked over my shoulder, and he frowned. Mark and Xavier twisted about to scan the room. I could have told them it was useless. The second we had learned my father's location, Lucy had run. Her presence had only been necessary to convince my grandfather that he was in control of this meeting, and now it was up to me to stall things until my friends found my father.

The corners of Franc's mouth tightened in a tense scowl. "Where is she?" he asked me.

*In a car with Lottie getting the hell away from here.* I shrugged.

A hand landed on my shoulder, the hold grinding the delicate bones in my collarbone together. I winced, and Xavier said, "Time to go. We're beginning to draw attention."

My grandfather nodded and rose. I couldn't refuse to go with them without raising their suspicions. They had my father and, as far as they knew, I was alone. The best I could do would be to slow our progress to the garage. So I stood and the four of us walked toward the exit. Xavier walked beside me, his arm thrown across my shoulders in a bruising grip, while Franc led the way and Mark followed us.

"Six people just got up to follow the four of you," Asher warned from his hiding spot. "All Protectors, I think. I have to change locations so they don't spot me. Go ahead and lead the way to the car park. We'll overtake them there once Gabe finds your father. I'll be right behind you."

That meant that I would be on my own for the walk to the garage. Me against eight Protectors and my grandfather. The odds sucked. *Stay calm, Remy.*

As we crossed the Grand Salon, Xavier said, "Your grandfather thinks you're naïve, but I know better." He sent me a sidelong glance. "You planned to get your sister out of here."

I gave him a vague look. "I don't know what you're talking about."

His grip on my shoulder tightened, but I met his glance defiantly, refusing to cry out. "I don't believe you," he said slowly. "You have a plan. I just wonder how many steps you are ahead of him." He tilted his head at my grand-father's back. Then he spoke over his shoulder to Mark. "I'm betting she has backup. Keep an eye out for anyone following us."

I hoped everyone heard that command through the com and stayed hidden.

Our odd group reached the sidewalk outside the British Museum. My grandfather shifted to walk at my side, and I prayed my hair still hid the earpiece I wore. I fought against the urge to fidget.

"You told your sister to run if your father wasn't with us," Franc said. It wasn't a question, and I wondered if he'd heard Xavier. It didn't make sense to deny it any longer.

I stared straight ahead. "You broke your side of the deal, so I broke mine. Did you really think that I would let you get your hands on her after what you did to me?"

My grandfather almost looked proud.

"You don't need her, you know. She's powerless," I added.

Franc nodded like I'd confirmed what he already knew. "So your father said after we tortured him."

His words had their desired effect. A fresh wave of agony flooded through me as I imagined what they had done to my father in the last six months, and I stumbled. Only Xavier's hold on me kept me moving forward.

"I hate you," I told my grandfather in a bleak voice.

For a moment, his eyes clouded like my words pained him, but then he gave a slight nod. "I can live with that."

We continued in silence, and soon I saw a sign that read BLOOMSBURY SQUARE CAR PARK. Panic swelled in my chest. *Not yet! I haven't heard from Gabe.*

I scrambled to find a way to stall my grandfather and latched on to a new topic. "You know my grandmother's ancestors started the war between the Protectors and the Healers."

"What are you talking about?"

"Did she ever mention a Healer named Camille Lovellette?"

His eyes widened, and he paused outside the car park entrance like I'd hoped. "Her ancestor. Did your mother tell you this?"

I ignored his question. "Camille married a guy named Martin Dubois in 1853. They had a daughter named—"

"Elizabeth," he finished. "She was a powerful Healer by all accounts."

"Did you know that she abused her power? Protectors died because of Elizabeth, and they finally rose up against her and the others like her."

"Are you saying that you agree with how the Protectors slaughtered the Healers?" Franc asked in a furious voice.

I shook my head, answering truthfully. "No, but I understand why it happened. The Healers abused the Protectors. The Protectors turned on the Healers. And before that, the Healers turned on the ones like me descended from both bloodlines." I held out both hands, palms up. "And now you want to bring war to the Protectors' doorstep again. Where does it end, Franc? How many people have to die?"

Part of me hoped that he could see reason. My upbringing had taught me an inescapable lesson. Violence just brought more violence in an unending cycle. If Franc killed the Protectors, they would simply turn the tables on him.

"It ends when I get what I want," he said. With Xavier and Mark and who knew who else in earshot, Franc didn't dare add that what he wanted was every Protector dead.

It was a dangerous game that he was playing, intending to double-cross these men when they could kill him with a flick of a wrist. I'd warn them, but they'd never believe me.

"No matter who gets hurt?" I challenged.

"Yes," my grandfather answered simply. He turned away, entering the car park, and Xavier shoved me after him.

Franc's answer prodded a fire that flared to life in my belly. "What about Erin? Alcais killed her. Didn't she matter?"

He looked away, and for a moment, I thought it was grief that I was seeing. Except when he turned to face me again, he shrugged. "There are casualties in every war."

Erin had died, and he dismissed her as if she were a stranger. She'd once looked up to him, trusted him to protect her. The same way his entire community believed in him. "And the Healers like Yvette that you've sacrificed to the Protectors? Were they just casualties, too?"

"Yes," he said, without a hint of apology. "I'm doing what I have to."

I opened my mouth to respond, but Gabe's voice suddenly blasted in my ear. "Remy, Alcais ran away when he saw us. We've got your dad, sweetheart. Get the hell out of there."

His announcement blew through my defenses and uncoiled the knot in my stomach. My chin dropped my chin to my chest as I struggled to contain my emotions. It was impossible, though. For the first time in six months, my father and sister were safe. Tears freely fell, and I didn't bother to hide them as I climbed into an elevator with Franc and six Protectors.

"Let's go!" Franc snapped when the elevator doors opened on another deserted level. We approached a black car with tinted windows. Gabe and the others were nowhere in sight. I spared a thought to wonder what they had done with Alcais when they took my father from him. Franc reached for a door handle, but I stopped. Xavier tried to push me forward, but I stood my ground as the other Protectors encircled me.

"Wait," I said in a calm voice. "I have something to show you."

"Remy?" Gabe asked. I ignored him.

My grandfather's brows drew together in confusion, and I reached into my coat pocket. I grasped the mobile phone, hit speaker, and held it up between us. The lit screen showed a counter ticking away the time that the call had been connected. The caller ID read *Erin's House*.

Franc swiped the phone from my hand. "Who's there?" he asked cautiously. I could see him trying to figure out what the person might have heard and what kind of damage it might have caused.

There was a long pause, and then Erin's mother whispered, "You bastard."

The helpless look on my grandfather's face satisfied a dark need for revenge. Only Asher knew about this part of the plan. *Protect the Healers.* In the end, I hadn't been 100 percent sure that Seamus would be on my side—he was a Protector, after all, and Protectors had spent a century killing Healers. Maybe that wasn't fair, but I didn't know Seamus well, and I'd learned that you had to choose whom you trusted with great care and prejudice.

"Remy said you betrayed us, and I called her a liar. But it was you all along. Everything that happened . . . The people who died. My daughter. Oh God, my daughter."

Dorthea's voice cracked on an agonized whimper, and her grief tumbled over me. I wished things could be different, and that I'd warned them sooner. Maybe Erin would be alive if I'd found a way to convince them. I guessed that Dorthea would blame me, too, and I thought she would probably blame herself. She'd put her trust in the wrong people, and it had cost her both children.

"Dorthea, they didn't die in vain," my grandfather pleaded. "This is a war we are fighting, and some people must be sacrificed. As much as it hurts."

As I listened to Franc, it struck me that the danger of a man like him was in his passion. His voice rang with sincerity. He believed in his cause as crazy as it was. Who knew how it affected Dorthea?

Then Franc added, "Ask Alcais. He'll explain it to you so you'll understand. Your son understands."

A movement on the other side of the car caught my attention. A shadow moved, and I realized Alcais hadn't run away after all.

Dorthea made a choking sound. "I heard what you said about him. You've turned my son into a monster like you."

"Dorthea, please—"

"No!" she shouted. "Not another word. You're finished with the Healers, Franc. I'm going to tell everyone what you've done, and we're going to leave this place. If you try to find us, I'll kill you myself. And you tell my son . . ." She took a deep breath. "Tell Alcais that he's dead to me."

She hung up, and two things happened. Alcais stepped out of the shadows, and my cheek exploded when Franc struck me with my phone. I fell to my knees on the concrete, raising a hand to the already bleeding gash.

"Remy?" Gabe shouted, and I could hear the panic in his voice. "Please, get out of there! Somebody help her!" When I didn't answer, he continued to shout for the others to get to me.

Once, fear would have swallowed me, but I had changed. I was not that girl who had trembled before Dean. I would survive this, too. I dropped my hand to my side and gazed up at my grandfather. Whatever he saw in my expression, he took a step back, and then scowled at his own reaction.

My steady voice echoed in the parking lot. "I'm just a stupid girl. That's what you thought, right? Easy to control, and easier to trick." I shook my head in disgust. "I knew you wouldn't bring my father here. Tell him, Alcais."

My grandfather watched Alcais approach, and ran to yank open the car door. Shock crossed his face when he found the interior empty, and he stared at Alcais with accusation. The boy wore a shattered expression, but I didn't pity him. He'd killed his sister, and now he couldn't return to his home. He'd made his decisions.

I rose to my feet, dropping my mental guard and flexing my power as I stood. I sensed Xavier and Mark retreating a few steps behind me, their fear of me tangible. The remaining six Protectors frowned as the surge of my energy caused them pain, but they didn't have the sense to back away.

"You lose, Franc. You have nothing. You are nothing. And this war is over."

His shoulders tensed, and he swung about in slow motion, pulling a knife from his pocket. "No, Remy," he breathed. "It won't ever be over for you. You may have rescued your father, but I'll find him and your sister. And when I do, I'm going to make you watch as I destroy them. You'll never escape me."

I'd never been hated with such an intense fire. The heat burned me from where I stood, and I knew that he was right. This would never be over because he had nothing to live for but his vendetta. He loved no one, and I suspected that the best part of him had died along with my grandmother.

"Let it go, Franc," I said. "Please. Before it's too late."

He threw back his head and laughed. "What do you

think you're going to do? It's you against all of us. You're alone."

"No, she's not," Asher said.

His voice sounded in my ear and echoed around me. I glanced over my shoulder and there they were: Asher, Edith, Ursula, Sean, and four of the Protectors who had watched over Lucy and me at the museum. They had come out of the stairwell instead of the elevator, and they spread out, slowly closing in on us.

I shared a glance with Asher. *Are you ready to do this?* He could no longer hear my thoughts, but he didn't have to. He knew me better than most, and he nodded in answer. We had to put on a good show for Franc and the others, or they would never leave my family alone.

Balancing on the balls of my feet, I turned to face my grandfather. My plan hinged on my grandfather's arrogance and his belief that I would sacrifice anything in my desperation to have some kind of family. But what if I was wrong? My fingers curled into fists, and I invaded his space, coming within inches of him, so that I had to peer up at him. It made me sick to get so close. "Last chance, Franc. Walk away or die. You choose."

For a moment, fear yawned across his face. Then my grandfather smirked as I'd guessed he would, and he stared into my eyes. "You won't kill me. Your heart makes you weak and in the end, you'll lose."

And there it was—his certainty that he knew me. He understood better than most that I could flip the pain back on him and still his knife slid between my ribs, slicing through skin and tissue with a wet sound. *Stupid man.* The pain slammed into me, and I sucked in a breath. Around us, the garage erupted with motion and chaos as my friends jumped into the fray to fight Franc's men, but my gaze never left my grandfather's face.

He twisted the knife, and I moaned at the new shock of

pain, laying my hand over his on the hilt of the weapon. He bent to whisper in my ear. "I always planned to kill you. Once I knew what you were, it made me sick to look at you. I'm only sorry that your mother died before I could make her regret betraying our kind."

"Thank you," I said.

His head jerked back in confusion. "For what?"

"For making it so easy to do this."

Violent red light struck him. His hand jerked under mine, and then fell away as he stumbled backward a step. The knife still protruded from me, but blood bloomed across his chest, staining his shirt as a twin injury ripped his skin open. His eyes widened in pain and disbelief as he stared at the growing scarlet stain. The blood loss weakened him, making him light-headed. I knew this because I felt the same. I swayed on my feet and yanked the knife out. It clattered to the ground when my cold fingers couldn't hold on to it. I forced myself to concentrate my energy enough to slow the bleeding in my chest—not enough to heal it because that wasn't my intent yet. I'd worried that I wouldn't have enough control to do this with my new powers, but it worked just like I'd hoped.

Franc dropped to his knees in front of me, and his fingers clutched at my waist. "Heal me!"

I shook my head and moved out of his reach. "I won't let you hurt my family again."

I'd thought that my fury would carry me through this moment, but my breath hitched on a sob. My grandfather's skin paled, turning a shade of gray, and I realized that I was still shaking my head, on the verge of hysteria. This wasn't me. I wasn't this person. I healed people. I didn't murder them.

But wasn't it justified? He would kill me if I didn't strike first. I'd even counted on him to wound me, so that I could use my injuries against him. An eye for an eye in the truest sense. So why did I feel so sick, watching my grandfather collapse on the ground? Bile rose up in my throat, and I covered my mouth.

*I can't do it. I can't murder him in cold blood. There has to be another way.*

The fighting continued around me as I knelt by Franc's side. Torn between my fear and my conscience, I hesitated a moment longer. When Franc's lungs seized on a breath, I stretched a hand toward him, still undecided.

I heard the gunfire a split second before the bullet slammed into my stomach. The force of it sent me sprawling to my back, and I lay there, listening to the shot echo over and over and over again. No, that wasn't an echo. That was another shot. Alcais stood over Franc, and I watched blood pool around my grandfather's body. I stared into his eyes until they lost focus.

Alcais knelt, clasping his head with the gun still in his hand. A keening sound ripped out of him, and he rocked back and forth. Some distant part of me realized that he'd reached the edge of a cliff and jumped over. He had nothing to hold on to, and no home to return to.

"Talk to me, Remy," Gabe pleaded. "Please."

My head rolled to the side as I searched for him, but everywhere I looked bodies lashed out at each other. No Gabe. *The earpiece,* I remembered.

"Gabe? Alcais shot me." I touched my stomach and warm liquid coated my fingers and spilled over my side. *I'm bleeding out.*

"Heal yourself, sweetheart."

I drifted for a second, unable to focus.

"Stay with me, Remy." His voice cracked, and the panic in his voice pierced the lethargy settling over me. Then he was shouting again. "Asher! Somebody! Help her!"

Asher appeared beside me, his head hovering over mine.

I almost didn't hurt anymore, and I drifted away again until he whispered, "It's bad, Remy. I'm afraid I'll lose control. Are you sure you want to do this?"

His face drained of color, and I snapped to awareness again. I'd known Franc or one of the others would hurt me. If they hadn't, I would have forced their hand. And when they did, Asher would be there to help me heal my injuries. With his powers only just returned, everyone would believe that he could lose control. That he would slip up and steal enough of my energy to take my power. After all, it was what we had feared when we'd first met. And if everyone saw it happening, I would be useless to my grandfather and the Protectors. They would no longer have a reason to chase me or to use my family against me. We just had to put on an act.

My teeth chattered, and I gave his trembling fingers a weak squeeze. "I'm sure."

He looked away, shaking his head. When I'd told him about this plan, he'd been worried. The reason people would believe he could lose control was because it was a very real possibility. He was scared that he wouldn't be able to pull away in time.

I lifted a heavy arm to touch my fingers to his jaw. "I trust you, Asher."

His lips tightened into a determined line. His defenses snapped down, and his energy flooded through me.

It was too much. I hadn't considered how the bullet wound had weakened me, or how stealing Erin's energy had changed me. The monster inside me latched on to his power with a greedy roar, ten times worse than what I had done to Seamus. A fire blazed to life inside me, melting the ice that had formed. I sensed Asher trying to retreat, but it was too late. I would take everything he had and kill him. The monster wanted all of it—all of that heat to fill the icy tundra left by my injuries.

"Remy, help me!" Asher pleaded, his green eyes narrowing in pain.

I couldn't speak, locked in a struggle inside myself. The Healer side of me fought to heal Asher. The Protector side wanted to steal his energy. The two halves of me splintered. Give. Take. Push. Pull. Healer. Protector. Fire and ice collided, and the pain that shattered through me nearly broke me. Asher cried out as my control slipped a little more, and I gritted my teeth.

*I am a Healer. I heal who I can, when I can.*

*I am a Protector. I protect the people I care about.*

It struck me that these two things were the same. Not two halves warring against each other but complementary elements adding up to the same thing—someone strong and fierce who would do anything for love. Not this monster who would kill a loved one to live.

*I am a Phoenix, born from the ashes of my charred body.*

At once, I pushed Asher's energy away and pulled inside myself.

My eyes opened. "Let go, Asher. Now," I ordered.

Suddenly released from the monster's hold, he shoved backward and I was alone in a storm. Fire rained down, scorching the air. Ice touched the blaze and turned it to ash. I'd been fighting both sides of myself for so long that I'd caused this chaos. No more fighting.

I gave in to the storm.

# CHAPTER THIRTY

*O uch.*

That was the first thing that popped into my mind as I drifted back to awareness. The fire and ice had dissipated, leaving behind a warm ball of energy in my belly. The energy flexed through me, bending and moving at my will, healing the wounds on my stomach, face, and torso instantly. There was no hypothermia afterward, and I instinctively knew that there never would be again. For the first time in my life, I did not fear my powers. They could no longer control me. I had hijacked the energy of both Protectors and a Healer. This is what separated me from Edith and the others Seamus protected—those women might live with Protectors, but they had never met a pure Healer like Erin or taken her life force. The two halves of me had melded and formed me into something new, the whole process ignited by the energy I'd stolen from both sides.

*I am a Phoenix, born from the ashes.*

With awareness, my senses returned. I opened my eyes and recognized Seamus's sitting room. I was lying on the couch, and Gabe sat on the floor beside me, his forehead pressed to my arm almost as if he was praying. The musty scent of an old room filled with books, and the pleasant acrid smell of burning wood filled my nostrils. The heat of that fire warmed my skin through my jeans. Gabe's hand pressed against my stomach, where I felt the liquid warmth of blood that had seeped from an injury that was no longer there.

Gabe's face turned toward mine. The silky strands of his hair slipped through my fingers when I smoothed it away from his forehead.

"Hey," he said.

"Hey."

He turned his cheek to kiss my palm. "Anything interesting happen since I saw you last?"

I appreciated him trying to keep the moment light. "Oh, you know. People trying to kill me. The usual."

All pretense of forced humor faded as he sat up in a jerky movement. Gabe's arms wrapped around my waist and he dragged me off the couch, twisting so that he cradled me in his lap on the floor. He held me so tight that I struggled to breathe, as he buried his head against my chest to listen to my heartbeat. His body trembled against mine, and I could only embrace him.

"I thought I lost you for a minute there," he said.

"I'm not going anywhere," I answered.

"Remy?"

I glanced up. Asher gripped the back of the couch with white knuckles. Seamus and Edith appeared behind him with expressions ranging from shock to disbelief, but I ignored them as Asher jumped over the back of the couch to land on a cushion behind Gabe and me. I raised my mental walls to protect Asher before I reached for him with one hand. He wrapped both of his hands around mine.

"Thank God you're okay," he said. "I thought I killed you." His green eyes still looked haunted by the thought, as he gave my fingers a last squeeze and let me go.

"I'm sorry I scared you. I guess our plan didn't work, after all."

"What are you talking about?" Gabe asked with a frown.

"Remy's idea to trick the others into thinking I lost control and stole her powers," Asher told his brother. To me, he said, "It worked. Just not like we planned." At my confusion, he added, "Remy, they think you're dead. Alcais saw me 'kill' you."

"But I didn't die," I said.

"Um, actually you did for all of thirty seconds," Asher said. "Your heart stopped and you weren't breathing. I cried over your body and everything. Someone should give me an Oscar."

He gave a flippant shrug, but I could tell that he'd been scared. He wasn't nearly as relaxed as he pretended. "I'll buy you a trophy. How did you bring me back to life?"

"I didn't. That was all you." He tipped his head as if trying to sense me. "Something's different. You're different."

Seamus walked over and dropped into an armchair. He eyed me for a moment, and I wondered if he understood what happened to me. He'd been a Protector of the Phoenix, after all. If anyone would know, he would. A stray bit of energy waved in the air, and I shoved it away without thinking. A small, satisfied smile curved Seamus's mouth, and I guessed he did know what happened, after all. Or at least, suspected. For some reason, he was choosing not to out me to the others.

"How are you feeling?" Seamus asked.

"Surprisingly good," I told him. It was true. I felt great. I used the moment to change the subject.

"Where are my dad and Lucy? Are they okay?"

"They're in a bedroom down the hall. Brita and Ursula are working on your father," Seamus answered. "He was in bad shape. They don't know that you were hurt." He shrugged. "I guess there's no reason to tell them now."

I swallowed the impatience to be with them. "What about your people, Seamus? How is everyone?"

He grimaced. "We lost two of my men, and four others were hurt. Edith has already seen to the injured."

"Sean?" I asked Edith, my voice low with concern.

She smiled. "He is okay. He stayed behind to cover any evidence that we were involved. He will make sure that the police do not know about you."

I didn't even want to know how he would accomplish that. Both the museum and the car park had to have security cameras. Maybe he had a way to erase the footage, but at the very least the police would investigate reports of gunfire.

"Xavier and Mark?" I asked.

Gabe scowled. "Xavier's dead, but Mark got away."

"For now," Seamus said in a calm voice. "He has much to answer for, and we will be speaking with him."

I thought he intended to do more than speak to him, but I felt no compassion for Mark. And perhaps it made me a bad person, but I wasn't sorry to hear that Xavier was dead. He'd caused us so much pain, and he'd done it gleefully.

"What about Alcais?" I asked.

Seamus shook his head. "Ben said that Alcais had already decided to let him go before we arrived. I think he only stuck around in the garage because he wanted to hurt you, Remy. After he saw you 'die,' he ran off. Asher told us to let him go."

"I figure he'll go back to his family or to the Morrisseys. Either way, it only helps us if he tells everyone that he saw you die," Asher said.

That hadn't been the plan. We'd wanted him to see that I was powerless, but this was better. I was useless to them now, and that meant my family and friends would no longer be collateral to be used against me. They were free. Elation and overwhelming sadness hit me at once. Happiness because they were free, and sadness because my "death" meant they had to be free of me in order to move on. Some small part of me had hoped I could find a way to stay in their lives, even if we couldn't live together.

I tuned back in to the conversation as Seamus explained that the police would find my grandfather and the gun that Alcais had used to kill Franc. At the thought of Franc, I did not feel grief. Once I had wanted to love him, but he'd destroyed that emotion.

"I want to see my father now," I told Gabe.

He helped me stand and placed a hand on my lower back to pull me close. "Not yet, sweetheart. You need to clean up, or you'll worry him."

I glanced down at my shirt and shuddered at the dark crimson stains on my stomach and torso. He was right. First, I would shower, and then I would I go to my father. He might not want to see me, but that was a chance I'd have to take.

Once I'd showered, Gabe led me to my father's room. I caught a look in his eye when he watched me, but his thoughts stayed hidden. Then all of my focus shifted to my family and the heartache that would come.

At the door, I paused. "I have to go in there alone," I told him.

I was terrified that I'd hurt his feelings, but Gabe smiled and dropped a kiss on my forehead. "Go ahead. I'll be around if you need me."

I hugged him in gratitude. Then I entered my father's room, closing the door behind me with the sense that I was closing a cell door. There was no way this was going to be easy. Franc had destroyed my family because of what

I was. The last time I'd seen my father, he'd just learned that I was something more than human. What had Franc's people told him about me?

My eyes adjusted to the dim light in the room. My father appeared to be sleeping, tucked into the middle of the oversized bed, while Lucy crashed in a chair on the other side of the room. My father's black hair stood out in stark relief against the white pillow beneath his head. The perpetual tan he'd always sported had faded, but he almost looked like the handsome man who'd brought me to his home and given me a family. All traces of his torture at Franc's hands had been wiped clean by Brita and Ursula, but that didn't change what had been done to him. Lines around his eyes and mouth remained, a testament to what he'd been through these last months.

Nerves clumped and knotted in my stomach as all of my old fears resurfaced. Would he hate me for everything that had happened? Would he be disgusted by what I was? Blame me for Laura's death and for the things Franc had done to him? *Stop feeling sorry for yourself, Remy. You've done the best you could.*

My attention turned to my sister. She looked exhausted and peaceful even in her sleep. I walked around the bed and knelt by her chair. "Lucy?" I whispered. I rubbed her arm.

She woke instantly, fear flooding her features until she recognized me. Then she fell into my arms, knocking me off balance. We both laughed and then we were crying, too.

"We did it," she whispered. "We got him back."

I'm not sure either of us had believed it was possible, but hoping had sustained us. An overwhelming tangle of emotions flooded through me as we sat on the floor, leaning against each other. Would Lucy forgive me when I sent her away? A sharp knife of pain stabbed me, and I shoved the thought away. *It's too soon. Don't think about it, Remy.*

I brushed a black curl away from her face. "I'm sorry it took so long." In an unspoken agreement, we spoke in quiet tones so we wouldn't disturb our father.

"It doesn't matter now. We're all together again." She bit her lip and looked at her hands. "He woke a while ago and asked about Mom. I had to tell him. He cried. I've never seen Dad cry."

I had once. My father had cried when Dean had hurt me after my mother died. The abuse he'd abandoned me to had become very real to him when he saw the evidence firsthand. Nothing had been easy between my father and me, from the day he'd shown up at the hospital in Brooklyn. Once, things had gotten better, but then I'd made the mistake of finding Franc. Anxiety gutted me. "Does he . . ." My voice cracked, and I had to begin again. "Does he hate me?"

"Remy?" I jumped at my father's voice, and I almost gave in to the urge to run away until he ordered, "Come here."

The stern edge in his voice was exactly what I expected, and my heart sank. I rose and walked over to the bed with my head lowered because I couldn't bear to see that the way he looked at me had changed.

"Dad, it wasn't her fault . . ." Lucy started, but she drifted off when he held up a hand.

"Remy, look at me," my father snapped. I forced myself to meet his fierce gaze and steeled myself for his hatred. But it wasn't hate that I glimpsed in his navy eyes. I couldn't tell what he was thinking. "Your sister told me everything, and Asher stopped by to fill me in on the rest."

What could I say to defend myself? I'd lied and kept things from him. I'd made so many stupid mistakes. I wanted to look away again, but I couldn't.

He continued in a gentler tone. "They told me how you kept everyone safe and how you put yourself in danger time and again to protect them. They told me that you nearly died trying to save your mother."

Tears threatened, and I blinked rapidly.

"Hate you?" He shook his head in disbelief. "Do you think I don't remember what you did in the forest before they took me?" He reached for my hand, and I gave it to him, unthinkingly. "Your grandfather ordered you to kill me, and you refused. You saved me instead."

Every bit of me wanted to let him believe that about me, but I couldn't. "It's my fault that Franc found us. Laura would still be alive if I hadn't gone to San Francisco."

I tried to pull away, but he held tight to my hand. Lucy touched my back in support, but it didn't help.

My father shook my hand, and the rough motion got my attention. "Were you driving the car that hit your mother?"

"No," I choked. "But—"

"But nothing. Xavier was driving, and he intentionally steered that car at her. It was his fault, or your grandfather's for bringing him there." He sat up and leaned against the headboard, wearing one of Gabe's T-shirts. "You know it kills me to see you standing there blaming yourself for this. Just like you blamed yourself for Anna's death."

"You don't understand," I told him.

"Don't I? That power you have carries a heavy burden, more than any one person should have to bear. You heal people with your touch, Remy. Do you know how that amazes me? How proud I am when I think of how giving you are when so much has been taken from you?"

That did it. The dam collapsed, and a measly blink couldn't stave off the tears that fell. My mother had never admitted she knew what I could do, let alone told me she was proud of me. My breath caught in a half-sob, half-gasp that hurt my chest and kind of squawked out of me. I thought I heard Lucy snicker behind me, and I didn't care.

My father's mouth held a hint of a smile before it straightened into a stern line again. "But your power doesn't make you responsible for the world. You can't save everyone, and nobody expects you to."

"But Laura—"

"Was the love of my life. And I don't know that I'll ever stop missing her." His eyes shone with unshed tears, and he cleared his throat. "But you didn't kill her. Don't put that on your shoulders. It's not fair. To you or Lucy and me. We need you, baby."

I inhaled, and when I exhaled it was like letting all of the baggage go. I'd thought my father would hate me and blame me, but he didn't. He was right, and he didn't even know how time was stealing away from us. If I couldn't have my family forever, I could have them for now. At least until they recovered enough to go home.

I climbed onto the bed and sat beside my father, my back against the headboard like him. It reminded me of the morning before my graduation, when we'd been happy. I tilted my head until it rested on his shoulder. "I need you, too. Both of you," I said.

His chest lifted as he exhaled in relief. Lucy sprawled across the foot of the bed, her legs thrown over mine. "Are you really okay?" she asked. "Asher said things got scary when you confronted Franc."

"Alcais shot me," I said. They both tensed, and I rushed to say, "I'm okay, though." I didn't confess that the others thought I was dead, or that she would have to leave without me soon. The guilt ate at me, but I shoved it away.

My father studied me long enough to see I wasn't hurt and nudged Lucy with one foot. "What did you call your sister again? Duffy?"

"Buffy, Dad. Buffy. As in Vampire Slayer."

"Oh God." We stared at my father's horrified expression. "Are vampires real, too?"

Lucy's gaze met mine. Her lips trembled, and mine followed. Then we were both laughing.

My father grinned. "Gotcha."

"Boo!" Lucy shrieked. "Bad joke."

They started arguing, and I was content to listen to them. There were things we hadn't said yet and the future we hadn't discussed, but right now it seemed that we had an unspoken pact to ignore everything outside this moment. We were a family again, and that was enough.

# CHAPTER THIRTY-ONE

*A* month passed and nothing of consequence happened at the O'Malley house. The outside world was a different story, though. The police never sought us out. Word got out to the Morrisseys that my grandfather had double-crossed them. They couldn't do much about it since Franc was dead and Alcais had disappeared. Scamus's spies did learn that they had taken out their rage out on Mark, a traitor for his part in working against the Protectors. His body hadn't been found yet, but then the Morrisseys had been *very* angry when they discovered that I was dead.

Seamus's spies had done their job spreading the word that Franc and Alcais had killed me. On sleepless nights, I wondered if Alcais's days were numbered. I guessed it depended on the Morrisseys' reach and how long their memories were.

As promised, Seamus had arranged to get Erin's body home to her mother. Dorthea had stayed long enough to retrieve her daughter, but the next day, the entire Healer community had uprooted and disappeared without a trace. Empty houses and disconnected phones were the only proof they had ever lived in Pacifica. Some of us speculated that they had scattered, giving up on the idea of a community altogether, but part of me hoped that they'd decided to start over somewhere new. Franc had betrayed them, but that didn't mean everything he'd done had been wrong. They had been happy together, helping each other to survive. It saddened me to think that had dissolved, too.

While all of this happened, my family existed in a kind of time warp where nothing touched us. Perhaps it was the months apart or maybe it was everything we'd lost, but nothing mattered except learning what we could about each other. Lies were revealed. Confessions were made. And we savored our time together. But it wasn't enough.

Everyone but my father and Lucy knew what was coming. I saw it in the compassionate looks that Asher and Lottie sent my way. And then there was Gabe and the silent way he watched me, like he expected me to break at any moment. He wasn't far off. My father and Lucy thought I would be going home with them, and saying good-bye to them was going to kill me.

Thirty-two days after the rescue, I walked into the sitting room to find my father and Asher in a deep discussion. Something about their body language made me turn around and walk right back out of the room. It was no secret in the house that my father was having trouble sleeping at night. His body might be healed, but his soul had been worked over by whatever he'd endured those months he'd been held hostage. It was the one off-limits topic, the thing he refused to discuss with Lucy or me. But if anyone could understand what he'd gone through, it would be Asher.

I sat on the floor in the hall, guarding the door so nobody would interrupt them. That was where Seamus found me. He leaned one shoulder against the wall next to me, crossed his arms, and stared down at me. One of his dark brows rose in expectation.

"What?" I asked when he didn't say anything.

Seamus had done everything in his power to make us comfortable, going so far as to treat us like family. He hadn't told anyone what he suspected had happened to me that day in the garage.

"You're a Phoenix," he said.

I willed my face not to flood with color and I met Seamus's eyes with more than a little guilt. I had worried that he would try harder to make me stay if I admitted what I was.

"No," I blurted out. "You're wrong."

His head tipped to one side as he continued to study me. "If you say so," he answered.

My hands grew clammy, and I wiped them on my jeans until Seamus's gaze followed the movement. *He knows I'm lying.*

"Do yourself a favor, and don't ever play poker. You bluff as well as you nurse." My mouth dropped open, and he tapped it shut before continuing. "Ah, well. I can't very well blame you for wanting to be free of all of this."

A hole had worn in the knee of my jeans, and I tugged on a loose thread. "You're not mad?"

"At who?" He threw up his hands and looked around the hall with exaggerated movements. "Nobody but me and a dead girl here. Can't stay mad at a dead girl."

I stood and bussed a kiss on his cheek. "You're a gentleman, Seamus O'Malley." I leaned against the wall beside him, crossing my ankles. "What will you do now?"

Seamus scowled. "Despite what I think, Brita, Ursula, and Edith have decided that they no longer wish to hide. Apparently, you have infected them with the belief that they can change things. It's Edith's theory that if the Protectors learn of their existence, then maybe the Healers will be safer."

I thought about it and guessed Edith could be right. The Protectors killed the Healers to feel something again, to remember what mortality was like. The three women could have the same effect on them without the killing. Going public could save the Healers that remained.

"Some people aren't going to like that." My mother had said that some Healers and Protectors would want to kill me because my power scared them. She'd been right, and the same would be true of the women if they made themselves known.

"Then the O'Malleys will be here to protect them, as we always have been."

"They're lucky to have you." I hesitated a moment. "When I first came here, why didn't you tell me about them?"

It had bothered me that he wanted me to trust him, but had lied by omission.

"You remember that painting of my wife?" I thought of the blond woman in the green dress. In the painting, she'd worn a necklace with a charm of a ruby-eyed phoenix. At my nod, Seamus continued, "She died a long time ago. One of the Phoenix murdered her." My eyes widened, and he said, "Just because a person appears to be an ally, doesn't mean they are. Until you know you can trust someone, it's better to be a little cautious, isn't it?"

I nodded in understanding. "Why do you want me to stay, Seamus? Won't I just cause you more trouble?"

He smiled. "I protect the Phoenix. It's who I am. I failed once when it mattered most, but watching over these women—who could become Phoenix—it's like a second chance."

That made sense to me. I had failed to watch over my family, too, and this time with them had been my second chance.

He continued. "If a woman were to become a Phoenix, there are things that she would need to know. Things a person like me could tell her." He gave me a sly look. "Hypothetically, of course."

"Of course," I answered in a dry voice. *Who's fooling whom here?*

"Say, for instance, she should probably know that she is mortal. She'll grow old and die just like the rest of the human race."

*Thank God,* I thought, but I said, "Is that right?"

"And a Phoenix can heal injuries instantly. Both her own and others'."

*Yep. Figured that one out the last time I healed Gabe.*

Seamus tapped a finger to his lips in thought. "And most importantly, there's the way she can make a Protector mortal in an instant, if she so chooses."

*WHAT!?!* I could make Gabe mortal if he wanted. Not in a few months, but now. I bit my lip, and then caved to my curiosity. "And how would she do that? Hypothetically, of course."

"Of course," he repeated, his eyes crinkled with laughter. "She would heal it like any other injury. Her body knows what to do instinctively."

The ramifications of that spiraled through my mind. "Is that why the Healers and the Protectors killed the Phoenix?"

His amusement faded. "The Healers didn't want people who could heal faster than they could. It threatened their way of life. And the Protectors . . . well, some of them never wanted to be mortal again. But the Phoenix are a powerful thing. You can't extinguish their spirit."

The door to the sitting room opened, and Asher exited, closing the door behind him again.

Seamus straightened. "I'll leave the two of you alone." Before he walked away, he glanced back at me over his shoulder, his eyes gleaming with amusement again. "If you find your way back to the living, there will always be room for you here."

My mouth quirked. "You never know. Who can guess what the future will bring?"

"An O'Malley can always tell the future," he teased. " 'Of every weather, ye are prophets.' Enjoy being a ghost, Remy."

He quoted from the tapestry in the hall, and I smothered a laugh. With a wave of his hand, he disappeared down the stairs to the first floor.

"He's not pressing you to stay again?" Asher asked, staring after him.

I shook my head.

"Good. Because I think it's time we all moved on."

My stomach clenched, and I had the childish urge to cover my ears to close out his words.

"You have to let them go," Asher said in a soft voice.

I glanced at the door to the sitting room. What had Asher and my father been talking about? Was he desperate to get away from here? Was being here making his nightmares worse?

Asher tilted my jaw up in a rare touch, forcing me to meet his gaze. "Not for them. For you. Nobody blames you for taking your time after everything that's happened. But it can't last forever. Not telling them is killing you."

I stared at his throat. "It's going to be worse when they leave." Red color flowed up Asher's neck to stain his cheeks, and I realized he looked guilty. I frowned, wondering at the possibilities, and it hit me. "You're going, too."

He nodded, tucking his hands in his pockets. "Lottie and I thought we would accompany your father and Lucy back to Blackwell Falls and watch over them for a while. Just to be sure nobody bothers them."

I rubbed the back of my neck and didn't say anything.

"You knew I wouldn't stay. It's one thing to know you and Gabe are together and another to see it."

My eyes flew to his. He didn't look angry or hurt. Just accepting that this was the way things would be. I sighed. "You're right. I know you're right."

"So you'll tell them?" he asked.

"Today. I promise."

"Good." He tipped his head and turned away.

"Hey, Asher," I said. "What made Lottie decide to go with you?"

He smiled with genuine amusement. "All my sister ever cared about was family. Lucy is part of our family now, and so is your father. She'll be in heaven trying to boss everyone around."

I pictured Lucy's reaction to that and the resulting battle that would ensue. In the end, Lucy was getting another sister. She really wouldn't be alone. A small part of me winced with jealousy, but most of me found comfort in that fact. "Thank you," I told Asher.

"We'll take care of them. I promise."

He kissed my forehead and I wished that none of us had to say good-bye. But that had never been part of the plan.

After Asher walked away, I went into the sitting room. My father stood in front of the Phoenix paintings. I approached him, and he glanced at me.

"You look a little alike," he said, tilting his head at the painting of Seamus's wife.

I'd hoped that knowing I was doing the right thing would make it easier to talk to my father, but I hadn't counted on how my heart didn't want to let him go.

"What is it?" he asked, his brow wrinkling in concern.

I twisted to face him. "I didn't tell you everything about the day we rescued you, Dad. You know the Phoenix that

Seamus talks about? I'm one of them. I'm more powerful than before."

It was the first time I'd said it out loud. I hadn't even admitted it to Gabe yet. The words didn't scare me like I'd thought they would. Rather, they filled me with pride.

The silence stretched on for a minute before he said, "I don't care."

I gave him a small smile like this didn't hurt and tucked my hair behind my ear. "Yes, you do."

He stared at the painting, avoiding my gaze. It didn't take a mind reader to understand that this news bothered him.

I touched his arm. "It's okay. You can tell me."

He finally looked at me. "I'm scared. Not of you, but of what happens if everyone finds out what you can do . . ." He gestured helplessly, leaving the sentence open-ended.

Misery appeared in front of me like a brick wall, and there was no way around it. "I've thought about that. A lot." I took a deep breath. "That's why when everyone thought I died the day we rescued you, we let them believe it."

Comprehension lit in my father's eyes. "You're not coming with us," he said in a voice heavy with accusation. "You never planned to come with us."

I tried to smile, but it felt like a macabre grimace. "So long as they think I'm dead, you and Lucy can go home. You can start over and live a normal life in Blackwell Falls."

"Don't do this, Remy," my father begged. "I know what I said. I'm scared, but we haven't had enough time together. Come with us. If not Blackwell Falls, then we'll find somewhere new."

When I'd thought of this plan, I'd never expected him

to fight me. I'd only thought of how desperately I wanted my family to be safe and away from this ongoing war.

I shook my head and ran my hands through my hair in frustration. "I can't do that. You know I'm right. This is the right thing to do. If I come with you, there would always be a chance that someone would find out who I am and what I can do. They wouldn't think twice about hurting Lucy to control me."

His face took on a hollow, glassy look of pain. "You're asking me to choose between my daughters. I can't walk away from you again."

He sounded so helpless that my defenses cracked a little more, and I couldn't stop the tears. "You're not walking away, Dad. I am." He opened his mouth to argue, but I threw my hands in the air to ward him off. "Can't you see that this is going to kill me? I've only had you and Lucy for such a short time. But if it will keep you safe, I will give you up. Gladly."

My father's throat worked, and he clamped his mouth shut. I wanted to take it all back, but I couldn't. This was the right thing to do, no matter how much it hurt.

"Asher and Lottie have agreed to go with you and see you settled. They're going to watch over you for a while to be sure no one bothers you. Don't be surprised if they show up at the house all the time. They'll be good for Lucy." *And for you.*

My father seemed to accept this. "What will you do?"

"I'm going to start over in a new place with Gabe, if he'll have me. Go to college if I can." My sigh sounded wistful. "Is it stupid to still want to be a doctor when I grow up?"

A rueful smile finally curved my father's mouth. It had taken him a couple of weeks to get used to the fact that I was with Gabe now. "Something tells me that Gabe will follow you anywhere you go. I've never seen a man so head over heels."

My cheeks heated in a blush. "It's mutual. He makes me laugh," I blurted out. It sounded lame to my ears, but it was too late to take it back.

"Well, then," he said in a soft voice. "He's given you the world, hasn't he?"

I smiled. "Yeah. He has." Then I sobered. "When will you and Lucy go?"

"Do we have to decide now?"

"The longer we draw this out, the more it will hurt," I confessed. I'd already waited too long to tell him the truth.

He hated my answer, but he nodded reluctantly. "Tomorrow, then."

I accepted his decision, even as my stomach burned. "Will you tell Lucy?"

"Yes. Promise me you'll find a way to visit. We're going to miss you."

Unable to get a word past the knot in my throat, I squeezed his hand. Then, because I was going to fall apart completely, I almost ran for the door. My father's broken voice called after me.

"You'll make a brilliant doctor, Remy."

Dinner was a party affair. Seamus had thrown together a feast, and everyone had gathered for a farewell meal. Through dinner, I managed to put on a bright show, teasing a morose Lucy into a better mood and reminding her of everything that waited for her at home. It worked. Too well. She and Lottie began to talk about all the things they planned to do, and I listened with a big, fake smile that made my teeth ache.

Gabe leaned over and whispered in my ear, "One more day, sweetheart."

He offered me his hand, and I squeezed it desperately.

This last month, I'd been so intensely focused on my family and the time I had left with them that I'd neglected Gabe. He'd moved into a room with Asher so that I could share my bedroom with Lucy. I'd missed him, though. We hadn't discussed the future. What if I'd blown it with him by putting him on hold?

I stared up at him. "I didn't mean to push you away."

Noise continued around us, the sparkle of it hurting my ears. Gabe bent to drop a small kiss on the corner of my mouth. "You didn't push me away. I'm right here."

"We have things to figure out," I said.

He smiled. "Tomorrow's soon enough. Don't worry about me, okay?"

He meant it, and relief flooded through me for one too-brief moment. Then the meal was over, and I followed Lucy to our room to watch her pack. She didn't have a lot, but every item that went into her bag felt like another piece of me being taken away.

"You know, I figured out why I don't have Protector powers like you," Lucy said out of the blue, landing on the bed beside me with a bounce.

"What?" I asked in genuine surprise. "What is it?"

"I'm adopted," she said.

I laughed, thinking she was joking, but her serious expression didn't change. "No way," I said. "Mom and Dad wouldn't have kept that from you. Besides, you look like them."

"No. I look like Mom, except I have black hair." She wrapped one of her curls around a finger, fidgeting with nerves. "It was the only thing that made sense. So I asked Dad and he told me the truth. Mom was pregnant with me when they got together. It was just an accident of fate that my birth dad had black hair, too."

I stared at Lucy in shock. "Where's your birth dad?"

"He was a soldier. Mom met him when he was on

leave, but he died before she could tell him that she was pregnant. And then Dad moved back to Blackwell Falls, and they started dating again, and here we are."

She rose and began to get ready for bed, changing into pajamas. She didn't look sad or mad, and I couldn't quite tell what she was feeling. "Are you okay with all of this?" I asked.

"Honestly?" She tipped her head, considering the question. "Yes. What does it really change? I guess I would have been upset a year ago." She paused and laughed. "Heck, I would have thrown a fit, and we both know it." She shook her head. "But with everything I know now, it doesn't seem to matter." She sat on the bed again, pulled her knees up, and rested her chin on them. "Blood doesn't always make a family. I was lucky to have Mom, and I'm lucky to have Dad and you."

"You've changed, Lucy."

"I've grown up. Because of you. Because of the example you set. I understand why you're not coming with us. You're doing it for me. So that I can have a normal life."

I nodded, too choked up to speak.

"I don't want to give you up," she said, her eyes filling with tears.

I hugged her. "It's not forever. We'll see each other again."

She wiped her face on her shoulder and stood up to go to the bathroom, pausing in the doorway with her back to me. "I'm not saying good-bye tomorrow. That's bullshit, and I won't do it. And you had better figure out a way for us to write to each other. I need you in my life."

The bathroom door shut behind her, leaving me alone in the room, and I wondered how I would make it through tomorrow.

★   ★   ★

The next day my family climbed into Sean's SUV and drove away, taking a huge chunk of my heart with them. I did not go outside to seek comfort. There was no sky big enough to fill the hole their absence had left behind. So I went to my room, closed the door, climbed into bed, and pulled the covers over my head.

# CHAPTER THIRTY-TWO

"*R*emy? Are you in here?"

The covers were yanked off my head, and Brita's face appeared. She wrinkled her nose. "No way. You are rank, girl. When is the last time you showered?"

"What day is it?" I asked, trying to grab the covers from her hand. I was pretty sure it had only been three days, but the nights had kind of blurred together. Sleep was the only time the pain went away, so I'd spent a lot of time seeking it out.

"If you need to ask, then you've blown way past the acceptable limits of personal hygiene."

"Shut up, Brita, and go away while you're at it."

"Fine," she said with an indifferent shrug. She let go of the covers, and I readjusted my cocoon. I heard her walking toward the door. "I just thought you'd want to know that while you were moping away in here, Gabe left."

That caught my attention. The covers fell to my waist when I sat up. "What are you talking about? Gabe wouldn't just leave."

She pointed toward the nightstand. "He left you a note." And then she flounced out of the room.

I vaguely remembered him coming in a few times, but I'd checked out. And now he'd gone. Panic sparked in my belly, quickly followed by anger. Okay, so I wasn't a prize these days, but give me a break. I needed a little time to get over saying good-bye to my family. For all of his promises of loving me forever, he'd jumped ship at the first speed bump.

I grabbed the envelope on the nightstand and slit it open. A piece of paper, a train ticket, a map, and some money fell out. I scanned the paper, and all of two seconds later, I was out of bed and running for the shower. The note didn't say much, but it said everything to me.

*Chase me, Remy.*


Four hours later, I climbed out of a cab at the Jardin du Luxembourg. Gabe had left me a train ticket from London to Paris. I'd showered and dressed in twenty minutes flat. Edith had been waiting with a packed bag, and Sean had broken some speeding laws to get me to the station on time.

The map marked a single location. Someplace called the Medici Fountain in the Jardin du Luxembourg. I hefted my bag over my shoulder and wandered into the park. Sudden nerves unsettled my stomach, and I was glad that I'd chosen to trade my usual jeans for a dress. The buttery yellow color made my skin glow and my hair look lighter than usual. Gabe hadn't seen me in a dress often, and I hoped he would like it.

I stopped a woman and showed her my map. She smiled and pointed me in the right direction. A few minutes later, I climbed a set of stone steps and inhaled a shocked breath when I spotted the fountain. A long rectangular pond sprawled under a grove of trees. The green canopy and greener water created a quiet, cool haven. Metal chairs were lined up alongside the pond and at one end, a giant sculpture stood majestically over it all. According to an inset on my map, the art depicted Polyphemus spying on two lovers, Acis and Galatea.

I didn't see Gabe, so I sat in a chair to wait. Ducks swam

in the pond, and birds chirped in the trees. Gradually, I felt myself relaxing for the first time in ages. There was something peaceful about being anonymous and knowing that nobody was looking for me.

"Mademoiselle?"

I jumped and shifted in my seat to find a short, older man with gray hair standing beside me. He smiled. "Remy?"

He pronounced my name with a strong French accent. When I nodded, he handed me an envelope, tipped an imaginary hat, and left. I stared after him, bemused for a moment, before I opened the envelope.

*Feel better? You're getting warmer.*

Below those five words, Gabe had written an address. I grinned as I stood and made my way out of the park to find another cab. He'd once told me, "Whenever you're upset, you go outside." So he'd sent me outside because he knew how sad I was.

A short time later, the cabdriver dropped me off on a street that overlooked the Notre Dame Cathedral. I paid him and walked the direction he pointed me toward. Soon I arrived at the address, and I laughed when I saw it was a café. Gabe was nowhere in sight, but I would have been surprised if he was. I found a table on the sidewalk so I could people-watch. It suddenly hit me that I was in Paris. The poor girl from the hovel in New York had managed to break free of her past. My mom would have loved to see this. My eyes filled with tears at the thought, and I blinked them back. *No more crying.*

A waitress with a mass of black curls and tan skin placed a white cup and saucer in front of me.

"Oh, I didn't order yet," I protested.

She shrugged, placed an envelope beside the saucer, and left.

I took a sip of the café au lait and closed my eyes in appreciation. I couldn't remember the last time I'd had a good cup of coffee. The O'Malley household had tended toward tea. I set aside the mug to open the envelope, pausing a moment to savor the anticipation.

*Have I told you that I love coffee? Especially when I get to taste it on you. You're almost there.*

I reread the note, imagining Gabe beside me. Kissing me, holding me, stealing my ability to think. I shivered and nearly scalded my tongue when I gulped the rest of the café au lait. Instead of an address, Gabe had included another ticket. It was for one of the boats, the *Bateau Mouches,* that took the trip along the Seine River to the Eiffel Tower. I spotted a sign for the boat company at the edge of the riverbank. I dropped money on the table to cover the coffee and ran.

At the water's edge, I handed my ticket to a man. He grinned and handed me a small, wrapped box before waving me onboard. I sought out the upper deck that offered a 360-degree view of the Seine and found a seat away from the other tourists. The *Bateau Mouches* pushed away from the dock and cruised along. I tried to look in every direction at once to take everything in.

Eventually, I studied the box in my hand. It was the perfect size to hold earrings or a ring, but I guessed that wouldn't be what it held. For a second, my mind drifted to another package, but I shoved that thought away. There was no place for thoughts of Franc here. I gave Gabe's present a slight shake, and something rattled inside. I gleefully ripped the paper off the box, impatient now. I opened the lid and stared at the contents.

A key. A very old-fashioned one that would open something equally old. But what? This time there was no note to explain. I held the key, flipping it in my hand thoughtfully.

"It opens the door of a beautiful apartment near the Jardin du Luxembourg."

I almost dropped it when Gabe slid into the seat beside me. The wind whipped his chocolate-brown hair in every direction, and he'd narrowed his eyes against the sun. The angle of his wide jaw was offset by high cheekbones and a sensual mouth. A mouth that I could taste whenever I wanted.

"Nothing to say?" he asked when I continued to stare at him. He carried on like I'd spoken. "It's close to several universities, including a medical school. And there's a music school nearby that I thought I might look into. You could live in the apartment alone, if you prefer. Or we could live there together."

Gabe rarely got nervous, but at that moment, he was almost babbling. So I leaned over and kissed him, sliding a hand into his hair to pull him down to meet me. Between one breath and the next, he stopped fidgeting and got busy reminding me what I had missed for the last month.

A throat cleared nearby, and I laughed against Gabe's lips as he pulled away. I glanced over his shoulder to find an old woman glaring at us. Rather than feeling ashamed, I smiled at her. I was in love.

Gabe tugged on the end of my ponytail to get my attention. He stared at me with a question in his eyes. Now, I was nervous. I settled back in my seat and clutched the key. "Can we go see it? The apartment, I mean."

"I thought we could have dinner at the Eiffel Tower and then head over there after."

I shook my head. "I'd rather go now. I think we need to talk." I glanced over his shoulder again at the woman who still stared at us. "In private," I added.

"Okay," he said. "We'll talk."

Gabe took the key from me and fit it in the lock. He pushed the black door open and stood aside to let me enter. The apartment wasn't huge. It wasn't even extravagant, though the furnishings looked comfortable. An over-stuffed, brown suede couch faced a set of shelves that housed a TV, books, and knickknacks that I couldn't wait to explore. I trailed a hand over the couch as I passed it on my way to the kitchen. I heard the front door close as Gabe followed me.

A square island occupied the center of the kitchen with two bar stools on one side. I rounded the counter and turned. Gabe stood in the doorway watching me with an unreadable expression.

"I'm sorry," I said. "That it took me so long to get back to you. Letting my family go . . ." Just thinking about watching them leave stole my breath, and it took me a second to continue. "I was sad."

That was the ultimate understatement.

"You're still sad," Gabe observed.

I gave him a small smile. "I'm less sad," I corrected him. "Soon, I'll be almost happy. And before you know it, I'll be Mary Freaking Sunshine. You'll hate how much I'll smile. But for a little while, I'm going to be sad."

"I can handle that. Just don't shut me out, sweetheart."

"Deal."

He started forward, but I held up a hand. "There's more."

He settled back against the doorway again and lifted one dark brow. "More? What could possibly follow Mary Freaking Sunshine?"

I turned to open a cabinet and spotted a box of Kraft macaroni and cheese and a bag of my favorite chocolate. I grabbed the chocolate, clutching it to my chest. "God, I love you."

"Me or the chocolate?"

"You?" I teased, and Gabe cracked a smile.

"Good answer."

I set the candy aside and opened another cabinet.

"Remy? Are you stalling?"

"Mmm–hmm," I said, looking at a shelf of spices.

"Are you trying to figure out a way to apologize for leaving me out of your scheme with Asher or a way to tell me that you're a Phoenix?"

I swung around so quickly that I almost tripped over my own feet. "You knew?" I shrieked.

He actually snorted. "I guessed and you just confirmed. You are the worst liar I've ever seen."

I blushed. "Seamus said the same thing. He told me to avoid poker." I stared at Gabe through my lashes. "I take it you're okay with this?"

He blew out a frustrated breath. "I guess I don't understand why you didn't tell me."

I'd hurt him, and I hated that. "I didn't think it was going to be as dangerous as it was. And people would only believe that Asher would lose control. Not you. And if we were wrong about the bonding being tied to my emotions . . . Well, there was a very slim chance that Asher and I might have bonded again, and I didn't want to upset you."

Thank goodness that hadn't happened.

"And the fact that you're a Phoenix? Why not tell me that?"

"Because I didn't want to think about it," I confessed. "I wanted to pretend that I was normal for a while, so maybe I wouldn't have to give up my father and Lucy. It was stupid, and I knew it while it was happening. But I couldn't let them go."

Except I had. And it still gutted me.

"Can you forgive me?" I asked.

"Apparently, I am incapable of holding a grudge against you," he answered ruefully. "You have to talk to me, Remy. I knew you needed time, but the last month has been hell."

"I'm so sorry, Gabe."

The tension in his shoulders finally released, and he said, "Come on. I'll show you the rest of the place."

He held out a hand, and I walked over to grasp it. He pulled me down a hallway, and I studied the muscles in his back. I let my defenses fall away for the first time in a month as my gaze traveled lower.

Gabe froze. Then he turned, picked me up, and backed me into the closest wall. His mouth owned mine for six separate kisses, though I might have lost count around four. His hands landed on my hips, and I could hear my blood rushing through my ears. I nipped his jaw and he sucked in a breath that made me smile. I kissed his neck. *I love you, Gabe.* I kissed the other side of his jaw. *I love you.* My mouth found his again. *I love you.*

"I missed hearing you," he said.

I pressed against his chest to gain a few inches of space so I could see his face. "What if you become mortal? You won't be able to read my mind then."

"I'll still have you, though."

He started to kiss me again, but I clapped my hands on his cheeks. "Gabe, if you could choose to be immortal or mortal, what would you choose? Honest answer."

His voice sounded quiet and intimate in the narrow hall. "I would want to be mortal again."

"Why?" I asked. His hand slid up from my hip to my ribs, and my eyes nearly crossed. I had to remember to breathe to focus again.

"This is a half-life, living without senses or the fear of time passing. I don't want that." Gabe's green eyes blazed with passion. "I want to experience loving you with my senses wide open, savoring every moment like it could be our last. I want to really live with you, to be alive in all senses of the word. That's what I would choose."

*Are you sure? Seamus said a Phoenix can make a Protector mortal in a second. We could do this now.*

Gabe didn't jump or outwardly react to my thought. Then he said, "Maybe tomorrow. I want to hear your thoughts a little while longer."

His mouth found my neck.

"You don't seem surprised," I said breathlessly.

"I expect the impossible from you, and you never fail to deliver."

I laughed. "Man, you come up with the best lines. I am putty at your feet."

He mock-scowled and traced his fingers over my ribs until I laughed again. "I'm being romantic here. Stop ruining the mood."

"You breathe, and I fall deeper in love with you."

Gabe's face took on a stunned expression, and then his eyes narrowed. "You almost had me with that one. What greeting card did you get that from?" I punched him in the shoulder, and he laughed. Then he stepped back and pulled me into his side as he opened a door. "This is the bathroom."

I had a brief view of a claw-footed tub before the door closed again. "You're not even going to ask how my powers have increased?"

"Nope."

Slightly disgruntled, I asked, "Why not?"

He opened another door, and I peeked into the room. It was a bedroom. A guest bedroom if I had to guess.

"Because it won't change anything," he said. "This could be your room. Or my room. You never answered my question, you know. About living here."

"You should care." At his blank look, I said, "About how my powers have changed." I sighed when he didn't say anything. "Now you're going to make me show you."

I held up my forearm. I imagined a small cut opening on the tender skin just above my elbow. It split open in a blink. A drop of blood spilled, and then I pictured the injury healing. An instant later, the skin closed with only the drop of blood left behind to prove it had ever been there. No sparks lit the air, and my teeth didn't chatter with hypothermia. Maybe because the push and pull of energy happened inside me now, perfectly balanced, perfectly controlled.

Gabe stalked forward and stared at my arm in shock. His eyes were huge, and he said, "Maybe you'd better tell me after all."

I sat on the edge of the bed and explained how my two halves—Protector and Healer—had gone to war when Asher unleashed his energy as part of our plan. I hadn't expected my injuries to be so severe that I might lose control of my powers.

"Asher couldn't get free of me, so I imagined a box and I shoved all of my energy inside it so he could escape. As soon as he got away, it hit me. I didn't have to be one thing or the other." I shrugged. "They're both part of me. As soon as I stopped fighting, the two sides melded somehow. Healer and Protector, bonded in a single person."

I couldn't think of another way to describe it. Since I'd met the Blackwells, my powers had been knocked off balance, as I absorbed bits of their energy. Then I stole Seamus's energy, really throwing things out of whack. That was why I'd been so quick to attack Erin, and why I hadn't been able to stop myself from absorbing her energy when she'd died. But stealing her power had rebalanced things inside me. I just hadn't known it until I was dying.

"I can control my abilities now. It's not a struggle like before. It's as easy as breathing. And I'm not immortal, Gabe. I should be after Erin, but it's like the energy that I stole from the Protectors canceled that out."

He listened to my excited explanation, and then he exhaled and stared at the ceiling. "Are you going to go back to Seamus's?"

"What?" I asked in confusion.

"It's okay if that's what you want. I know he thinks you belong with the O'Malleys, and if you want to be there, then we'll make it work. I bet we could still catch a train if you wanted to get back there tonight."

I stared after him in bewilderment as he disappeared in the direction of the living room. It occurred to me that I'd handled this all wrong. He thought I didn't want to be here.

I rose and followed him to the living room. He stood in the middle of the room, looking a little lost.

"Do you remember that last night in your kitchen in Blackwell Falls when I showed you what I imagined our future would be like?" I asked. He spun to face me, and I kept on. "I had it all wrong. Do you want to see what I picture now?"

He gave me a slow, hopeful nod, and I held out a hand to him. "Close your eyes." I waited for him to listen. I walked backward and pulled Gabe after me as I took small steps. Then I opened my mind and let the movie roll.

*We lived together in this apartment. I went to school to become a doctor. He studied music and played a guitar in the evenings while I did my homework. Some nights my family or his would call—because it was safe for them to do so now—and we would catch up on all we'd missed and talk. And even when he made me mad, he could say something and I would laugh, and an argument would end with lots of kissing. We were happy and in love and our life together began when I led Gabe down the hall to our room and we opened the door together.*

Gabe's eyes opened, and he lifted a hand to my cheek. "I love you, Remington."

I turned my face to kiss his palm and whispered, "I know. It says so right there on your chest."

His gaze shot down and he peered under his T-shirt. I

stood on my tiptoes to spy the design, a replica of the Sharpie markings he'd once tricked me into "healing."

"Wow," I said. "I did that without even looking. These new powers are going to be awesome."

Gabe smiled. "Guess what?"

"What?" I asked cautiously. He had the look of someone who was up to no good.

A second later, he whipped a Sharpie out of his back pocket. The same pen he'd used to write my scavenger hunt notes. His eyes promised retribution, and I took a quick step backward.

"Don't run, sweetheart. I might mess up and have to start over again."

He uncapped the marker, and I shrieked with laughter. The chase was on.

# ACKNOWLEDGMENTS

First and foremost, I want to thank the readers and bloggers who have loved this series from the beginning. Your notes, reviews, posts, tweets, and pictures put a smile on my face every day. I'm so humbled by your love for Remy and her world. Special thanks to the Mundie Moms for arranging the *Touched* blog tour and trailer premiere and to Jaime Arnold of Two Chicks on Books who live tweeted her reading of *Pushed* and *Ignited*, much to my enjoyment.

With every novel, I learn how to write all over again. *Ignited* required frequent phone brainstorms and panicked meetings at Mel's Diner and/or Starbucks to work through twisty plot points. Lots of love to Kari Young for listening to me blather on about "emotional continuity." You have the patience of a saint, friend.

To my agent, Laura Bradford, I'm so glad you loved this series and that you made it possible for me to write the whole thing. Thank you for letting me discover who Remy would become.

I owe my editor, Martin Biro, a big basket of Ghirardelli chocolate for his work on this book and the series. Thanks for everything you and the team at KTeen do to get these books out into the world, with special gratitude to Vida Engstrand, Craig Bentley, Arthur Maisel, Alicia Condon, Alexandra Nicolajsen, Michelle Forde, and Megan Records, who encouraged the direction this book took. I also want to give thanks to the team at ThienemannVerlag who contributed edits and input to the series, especially Heike Brillmann-Ede, Bettina Traub, Heidi Lichtblau, and JuttaWenske. Thanks to all of you for letting me discover who Remy would end up with.

AC Gaughen and Tracy E. Banghart, your notes were brilliant, especially the lusty ones about Gabe. Thanks for making this book far better than I could alone! The same goes to my crit group—Kari Young, Jay Lehmann, Stephanie Kuehn, Karen Langford, Angelica Hagman, and Justin Sloan—who were always there to celebrate my successes and give me a shove when I was ready to give up.

To the Class of 2k12, Bookanistas, Apocalypsies, and YA Rebels groups, I couldn't have made it through the last two years without you.

And last, but never least, to my family, thanks for putting up with me. I love you more than salted caramel mochas with whipped cream and those little salt sprinkles.

# FOOD FOR THOUGHT

1. Four months have passed since the end of *Pushed*. How has life changed for Remy, Asher, and Lucy? How has life on the run affected their relationships?

2. In *Touched*, Remy was isolated and traumatized by the physical and emotional abuse inflicted on her by her stepfather, Dean, and her mother. How has she changed over the course of the series?

3. In *Pushed*, Asher was kidnapped and tortured by Franc's men. How did this experience change him? How has it impacted his relationship with Remy?

4. Lucy blames Remy for their changed circumstances, including what has happened to their parents. Is she right to punish Remy? Could Remy have done anything to change the outcome? How does Lucy change over the course of the series?

5. Remy discovers that Erin has also been abused. How did they each deal with the abuse? How does Remy's discovery affect her relationship with Erin? Why do you think Erin makes the choice she does at the end of the novel?

6. In *Touched* and *Pushed*, Remy struggles with how others view her abilities and how she chooses to use them. Sometimes the others call her a martyr or criticize her willingness to sacrifice her well-being. What drives Remy to put herself at risk? Does her view of her own abilities change in *Ignited*?

7. Remy is torn between Asher and Gabe. Do you believe it's possible to love two people at once? How does her love for each of them differ? How does their love for her differ?

8. Remy has often been disappointed by her family, but in *Ignited,* her ideas about a family unit change. What does a family look like to her? What does each member of her group bring to their family? Does having a family change Remy? If so, how?

9. How is the Phoenix symbolic of Remy's internal and external journey over the course of the series? How does it reflect who she has become?

10. At the end of the novel, Remy is beginning a new life. Is her ending a happy one?

# SOUNDTRACKS

When I begin a book, I create a playlist. The songs I pick fit the mood of the novel, or the lyrics may reflect a certain moment or character. As I write, I listen to these songs over and over. By the time I finish a book I've listened to each song upwards of 100 times. They become so much a part of my process that they feel like the backbone of the story. Below is a partial list of songs that I listened to while writing the Sense Thieves series. A lot of these bands may be new to you, but I hope you check them out

## *Touched*

*Song (Artist)*
Because of You (Kelly Clarkson)
Waiting on an Angel (Ben Harper)
Daughters (John Mayer)
Breakable (Ingrid Michaelson)
Yes I'm Cold (Chris Bathgate)
Trouble Is a Friend (Lenka)
You're Not Sorry (CSI Remix) (Taylor Swift)
Hangin' by a Thread (Jann Arden)
Falling (Tyrone Wells)
Inside My Head (Clare Reynolds)
Come Down to Me (Saving Jane)
The Death of Us (The New Amsterdams)
Hero/Heroine (Boys Like Us)
Falling (Keri Noble)
Next to You (Tim Easton)

Closer (Kings of Leon)
Hang On (Isobel Campbell & Mark Lanegan)
So Long Sweet Misery (Brett Dennen)
Winter Song (Sara Bareilles & Ingrid Michaelson)
Arrivals (Aqualung)
I Would Die for You (Jann Arden & Sarah
    McLachlan)
That'll Be the Plan (Daniel Martin Moore)
The Night Will Go As Follows (The Spill Canvas)
All I Can Do (Tyrone Wells)
Don't Give Up (Clare Reynolds)

## Pushed

The Light Song (The Homes)
Come Over Here (Sarah Bettens)
Someone to Fall Back On (Aly Michalka & I Can't
    Go On, I'll Go On)
The Fear You Won't Fall (Joshua Radin)
The Road Knows (The Homes)
Stay Over (The Rescues)
Youthless (Beck)
Into Dust (Mazzy Star)
Safe & Sound (Taylor Swift)
Sit With Me Tonight (Garrison Star)
Jungle (Emma Louise)
The Trapeze Swinger (Iron & Wine)
The Only One (The Black Keys)
Lonely Hands (Angus & Julia Stone)
Fever (Adam Freeland & Sarah Vaughan—Verve
    Remixed 3)
Run (Katherine McPhee & *Smash* Cast)
Firefly (Ed Sheeran)
Call It Off (Tegan and Sara)

The House That Built Me (Miranda Lambert)
Somebody That I Used to Know (Gotye)
Free (Graffiti6)
If Not Now, When? (Incubus)
Falling Awake (Gary Jules)
Live Forever (Drew Holcomb & The Neighbors)
Sail (AWOLNATION)

## Ignited

Cripple Me (Elenowen)
You Can Close Your Eyes (feat. William Fitzsimmons)
   (Brooke Fraser)
Belong (Cary Brothers)
Falling (The Civil Wars)
Titanium (Madilyn Bailey)
I Will Fall (*Nashville* Cast Album version)
   (Clare Bowen & Sam Palladio)
Too Close (Alex Clare)
Turn into Earth (The Yardbirds)
Half Moon (Iron and Wine)
Can't Go Back Now (The Weepies)
High Hope (Glen Hansard)
Stubborn Love (The Lumineers)
Counting Stars (OneRepublic)
Ho Hey (The Lumineers)
All Your Gold (Bat for Lashes)
Into the Wild (Lewis Watson)
If I Didn't Know Better (*Nashville* Cast Album
   version) (Clare Bowen & Sam Palladio)
Stay Over (The Rescues)
Feel Again (OneRepublic)
Fade into You (*Nashville* Cast Album version)
   (Clare Bowen & Sam Palladio)

Heavy Cross (Gossip)
I Will Follow You into the Dark (Death Cab for
  Cutie)
Home (Gabrielle Aplin)
Carry (Chris Ayer)
Overwhelmed (Tim McMorris)

See how Remy's journey began in Corrine Jackson's

# *TOUCHED*

You'd think being able to heal people with a touch would be a blessing. But to 17-year-old Remy O'Malley, it's more like a curse.

Every injury Remy heals becomes her own. She lives in fear of the day she's forced to mend a wound from which she can't recover—and she's desperate to keep her amazing ability a secret.

Enter Asher Blackwell, a scarred eighteen-year-old with dangerous powers of his own. Asher seems to know more about Remy's abilities than she does—and maybe more than he's letting on. If she opens up to him, she might find out what it truly means to be a Healer. But she'll also expose herself to capture by an old and very determined enemy. And if they catch her, they won't just injure her.

**Turn the page for a special excerpt.**

A KTeen trade paperback on sale now

*Okay. This is going to hurt like hell.*

Taking a deep breath, I stepped into the room, my movements piercing the alcoholic haze insulating Dean. He straightened to his full six-foot-three when he noticed me, his eye twitching when I stared back unblinking. Maybe he suspected I was a freak and it scared him. Maybe he was scared of himself, of what he wanted from me. I figured that's why he mostly hit my mother when I wasn't around.

Unknotting my hands from white knuckled fists, I hoped to defuse the tension before it exploded.

"You're home early," he said, his heavy-lidded stare straying over me without meeting my eyes.

Tall and plain, I was skinny with no curves, but that didn't matter. My skin crawled when his pale blue eyes tracked me through a room. I went out of my way to stay away when he was alone in the apartment, but sometimes he managed to corner me in the shadows of our dim hallway. Sick in ways I couldn't cure, he'd crowd me with his hulking body and laugh when I'd lurch away to avoid his touch.

The funny thing was that Dean looked like the grown version of that charming, innocent boy all the girls crushed on in high school. He had soft, blond curls and a friendly, open face that charmed the unaware. Perhaps that's what had attracted Anna to him in the first place.

"Maybe I should call ahead next time?" I mused. "That way you could plan to finish beating my mother by 9:05, I can arrange to have the ambulance here by 9:10, and we can all be in bed by midnight."

My flat voice held no sarcasm, only bitter resignation. Dean's hands tightened into fists that could feel like steel. I'd stayed too long, trying to protect my mother, but Anna loved Dean more than anything. More than me. Dean loved how my father's child support checks kept him drinking down to the worm at the bottom of his tequila bottles.

He stepped closer. "Gonna stop me, princess?"

My indifferent act never fooled him. After seeing Anna's unconscious body on the floor, I wished I could kill him. I shuddered in anticipation of the brutality to come and the moment I would touch Anna. Never taking my eyes from him, I slid sideways to keep the threadbare couch and scarred coffee table between us. Anna moaned, and Dean's gaze flicked to her, his lip curled in disgust.

"You think you're a man because you beat up women?" I taunted to distract him.

His smile raised the hair on my arms. It was a smile of warning—a smile to predict the weather by because hell was sure to rain down on its recipient. "You think you're better than me, kid, but you're gonna respect me." He whipped his belt from the loops of his dirty jeans. The buckle glinted in the light when he wrapped the black leather around his fist—a bright, shiny weapon.

Hate speared through me, along with paralyzing fear. *Better to make him angry,* I decided. Then, maybe, it would end faster. I sneered while sidling closer to Anna.

"Respect you? You're barely human. A pathetic coward. You want to hit me, don't you, Dean? Go ahead."

I'd never ridiculed him before and, within two feet of Anna's limp body, my courage faltered. *Stupid. Stupid. He'll kill us both.* At least the ghoulish waiting game would be over. He'd come close enough to touch me when I whispered, "I dare you to try."

He charged and pulled back his arm to hit me as I stepped in front of Anna. His fist landed in my stomach, and I tripped over her. My head bounced off the wall with a dull thud. Dean's hand clamped around my throat, stalling my fall to the ground as he pinned me, and I inhaled the stale mix of sweat and tobacco wafting from him. Cutting off my breath, he smiled and squeezed his fingers until the pain weakened my knees.

Anna rolled at my feet and screamed, "No!" She jumped on Dean, trying to drag him off me, her red fingernails biting into his forearm. Desperate for air, I clamped one hand on his arm and clutched my mother with the other.

My eyes squeezed shut. *I'm dying,* I thought. Then my ability to think fractured. The mental wall barricading my power collapsed and, without the defense, Anna's pain thundered through me, allowing me to see inside her body. I noted two broken ribs, a concussion, black eye, and bruises scattered all over her body. Dots of color popped against my closed lids in a spectacular fireworks show. My lungs constricted, and I embraced Anna's aches, healing them and grafting her pain to my own.

Dean's grip loosened as he stumbled beneath Anna's attack, and he yanked her hair to toss her away. She sobbed, and the storm inside me doubled and tripled in size. I had failed to protect her. Filled with rage, I imagined all my pain striking Dean down like fiery lightning.

Violent red light sizzled between my hand and his arm. His face froze in horror as his body jerked and convulsed. A loud crack splintered the air—his ribs breaking or mine—and I passed out.

3/94 Ingram 1395/ 837

# WITHDRAWN
# ONE PARTICULAR HARBOR

| DATE DUE | | | |
|---|---|---|---|
| APR 12 '94 MY -2 '02 | | | |
| APR 20 '94 | | | |
| MAY 6 '94 | | | |
| MAY 11 '94 | | | |
| MAY 27 '94 | | | |
| JUN 7 '94 M Lamar 7-20-94 | | | |
| JUL 06 1994 | | | |
| JUL 27 '94 | | | |
| ILL Alamosa 8-29-94 | | | |
| FEB - 3 '98 | | | |